P9-BAU-442

DEEP WAR

PREVIOUS BOOKS BY DAVID POYER

Tales of the Modern Navy

Hunter Killer
Onslaught
Tipping Point
The Cruiser
The Towers
The Crisis
The Weapon
Korea Strait
The Threat
The Command
Black Storm
China Sea
Tomahawk
The Passage
The Circle
The Gulf
The Med

Tiller Galloway

Down to a Sunless Sea
Bahamas Blue
Louisiana Blue
Hatteras Blue

The Civil War at Sea

That Anvil of Our Souls
A Country of Our Own
Fire on the Waters

Hemlock County

Thunder on the Mountain
Winter in the Heart
As the Wolf Loves Winter
The Dead of Winter

Other Books

The Whiteness of the Whale
Happier Than This Day and Time
Ghosting
The Only Thing to Fear
Stepfather Bank
The Return of Philo T. McGiffin
Star Seed
The Shiloh Project
White Continent

DEEP WAR

THE WAR WITH CHINA—THE NUCLEAR PRECIPICE

DAVID POYER

ST. MARTIN'S PRESS
New York

This is a work of fiction. All of the characters, organizations, and events portrayed in this novel are either products of the author's imagination or are used fictitiously.

 For information, address St. Martin's Press, 175 Fifth Avenue, New York, N.Y. 10010.

www.stmartins.com

The Library of Congress Cataloging-in-Publication Data is available upon request.

ISBN 978-1-250-10110-5 (hardcover)
ISBN 978-1-250-10111-2 (ebook)

Our books may be purchased in bulk for promotional, educational, or business use. Please contact your local bookseller or the Macmillan Corporate and Premium Sales Department at 1-800-221-7945, extension 5442, or by email at MacmillanSpecialMarkets@macmillan.com.

First Edition: December 2018

10 9 8 7 6 5 4 3 2 1

I am here; more than that I do not know; farther than that I cannot go. My ship has no rudder; it drives with the winds that blow from the remotest regions of death.

—FRANZ KAFKA, "THE HUNTER GRACCHUS"

I

I AM HERE

1

The East China Sea

ON fire. Her ship was on fire.

The commanding officer leaned over the splinter shield, peering aft through the exhalation-fogged plastic of her gas mask.

Dead in the water, the cruiser was slowly pivoting. The wind was turning her stern to the enemy coast. The choking black smoke blowing forward erased sight, but deep within it glowed the ominous amber of fuel-fed flame.

Commander Cheryl Staurulakis, USN, was slight and blond. One arm hung in a makeshift sling contrived from an olive-drab-and-black shemagh and tucked into blue shipboard coveralls. She wore heavy black flight deck boots and a Kevlar helmet stenciled CO. Her hands were streaked with blood.

USS *Savo Island* drifted alone on a deserted sea. The whole starboard side was aflame, from the waterline up to the bridge level. Oblong holes perforated the steel Cheryl leaned on, as if from a load of square buckshot. Beside her on the bridge wing, the lookout muttered, "Jesus, save us." He scanned the horizon with binoculars. "Jesus . . . Jesus. Save us."

She lifted her head. Above them, a cerulean sky. A blazing dawn, with the sun a thumb's width above a flashing sea of molten brass. She shaded her eyes to examine lilac-glowing contrails. Truly beautiful . . . Truly terrifying.

If only Eddie could still be up there. But according to last night's message, he was dead. Shot down in his fighter, defending the retreating task force.

She squeezed her eyes shut. Can't think about him. Can't mourn. Not now.

If those lavender tracings were another salvo of supersonics on their way, her ship was finished, and her crew as well.

THE war had begun two years before. China had intervened in a battle between Pakistan and India. When the U.S. imposed a blockade, the People's Empire knocked out communications and reconnaissance satellites.

Then Senior General and Chairman Zhang Zurong hammered Taiwan and Okinawa with missiles and invaded. When a U.S. carrier battle group sailed, he destroyed it with a thermonuclear warhead, killing ten thousand servicemen and -women.

Backed by Beijing, North Korea invaded the South while Japan and the Philippines stood aside. Battles still raged in India and Vietnam, but the Chinese had seemed to be winning them all.

Until Operation Recoil. Secretly assembled after months of retreat, the first Allied strike against the Chinese homeland was intended to break up the second phase of Zhang's strategic offensive, outward toward Guam and Midway.

Task Force 76's flagship had led the attack on the Ningbo base complex. *Savo*'s mission: Clear the way for the carrier strike. Then, after covering the main body's retreat, withdraw to rearm and resupply.

Only it hadn't worked out that way. With enemy fighters headed for the carriers, the admiral had ordered Cheryl to "squawk flattop": imitate the higher-value unit, to draw the strike to the cruiser.

Four warheads had connected. Two hit high, wrecking the upper helo hangar, the Army-manned Stinger launcher, one of the radar-controlled 20 mm's, the after stack and intakes, and half the ship's thirty-eight antennas, including both after phased arrays. Another exploded at the main deck level. The last had punched through the hull, detonating in an engine space.

Now USS *Savo Island* rolled helplessly, magazines empty, a hundred miles east of Shanghai.

THE phone talker at Staurulakis's elbow buzzed like a dying cicada through his mask's speaking diaphragm. "I can't make out a fucking word you're saying," Cheryl snapped, pushing past him into the pilothouse. She dogged the door and stripped off her mask, sucking air freighted with fuel smoke and the nitrate bitterness of explosive. As the men and women on watch stared, she tried to steady her voice. "Keep calm, and say it all again."

The young talker gulped. "Doc Grissett reports fifteen wounded and three dead in sick bay, and more on their way down. Corpsmen are triaging—"

And the rest of her crew, the other three hundred and fifty-some, were going to die too, if she didn't think of something fast. "Very well. What's DC Central got?"

The officer of the deck said, "Damage Control reports. Four-foot hole at the waterline, frame 220. Major blast and fire damage in Number One Main Engine Room and Aux 1. Multiple superstructure and main deck penetrations. Fires from there to the boat deck and quarterdeck. Blast damage. Frag damage. No hose teams in sight."

She coughed into a bloody fist. "Ask the master chief, where the hell—"

"Central reports, lost firemain. No point exposing hose teams till they regain pressure. Preparing to counterflood, to fight the list."

"Belay the counterflooding. Hear me? Every ton we take on makes us less stable. We have spaces open to the sea." Stepping to the 21MC, she snapped the lever before biting her lip. "Shit!"

"No power, Skipper," the officer of the deck said. "If you want Main Control, they reported major fires, both engine control panels tripped off, all engines off-line. Number One switchboard's gone. Number One gas turbine generator is wrecked. And the emergency switchboard's out."

Major fires, yet all her fire pumps were electrically driven. "We need Number Three GTG on the line. It's all the way aft, so it should be undamaged, right?" She asked the young woman at the helm console, "Can you cycle the rudder? Try it again."

"No rudder response, ma'am."

The officer of the deck said, "Main Control says they won't be able to answer bells until they get a generator restarted. And they can't do that until the switchboard's circumvented."

Cheryl bit back a curse. Without power, a ship couldn't communicate, navigate, or fight. Was there really nothing she could do?

SHE'D been in CIC with Admiral Lenson the night before, when the task force emptied its magazines. Blazing light had blanked the deck cameras. Flaming stars lifted, steadied, and dwindled, transmuted into digital displays as *Savo*'s powerful radars tracked them to their targets. They'd hit radar sites, missile sites, communication and command nodes, antiaircraft batteries, and airfields.

Over two hundred attack aircraft had followed, from *Nimitz*, *Vinson*, *Reagan*, *Truman*, and *Stennis*, accompanied by combat and jamming drones. The heaviest punch the Navy had thrown since World War II. After the swarm and the fighters, the attack squadrons had unloaded, obliterating oil refineries, power stations, container piers, munitions dumps, bridges, handling cranes, and any ships that had thought being in port kept them safe.

Arriving after a seven-hour flight from Alaska, Air Force bombers had brought fifteen more minutes of unadulterated inferno. And an hour after that, a final wave of Tomahawks decimated firefighters, police, medical personnel, repair crews, and anyone else who exited a shelter, dazed and concussed, thinking the attack was over.

By this morning, the Shanghai/Ningbo complex should no longer be able to support a renewed offensive. But that didn't mean they couldn't muster forces to sweep up cripples. And there could be submarines out here too.

She kept trying not to think about the grisly fate of USS *Indianapolis*.

THE heavy little radio clipped to her web belt, the Hydra, clicked on. "*Skipper? Comm-o.*" It was Dave Branscombe, *Savo*'s communications officer.

"Go."

"*Bad news. Red Hawk doesn't answer up.*"

The ship's helicopter, which had left the deck half an hour before with several wounded and the admiral aboard. "Emergency channels?"

"*No joy. Just a weak signal from* McClung *on 2182 kilohertz distress.*"

"Pass them our Mayday and location. Ask them to stand by us."

"*Already done, ma'am. They're forwarding request to task force commander, but say he's not answering up.*"

"What about standing by us? Helping us fight these fires?"

"*They're retiring with the main body, ma'am. I don't know how much longer we can maintain comms.*"

Cheryl scratched the itchy place between her fingers, then gritted her teeth. She was scratching them bloody. "Ask *McClung* to query USS *Hampton Roads*. That's where Lenson was headed. If he didn't reach it . . ."

But she didn't finish that sentence. If he hadn't, and they'd lost comms with the helo, she could only assume the worst. That he'd crashed, or been shot down. And that now she and *Savo Island*, left behind, were truly on their own.

The Hydra crackled again, and simultaneously the talker began a report from Damage Control. Chief McMottie, Commander Danenhower, and Lieutenant Jiminiz were working to get the generator and switchboard back in operation. The casualty-recovery teams reported wounded and bodies clear of the main deck. She issued terse orders, then ducked to peer out to starboard. She tensed as she caught sight of the lookout pointing out something on the horizon to the machine gunner. But the gunner shook his head; apparently it was nothing. Yet.

Okay, if no one was coming to help . . .

At her questioning glance, the quartermaster chief unrolled a chart. Securing it atop a table with masking tape, he outlined their options. Cheryl paced off distances with dividers, then stood over the chart, shoulders hunched, staring down.

Taiwan lay far to the south. Korea, divided still but with its south now occupied by China as a "protectorate of the People's Empire," was nearly as far north. *Savo*'s only avenue of escape lay to the east, where a scatter of small islands stuttered down from Japan. The Ryukyus were Chinese-occupied too, but carrier strikes on the way in had closed their runways. At least, for a few more hours.

She clicked the Hydra again. "Main Control, CO: Commander Danenhower down there?"

"Here."

"Bart, what's going on? I have to make decisions."

"Just about to report: halon and CO_2 *dumps have quenched the fire in Main 1 and Aux 1."*

"Good. Excellent. Any progress on regaining power?"

"We've routed casualty power. Getting ready to try to start Number Three GTG locally. Once we localize the grounding issue on the engine control panel, we'll switch the start loads to alternate power. Then try to spin up whichever engine looks best. Just hope we have enough HP air."

Ticos had no "emergency" generators, just main generators. With all three off-line, the ship was dark until one could be restarted with high-pressure air stored in heavy steel flasks, since bleed air wasn't available unless the propulsion turbines were running. She clicked an acknowledgment and returned to studying the chart. "Lay me the shortest route through," she told the chief.

Back on the open wing, she eyed the plume of black smoke streaming away downwind. The enemy had proven resourceful at deploying fragile, datalinked UAVs to surveil large areas of ocean. Nor could a sub miss that smoke with even the briefest periscope exposure.

She still had a few torpedoes left, a few rounds for the guns, but until they had power back the ship was helpless. They might be able to fight off a sampan with the machine guns, but that was about it.

So all she could do was wait. And stare up at the sky. She closed her eyes, her lips moving silently. *Eddie, if you're there . . . if you're anywhere you can hear me . . .*

But she didn't expect an answer.

FIFTEEN of the longest minutes of her life later, a *clunk* sounded from the helm console. A muffled whine of motors and fans powering up chorused from around the bridge, and the 21MC comm consoles went *pop.* Pilot lights lit. The wipers cycled noisily on the windshields, scraping at the dry glass, until the boatswain went to turn them off. The helmswoman spun the wheel left, then right. "Regained helm control, port synchro, port pumps," she reported. "No course given."

Chief Van Gogh, at the chart table: "One-zero-five degrees will take us between Akuseki-shima and Ko-lakara-jima. Distance, a hundred and forty nautical miles."

Cheryl frowned. "Depth between the islands?"

"Two thousand feet."

The 21MC said, *"Engine Room reports: ready to answer bells, limiting speed four knots."*

Not good, but better than zero. She nodded to the officer of the deck. "Make it so."

After a last look around, she went to the door that led down. Started to reach for it but winced; her arm; the greenwood fracture was starting to really hurt.

Her head swam; she leaned against the bulkhead. No sleep for the last two days, during the approach phase and then the battle. The corpsman had offered morphine, but she couldn't lose alertness.

Gritting her teeth, she shoved herself vertical again, and made for the ladder down.

TWO decks down, in the Combat Information Center, some of the displays had lit again. Otherwise the space was dark, and hotter than usual. The ventilators were still off, and an eye-watering smoke-stench lingered. Only a few consoles were occupied. Most of the technical ratings had tailed on to firefighting parties, or helped drag wounded out of danger. She halted at the command desk, which faced four large-screen displays ranged against a black bulkhead.

"We have the SPY back," Matt Mills told her. Tall, blond, and good-looking, but not just a pretty face. He was her best tactical action officer, charged with fighting the ship when she herself couldn't be in the command seat. "The forward transmitter, anyway. Degraded, but we have an air picture."

The SPY-1 was a high-powered phased-array radar that functioned in both the antiair and the antiballistic missile modes. Unfortunately, with the aft transmitters destroyed, they were blind in two quadrants. She leaned over Mills, cradling her broken arm, and swept her gaze across the East China Sea. Small contacts skittered here and there over the base they'd just struck. Helicopters, she guessed, evacuating wounded and moving in repair and command teams from other bases.

"No fast movers yet," Mills murmured.

"Iwakuni?"

"Nothing yet. We hit 'em hard."

More callouts blossomed as the computers linked with those of the main body, far ahead. Eighty miles away, and scooting east at flank speed. She picked out the other cruiser, and wondered again where Lenson was. She tried the Navy Red phone. The light lit, the circuit synced, but no one responded. No surprise. Both sides had jammed and spoofed each other's communications, even replicating individual voices with digitized imitations, to the point that no one trusted anything but face-to-face speech now.

Mills rattled the keyboard. "Where we headed, Skipper? What's our plan here?"

"We're on our own, Lieutenant. At the moment we're in creep mode. Get-home speed. If we can sneak out the back gate, we might be able to limp back to Guam."

"At four knots, that's . . . two weeks?"

"I'm hoping we'll do better." Cheryl ran her gaze over the other displays, computer status, radio call signs, weapons loadouts. Her magazines were nearly empty.

"What's the intent, Commander?" said a deep voice behind her.

She turned. "Captain Enzweiler."

Enzweiler was Lenson's chief of staff, or deputy. As a four-stripe captain, he outranked her. Somehow that didn't console her. He didn't know her ship the way Lenson had. In fact, she wished he'd stayed wherever the hell he'd been until now. "Uh, Captain, good to see you. As you know, we took four hits. We're fighting major casualties and flooding. Our helo, with the admiral and the Korean liaison aboard, is missing." She fought for breath, but having to make a report, that oh so standard naval procedure, seemed to steady her. "Main space fire's out. Casualty power's restored, as is Number 1B gas turbine motor, giving us a minimal maneuvering capability. We have Aegis back and are datalinked with the main body."

Enzweiler looked disturbed. "I tried to go with him. He said it would be better to take the most seriously wounded."

"I understand, sir."

"So I may be in charge of the task force."

"With all due respect, Captain, my reading would be that the admiral's departure relieves you of that responsibility. Our comms are still basically nonexistent, and the task force is withdrawing without us." She looked away, anxious to get back to what mattered. "We need to concentrate on staying afloat and getting home. Sir."

He sighed. "You're probably right. What about high-side chat? Can I report?"

"Sir, chat's been cyber-compromised. We got a Mayday off via *McClung*, but there's no response on satcomm voice or Navy Red. We're on our own. I intend to head for the Okinawa Strait and try for Guam."

Enzweiler nodded. "Sounds reasonable. For now. I'll put the staff at your disposal. What can I do?"

"Well, sir, if I could keep Commander Danenhower on the engineering casualties, that would really help. And if you could—yeah, actually, if you could bird-dog exactly what happened to the admiral, that would be great. I've been concentrating on the ship, but—"

"Danenhower, sure. On Lenson, point me where to start."

She told him that would be the helo air controller, and to try to generate a last known position to pass to Higher. At the moment, though, there didn't seem to be any ongoing search-and-rescue activities. In fact, the Aegis picture showed nothing at all between *Savo* and the coast, from which they were now receding at a little better than a walking pace.

Her husband might be out there. Still alive. In the water.

But the message had been pretty definite. Shot down over Ningbo. No chute.

She bared her teeth. He'd only just transitioned to the F-35. He wasn't familiar with the aircraft. And the bastards had sent him into the heaviest antiair defenses in history.

She'd find out who'd sent him. And somehow, make them pay.

A jittering, a flicker, and the screens went blank again. "Shit," Mills muttered. He yelled across to the control station, "Where's my data, Chief?"

"Just a fuckin' minute . . . we're being fucked with, for sure. I'm not getting anything from the main body, or the Japanese either."

Despite being officially neutral, the Japanese had been feeding them a radar picture during the strike. But losing data, plus their own damage, made *Savo* blind to any renewed attack.

She was raking at her fingers again when the 21MC clicked on. *"CIC, DC Central, Skipper?"*

She hit the switch. "CO."

"Lieutenant (jg) Jiminiz. Ma'am, we seriously need to counterflood."

She suddenly realized she was looking downhill at the port displays. The list had increased. "We're still taking water?"

"Affirmative. One gen's not enough to power self-defense, maintain firemain pressure, and run the pumps. Main 1 fire's out, but we've got toxic gas leaks into Aux 2 and Main 2, from the halon flood. Halon turns into phosgene at high temperatures. At current flooding rate"—a pause, during which Cheryl could hear someone protesting in the background—*"at current rate, we're pushing stability boundaries in an hour."*

She told him, "I'm hearing this, but heating halogenated hydrocarbon inhibitors in enclosed spaces doesn't produce phosgene, Lieutenant."

"Sorry, ma'am, but the book says halon breaks down to mixed chlorine and bromine toxics: Fluorophosgene, hydrogen chloride, carbon monoxide. Our guys in Aux 2, MER 2, and Shaft Alley are working in masks."

"Okay, I stand corrected. We counterflood, then what?"

A new voice: the senior engineering chief. *"McMottie, ma'am. Then we get 1A GTM running, then Number Two GTG on the line. That gives us full electrical power and propulsion on the starboard shaft. At that point Main 1 should be cooled down enough we can get a repair team in and start patching and dewatering."*

"And the port shaft?"

"Forget that, ma'am. Main reduction gear's gone, turbines are junk. We're a one-shaft pony from here on."

Okay, Ticos could run at almost twenty knots with one screw. If she had electricity restored, got the side patched, and the flooding contained . . . "Sounds like a plan. What do we need to do up here, Chief?"

"You know that better than me, Skipper. Keep our heads down until we can get things running again, I guess."

She double-clicked the Transmit lever and sat back. "Still no data," Mills murmured.

Cheryl stared at the display, more and more disturbed by the lack of visibility astern. The most threatening quarter for any renewed attack. "Donnie? Chief? How far left do I have to come to get a look over my shoulder?"

He said twenty degrees left or right of their base course would do it. She checked the pit log. Six knots. Better, but still . . . she hit the intercom to the bridge. "OOD, CO here. Come left to zero-eight-five degrees. Hold for one minute, then return to base course."

TWO hours later they were up to twelve knots. But the list had increased, and Damage Control reported difficulty getting the flooding isolated and shoring into place.

"Feel it?" Jiminiz was wading ahead of her through the gloom of Main 1. Teams were at work clearing wreckage and removing bodies. The space had been desmoked, but he was coughing and wheezing. "How she's taking longer, to come back?"

Cheryl nodded, shining a flash on the grating beneath their boots. She sensed that wrongness. The ship rolled harder, stayed over longer, and came back grudgingly. It wasn't just that they were losing buoyancy. With each added ton of "free surface"—water that could shift back and forth, gaining momentum with each roll—the righting arm that levered them back to vertical shrank. When it reached zero, nothing in this world would keep ten thousand tons of steel from turning turtle.

She half hiked, half skated along a slick canted catwalk of perforated steel. The urine gleams of battle lanterns probed the dark. The thunder of pine wedges being hammered in reverberated in the choking dim. She peered down through the catwalk to a dully gleaming, oily blackness that surged this way, then that.

At the hole in the side coveralled figures toiled like miners at a coal seam. They were struggling to heave a steel I beam into position against a stringer in the overhead. Once there, it would brace a plywood-and-mattress soft patch set athwartships the hole. There were other gaps too. She could see daylight, and with each roll water burst through, running down first in trickles, then sheets, to cascade through the gratings into the bilges. Men and women groaned together in the effort to lift the beam. She stepped forward and added her shoulder, twisting to protect her fractured arm. The burden rose, but halted, wavering, just short of the stringer.

The straining sailors groaned louder, and it lifted another inch.

Suddenly it slipped away, barely missing a seaman's head, and slammed down with a booming splash. The sea bulged darkly, and a huge surge burst through, knocking sailors to their knees. They retreated, scrambling as wood and sodden mattresses tumbled end over end, knocking more people down. A petty officer hauled Cheryl back as another beam slammed down at her boot-toes.

"I don't get it," Jiminiz muttered. "We got three pumps running. Shouldn't be taking water this fast."

Cheryl glanced down again at the black surface below. Her imagination, or was it already closer? "Are we sure this is the only penetration?"

The Damage Control assistant scratched his ear. "The only one reported."

"So this is flooding both the MER and Aux 1."

"Yeah, but we got the hole in Aux 1 sealed."

"Is the level there rising, or dropping?"

"It's holding steady." He shrugged.

"Then we've got another penetration somewhere," she told him. "We need to get somebody over the side, check it out. Let's do it while we still have daylight."

THE diver found another hole, below and aft of the one they'd been trying to patch. But by the time he confirmed that, *Savo* had lost another two hundred tons of buoyancy.

Leaving Cheryl, back in the pilothouse, pondering a dilemma as she looked down on a forecastle that was already noticeably closer to the water.

Savo still had power, though they'd had to drop to ten knots again. But the flooding was gaining. Slowly, but the end could not be many hours away.

Abandon ship? Unfortunately, they didn't have enough boats. One rigid-hulled inflatable had been destroyed in the fire. A third of the life raft inventory was gone too, holed by fragments or destroyed in the fires.

She couldn't help thinking again of *Indianapolis*, torpedoed in 1945 and forgotten by the chain of command. Hundreds of men had drifted for days, baking in the sun, ravaged by sharks. . . . She tried to raise Higher again, then broadcast a general Mayday. With no response.

Danenhower let himself onto the bridge. The engineering officer looked utterly weary, coveralls stained with grease and soot. He joined her on the wing, hacking black phlegm into a tissue. "The warhead separated from the airframe just before it hit. Both parts went through the hull."

"Can you patch it?"

"We can't reach it to patch, not with the rounded hull form. And we can't compartmentalize it." He grimaced. "We tried concrete, but it runs out the bottom. That whole area of the hull's shredded. I'm running every pump, but eventually the ones in Aux 2 will be submerged. The failures will percolate aft as we go down by the head. Until . . ."

"I see." She glanced inside; anxious faces stared back. "How long? Can we hold it off overnight?" With twelve more hours, they might get through the strait. Still in trouble, but at least whoever picked them up might not turn them over to the enemy.

"Lemme do the math again." Danenhower punched the screen of his PDA. Finally he shook his head. "No."

A clank as the door undogged. Van Gogh let himself out, followed by the sonarman chief. “Skipper, Commander,” he muttered.

She nodded. “Guys?”

“Looked at the chart again, ma’am. Thought you might want to see this.”

Cheryl flattened the paper. A penciled circle around a blue area. “There’s nothing here.”

“It’s a seamount,” the sonarman said. “Part of the same chain as the Ryukyus, but it doesn’t break the surface.”

Zotcher handed over a printout of classified submarine hydrography. It showed the depth as ten to twelve meters. Last, Van Gogh produced an old book with blue damp-warped covers. “Found it in a Royal Navy survey, too. They note it as a ten-fathom reef, but it’s a submerged atoll. A flat-topped seamount.”

She coughed into a fist, doubt worming her stomach. Scratched furiously at the itch between her fingers, breaking the scabs. Fuck, it was going to start bleeding again now. “So which is it, ten meters, or ten fathoms?”

“I’d trust the later survey,” Danenhower put in.

“And how far?”

Van Gogh said, “Thirty-two miles, bearing one-three-seven true.”

They waited. She thought of asking Enzweiler. Then steeled herself. The chief of staff outranked her, but he wasn’t the skipper.

She held their gazes, smothering any uncertainty or irresolution. She could mourn, for her husband, for her dead. But they didn’t want to see her doubt, or be weak, or show fear.

She took a deep breath. Lifted her chin. “Monitor the rate of flooding,” she said, startled at the firmness of her own voice. “Keep me informed. For the present, maintain course. Another hour, and then I’ll decide.”

2

In the Karakoram Mountains

THE old mirror was wavery, speckled, dim. Holding it against the pick-pocked, just-excavated rock face, Master Chief Teddy Oberg inspected his own warped visage.

His beard was going gray. Scars radiated from his nose like ejecta from a lunar impact crater. His eyes: blue, cold, the corners seamed. His skin: bronzed and rough. Hair: shoulder length, longer than he'd worn it on the Teams, twisted back into a knot.

"*Zhè rúhé bangzhù women?*" And this does for us exactly what? Nasrullah, the rebels' supply honcho and go-between to the lowlands, pointed to the mirror. He spoke in the pidgin Han that was the main tongue Teddy and the rebels shared. Though Teddy was making some progress with Uighur. . . .

Obie angled the mirror down the new tunnel. Rays from the entrance, glary with snow, ricocheted into the darkness. Mujahideen, bent double, chipped laboriously, chewing into the mountain's guts. One raised an arm, shielding his eyes from the sudden dazzle.

"We want all the mirrors we can get," Teddy told Nasrullah. "I saw this in the White Mountains."

"Al-Qaeda?"

"Exactly."

"You fought Muslims then. Why soldier beside us now?"

"What can I say, the world changes." Teddy shrugged. He lowered the mirror. Set it against the granite wall, reslung his rifle, and limped for the main entrance, favoring his injured foot.

He was still a SEAL, but he barely felt like one anymore. Salena, the cop he'd been dating back in LA, was a distant memory. A scene from a film he'd watched too long ago to really remember. Hollywood? He could hardly believe he'd wanted to make movies once. No, that was all gone. Blown away like poppy pollen on the thin cool winds of war.

After escaping from a POW camp, he and "Ragger" Fierros had stumbled down out of the mountains in time to witness a mujahideen attack. Since the Americans had been firing back at the government troops too, the rebels took them along when they withdrew. After a jolting ride in the back of a pickup, then a long, blindfolded climb, the captives had been shoved into this same cave complex to be judged.

And nearly executed. But Teddy had saved them with a lie: that he was with the CIA, and could provide support for their revolt against Beijing.

Today he'd find out whether he could make that lie into something closer to the truth.

If not, he could face that same court again.

The outside air was icy keen. As snow blew past he drew his blanket close, huddling near the entrance so as not to stand out to any overhead surveillance. Doubtful in this weather, but best to play it safe. He wore the same threadbare shalwar kameez as the Uighurs, the same flat wool cap, and over his shoulders the POW-issue blanket that had covered him during the escape. He fingered the Chinese rifle's stock. He'd taken it from a trooper shot down by the muj during the attack on the town.

Before and below spread the valley. Not a building within sight, though in summer flocks would pasture down there. Rock. Snow. Low brush, at the lowest altitudes. Knife-sharp ridges, deep ravines, a deserted, rugged Mars-scape, shadowed even in daylight.

He blinked across snow-hazed miles to a wall that blocked the sky: the snow-covered, frowning Pamirs. Remembering another snowfall, another high mountain pass. The mission to kill bin Laden.

He hoped this turned out better.

A hiss, a crackle. He pulled out the cheap walkie-talkie and faded behind a rock rampart. But the transmission, mountain-faint and scratchy, was in Uighur. "*Qing shuo hányu,*" he snapped. Speak Han.

"*Yes, Lingxiù.*" Chief, sort of, what he'd asked them to call him. "*This is Tok. Have man with us now.*"

Tok was "Tokarev," given name Guldulla, the co-head of the guerrillas. "Copy. What's he like?"

"*Hard to say. Maybe Russian?*"

Obie frowned. "Russian?"

"That's what he looks like. He will not say his name. Says, only to you."

He cradled the radio, pondering. He'd asked Fierros, when his fellow escapee had decided to try for the border, to send someone back if he could. There was an opportunity here for the Allies. But a Russian?

He could be a spy, a double agent. If there was any possibility of that, he couldn't bring him here.

"Meet me at the spring." He jacked a cartridge into the rifle, then began limping down the mountain.

THE guy looked Slavic, all right, with salient cheekbones. His dark stubble was rimed with ice. A straight, thin blade of a nose. Deeply hooded, altitude-bloodshot eyes in a hue Teddy couldn't quite make out. He stood beside the frozen stream in hiking boots and an ancient greatcoat that could have been issued by the army of the tsars, but at least looked warm. Thin insulated gloves were modern, but the earflapped fur hat said Russian again.

"So, you walked in?" Teddy asked warily. In English.

"All the way from Manas. Master Chief Theodore Harlett Oberg, USN, I presume?"

No discernible accent. East Coast Standard. They shook hands guardedly. Teddy said, "So, where are we from? You're not a Team guy, are you?"

"Former Ranger. Call me Vladimir."

"You *look* Russian."

"I've passed for that."

"So did I, after we escaped. Pretended to be hunters."

A squint. "Did it work?"

"Not all that well. So what's the news? We winning the war?"

"It's not going all that well, no. Oh. I was told you wanted one of these." Vladimir dug into his greatcoat, and the Uighur behind him lifted his shotgun. Teddy gestured him to stand easy.

"Fierros said you wanted a good thin-blade," the CIA man said. "A Boker fighting knife, ceramic blade, that do the trick?"

Teddy turned it over in hardened, cold-blistered fingers. Flicked it open, then closed. "Nice," he grunted.

It would do for a bona fide. Unless of course the Chinese, or their Iranian allies, had captured Ragger and were running this guy in. But you couldn't start a revolt without taking risks.

"Let's go on up to the main cave," Teddy muttered. "It's too fucking cold to talk here."

BATS twittered and squeaked far above. Worn carpets and low tables of rough wood were scattered across water-eroded limestone. To one side dozens of ancient Buddhas lay toppled, shattered, faces gouged back into emptiness. Carvings on the rock walls were scarred by bullets. A crushed mass of ancient parchment shoaled the corners, layered with centuries of bat guano. Black banners hung behind a lectern. "Dandan!" Teddy yelled into the recesses of the cave.

The field officer revealed a tactical vest, a maroon turtleneck, and a holstered Glock as he unbuttoned to sit cross-legged on a bare-napped carpet, sweeping the tails of his coat aside. A fire of dry brush crackled in the far corner, eddying a silver snake of smoke along the ceiling. "Cozy," Vladimir said, looking around at reclining men chatting over tea as they took a break from digging, at the sleeping pallets, at the crack in the rocky overhead that sucked the smoke up to vent somewhere higher up the mountain.

Teddy nodded. "Used to be some kind of hermitage."

"How's the leg? You were wounded on the Woody raid?"

"Yeah, it's never really come back." He massaged his calf, where the muscles knotted at night in agonizing spasms. "I take it Ragger made it back in one piece."

"He was in bad shape when he got to Bishkek. A week before he could talk. Then we couldn't shut him up. Quite a story, escaping from the toughest hard-labor camp in China. Oh, and we passed your message on to your old girlfriend. 'The guy she knew is dead.'" Vladimir looked around again. "How many effectives?"

"Not that many yet, but the possibilities are there—Dandan! *Ni zài na?*"

A slight figure in black materialized from the gloom. His slave girl was barefoot, face so swathed in black cloth that only one dark eye showed. Teddy ordered her to bring chai and naan, and lay back on a musty-smelling pillow.

Vladimir stared after her as Teddy asked again about how the war was going. The operative said the Indians and Vietnamese were holding their respective lines, but didn't seem to want to discuss what the Allies had planned. Then he was asking the questions again. "Numbers, Ted. If you want us to supply you, we need quantification."

Obie said reluctantly, "I have forty-some right now. But we could triple that if we tried. From there on, if we train the trainers and get the arms, I can double the numbers every two weeks."

"How many in a month or two? Fighting men?"

Teddy said reluctantly, "Maybe . . . three hundred?"

The CIA man didn't look impressed. The girl, silent, returned to set down a tray with hot tea, small brass cups, and cold bread. They ate with their fingers. Vladimir drank off a cup, then poured more.

"What about it, amigo? Agency gonna help out, or not? Way I see it, golden opportunity to put an itch on Zhang's balls."

Vladimir murmured, "The colonel told us what you propose. Essentially, what we did in Afghanistan against the Soviets. Recruit a resistance. Foster a sectarian rebellion. But is that going to actually hurt Beijing? Or just end up sucking down resources, and getting a lot of more-or-less friendlies killed."

"Since when does Langley worry about losing ragheads?"

Those colorless eyes regarded him levelly. "I'll take that as a rhetorical question, Master Chief. Or some kind of satire."

"Take it how you like. These guys were busting heads before I showed up. Low-level, but they kept Internal Security hopping. Raiding police stations. Shooting up marketplaces. Bushwhacking foot patrols. The Hans have oppressed them for centuries. Stolen their land. Cut off their beards. We've gotta be thinking about destabilizing the enemy, right?"

"Your proposal was accepted," Vladimir said carefully. "But with caveats."

"What?"

"We direct operations. Not the local leadership, whoever that is. If we're going to underwrite a rebellion, we specify the targets."

Teddy said that seemed fair. "So what's our first mission?"

Checking that no one was looking, Vlad slipped what looked like a cell phone from the greatcoat and palmed it over. "We'll drop a squirt transmitter for backup, but Jetwire'll be our main comms. Lets us talk direct, without the indigenous overhearing. Uplinks to a MOUSE satellite."

He initialized it and called up a map. Teddy squinted at it, wondering if he shouldn't ask for reading glasses too. "First priority: recruit. But as soon as you muster two hundred effectives, we need you to hit a major pipeline and high-voltage line."

Teddy scrutinized the map as the other explained that before the war China had committed a hundred billion dollars to secure an overland flow of liquefied natural gas and oil from Iran, via Pakistan, along a China–Pak Economic Corridor. "The line runs from Islamabad north along the route of a mountain highway. It crosses the border from Pak-occupied Kashmir at the Khunjerab Pass and goes to Kashgar, China.

"This has been Zhang's main source of imported oil since the blockade started. Running alongside it, a high-voltage DC transmission line takes power from the wind and solar installations in the desert south to Islamabad. Fossil fuel one way, electrical power the other. So cutting it will impact them both."

Teddy sucked a breath. "That's got to be . . . a hundred kilometers from here."

"Right. Not far."

"But over the roughest terrain in the world."

"Your guys are mountaineers, right?"

"Not all of them." Teddy cleared his throat; the dried bat shit, or whatever, clogged him up. "Look, all we've got are small arms and a couple RPGs they stole from a police station. The Hans patrol these mountains with drones. Copters. We need weapons. Serious cold-weather gear. Night vision. Stingers."

The CIA man lowered his voice further. "I'm here to elucidate your requirements. But the first drop's tonight. They're waiting on my call."

Teddy sighed, trying not to show how pleased he felt. A drop was a commitment. "I hope it includes boots."

"Of course it includes fucking boots." Vladimir winced, as if he hadn't meant to drop the F-bomb. "Sorry."

"Hey, you didn't offend me . . . it's actually good to hear English again. Boots and—?"

"Figured you wanted to stay with the AK platform. So it's 7.62×39, RPDs and RPGs. And we—"

"Kim bu?" The short slim old man bowed, smiling, his wispy beard falling to his chest. A taller man, with a mustache half white, half black, stood behind him, holding a rifle.

Teddy lurched to his feet, favoring his bad leg. The rebels' religious leader was asking who this new guest was. Vladimir stood too, and Teddy introduced him, lapsing into his prison Han. "Imam Akhmad, this is our contact man with the CIA. We can call him Vladimir, but he is American, not Russian. That is only his war name. Like Tokarev here." He nodded at Guldulla. "Let us sit down to tea. Dandan! More!"

No reply. But the scuffle of bare feet in the dark told him she'd heard.

THE sun fell behind the peaks. Their shadows merged, painting the world black beneath a glowing sapphire sky. Miles from the cave, Teddy shifted uneasily atop a donkey. At least he didn't have to walk. The bitter wind chilled him to the bone. To his left Vladimir sat on another donkey, chatting in low tones to Tokarev. To his right, Nasrullah muttered with one of the bodyguards he'd assigned to Teddy. Obie wasn't sure if it was to protect him, or to keep an eye on him.

At last he swung down and found shelter in a rock crevice. The CIA contact joined him, cupping his gloves to torch a cigarette with a black Zippo. He offered one, but Teddy grimaced. "Akhmad runs a tight ship. No alcohol. No smokes. Prayers five times a day."

"What, are you turning into one of the Faithful?"

Teddy wondered how to explain whatever it was he'd experienced in the Tien Shan. But he didn't understand it himself. Vision, hallucination, mystic insight?

Shivering on the icy ridge that night, eyes wide open, Teddy Harlett Oberg had left his body.

The mountains had glowed with a light he'd never seen before. They were folded out of rock, like origami. The way the world itself was . . . folded . . . out of . . . nothing.

An enormous voice had spoken, but without words. It revealed how one single Will underlay the world. The mountains. The stars. Everything that had happened, or ever would. All had been foreordained, before Time itself had existed.

Which meant: Choice was an illusion.

All was one thought. One act. One creation.

The vision had left him shaking on the ground. When it lifted, like an immense black saucer departing for the stars, he'd screamed for it to take him. Hating to return to his starving, agonized body. His time-bound, ignorant mind, pinched as in a coffin.

No . . . some things couldn't be talked about. Reducing it to words would make him sound insane. Finally he just muttered, "It's complicated. I'm sort of falling in with the way they think, maybe. So, when's the drop?"

"Any minute now." The liaison studied his own phone. "And . . . here it comes."

A shape slid against the stars. Before Teddy could react, something heavy thudded down onto the gravel fifty yards away. Black wings collapsed above it, fluttering in the wind. Guldulla's shout sent men running to drag it back into the warren of rocks where the donkeys were hobbled. Others scanned the ridgeline, aiming rifles with, Teddy knew, nearly empty magazines.

But apparently the drop was undetected. Daylight, though, could change that. So as chute after chute collapsed fluttering, he and the other leaders kept the men humping. They hauled the crates to where drivers lashed them on panniers and chivvied the animals on up the mountain. When the stars had wheeled two hours on, all the parachutes were collected and the packaging was policed up. They left the streambed unmarked.

CUMIN-RICH smells of lamb and rice and naan met them as they pulled off blankets and coats back in the main cave. As the men pried the crates open, Nasrullah inventoried them on a grade-school tablet. Teddy inspected a new-looking AK. "It's stamped in Chinese," Vlad said. "But it was made in Charleston. The ammo's Ukrainian."

There were two hundred rifles and over a quarter million rounds of ammunition. Enough for training and a couple of engagements. Teddy was inspecting a case of road mines when Nasrullah came up, carrying an irregular bundle. *"Bu oyoq seniki bo'lishi kerak,"* he muttered, of which Obie got only about half. Accepting it, he stripped off Bubble Wrap to reveal a complexly curved fabrication. Aluminum? Titanium? Bending, he held it to where the damaged foot dangled. He buckled the straps and stood, testing it. The brace took his weight, and, miraculously, without pain.

"Nice," he muttered. "But I don't see any Stingers. Nothing to bat down drones. Or any night vision. Did I miss those?"

"Got to earn the advanced technology, Teddy. Hit that pipeline. Show us results, the good stuff arrives. And we do have good stuff on tap."

Dandan nudged his elbow with a mug of hot tea. He patted her behind through the black cloth, and watched with interest as she shuffled off. Then re-collected himself and walked slowly, not limping for the first time in months, toward several ragged young men who squatted at the back of the cave.

New fish. They regarded him with something between apprehension and awe as he forced a smile. *"Isyon xush kelibsiz."* He hoped that was passable, and repeated the words in Han and Russian. *"Huanyíng lái dào pànluàn . . . Dobro pozhalovat' v vosstanii."* Welcome to the rebels, welcome to the resistance. *"Hal yujad huna ahd yatakallam alerby?"* Anyone here speak Arabic?

No takers, which was good. The guys who came in from the cold tended to be uneducated: shepherds, peasants, truck drivers. He could work with that. He shook hands with each, and led them past the guys unpacking the crates, noting how their gazes homed in on the weapons. Back to rows of carpets, steaming pots of tea, and covered dishes the slave women were carrying in.

The food was hot, the air warm, and a song was wailing and jangling on a player, heavy on the drums and guitar, when one of the original muj lowered himself beside him. A chunky fellow with a reddish beard. Alimyan. Teddy nodded companionably. Alimyan helped himself to tea. Then asided quietly, "He is truly CIA?"

"As best as I can tell."

"You will use us as food for cannons. We cannot trust CIA. Or America."

Cannon fodder, he must mean. Teddy debated how to answer, since he'd just accused Langley of the same thing. Vladimir was eyeing them from across the feast. One of the new recruits was holding the officer's hand. . . . "Uh, not sure what you mean. Food for . . . ?"

"America will supply guns as long as we fight Chinese. But you will abandon us after the war. Bomb us, as you did the Taliban after the Communists withdrew."

Teddy shifted, like a man on the hot seat. From his other side, Akhmad was listening too, blinking watery old eyes. The imam's cataracts didn't seem to keep him from reading the Koran, or maybe he'd memorized it by now. Turning back to Alimyan, Obie murmured, "There are other versions of this history. We are allies now. America will stand by you to the end."

"The end of what? Of the Uighurs, at the hands of the Han? No, too many abandonments." The fat muj raised his voice, glaring across at the contact. "I tell you, I do not trust this man. Him, or any other foreign unbeliever."

Teddy deliberated. "Foreign unbeliever" had to mean him, too. The voices around them were falling silent. Others had heard the challenge. He had to meet it.

As to how . . . these guys operated on two things: religion and honor. He didn't share their religion, but maybe they had the other in common. "Then I will swear you a solemn oath." He raised his voice too, so all could hear. "I will stand by you to the end, no matter what that end may be. I, the Lingxiù, will not abandon you. *'Uqsim fi sabil allah:* In the name of Allah."

Alimyan still looked skeptical, but the old imam laid his withered hand on Teddy's arm. He blinked rapidly. Then intoned, "We will walk this road together. As you said: In the name of Allah."

Oberg blinked too, covering a sudden rush of unexpected emotion with a reach for a handful of lamb. What the fuck? Had he meant that, what he'd just promised?

Even he wasn't really sure.

THAT night, after the fires were banked and he'd seen Vlad to another chamber, stationing an armed guard outside to protect him, he attended prayers with the others in the main cavern. Sitting and kneeling in unison, turning his head to left and right to greet his co-worshippers, he felt a sudden qualm. Maybe the doubting Thomas, Alimyan, was right. Maybe he was leading them all to the slaughter.

Fuck that, Obie. They're all volunteers. All grown-ups.

Except maybe the fifteen-year-old beside him. Who looked actually more like thirteen.

They're still volunteers.

Volunteers who think you're leading them to paradise?

Who think I'll lead them against the Chinese.

Who'll mow them down.

Not if we do our planning, Tok and I. Plan hard, hit hard, then disappear. Billet most of the rebels with their families, in towns and villages, or their home farms. As far as Internal Security knows, they're civilians.

The old imam intoned the rak'as as they faced Mecca, and Teddy murmured and prostrated himself along with the rest. The old guy's

Arabic was terrible. As the prayer ended and the men held up their hands and muttered their dhikr, he made a mental note to ask Vlad to send him a Koran with a pronunciation guide.

DANDAN was waiting in his own cave-nook, which had an entrance so low he had to stoop double to crawl in. But that let him block it with a crate, and he laid his rifle, fully loaded and with the safety off, beside his pallet.

The Han girl looked frightened. *"Ba ni de yifú tuole,"* he told her, and pulled up the black caftan. She was naked underneath, naked and scrawny and with blue bruises on her throat. Her suddenly revealed face was ashen, and she shrank away, covering herself with her hands.

At his peremptory gesture she lay back on the pallet and hastily spread her legs. Holding her by the throat, half choking her, he pulled down his pants and rammed up into her bony hips with hard, rapid strokes. Face turned away, eyes squeezed shut, she shuddered. A tear winked in the candlelight when he rolled off, breathing hard.

Hey, Teddy Oberg thought, lying on his back, watching the firelight flicker on the overhead. This might not be too bad of a way to live. Training, and leading men into battle, and in the evening feasting and screwing slave girls . . .

There might be something to this.

3

Cast Away

THAT day dawned like all the others since the crash. Cloudless, and it would soon be hot. The surf was booming out on the reef, a deep growling like faraway drums. A reverberation so endless, beneath the sigh of the wind in the palms and the cries of gulls, that he never noticed it unless he consciously listened.

And someone was screaming, not far away.

Daniel V. Lenson rubbed grit from swollen eyes. Scratching at sand flea bites, he lay staring out at the sea from a pile of plastic bottles, discarded fishing floats, driftwood, and thin plastic bags wadded up and hammered into makeshift bricks. The shelter he lay in was floored with pandanus leaves. The roof was more leaves, high enough so he could crawl under, but not sit up. It was warmer at night that way.

The horizon was empty. Vacant. Untenanted. As it had been since they'd landed here, though occasionally high contrails scratched the blue.

The island—they didn't know its name, if it even had one—was less than half a mile long and not quite ten feet above sea level at its highest point, except perhaps for some craggy exposed rocks at one spot along the shore. Rugged and black, they were obviously part of whatever ancient volcano had vomited up the island before eroding into what was left. The place was uninhabited, though a rotten, abandoned lean-to on the eastern spit testified that someone, probably fishermen, had camped there long ago.

Their helicopter had been shot down after the strike on the mainland. Lenson, in charge of the surface strike group, had been en route from the stricken and burning *Savo Island* to her sister cruiser,

Hampton Roads. Wilker said the missile had come out of the blue. Best guess, one of the German-licensed antihelo weapons the Allies had discovered Chinese submarines carried.

Only three men had made it out of the inverted, sinking airframe after the crash: Dan; Min Su Hwang, the South Korean liaison officer; and "Strafer" Wilker, the pilot. Dan had tried to pull the wounded out. He'd been taking them to *Hampton Roads* as well. But he'd failed, foiled by their entanglement in their litters and their inability to help free themselves. Grabbing a bailout bottle as the water submerged their screaming mouths, he'd swum forward to cut the pilot out of the smashed-in cockpit. But all the others—the crew chief, the co-pilot, and the wounded—had died, spiraling down into the blue-black abyss.

Leaving the three of them, all stove up to some degree, on a bright yellow life raft meant for two. They'd drifted for days, running out of food first, then water. Fumbling desperately with the patch kit as taut rubber wrinkled toward uselessness. Bobbing oh so gently on the blue, eyeing circling fins. And the gulls too had circled, lower and lower. . . .

He'd understood the birds, there near the end. What they were saying. It was simple. They were shrieking, *Die. Die.*

Now Wilker was screaming again. "Oh, God," he sobbed. "Oh, God. No."

Dan dug at his eyes again—the pussy salt-crust that had formed during long days in the raft had never quite healed—and pushed aside the crumbling body board that walled out the coconut crabs. Unless you barricaded yourself inside, they'd eat you alive at night. And the less said about the flies, the better. That was why they'd set up camp on this beach. The wind, nearly always from the southwest, blew the insects back into the interior, which was a festering jungle.

He crawled out and stretched, brushing sand and leaves from faded, salt-stiff khakis.

Hwang was crouched over Wilker when Dan got there. Always thin, the Korean had gone from willowy to ephemeral. They spent all their waking hours looking for food. Coconuts. The yellow fruits of the pandanus, stringy and probably not all that nutritious, but they filled the belly. Seaweed, soaked in rainwater. Roots, boiled in their prize possession, a tin pan found discarded near the abandoned camp. And the fruits of the sea, of course: bêche-de-mer, conch, shellfish. They'd tried to spearfish, but it was impossible to pin a silver-flicker with a makeshift shaft of sharpened bamboo. Hwang had found a sun-corroded net on the beach, complete with glass flotation globes. This had allowed them to catch a few reef fish, colorful little wrasses and gobies whose brilliant hues swiftly bleached in the air, before the ancient polymer disintegrated.

"Admiral," Hwang mumbled. He'd lost his front teeth in the crash, which made everything that included a fricative hard to decipher. *"An yung ha see yo?"*

Dan knelt. "Morning, Min Su. How we doing, Ray?"

"Fucked up. Fucked up. Oh, God, it hurts." Wilker clawed at his face, sobbing.

Half buried in a pile of plastic trash, the pilot shuddered. His face was ruddy, choleric, and blackened with bruises. The windshield had smashed it in and broken his jaw. Never again would he haunt the erotic dreams of the female crew. His legs were both shattered. Dan had found driftwood boards and lashed his thighs and calves to them, straightening the fractured bones as best he could, but neither he nor Hwang was medically trained, and they'd had to back off when Wilker's shrieks grew too appalling to bear.

And the days had stretched out into weeks. . . .

"I'm dying," Wilker muttered, between teeth clenched tight in the swollen, inflamed jaw. "And it won't . . . be a minute . . . too fucking soon."

Dan sat back on bare heels in the sand. They'd left their boots in the wrecked chopper, or ditched them from the raft. A mistake, in retrospect, but nothing they could do anything about now. Like so much else.

"What will it be thif morning, thir?" Hwang asked. "Coconut?"

"Yeah," Dan muttered. "Coconut. Again."

"It is your turn. Thir."

"Don't fucking bother, either of you fucking cocksuckers," Wilker muttered. "I'm fucking finished. Just leave me the fuck alone."

They'd taken turns chewing up food for the pilot, since he couldn't. Fortunately, there were plenty of plastic spoons.

Really, Dan thought grimly, the garbage had litter-ally saved their lives. Untenanted though they were, the beaches were strewn with flotsam. All kinds of plastic trash—bottles, fishing floats, life preservers, bleach containers, discarded toys, butane lighters, six-pack rings, balloons, toothbrushes, plates, bottle caps, and thousands of slowly disintegrating plastic bags—lay scattered wherever the waves touched, left by the tide or half buried in the coarse brown sand. Which meant that once they'd succeeded in kindling a fire, after two days of frustrating failure, they'd never lacked fuel.

And the weeks had gone by one after another. . . .

A plastic bag dangled from a branch stuck in the sand. The ground under it was scribbled with the tracks of the murderous crabs. He pulled it down and peered inside. Five small yellow fruits and half a coconut gave off a stench of glue and ferment. Grimacing at the taste, he masticated one, then squatted and spat it onto a spoon. Held it out.

Wilker squeezed his eyes closed. He shook his head.

"Eat it, Strafer. Eat your food."

"Fuck you. Fucking bastard."

Hwang sighed. "Don't be like that. The admiral chewed it up good for you. Tafety, tafety fresh fruit."

"Fuck you. Fuck both of you. Goddamn vultures. Just let me die."

Christ, it was like getting Blair's cat to eat. But he couldn't imagine what tortures the airman was suffering. The worst thing about it was that there was nothing they could do for him.

"Just a little, Strafer. Come on," he coaxed. "You have to eat something."

The pilot only turned his face away.

HE and Hwang had walked around the island—a twenty-minute stroll, if they took their time—many times in the days after they'd arrived. Hoping they'd missed something, or someone. Then, reluctantly, ventured at last into its seething heart.

Once the sea was out of sight the racketing silence of the jungle surrounded them. Insects cheeped. Mosquitoes whined. Birds cawed and honked overhead. The light turned green. The heat clamped down, windless and humid. They clawed their way through heavy, clinging undergrowth laced with thorns that grabbed their ragged clothing and clawed their skin and punctured the tender soles of their bare, exposure-swollen feet. Fine silky webs clung to their faces, and the spiders bit savagely as they tried to shake them off.

The island was deserted. The only sign of human visitation had been the tumbledown hut on the spit. Until, deep in the interior one day, desperately hungry, grubbing for edible roots, Dan had stumbled over the remains of an outrigger canoe.

He lost, after a moment's inspection, his momentary flare of hope.

Scooped from a single log, with the adze marks still visible, it had been left abandoned, or had washed up in some ancient typhoon, sitting upright. Rainwater had rotted through the bottom long ago. The sides were crumbling. When he yanked on a gunwale, it fragmented away in his hand.

Termites boiled whitely beneath, amazed by the sudden light.

He recoiled, then recovered himself. He stared down, suddenly both attracted and revolted. Remembering how chimpanzees used a thin straw to tempt termites out of their nests.

So that they could . . . eat them.

After some gagging, he got one down. It tasted odd but not bitter, like he'd expected. Slightly crunchy, buttery, and at the same time a tiny bit tart. The taste wasn't unpleasant. Actually, it wasn't bad at all. If you didn't think about what was writhing in your mouth before you bit down.

He bent, panting, waiting for his stomach's reaction. Then began tearing apart the rotted wood, and feasting on the teeming multitudes within.

STRAFER got worse in the afternoons. Today was no exception. The screaming lessened, trailing off into long agonized groans. Then, even more ominously, into silence. Dan checked on him again. He rearranged his plastic-bag blanket, then stood motionless above him. Shaken by helpless rage.

If he hadn't shifted his flag, this wouldn't have happened. Who exactly had he thought he was? Commodore Perry, at Lake Erie? He'd abandoned his old crew. Left his old ship, to fend for herself without him.

Yeah, he was the strike group commander. It made sense tactically. You could even argue it was what he'd *had* to do, once his flagship lost power, lost connectivity, rolling dead in the water in an enemy sea. But he couldn't shake the guilt.

"I'm so sorry," he muttered, as much to the dead as to the dying man at his feet.

A writhing pang in his gut reminded him he had other urgent business. An urge that had struck every other hour since they'd landed, and, parched from thirst, drunk greedily from a scummy puddle above the tide line. Ever since that fatal draught, diarrhea had racked their guts, weakening them so much at times they could barely crawl.

He panted, squatting in the surf. Then, when the crisis passed, belted up and tottered inland. Intent on the next task. Not just for himself, but for the broken, dying hulk he cared for.

Fish today? Clams? Or coconuts? His stomach turned at the thought of more pandanus fruit. Stringy, pulpy, the stuff tasted like Testors. Seaweed was filling, but tough to chew unless they boiled it into a slimy mess. Leaving you, in the end, doubting whether the energy you'd expended was worth what you got out of it. He lurched on down the beach, forcing each step. Go on. Make the tour. Maybe something would turn up. A dead bird. Seagull eggs. Hearts of palm. They'd managed. So far.

His thoughts went to everything he didn't know. What had happened to his old ship? To his strike group? To the war, heating up on three fronts, and with the homeland itself under a tyrant's dire and all too credible threat?

Of course no answers came. He dragged along, sweating. He clambered over black weathered lava, then down to the sand beyond. He stepped over the boles of fallen, half-buried palms. Skirted where he and Hwang had piled up more of them, heaping the makeshift pyre with plastic bottles, milk crates, life preservers, whatever they could scavenge that would burn.

As he rounded the point to the spit, coming out on the leeward side, hordes of mosquitoes found him, followed by the biting flies. He windmilled his arms like a lunatic, slapped his brow, but it barely discouraged them. Well, he couldn't blame them. Probably the first warm-blooded meal they'd had for years.

Strafer would die, and soon. That was obvious. They couldn't do anything, even to ease his pain. And not long after, he and Hwang would too. Either of infection, or starvation, or exposure, if a typhoon happened along while they were stranded on this all-too-low patch of wasteland.

He stood motionless. A faint wind cooled him, and drove a few of the flies away. He fanned a persistent one away from his eyes with a hand. So, if this was it . . . what had it all amounted to?

One thing about being cast away on a desert island: it gave you time to think.

His life, his career, his marriages? The relationships . . . lovers, wives . . . he didn't regret those. Maybe that he'd been too hard-hearted, too abrupt. Too concerned, too often, about himself over others.

His career . . . "star-crossed" was the usual euphemism. He held the

Medal, true, but not for himself. Paid for by others, most of them dead, on the ill-fated Signal Mirror mission to Baghdad. As to the rest . . . he'd tried to act honorably, but by his own lights, not necessarily by the Rocks and Shoals.

He thought he'd been a decent skipper aboard USS *Horn*. Done some good at the Tactical Analysis Group. Helped defuse some sticky situations. But he'd screwed up, too. Nearly lost a squadron in the Taiwan Strait. Hazarded a hunter-killer group in the central Pacific. And along the way, made powerful enemies, both in the Navy and in the government.

Maybe after all, what they whispered was true: that he owed whatever he had to his connections. To his rabbi, the chief of naval operations. To his wife, high in the previous administration, and now part of this one, too. That he didn't deserve the stars on his collar. And even that rank was good only for the duration.

He kicked a bleach bottle out of his way. A hermit crab scuttled out, tiny pincers raised in threat, and backed away.

But did all that really matter?

No. It didn't.

So what did?

Maybe, that he'd always tried to do his best.

That he'd put the welfare of his crew before his own, and saved lives whenever he could.

He was pretty sure he'd made Blair happy. If she loved him, he couldn't have done too much wrong.

And the one bright and untarnished thing he could truly cherish: his daughter. If Nan was safe, that would be reward enough.

Despite hunger, and fear, Dan Lenson smiled, alone on the sea-swept strand.

If she remembered him, if she missed him, that would be enough.

HE was trudging back to camp, squinting toward the surf-line in the blinding light, when he saw it. Far off, against the horizon. A tiny speck.

He glanced away, then back. The dot was still there. He shaded his eyes and created a pinhole with a fist to inspect it more closely. Still only a speck; he couldn't even tell if it had a mast.

But it was the first craft they'd seen in all the weeks they'd been stranded.

He folded, elbows on knees, suddenly overcome by the dizziness of mingled hope and agonizing abdominal cramps. He breathed deep, sucking in briny air. Mustering all his strength. Then straightened, and looked again.

Still there. And unless he was imagining it, the tiny shape was bow on.

Headed for them?

Yes. Headed for them.

He bawled aloud, shaking both fists over his head, a mindless, animal outburst of sound. Tears streaking his cheeks, but not caring.

He lurched into an uneven, staggering run, bare feet thudding in the sand.

4

The Pentagon

A watery winter sunlight oozed through thick shatterproof windows as the tall, pale woman marched down the E Ring, heels clicking unevenly. A slight limp marred her stride. Two male staffers hurried after, one gripping a briefcase, the other a notebook computer. She looked tense, abstracted, not meeting the glances of the uniformed officers who passed. A sleepless night had creased her forehead and left smudges under her eyes. She fingered her left ear, then pulled down a lock of hair to hide it.

Maybe time at last to go gray, she thought. This war . . . She wheeled at a corridor, heading for a security station, and the staffers turned with her, almost in step. She pulled an access card on a chain out of her blouse.

A sign read NATIONAL MILITARY INTELLIGENCE CENTER.

THE Blairs had been active in national politics since 1831, when Francis Preston Blair had moved to Washington to start a pro-Jackson newspaper. Five generations on, Blair Titus had begun her career at the Congressional Research Service, then been hired as Senator Bankey Talmadge's defense aide. As he gained seniority over the years, she'd risen too. Staff director at the Armed Services Committee. Then, a DoD position in the administration before this.

Narrowly defeated in a bid for Congress, she'd accepted an offer from the opposition party, to help bridge the expertise gap as the country plunged into war.

"We'll fast-track Senate confirmation," Edward Szerenci, the national security adviser, had mused a year ago. "Your people say they want a coalition government. I thought about NSC staff director, but I need at least one girl with brains in the Puzzle Palace. How's deputy undersecretary for strategy, plans, and forces sound? The current guy isn't impressing anybody. And you still have juice on the Hill. That work for you?"

She'd wrestled grave misgivings. She and Szerenci had clashed before. To some extent, she blamed him for the war. Certainly he hadn't worked very hard to avoid it. The president seemed paralyzed, indecisive, unsure. Plus, joining would mean ostracism by the peace wing of her own party.

But at last she'd decided. The country needed her, as much as if she were in uniform, like so many others. "I'll work *with* you. But not *for* you," she'd finally told him. "And when I think you're wrong, I'll push back."

He'd shrugged. Smiled that remote smile. Acquiescence, or only a temporary truce? With Szerenci, who knew.

And now she was a widow. Not officially—Dan was still listed as missing in action, after his helo had vanished—but after more than a month, no one was holding out hope any longer.

She touched her ear again, then snatched her hand down. Well, *tant pis*, Blair. A lot of people had died since this war had started. And losses and damage weren't limited to the Pacific. Chinese cyberattacks were becoming steadily more effective, driven by Jade Emperor, a massive self-programming neural network. Terabytes of vital data had vanished in the Cloudburst. Financial networks collapsed. Credit cards were history. Power outages crippled war production. The draconian "Defense of Freedom" Act had suspended trials, confiscated weapons, drafted the undocumented, and nationalized the internet. Looting, riots, rationing, hoarding, the rise of violent militias and apocalyptic sects, made her personal problems—a dead husband, a million dollars of debt after the failed House campaign, and vilification by the isolationists—seem paltry. Compared to the danger.

Regardless of what happened in this war, the U.S., and the world, were going to look very different afterward.

The guard slid their phones and the notebook into a plastic bin, and waved them through. "Go ahead, ma'am." She smiled, lips compressed, and went on in.

THE Joint Chiefs' Pacific War Working Group, acronymized to PWWG, met twice a week. Today the principals were tasked to reexamine offensive options. She'd worked all night pulling together the alternatives with her staff and mustering her arguments.

The meeting room, opening off the already highly secure Intel Center, looked like any windowless conference space. But it was as heavily shielded electronically as anywhere on the planet. No phones or computers were permitted, and a staffer in a soundproof booth ran a console that detected any recording or transmitting devices.

"So we're back to yellow pads and pencils," she murmured to General Ricardo Petrarca Vincenzo at the coffee-and-pastries table. "How retro."

The chairman of the Joint Chiefs muttered something inaudible from behind a pecan sticky. Several ops deps, operations deputies, settled along the wall. They could be called on for clarification, but were there mainly because they'd have to execute whatever was agreed on. She greeted the other attendees as they filed in. General Glee, the Army chief of staff. Gray, sparrowish Absalom Lipsey, Joint Chiefs J-3, operations. The blue-suited bulk of Admiral Barry "Nick" Niles, chief of naval operations. General Randall Faulcon, rangy and taciturn, with three stars won in Ashaara, Afghanistan, and Iraq; now he was the deputy Pacific Command, under Jim Yangerhans. Dr. Kevin Glancey, an expert on war termination from Stanford. And others, all high in the pecking order, including reps from State and CIA.

Compact, gray-suited, platinum-haired, the national security adviser gave her an avuncular smile as he took his seat. "Ed," she murmured unwillingly.

"Finally, no more 'Dr. Szerenci.' About time." He took off horn-rims and polished the lenses with a handkerchief. Without their frames his face sagged like wet clay. "Any . . . news about Dan?"

She shook her head, looking down, focusing on her notes.

A Marine colonel opened with sobering news, the kind you didn't hear on television. Iran was taking over islands and oil platforms in the Gulf. The Saudis were fighting back, but losing. A new crisis loomed on the southern front, where Vietnamese forces faced the Chinese on a line south of Hanoi. The Vietnamese army was reeling back under a massive ground offensive, with horrendous losses on both sides. The Chinese were also reopening their offensive against India, where the mountain fighting had stalemated up to now.

"The war's still spreading," the briefer said. "One or more of our frontline allies—Saudi, India, Vietnam—may be knocked out. Forced to ask for terms."

Szerenci rubbed his face. “Someone mentioned sending reinforcements. To stiffen them. The Viets, I mean. An armored brigade. Is that possible?”

Beside her Vincenzo shook his head. The chairman said, “We’ve discussed this, Doctor. The Army’s not ready for sustained major-power ground war. We let our heavy units rot while we fought counterinsurgency in the Middle East.

“It took nearly two years in the last war before we could seize the offensive in the Pacific. Until the middle of ’43. And in some ways, we’re not doing as well this time.”

“Are *any* forces available?” Szerenci massaged sunken eye sockets.

“We’re working on it. But if we commit untrained troops, the slants will grind them up.”

“So what’s our response?”

“Continue to build up in depth. Bring the new weapons forward. Stockpile a robust inventory. Train. Ask me again a year from now, I might say yes. Even then, I’ll fight any landing on the mainland.” He sighed. “For Vietnam . . . maybe a second bomb wing to the base at Da Nang. Step up weapons shipments. But they’ll have to hold on their own.”

“I see,” Szerenci said. “Any other opinions?”

Faulcon cleared his throat. “I don’t mean to disagree. But I’ve studied Grant’s campaigns. Usually, in a battle, there’s a lull after the first engagements. Whoever renews action first usually ends in possession of the field.

“The chairman’s right about needing to work up ground forces. But we should move sooner rather than later.”

“Thank you, General Faulcon, General Vincenzo. We’ll leave the final decision to the president, advised by the SecDef.” Szerenci nodded. “But I’m sure he’ll take everyone’s opinion into account. Blair, will you—?”

“I’m seeing the secretary right after this meeting.”

The briefing resumed. The DIA rep explained a split in what he called the “consensus of the intelligence community.” The questions were whether Zhang was contemplating further aggression, and how much the People’s Empire was hurting internally.

“We get varying indicators. Special intelligence sources confirm a pullback of air and remaining naval forces in response to Operation Recoil. Apparently our invasion of Itbayat and the raid on Ningbo were successful in interrupting any plan for a second pulse eastward, to the Marianas and Guam.

"Internally, there's unrest, yes, and some indications of spot famine. But the Internal Security forces are still robust and General Chagatai's repressions in Hong Kong seem to have quieted things down. We have hopes of nurturing trouble in Xianjiang, though."

Blair had been doodling on the edges of her yellow pad. A bee. Then another, on the page beneath. And another, each in a slightly different position. "My concern," she put in, "is the recent statement of support from Moscow. Support for Zhang, that is. Is Russia going to take part? That would put a different complexion on the war."

"I agree. We can't take on another enemy just now. Shira, anything to contribute?" Szerenci turned to a slender, small-boned black woman.

The State rep was about Blair's age, in a hip-length slate tunic and fitted black trousers. Blair knew Shira from her time with Armed Services, in the Senate. Salyers wore smooth, straight bangs across a high forehead. "State suspects Moscow may take this opportunity to move on the Baltic states while we're occupied in the Pacific. But we don't see them overtly taking China's side."

"Elaborate, please," Szerenci said. "Can the EU hold the line in eastern Europe? Right now, all our forces are in the Pacific, except for placeholders opposite Iran."

"Um, well, as far as the EU . . . they're debating their response. The Russians are also selling Beijing arms, of course. Missiles. Updates to the Shkval torpedo. The new tanks."

The CIA rep lifted a hand. "Apparently, one reason Russia's supporting Zhang—other than that he's fighting us—is that the premier's threatened Mongolia and the Russian Federation republic of Tyva. Essentially, 'Stand behind me, or Russia loses territory in the east.'"

Drawing another bee, Blair murmured, "Could we delaminate the two? Surely their interests diverge. And Russians don't react well to threats."

State, her head down, said, "We're staying alert for any opportunity. Um, on the plus side, the Japanese are moving toward renewed participation in the war. They want to retake Okinawa."

Vincenzo explored his teeth with the point of a pencil. "Will they help elsewhere?"

"An open question. You can put that peer-to-peer with the Self-Defense Forces leadership. At least, they might cooperate on logistics and air and missile defense. The way we did before we had to withdraw from Korea."

"We can offer support in the Ryukyus," Blair said. "Reintegrate them gradually into joint operations."

"They're still wary," the State rep pointed out, fingering her bangs. "Until they get their own deterrent in place, um, they're going to be skittish about an overt alliance."

An Air Force general leaned forward. "We can offer deterrent coverage."

"Why trust us?" Vincenzo said bluntly. "Zhang wiped out a whole carrier group with a nuclear weapon, and we held back. That doesn't inspire confidence in our willingness to protect anyone else."

"The president wants . . . ," Szerenci began, then fell silent. Blair frowned. What had he been about to say? But the usual smooth emendation emerged. "He wants recommendations. What are we going to tell him? Nick?"

Admiral Niles lumbered to his feet. He'd always been big, but the stress of the past year had thickened the CNO's frame even more, as well as thinning his never-all-that-plentiful hair. "The destruction of the Chinese wolf pack in the central Pacific by Admiral Lenson"—he gave Blair a nod—"and others has cleared our supply lines. We're completing fleetwide upgrades. Improved missile defense, better antitorpedo capabilities, uparmoring, and enhancing signature management for self-protection. A new cruiser class, more jeep carriers, and forty more autonomous submarines will be operational soon."

He cleared his throat into a fist. Really, she thought, he didn't sound healthy. "We're isolating what will be the ultimate battlefields. Our subs are continuing the blockade of the South China coast. They're taking losses. We don't know why . . . they just don't report back in. But Admiral Lianfeng's Southern Fleet is either wiped out or sealed into their ports. Our drone subs, recharged from isotope-fueled supercapacitors on the seabed, are cutting Taiwan off from the mainland. Eventually, we may be able to strand half a million occupation troops.

"The carriers. *George Washington* has finally been repaired and will be operational again soon. We'll have the new *FDR* in workup shortly as well. With *Nimitz*, *Vinson*, *Stennis*, *Reagan*, and *Lincoln*, that will mean seven carrier battle groups in the Pacific this spring, plus another eight light carriers optimized to handle deep-strike AAVs. Pretty certainly, that'll be as many as we'll ever be able to surge."

Niles took a turn around the room, big hands locked behind him. "Operation Recoil dented their confidence. But two years into the war, I agree—we've got to take the offensive. Or, as I've said before, the situation on the ground becomes the status quo.

"Plus, even a peripheral offensive could take the pressure off the Vietnamese and Indians." He stretched massive arms until the joints cracked. "Iran's making hay in the Gulf. But we can't stop them."

"We can deal with that after China's defeated," Vincenzo said.

"Well, I believe you're right, Mr. Chairman," Szerenci said. "But, unfortunately, so is the CNO."

The national security adviser folded his hands and rested his chin on them, peering into the far distance. He murmured, almost too low to hear, "This is what Ehrenburg called 'Deep War.' Like the Somme. Or Stalingrad.

"Blair, I know you're uncomfortable with our suspension of habeas corpus and the First and Second Amendments. So am I, frankly. But we're finally committing to total war and total victory. The Hill's approved a full military draft, including women. Industry's still clearing the wreckage from the Cloudburst, but we're fully converted to defense production."

He nodded to Vincenzo. "Ricardo, I understand we're still not that well trained. But Nick's right too. Recoil threw a stick in their wheels. Now we have to start running the game."

He pointed to Lipsey. "Abe, what's Plans come up with?"

The sparrowlike general hopped to his feet as a wall screen came on. The JCS logo: four crossed swords behind a shield, encircled by the laurel wreath of victory.

"Utilizing mainly naval, air, and Marine forces, but with limited Army participation, J-3's planned a two-pronged offensive. Attacks on both coasts, to divide their forces. Preceded by intense information-denial operations and cyber raids, to confuse and interrupt command and control."

The screen showed the southern coast of China.

"The southern phase will be called Operation Uppercut. A major raid on the naval bases on Hainan Island, accompanied by strikes on other military assets along the contiguous coast to Hong Kong. Supported by light carriers, it will include Australian, Indian, and some Vietnamese participation. We envision it taking place in three phases, extending over roughly a week, and ending with the destruction of the Southern

Fleet and reduction of their air power and ability to stage further aggression in the South China Sea.

"As a downstream benefit, regaining battle space dominance will free us for follow-on strikes along the flank of the enemy armies in northern Vietnam, keeping Hanoi in the war."

The Plans chief called up a third slide. "The northern phase will be the step we've discussed before as a possible follow-on to the seizure of Itbayat: the landing on Taiwan and the eventual liberation of that island."

Vincenzo was shaking his head already. Blair tensed, leaning forward in her chair.

"Following a carrier surge west, Operation Causeway would land a full U.S. Marine division and supporting forces to link up with General Luong Shucheng's guerrillas in the eastern mountains. Simultaneously, an Army corps will land in the south. It'll be a bitter struggle. But since we'll control the air, with the carrier groups and Air Force support out of the new field at Itbayat, we can reinforce as the Guard divisions complete training and come online."

Silence haunted the room. At last Szerenci said gently, "You left something out. About Hainan."

Lipsey looked away. "The sub pens are under a mountain. Protected by millions of tons of rock and concrete. Conventional penetrating bombs won't destroy them. We're considering a penetrating nuclear warhead. Unfortunately, or perhaps by design, there's a city, Sanya, half a million people, only a few miles away.

"As I said, we're still modeling. The results aren't conclusive yet."

Szerenci gestured around the table. "Opinions? Objections? On the plan as a whole, or on either prong?"

He was looking at her. She thumbed the edge of the legal pad, making the pages flicker so the bee darted angrily back and forth. Finally she murmured, "I'm inclined to agree with Nick. It's time for an offensive. At least a limited one. Not on the mainland—I'm with Ricardo there.

"But . . . listen." She spread her hands. "I've seen war. In the Gulf, in Ashaara, in Iraq. But even war has to have limits. Restraint's the only way to end this conflict without major losses on both sides. Yes, China went nuclear. And hurt us. Badly. But if we escalate too . . . there's no telling where this will end. Nowhere good, for anyone."

Szerenci nodded, lips pursed. He turned to Glancey. "Doctor?"

The professor lifted his eyebrows. "Unfortunately, modern wars don't terminate when both adversaries are equally balanced. Unless both are totally exhausted, their economies wrecked. And often, not even then.

"In this case . . . I have to come down on Ed's side, Blair. Overwhelming force has to be demonstrated by one side, so the impossibility of victory is accepted by the other. Sometimes that happens militarily. Sometimes psychologically. In a few cases, by economic collapse. Human beings seem unable to accept stalemate." He sighed. "Especially after sacrifices have been made, outrages publicized, populations mobilized."

"Thanks, Kev. Anyone else?"

Vincenzo scowled down at the table. "Hainan, a raid—okay. But Taiwan's a bridge too far. Like I said, we're not ready. We don't have the forces. We don't have the surface connectors—the landing craft. Our studies say five divisions. Even then, we might get kicked back into the sea."

Szerenci pulled off his glasses again. Leaned back, as if he were lecturing in the classroom once more. "All right. Thank you for your opinions.

"As far as second use. I respect your arguments, Blair. But we have to get past squeamishness. We let them achieve strategic parity. I warned about that years ago, but we didn't act. Then, when hostilities began, we didn't retaliate against their first use of nuclear weapons. A major mistake, I think, but I was overruled. They perceived weakness, and may well strike again.

"These are unpleasant truths. But we have to rid ourselves of illusions."

He closed his eyes and massaged his cheeks. "We had to kill five percent of the Japanese population to convince them to surrender. The only way to win this war may be the same: kill enough Chinese that they turn against Zhang.

"Unfortunately, you can't regenerate a heavy deterrent overnight. And the previous administration didn't leave us in good shape."

Was he looking at her? "It was Congress that imposed sequestration," she corrected. "They postponed strategic modernization. Not the White House."

He shrugged. "Whatever. But we fell behind, while Beijing accelerated. We've doubled the warhead numbers on our heavy missiles. Reactivated three thousand tactical nukes from inventory. And improved our antimissile defenses.

"If Zhang wants a showdown, toe to toe, we may finally be able to take him on." Szerenci paused. "But only if we strike first."

Blair had started to set the bee flying again, but at his words a shudder threaded her spine. The old injury in her hip flamed. "A central nuclear exchange?"

Niles grunted, "Zhang started this game. When he wiped out our battle group."

She felt unreal. Detached. As if she could leave her body and float up from this long table, at which the end of the world was being discussed as if it were a video game. She forced words through breathlessness. "I'm sorry, that's just . . . insane. Not retaliating is the one thing we've done right so far in this war. The only way we can hope for a final decision without destroying both countries. What's going on backchannel, to see if there's some other way out? Or is it going to be bomb, bomb, bomb from now on?"

A few looked at her somberly; the rest, down at the table.

"The president will make the final decision," Szerenci murmured.

Vincenzo rapped the table. "Then let's conclude. I suggest a consensus. Yes to Operation Uppercut, in the south, with the nuclear option on the table for now. I still believe we're not ready for Taiwan. But if the political, I mean, the strategic realities demand an offensive, and if the commandant concurs, we'll support amphibious raids. To the extent possible. Ed? Is that responsive?"

"It'll be up to POTUS." The national security adviser smiled grimly.

They all looked down the table, at the commandant of the Marine Corps. Who said nothing, but simply nodded.

"All right, put that in the minutes. All in favor?"

The vote was six for, one against.

SHE was leaving when Szerenci called her aside. She clenched her fists, but kept her tone level. "What is it, Ed?"

He took her arm. "Don't be like that, Blair. Don't make this personal."

"You're playing poker with millions of lives. How can it not be personal? And let go of my arm, please. Now!"

He patted it and released her. "I have a request. We want you to serve on the UN Committee on War Crimes and Atrocities."

"What?" She blinked. "What the hell are you talking about? And who's 'we'?"

"They're meeting in Dublin next week. Setting up an oversight committee. We need an observer there. To make sure we don't get tarred and feathered, without having a chance to balance the membership."

The State rep had come back in. She stood a few feet away, obviously unwilling to interrupt. Blair tugged at her own ear, trying to keep her expression neutral. Was he trying to get her out of the way, so he could push his nuclear option without objection? Then say it was unanimous? "Dublin? Dublin, *Ireland*? Isn't that a State job? Or the UN ambassador's business?"

"State'll be there too. But the president asked for you by name."

Oh, right. So he could blame it on her if it turned sour. But the short man was saying, "You mentioned a back channel. Well, the Chinese will want to observe too. You may not be the only one thinking about opening a conversation." He half turned to the waiting woman. "Something for me, Shira?"

The State rep shook her head. "No, sir. Actually, it's for Ms. Titus."

"All right, what?" Blair snapped.

A slow smile curled the woman's lips. "Actually, I have some really good news for you, Blair."

5

Camp Pendleton, California

THE rifle squad's been split into fire teams. Team One crouches in a wrecked basement into which an apartment building has collapsed, leaving shattered beams of reinforced concrete tumbled like dead bones. A fire crackles somewhere, and the air, even down here, is hazy with smoke and rubble dust.

Hector Ramos crouches with them, peering intently into what to a merely human eye would be complete darkness. But his goggles give him vision without light, and data to inform his actions—though there isn't much just now, and he has to strain to understand what's streaming from the sensors the team set up outside, and from the single remaining quadcopter buzzing faintly far above.

Sergeant Hector Ramos is twenty years old. An E-5, even though he's been in the Corps for only two years. War speeds up promotion. He was slight when he joined but has put on twenty pounds since. His black hair is buzzcut. He wears a chin tuft and an eagle, globe, and anchor tattoo. He joined to avoid being deported, but he's a citizen now. The backs of his hands are deeply scarred from the Kill Room of Uncle Seth's Poultry Processing Plant #14, where he worked before being "volunteered" for the Corps.

The burns on them, though, are from battle. Ninth MEB was the spearhead for the seizure of Itbayat Island, the first bite off the People's Empire. Ramos holds a Purple Heart, the Combat Action Ribbon, and the Asiatic-Pacific Campaign Medal for that battle.

This morning the platoon hit the beach half a mile back, following a wave of cruise missile and air attacks. Far above, armed drones surveyed the surf-line and the dunes. When their operators detected an enemy, fire lanced downward, detonating either shrapnel or a shaped charge, depending on the target.

At last, with attack helicopters sealing off the flanks and inland approaches, the amtracs stormed ashore.

But just now things aren't going so well. The marines have penetrated the wrecked city, but an enemy force has circled behind the lead platoon, cutting them off. The fire team leader, a rookie corporal, doesn't seem to have a clue. Ramos explains again, sketching on his tablet. The Glasses of his squad gleam faintly, imaging the tactical situation as he outlines it. But he doesn't tell them what to do. That's up to the fire team leader. Who so far is showing zero leadership.

The marines wear "jelly" body armor with reactive inserts. Over that go the baggy new Cameleons, digital utility uniforms that change color and reflectivity according to the background. Each man or woman carries a chip under the skin of his or her upper back. The chips carry their medical history and individual ID. Their Lightweight Integrated Combat Helmets have night vision and a BattleGlass interface that feeds them ranges and threat evaluations wherever they look, as well as passing commands from Higher. The Ka-band link in the helmets connects them to the intraplatoon net. They grip weapons strange to Hector, who joined up before the tide of new equipment arrived.

One thing that hasn't changed is the Pig. Hector trained on the black 7.62 machine gun as a private, and fought with it as a gunner. But now it has a new optic and an autofire attachment, so a gunner can leave it to scan and interdict a sector on its own. The squad also has a recoilless rifle. The "Goose" fires antipersonnel, antitank, illumination, and smoke to an effective range of nearly a mile. Instead of the old 5.56, each rifleman carries an experimental shoulder weapon. It pings ranges with a laser, then sets its high-explosive projectile to detonate above the target. It has buckshot and flash-bang rounds for close-in work as well.

They also carry pistols in leg holsters, a rigger belt, a multitool, grenades, water-purification tablets, and LED flashlights. In their assault packs are a CamelBak with a hose, a 500ml intravenous bag with starter kit, MREs, poncho and liner, spare batteries, and a personal hygiene kit. In their main packs are a sleeping bag, undershirts, socks, more MREs, a sleeping pad, and a combat lifesaving kit. All in all, each man or woman carries 130 pounds of clothing, gear, weapons, food, water, and ammo.

Hector himself isn't part of the squad. He'd rather have just stayed on the Pig, but the Corps hasn't given him a choice. There are all too few veterans, and though he didn't exactly come out of Itbayat as a hero, he has the Heart and the burns to show he's been in combat.

Okay, gotta do something here. But the fire team leader's still staring into her Glasses, frozen. Hector tongues his Talk button. "Enough fucking *thinking*. What you gonna do?"

"Well, I'm not quite sure. . . ."

"Can't fucking *sit here*, Corporal. You're gonna get smoke checked. Keep ahead of the enemy. Disrupt his decision cycle. And remember to sweep for snipers. Urban terrain like this, Charlie Sierra can be anywhere." He gives her another couple of seconds, then sighs. "Remember, you got Chad here. Is this a mission for him?"

Beside them, crouched like them, yet profoundly unlike the other troops, a figure slowly gets to "hands" and "knees."

The Combat Humanoid Autonomous Device is a powered skeleton of carbon fiber and aluminum, programmed to respond to voice commands. It usually just follows them, hauling spare ammo, water, batteries, and chow. But it carries a rifle, too, and can acquire a target. Usually it requires verbal authorization to fire, but like the machine gun, it also has an autonomous mode, in case it has to cover a retreat. Along with a self-destruct charge, so the enemy can't get their hands on it.

Hector's wary of the thing. It seems both dumb and ominous, and his previous experiences with machines haven't been good. A robot cart went haywire during the Itbayat assault and raced off downhill, taking their ammo with it. But it's been assigned to them tonight, so they're pretty much stuck with it.

Still no action from the corporal. He leans in and hisses in her ear. "Let's fucking *act*, bitch!"

"Uh, Chad. I need you to go out the exit to your left. Find cover out there and lay down fire on a bearing of . . ." She hesitates. Hector was trying to visualize it too, but he's never been good with numbers.

"*Incomplete command*," Chad hisses, sibilant, pitched low.

In Hector's earbuds the computerized purr of Iron Dream, the seduction-voiced tactical adviser the troops call Wet Dream, prompts, "*Two-seven-zero to zero-zero-zero.*"

The fire team leader says, "Chad. Find cover out there and lay down aimed fire on sector between bearings of two-seven-zero to zero-zero-zero."

Chad hisses, *"Exit cover. Find new cover. Lay down. Aimed fire on sector between bearings of two-seven-zero to zero-zero-zero."*

She mutters, "Close enough. Confirm." The other squad members wriggle aside, and the machine creeps between them, motors whirring. It orients to the chink of light that marks the exit, lowers itself to its "elbows," and crawls through, bent awkwardly on all fours like a metallic reptile.

Thirty seconds later a thud marks the first departing round from Chad's rifle, followed almost immediately by an explosive *crack*. Hector clicks to its video feed. Chad's point of view, in infrared because it's night. It's in position, covering the approach, but the black cloud of high explosive it's just fired is too close amid the tumbled rubble of the wrecked city.

"Chad: Lengthen your range," the fire team leader orders. Good, Hector thinks. "Set your elevation to three hundred meters."

The next shot bursts above and behind a wrecked bus some three hundred meters off. "Good boy," she mutters. Hector blinks; why praise a machine? But when he turns back to the leader, she's staring into her Glasses again.

"Okay, what next?"

"I'm . . . not sure."

"You're taking too long. They're gonna target you. Move 'em out, goddamn it!"

She flinches. She snaps terse orders and flicks a go-ahead signal. As they crawl past, Ramos examines each face. They're newbies, draftees, and even after war-accelerated boot camp and infantry school, unsure of themselves. Frightened, though they haven't seen a single casualty yet.

They haven't seen war yet.

Boys trodden into bloody pink paste by amtrac treads . . .

He closes his eyes. Not wanting to go back.

But the ground gives way beneath him

fuck it fuck it fuck it I can't stop it

Figures running, staggering, fitfully illuminated by explosion-flashes.

The wreck of a powered mule. Hundreds of cartridges lie scattered across the dirt. The driver's been blown into shreds of meat. Strips of flesh hang, swaying in the wind.

Lasers search the dark, searing retinas to blindness.

A flash illuminates a mashed-in, concave mass of blood and bone that somehow still breathes. Bubbles burst and slide. Until Hector rams the butt of the Pig down, caving in the Chinese's skull.

His assistant gunner lies half in, half out of the caved-in fighting hole, chin back at an unnatural angle. In the light of the falling flares a scarlet well pulses at his throat, in which is wedged something small and black with stubby wings.

A helmetless head, dark braids unraveled. Olive skin and a hawk-like nose. One leg lies several yards away. She's cold. Bled out.

The fire team leader touches his hand, and he realizes he's groaning aloud. They're waiting at the exit for him. Sweat pulses over his cheeks. He shakes her hand off. "Forget about me. Get the fuck out of this hole! Take some action, or your people're gonna die here!"

She suddenly shakes herself. Maybe seeing him like this shocks her. She pushes her team out of the hole, then follows them. Rifles thud.

When he scrambles out from cover the high-pitched clatter of Chinese fire echoes off wrecked buildings that stretch from here to the smoky horizon. Overhead the black sky is solid smoke. Even in the infrared spectrum the stars are invisible. But small objects are darting overhead, and he cowers instinctively as a rabbit at a hawk-shadow. Bullets whine past, cracking into concrete. Strangely, though, the fragments don't sting. He lurches after the team in the stumbling bent-over jog of the battlefield. Then halts as he collides with the robot, which has suddenly jumped to its feet.

The Chad stops dead. Its "head" angles, then slowly tracks around.

A bullet clangs into its "shoulder." It sways, but stays upright. Its head lifts. A faint red light glows on the back of its metal skull.

"*Targeting*," the fire team leader says into the circuit. "*Active sniper, fourth floor, top deck, second window from the left. Lasering.*"

Another shot, this time full in the chest, hits the robot. It reels, starting to lose gyro control. But again, stays on its feet. Around them, amid broken concrete, steel beams, a toppled and dented bathtub, the team's firing up at the building. But their projectiles detonate a hundred yards short, bursting in the air. "*Shit*," someone mutters over the circuit. "*He's got something that explodes our rounds early.*"

"*Targeting*," Iron Dream's dulcet voice confirms. "*Acquired. Mark on top. Missile away.*"

Faster than the eye can follow, a fiery lance penetrates the roof opposite. White flame blasts out the windows in a glittering hail of glass, succeeded by smoke. Hector's goggles blank at the flash, then regenerate.

The robot takes one last step and crumples. Its head smacks a chunk of concrete curbing as it goes down, and a piece of plastic sheathing flies off. The red light dies. Motors whine down the scale to silence.

Hector stares at it, unable to move. The fire team leader, who's started off on foot, signals to one of the riflemen. Who grabs Hector's arm, tugs him along. The fire team leader grabs the other.

Hector whirls, taking her down to the ground. His knee's on her chest. He rears back, ready to bring the butt of his weapon down.

Just at that moment, Dream says in all their earbuds, *"Attention. Attention. Scenario is terminated. LVT is secured."*

Hector pants, recalled suddenly. The fire team leader's blinking up, eyes wide behind her goggles. He pats her shoulder. "Uh, sorry about that. Got carried away."

"Yeah," she mutters, rubbing her neck. Getting up, she turns away, suspicious of him. As the dirt and crushed concrete beneath them turn a pale washed-out blue.

"Better learn to take it. Gonna be a lot worse than that, where you're going."

Unfortunately, one of the men snickers. Hector wheels instantly. "Who the fuck just laughed?"

They all stare back wide-eyed. "Nobody, Sergeant."

"You sad little motherfuckers. Do you hate the Chinese?"

They stare back, silent. Ramos covers his face with both hands, then flings them away. "I asked, *Do you hate the fucking Chinese?*"

The fire team leader puts her hand on his arm. "You asked us that this morning, Sergeant. We hate 'em. We told you that then."

"Yeah, but enough to blow their fucking guts into the dirt? And stamp on them?"

Hector whirls, and slams a helmet with the heel of his hand. "You, you gay-ass little motherfucker, you hate the fucking Chinese?" He punches the next guy's helmet, the next woman's, ringing their bells one after the other. "Wise up, people. There won't be any replays in combat." He clutches his head as their faces reel around him. Bleckford. Breuer. Titcomb. Conlin. Schultz. Evans. Vincent. Orietta, Whipkey, Hern . . .

The tumbled masonry around them begins erasing, line by line. "Where we headed, Sergeant?" one of the team mutters. "After training? You know, right?"

Hector shakes his head, turning away. As ever, the grunts are getting the mushroom treatment.

"LVT is secured," Dream purrs again. *"Scenario four is terminated."*

The scene pixilates around them, erasing from their goggles. The Chad vanishes; then, line by line, the computer-generated imagery of the ruined city. Sweating, Hector snatches off his goggles. Revealing pale blue walls and, overhead, the pale blue spotless floor of an immense area that not long before was a DreamWorks soundstage.

"Live Virtual Training session complete," the soft voice coos in his earbuds. *"Fifteen-minute break. After which training will resume."*

THAT night, lying on his bunk in his hooch. Hector shared it with another drill sergeant, Ahoh. Who, at that moment, was reclining on a weight bench, doing curls. Ahoh was from Minnesota, second-generation Somali. Despite his name, which might normally subject him to scatological ragging, no one joked about him. Erotic tattoos covered most of his body, and he took off his shirt at every opportunity to show them off.

Like now, as he finished his curls nearly naked in boxer shorts and boots. His body gleamed darkly, coated in sweat. Hector lay back, studying the report the lieutenant had handed him after the day's training. Another reprimand. Harsh language. Striking a trainee. Second warning.

What the fuck did they want? These kids had no idea. They needed toughening up. He crumpled the paper in his fist, bolted a concussion pill, followed by another deep pull at the can of Upgrade. Energy drink, protein, and rumor said some kind of meth. The supply sergeant let the trainers have all they wanted, since they were running sims fourteen hours a day. "It's fucking hopeless," he muttered.

"You talkin' to me?" muttered Ahoh. The weights clanked as he set them down on concrete. "Or to yourself, again?"

"These fetuses they're sending us. They're gonna shit themselves when their friends die, then die themselves." He sucked the last drop down and flung the can across the room. It clattered off the metal wall, spun, and joined the others on the concrete-slab deck.

"You got to lay off that macho juice." Ahoh sneezed, then reached back over his head to pick up the heavy bells. He dropped them to his chest, then lifted, concentrating on his bench press. "They're makin' you even more nutzoid than you already is."

"Fuck you, A Man."

"Beyond your grade, Ray-mose. *Way* beyond your grade." Ahoh blitzed out ten quick ones, fast as he could, then racked the weight and flexed, admiring his biceps. Grunted, "One," and started the next set. "Hey, wasn't chu due leave?"

"Not for a month."

"How long?"

"A week."

"Goin' home?"

"Think so."

"I'll get Samantha to move in here. While you're gone."

"No you don't. Keep that fucking skeeze-whore out of my fart sack."

"Hey, no sweat, Chicken Man. What you don't know don't hurt you." Ahoh chuckled. His gaze traced the curved corrugated metal overhead as his arms pumped iron.

Hector picked up a computer game, but it didn't interest him. Who gave a fuck how fast he could build villages into cities? He liked first-person shooters, but Corps had banned them. Something about interfering with training.

He reached down for the report chit, smoothed it out on a knee, and read it again. *Typically effective in the trainer role, but prone to outbursts of anger. Sometimes less than attentive to duty. Is only being retained due to his combat experience and the needs of the Service.*

"I told you not to call me that," he muttered.

Ahoh gulped air between reps. "What'd ya say?"

"I said, don't call me that."

"Hey, mean nothin' by it. You're the one told me where you used to work . . . Chicken Man."

Hector twisted suddenly, grabbed the weight, and leaned on it. Taken by surprise, Ahoh pushed back only when the bar got within an inch of his throat. Hector threw himself atop the other sergeant. Hung there, face inches above Ahoh's, which was darkening as he fought the combined weight of barbells and hoochmate. "I told you," Hector said softly.

"Didn't . . . oof. Get out of my face."

"You like four hundred pounds on your fucking throat . . . asshole?"

Ahoh squinted. Sucked air.

With a sudden thrust he kneed Hector in the groin and rotated the weight, throwing it and Hector off the bench to one side. Then landed on top of a gasping, doubled Ramos, who still managed to get in a solid punch. They wrestled on the cold concrete, wheezing and grunting, trying for holds.

Banging on the wall. "Knock it the fuck off in there!" someone yelled from next door.

"You gotta get a grip, Heck-tor," Ahoh muttered, getting up slowly, still watching him. He tucked his penis back into his boxers and straightened his shoulders. Punched the air. "Or I'm gonna have to take you apart, put you back together with that fucking head on right."

Hector started to banter back, but gave up. "Fuck you," he grunted, and threw himself onto the bunk again. The black depression that had dogged him all day rolled in again, like storm-tossed surf. He reached for another Upgrade, but there were no more left.

A double rap at the hooch door. "Yeah!" Ahoh yelled.

One of the sergeants from next door. "You guys okay in here?"

"Just fucking Heck-tor up the dirt road," Ahoh said. "Want some?"

"Huh-uh. Hey, hear the scuttlebutt?"

"What you got?"

"Fobbit heard it from his girlfriend, she works in the head shed. We're prepping for a landing. Something called Causeway."

"She say when?"

"Don't know."

"So that's it, you don't know nothing else?"

The NCO shrugged. "All I got is what I got."

Hector lay motionless, digging his fingers into the seams of the mattress. Face deep in his pillow. No use. Eyes closed tight. But still. Can't stop it.

Seeing it all again.

Fleshy pink paste, in the treads of a tank.

A severed head, still in its helmet.

His own hands, hanging the birds one after the other.

The Line, steel chains chiming and swaying as it jolted into motion.

Taking the pinned and helpless birds, fallen silent now, as if they knew what lay through the slot in the wall, on into the Kill Room.

6

Tripler Army Medical Center, Honolulu, Hawaii

IT took two days before Dan realized he was in an Army hospital. The plain green scrubs gave no clue, and as far as he could tell, most of the other patients in his wing were Navy or Marine. Also, he'd been unconscious most of the time, and in a private room to boot.

He was on the fifth floor, to judge from his room number. Just now, the first morning he actually felt like sitting at the window, he was gazing down on what seemed all of Honolulu. The sea flashed scarlet beyond the towers of the oceanfront hotels. Violet mountains rose to his left. The sun was ballooning up like a nuclear detonation over Ford Island and the Pearl Harbor basin. He couldn't quite see which ships were in at the moment, just the distant upperworks of a Burke-class, and maybe one of the new jeep carriers.

The funny thing was that for the first time in his life, he didn't really like looking at the sea.

The fishing craft he'd spotted east of the island had never approached. But it had obviously seen their smoke. They'd built the rescue pyre piece by piece over their weeks on the island. A fifteen-foot stack of driftwood, plastic trash, tires, and coconut boles, set atop the highest point of the volcanic rocks. The rolling black billows it produced must have been visible for many miles. The hydrocarbon stench had set the castaways coughing and retching.

But someone had radioed it in. Because the next day a recon drone buzzed over. Dan and Hwang had waved and capered like the desperate, starving strandees they were. Pointing to the letters they'd scraped in the sand with a driftwood plow. USN HERE. The aircraft had darted around the island, obviously searching for other survivors, then departed, shrinking into a humming dot before disappearing eastward.

The day after that, the Self-Defense Forces had shown up. A Japanese coast guard cutter, not all that big, but easily the most welcome seaborne sight Dan had ever feasted his eyes on. They'd hove to and run a boat in to the spit. Heavily armed troops jumped off and advanced warily, suspicious at first of Hwang, until Dan identified him as Korean and himself as American.

It seemed that while he'd been out of touch, Japan had reentered the war. Which couldn't help but be good news.

His recollections got spotty after that. A medical bay, then a clinic. An aircraft. A short stay somewhere, then another plane.

And now, Hawaii. He sighed, examining his reflection in the window glass. Thinner, definitely. In fact, pretty fucking gaunt, though they'd been feeding him, first with an IV, then with heaping trays. His doctor was a smart, attractive brunette. Greek by extraction, he guessed. "Exposure, intestinal parasites, et cetera, et cetera," she'd told him. "What I'd expect from somebody stranded on a desert island in the tropics, and forced to eat pretty much anything he could find."

The good news: *Savo Island* had survived. Heavily damaged, but Cheryl and the crew had brought her through. For which he was profoundly grateful.

Phone connections to the mainland were intermittent. He'd managed to leave a message, but Blair hadn't called yet. Still, the Navy would get the news to her.

After he'd come to, he'd asked where the others were. His nurse said Captain Hwang was next door. Dan could see him whenever he liked. He'd tottered over to find the Korean liaison, head thrown back in a chair, being worked over by a dentist. Actually, of the three, he looked the least affected by their ordeal, smashed teeth aside.

Wilker was in critical condition, in the recovery ward after surgeries on face, jaw, and legs. When Dan visited, the pilot had been asleep, but he'd sat with him for an hour, and left a request that he be kept informed about his condition.

"Admiral? Breakfast." His server set down the tray. Dan nodded, suddenly ravenous. His stomach growled.

He watched television while he ate, but didn't learn much. Reportage had been replaced by sanitized "government bulletins." The various channels, CNN, Fox, MSNBC, did agree on a few salient facts. A full draft was in effect. Everyone had to register, either for the military or for labor. Including women. Every ad trumpeted that company's contribution to war production. A major battle was under way in Vietnam. The Chinese were suffering heavy losses there, but U.S. forces didn't seem to be involved. Citizens were warned about impeding the war effort, and asked to report anyone criticizing the government to the Internal Enemies Hotline, phone number 1-800-PATRIOT.

Just as ominously, unrest and shelling were starting again in Latvia, and something called the Visegrad Group was mobilizing. The Germans were debating sending troops.

He clicked from channel to channel, but there was zip about the Pacific. As if every mention of it had been blacked out. Even the fact that the Japanese were back in the war.

Which left him with . . . not very much. Confused. Out of the loop. In a bubble.

Which was pretty much where he figured he'd be for the rest of the war.

AFTER breakfast he decided to look in on Wilker again. The staff raised a fuss if he tried to walk. They wanted him to use a wheelchair, but he refused. A cane was bad enough.

He trudged slowly down the hall to the elevator. When he tapped at the pilot's door, Wilker was awake this time. A brace locked the lower half of his face, but the bruising was fading. An IV dangled, and a complicated apparatus pinioned both legs, which were cast and bandaged. He raised a finger in welcome, then pointed to a chair.

"Feeling better, Strafer?"

A muffled reply from between locked teeth. "Almost human. Thanks, Admiral."

Dan patted his arm. "Let's keep it Dan."

The aviator closed his eyes. Laid his head back on the pillow. Then opened them again. "Don't think I . . . actually ever thanked you. For pulling me out of the cockpit. Guess I was . . . not so happy to be alive. On the island, I mean."

"Forget it. You don't need to say anything, if it's too hard to talk."

"Not hard. What's hard is all I get is . . . fucking smoothies. Can you really understand me?"

"Pretty well. Anyway, you were stove up pretty bad back there. I didn't take it amiss."

"If I didn't say it then, I will now. Thanks."

Dan rearranged the pilot's covers. "What do they say? About your legs, I mean."

"Think they can save 'em. But not sure yet, I guess."

Dan nodded. They rested in companionable silence for a few minutes. Then Wilker's lids popped open again. "*Savo*. She make it? Did you hear?"

"Commander Staurulakis brought her back. She's safe. The ship, I mean."

"Great. Great. Any word on the det? My maintenance guys?"

Dan said he hadn't gotten anything firm on casualties, but he would ask.

Wilker sagged back again. Then, as if recollecting something, waved at a newspaper on a tray table. "Uh, saw your name. Didn't read the story. But it's in there."

"My name?" Dan glanced toward it. He didn't want to read it. But got up at last and picked it up.

The *Navy Times*. Page 4. A short article about Rear Admiral Daniel V. Lenson's loss somewhere in the western Pacific. Less an obituary than that he'd been proposed for the Cordon of the Order of Military Merit, First Class, by the acting minister of national defense of the Republic of Korea, Admiral Min Jun Jung. It had been awarded to his widow by the ambassador from South Korea, at a short private ceremony at the Pentagon. Also, at the request of that officer, seconded by the chief of naval operations, Admiral Lenson had been proposed for a Defense Distinguished Service Medal. The latter award had been denied, though, due to objections in Congress. Members had questioned the admiral's abandonment of his flagship in the middle of the battle.

He folded the paper, face burning. He knew where the objections had come from, but finally just shook his head. Did it matter? Nope. It really didn't.

"Anything interesting?" Strafer mumbled from the bed.

"Just the usual political bullshit."

"Can you . . . uh, you mind . . . ?"

"What do you need?"

"I hate to ask."

"Hell, Ray, I was wiping your ugly ass with dried seaweed for weeks. What the heck do you want now? At least we have real toilet paper."

"Yeah, the bathroom—"

"Forget it, Strafer." Dan hobbled over to the bed and pushed the Call button.

BACK in his room, he felt dizzy after his excursion, brief though it had been. He was about to lie down for a little nap when someone tapped at his door. Probably the nurse, taking vitals. But she usually just breezed in. "Yeah," he called.

Then blinked, astonished. Not believing his eyes. Until she set down her briefcase, leaned over, and kissed his forehead.

"Blair?" he whispered, not really sure if he was still awake. But he could smell her perfume.

"It's me." She pulled a chair over and plopped down, taking his hand and crossing her legs. Those long long legs . . . He couldn't help staring. Until she raised her eyebrows. "What is it? What's wrong?"

"Only that you're the sexiest thing I've ever seen."

"Keep thinking that." She looked around the room, then leaned forward and kissed him again. This time, on the lips. "They told me you were dead," she murmured, closed eyes hovering above his. So near he could feel her warmth. "I am so glad. God, just . . . so glad."

He groped for a reply, but words all seemed inadequate. So he just pulled her down, and kissed the misshapen, withered stub of the ear she kept hidden under a lock of blond hair. She flinched. "Don't do that. Just hold me," she murmured into his neck. "Hug me. Like that. Yeah."

When he let her go at last she held him at arm's length and sighed. "You're so *thin*."

"Yeah, lost that little potbelly you like. What there was, we had to root hard for."

"What's your status? What's the hospital say?"

He shrugged. "They pumped us full of antibiotics, and poison for the parasites. Other than that, I'm not sure I need to be here."

"But they insisted."

"Correct."

She kissed him again, one quick peck.

"Does Nan know I'm okay?"

"Yes. The Navy notifies both primary and secondary next of kin." She glanced at the window. "They gave you a good view, at least. I'll check with your doctor when he comes by."

"She."

"When she comes by. When is that, usually?"

"After lunch, I think. I'm really surprised to see you here, hon. This is a long way from DC."

"Ricardo . . . the chairman gave me a plane. When he heard you were alive, they'd picked you up. I'm supposed to touch base with the cybercommand, too, while I'm here. And have a sit-down with Jim Yangerhans. PACOM. Oh yes. You know him." She rubbed her brow. "I'll put in a word for you when I do. About what you can expect, once you're back on your feet. Or if there's something specific I can say you want?"

He was about to give her the usual song and dance, about how he didn't want her trying to advance his career, but remembered the *Navy Times* article and didn't. This might be the time to call on a little favoritism, if he had any left. "Uh, well, maybe you could just sort of put out a ping. See if there are any, um, plans."

"But what do *you* want? Surely not to go back to sea. Not after what you've been through."

He thought about giving her the old 'sailors belong on ships, ships belong at sea', but just now he wasn't at all sure he did want to go back. Ever. And as for facing battle again, well . . . he didn't want that either anymore, to be perfectly frank. Maybe somebody else deserved a shot at glory.

He coughed into a fist, apprehensive and guilty. This wasn't how Certified Navy Heroes were supposed to feel. "Uh, lemme think about that. Okay? So, what's going on in DC?"

She glanced at the half-open door. People were passing. Carts rattled past in the corridor. "Not much I can tell you. In a nonsecure environment."

"Anything? All I have's the TV."

"Just . . . we're not in good shape. Your operation set the primary enemy back on their heels. But other developments don't augur well. In the Gulf. Or eastern Europe."

"There was something on the news about that. What's the 'Visegrad Group'?"

"That's the Czech Republic, Hungary, Slovakia, and Poland. The Russians are taking advantage of our being tied down in the Pacific."

"Uh-huh. What else? Are we going over to the offensive? That was the idea of Recoil, wasn't it? A spoiling attack, to set us up for a counterpunch?"

"Like I said, can't comment." She smiled apologetically and glanced toward the harbor. "You've got a great view."

He sighed. "You said that already. Don't change the subject."

"All I can tell you is, we're presenting various options to the NCA. Some are more aggressive than others. It's going to be up to the president."

"And Ed Szerenci. How are you two getting along?"

She spared a smile. "It's complicated."

"I'll bet. Wish I could be there to watch the two of you butt heads."

"There'll be an offensive. At least a limited one. But we've got to keep the danger in mind too."

"That Zhang keeps threatening nuclear war? On the homeland?"

She looked disturbed, as if he was getting too close to something. Time to steer away. "So what's your part in this?" he added.

"I'm going to Ireland."

Did he hear that right? "I'm sorry . . . did you say Ireland?"

"Dublin. There's a UN meeting on documenting, and thus, they hope, preventing war crimes and atrocities. The administration wants me to go. I'm not sure why, or what they expect me to do. But apparently the president's asked for me by name."

Dan gave it exactly two seconds' thought. "So they can blame it on you when it goes down in flames."

"That's what I think too."

"So why participate?"

"I just might have a chance to make a difference. The same way you do, when you get orders you don't much like."

He sighed and took her hand again. "Wish I could go with you. But I have no idea what happens once I get out of here. When do you leave?"

"In a day or two."

"And there's two other commitments. So we might just have now?"

"I'll try to come again. But . . . yes. It might only be this visit." She glanced at the door, then back at him. Her brows lifted. "You're not feeling like—?"

He nodded. She gave him another close, scrutinizing look, then got up. Surveyed the corridor, then eased the door closed. There wasn't a lock, so she pushed the visitor's chair against it.

"Sure you're up for this? You look like you can barely—"

"Judge for yourself." He threw the covers back, inviting her in.

A mischievous grin. She began unbuttoning her blouse. "That's evidentiary, all right. How do you want to approach this?"

He was telling her exactly what he had in mind when the door slammed against the chair. She sat back quickly, rebuttoning, brushing hair out of her face.

"Sorry to intrude," said the nurse. She examined Blair, then switched her attention to him. "But you have a call, Admiral. Office of the chief of naval operations."

"Take it," Blair said, putting her finger over his mouth as he was about to refuse. "He'll take it," she said.

"Just lift the receiver by the bed."

"Mr. Lenson?"

Mister? "Here," he said warily.

"Can you hold for Admiral Niles?"

Nick Niles, chief of naval operations. His old enemy, and current rabbi . . . if that relationship still held. "I'll hold." He raised his eyebrows. Blair nodded, and he put the phone on speaker.

"Dan. You there?"

"Yes sir."

"How're you feeling?"

"Better, sir. I'm at Tripler, in Honolulu."

"I know where you are. I just called you there, Lenson. I told Blair. She should get there later today."

"Actually, she's here right now, Admiral."

"Hello, Nick," Blair said.

"Blair, hello. Look, I'll make this fast. Tell me why you were on that helo."

"Sir, we were extricating after the operation. *Savo* lost power and comms, but I had the rest of the strike force to think about too. I was shifting my flag to *Hampton Roads*."

"Okay, that's what I figured. And got shot down en route?"

"Correct, sir. Not exactly sure by what. Maybe a—"

"All right, well, we're taking heat over your actions. It was OBE since you were MIA, but now you're back, so are the accusations. I'll try to defend you, but I can't tell yet how it'll turn out."

"I understand, sir. Appreciate the backup."

"Meanwhile, get well. Blair, my best."

"Thanks, Nick."

The rattle-click of a disconnect.

"Shit," Dan muttered. He'd fought the strike group in to the target, accomplished every objective. Now they were hanging him out to dry, because one congresswoman with an ax to grind had it in for him?

It didn't leave him in the mood at all.

But after a little while, with the chair jammed against the door again, Blair was able to change his mind.

II

FARTHER THAN THAT I CANNOT GO

7

Xinjiang

HALF an hour before dawn, Teddy Oberg lay prone on a western-facing step below a ridge. His shadow stretched before him like a dark Other lying dead on the bare rock. Below and around other shadows crept ever forward. Toward a strip of empty pavement bowled in a greening valley, between plunging walls of gray mountain too barren and steep for even brush to gain a foothold.

Two months had passed since their first weapons drop. Occupied, mainly, in recruiting and drilling young men (and some not so young) who'd sidled up to Nasrullah's contacts in the hamlets and compounds that dotted the valleys. From Yengisar to Yitimukongcun they streamed, drawn by murmurs in the bazaar and tape-recorded sermons, martial songs and exhortations to resistance.

And the timeless beckoning of battle.

"Vladimir" had left after a week, leaving Teddy to run the buildup. They'd checked in from time to time on the Jetwire, and twice supply drops had fallen like silent snow from the night sky. The last had nearly been intercepted by a Chinese patrol, but the drop party had starbursted on contact, as trained. And, as trained, the three rebels security had surrounded had shot themselves before they could be captured and interrogated. He'd established other complexes, built and building, tunneled into the stark mountains west of Poskam, the nearest thing to a city that existed in these isolated reaches of the new People's Empire.

It had taken four days to travel a hundred kilometers, moving by night and sleeping by day. With the lead platoon fifty meters up and the rest in column, they'd crossed three mountain ranges by passes and gorges only the locals knew. Negotiated precipitous ravines floored by rushing streams so deep with snowmelt they'd lost two bearers by drowning. Toiled up nearly vertical rock walls via goat trails that had probably been ancient in Alexander's time. Two hundred picked men, in four squads.

He'd organized them SEAL-fashion, into forty-man platoons. Each platoon commander directed four squads. Each squad was divided into two five-man fire teams. He had no headquarters or targeting elements yet. Nasrullah ran the logistics, mainly donkeys and women. The bearers, Han and Manchu slavewomen, proved surefooted on rugged terrain with heavy burdens. Teddy had built his fire teams around light machine guns and designated RPG crewmen, in case the Han brought in light armor. His main remaining worry was enemy air, but the Agency had refused to provide man-portable missiles despite repeated requests.

Still, in this terrain, he didn't think they'd run too much of a risk during the approach phase.

That would change in a few minutes. They'd moved the last miles to contact by bounding overwatch, with one platoon covering the next from a firing position while the other moved forward, then exchanging roles. Now, using the hand signals he'd taught them, he signaled the right-hand platoon out to cut the road. The left-hand one was already in place, dressed in stolen police uniforms. He himself wore shalwar kameez: baggy trousers and a long, loose shirt, topped off with a *pakul* hat and a heavy, wide-sleeved wool coat.

He checked his watch again. Just about now, two fire teams would be assaulting the security station nearest the border. Any quick-reaction team would be vectored south.

The real target lay below, emerging into sight as he trotted downhill. His bad leg jolted with pain, but still supported him thanks to the brace. He carried his rifle, a bag of grenades, and a Makarov, tucked into his belt, in case he was captured.

The Chinese had already tortured him once. He didn't intend to give them another chance.

A crackle of distant small-arms fire, barely audible over the wind. Below, against a patchwork of green, the road switchbacked upward. Four hard-surfaced lanes. They'd overwatched it for a day. He was tempted to hit a convoy, but decided to stick to the plan.

The road wasn't the mission. His targets ran alongside it, a few yards uphill. A white-insulated pipeline, four feet in diameter, elevated six feet above ground on steel girders concreted into footings. Above that, still farther uphill, rose the trussed green pylons of a high-tension line.

The walkie-talkie crackled. Relayed up the valley from boys crouched behind boulders. *"Yo'l yopiq."* The road was closed. Four minutes later came the same word from the other direction. Teddy clicked acknowledgment, then switched to Guldulla's channel. "Tokarev? Lingxiù here."

"I would know your voice in Sheol, my friend."

"And I yours. Stand by . . . *execute.*"

His demolition team broke cover a hundred meters from the road and sprinted across, bent double under their loads. Sinking to perch on a flat rock, Teddy focused his binoculars on them, noticing particularly Alimyan, the fat muj who'd braced him at the feast. He seemed brave enough. He'd volunteered for demolition training. But a doubter. Maybe, a troublemaker.

Two fire teams splayed out, setting in RPKs to cover the demo guys. He'd have preferred to set the charges himself, but didn't trust himself to manage a long run uphill to escape. But he'd calculated the placement and wrapped the C-4 himself. All they had to do was duct-tape them to the pipe and the support pylons, press in the primers, and hit the timers. Guldulla crouched holding an RPG at his shoulder, aiming alternately up the road and down.

Teddy examined each end of the highway where it bent out of sight around hairpins. Still empty. Drilling again and again, he'd squeezed emplacement and withdrawal down to eight minutes.

He checked his watch again. Seven gone already.

Then all they had to do was evade and escape an alerted enemy with overwhelming numbers and total mastery of the air.

He tried for patience, but two minutes later finally had to click the little radio on again. "Tokarev, Lingxiù. What's the fucking holdup down there?"

"A problem . . . the electrical thing is done. Just holding off on setting the timer. The problem is the pipeline. The covering is wet. The tape does not stick."

"Oh, fuck me," Teddy muttered, comprehending instantly. The chilled liquefied natural gas kept the line, even its insulated exterior, colder than the surrounding air. So any humidity was condensing on it. And the fucking adhesive wasn't up to it. "Have them set the charges on top. Or lash them on with something. Hurry up, the QRF's going to be here any minute!"

He hesitated, clutching the other radio. Withdraw his flankers, or leave them in place until the charges went? They were the most vulnerable, at either end of the road.

Then he heard it, echoing through the valleys.

The flutter-whack-whack of faraway blades, en route from the Internal Security base at Kargilik.

He hit Transmit again. "Tok, they're incoming. Helicopters. Set the charges as best you can, and get out of there."

"One minute more. We are tying them on with our bootlaces."

"No time, guy. Retro! Now!"

"One minute more—"

Teddy radioed the flankers. Instead of pulling them back into the hills, he ordered them both in toward him, on the double. He wanted everyone concentrated. Three or four helo loads of troops, he could deal with. Anything beyond that, the muj would find themselves the filling in the classic shit sandwich.

When he glanced up again the golden rays of a rising sun glinted off spinning blades.

The gunships came in fast and low, bursting out of a ravine and wheeling instantly into line abreast, as if they'd rehearsed the move for the last week.

Their black shark-silhouettes brought back bad memories. Woody Island. Echo Four, caught in the open by gunships with searchlights. A thousand suns rising over the dunes. The rotor wash blasting down brush and trees. He'd pulled his SIG and pumped round after round into the pterodactyl shadows, even knowing the full metal jackets would bounce off the bottom armor of a battle copter. The miniguns had blazed like red flashing eyes, a white-hot stream of incandescence searching the dunes. The final image so many insurgents, Taliban, al Qaeda, ISIS fighters, must have seen.

He pawed his face, clawing himself back to now. Three Z-10s, in a tight formation that said these guys knew how to maneuver in mountains. He held absolutely still as they flashed overhead, obviously missing the small party crouched under the pipeline as they headed for the border station. Teddy radioed the border party to take cover, hoping he wasn't too late. Then to Guldulla again: "Extract. Extract! Before they come back."

"Men eshitish va itoat qiling, Lingxiù." Which he didn't quite get, but hoped meant something like "Roger, wilco, out."

The *brrrr* of miniguns echoed up the valley. Teddy jumped to his feet and signaled the flank teams in. Disemplacing the machine guns, they straggled back across the road, shockingly exposed. He held his breath until they were climbing the hillside again, then pointed left and right, spreading them out. If they clumped during a firing run, they were toast.

Four more helicopters emerged from the same ravine as the first flight. Heavier, hanging clumsy in the air: troop carriers. They too roared overhead, but flared out and settled five hundred meters down the road. A blocking force, to cut off the retreat of whoever had attacked the border post.

One advantage, then; they still thought that was the main body. They didn't realize another force was behind them. Teddy crouched again, staying low as black-clad troops in body armor spilled out of the squatting helos. As soon as the last soldier disembarked, the racket of engines grew again. The heavy black bodies lofted. A man downslope raised an RPG. Teddy yelled, *"To'xta! olov qilmang!"* The muj lowered his weapon, but looked puzzled.

The radio from the southern element crackled. They were pinned down by helicopters, taking fire from troops. Teddy ordered them to the southern slope, to take shelter during strafing runs, and advance to engage the force to their front.

Guldulla joined him, breathing hard after the run and climb. His half-white mustache looked wilted. His fingers were stained with blood, and his boots gaped laceless. Teddy gave him his orders.

The charges went off. First on the pylons, with cracks that echoed down the valley, accompanied by puffs of dirty smoke. For an endless moment the lofty structures stood proud. Then, one after another, they toppled.

The charges on the pipeline went off as the pylons crumpled, draping electrical cables over the raised line. A crack, a flash of electricity lanced among the snarl of wiring.

A blue-yellow fireball wiped out vision. The heat-flash seared his cheeks even two hundred yards uphill. It was smokeless, glareless, an enormous release of pure energy, but the dust boiled up and concrete and gravel and pieces of steel rained down all around him. Covering his head with one arm, he jumped to his feet. *"Hujum!"* he yelled. Forward, attack! *"Ularga hujum! Xitoy o'ldiringlar!"*

Another flash, another searing pulse. Driven by pumps, the severed pipe was still spewing liquefied gas. An immense torch lit up the still-dawning valley like a series of magnesium flares igniting one after the other. Teddy had figured it would cut off once pressure fell, but either there wasn't a shutoff or it hadn't tripped yet. Down by the road the grass was aflame. The asphalt pavement was boiling and burning, the melted area spreading in a circle around a roaring volcano.

Pulling his attention from that molten eye, stumbling forward, he waved his rifle. "*Hujom! Hujum!*" Then knelt, set the selector for single shots, and began sniping the dark figures that had deployed across the road, backs to him.

A ripple of fire clattered from his own line. Not heavy, but that was good. He'd drilled them over and over to aim carefully, to fire one shot at a time. Two or three of the blacksuits spun and crumpled before the troops reoriented to the threat from their rear and began firing back.

Guldulla, beside him, kept firing as he advanced. "Got 'em in a pincer!" Teddy yelled, knowing the guy didn't speak English, just to encourage him. "Put 'em all down before they get reinforced." He fired and rolled over, switching to another target. The bullpup was zeroed, and the butt jolted his shoulder as he put three fast rounds into another Chinese. From down the road more fire snapped, the 7.62s from the RPKs deeper than the smaller-caliber, higher-velocity Chinese rounds.

Then he heard it. The higher-pitched, fast near scream of approaching gunships. And in front of him, a bulky, low silhouette he recognized.

Alimyan. Teddy glanced around quickly. No one was looking their way. He went to one knee, fired out the last of his magazine into the tubby Uighur, and dropped to roll behind a boulder.

Just then the miniguns unleashed. Droning straight up the highway three abreast, the attack helicopters unchained hell on both sides alike, entangled as they were. RPGs lanced upward, but missed as the black birds tore close overhead, then lifted into the golden-red sky, gaining room to wheel back for another pass.

A blow knocked him down. He staggered to his knees as blackness submerged his brain.

HE swam up reluctantly through a scarlet haze. Men, too many of them his, lay along the sloping berm, some screaming and writhing, others motionless. Dust and smoke hazed the breeze, and a thick petroleum stink from the burning asphalt. The rebel he'd shot, Alimyan, lay a few yards away. Teddy crawled over to make sure he was dead, then stood.

Couldn't make a stand here. He had nowhere near enough effectives or ammunition to hold against the squads that would be arriving on the next transports, or the battalion that was probably mounting up in light armor back in Kargilik. Their only hope was to melt back into the fastnesses. Extract as many as he could, and use the survivors as cadre to rebuild for the next action.

"Pull back!" he yelled in Han. "Withdraw! Take the guns. Shoot the wounded." No way they could carry anyone who couldn't walk. Not over three mountain ranges, moving by night.

Which might leave him out too . . . He uncupped his shoulder to inspect a gaping tear in cloth and flesh. Plenty of blood, but no fountain pulsed; no arteries damaged. He shook on clotting agent and taped on a pressure bandage. "Good to go," he muttered.

But distant specks in the sky wheeled even as he blinked up. The gunships were returning. He waved the left two platoons, now inextricably intermixed, up the slope, leaving scores of crumpled bodies—far more than he'd expected to lose—and pointed his RPG and machine-gun teams at the incoming helos. "Do not fire too soon," he told them. "You are the rear guard. Songs will be sung about you. But you must stay until your ammunition is gone. Now is your time to gain martyrdom. But do not let them take you prisoner."

Their sergeant nodded grimly, wide mouth rimed with powder-smut. He stamped in the bipod legs of his machine gun and writhed his pelvis down into the loose scree. "Go with Allah, Lingxiù. We will die here," he muttered. The rest of his fire team looked scared, but no one made a move to leave.

Teddy wanted to stay with them. But he couldn't. "Go with Allah," he muttered back. He unslung his grenade pack and dropped it beside them. Then turned away, eyes burning, and limped up the slope.

They'd accomplished the mission, but at far too high a cost.

You will use us as food for cannons.

In a very little while, firing erupted behind him, and the roar of rockets. He did not look back.

8

San Diego, California

THE deputy J-4—Pacific Command, Logistics, Engineering and Security Cooperation Directorate—sat Dan down before he left Honolulu. "Good morning, Captain," the Coast Guard captain had said. "Honored to meet you, sir. Welcome to the staff. We all heard about your . . . stranding on that island." He looked as if he wanted to know more, but glanced away instead.

Dan had nodded, easing himself into the chair in front of the deputy's desk. He was back in khakis, instead of a hospital gown, but still felt weak. Not much of what he ate seemed to turn into what it was supposed to. His orders read *limited duty, medical restrictions.* And he was wearing eagles on his collar again. Reverted, as those orders had directed, to his permanent rank. "Nice of you to say so." He smiled, as affably as he could.

The coastie said, "I'd like to make this a long chat, but I've got a meeting in five minutes. I understand you're available for TAD."

Temporary additional duty was a euphemism, in this case at least, for the Navy not knowing exactly what to do with him. He cleared his throat. "Correct."

"Admiral Yangerhans wondered if you could act as his eyes and ears at the shipyard level for new construction. Are you familiar with the Asia Victory Program?"

"In general. Not in detail."

"That's the major defense buildup Congress approved as soon as the war went hot. The Army, tripled to ninety brigade combat teams. The Air Force, more combat aircraft. And the Navy, expansion to fifteen battle groups and five hundred combatant ships, plus UAVs, industrial expansion, submersible drones, space assets, et cetera."

Dan nodded. The other went on. "Carrier production was accelerated, and the jeep carrier program initiated."

"I had *Gambier Bay* under my flag. In the central Pacific action."

"What's your opinion?"

"Helpful in antisubmarine actions, but not up to full combat standards. I'd, uh, look into making them more seaworthy, and if we could, more survivable. The container stacking—"

"We'd be interested in a written report. If you can summarize your recommendations." Though the guy didn't look that eager. "Just bear in mind, it's too late to make major changes. Additional conversions are coming out of the yards now. Newport News will deliver two new strike carriers next year too. And two more have been authorized.

"But the admiral wants you to concentrate on the surface combatant program. Forty new Flight V Improved Burke-class destroyers, and twelve of the new cruisers—they don't have a class name yet, we just call them the CGW class. W for 'wartime,' I guess."

Dan nodded. "I've read about them." The new cruisers were based on Zumwalt destroyers, with an improved hull and the ability—which *Savo* had never really possessed—to conduct simultaneous antiair and antiballistic missile defense. Half were to be powered by a new type of compact nuclear reactor, the rest by gas turbines. Both were electrically driven, with railguns and advanced beam weapons. Perhaps most important, they were hardened to survive near hits with nuclear weapons.

The J-4 went on. "We weren't ready for a major war. Had to rebuild the industrial base nearly from scratch. On the West Coast, we had NASSCO, Gunderson and Vigor in Oregon, and the other Vigor yard in Seattle. We pressed the smaller yards into service to repair battle damage, but most new construction's got to be sourced from the East and Gulf Coasts.

"The exceptions are the BAE yard in San Diego and Long Beach Naval Shipyard. We BRAC'd Long Beach years ago, but reactivated it when the war started. Three of the new cruisers are under construction there. Vigor's building the escort carriers, and BAE has three shifts cranking out Flight V Arleigh Burkes. The bottleneck's a lack of skilled workers and a withered supply chain. We're having labor difficulties, too.

"Admiral Yangerhans wants somebody who can identify choke points, ream them out, and get those ships to sea. I hesitate to say carte blanche, but he'll back you up."

Dan pondered it, though the answer didn't take much thought. "What's my relationship to SUPSHIPS? They manage new construction, right?"

"Correct, and you're not to interfere in contract management. If you identify problems at that level, notify us. We'll work with the appropriate folks at NAVSEA. That'll play better than trying to push things on your own. If we're clear on that?"

Dan had smiled and accepted. He'd gotten up, and shaken the captain's hand. Remembering what Blair had told him, in their all too short tryst in the hospital. *The chance to make a difference, when you get orders you don't much like.*

After all, he was still in the war.

Just not in the front line anymore.

HIS welcome that morning, at an old waterfront building in Long Beach, wasn't exactly warm. Supervisor of Shipbuilding, West Coast, managed the contractors in California and Washington. Hundreds of engineers and accountants were working 24/7 to build the fleet that would retake the Pacific. Walking the corridors, Dan saw heads bent over screens, sensed near desperation. He was supposed to ream out bottlenecks? More likely, he'd just get in the way. A civilian rep muttered a cursory greeting. A yeoman showed him to a room that looked as if it had been hastily cleared of cleaning supplies.

Two officers looked up from keyboards as he stood at the door. A commander and a lieutenant. Both bolted to their feet.

"Carry on," he muttered, looking at the door again. A taped-on sheet of pink bond, obviously from a desktop printer, read PACOM REP. "I'm Dan Lenson. Are you working for me?"

They introduced themselves. The commander was Kitty Pickles, a stocky, fortyish brunette with the tightly braided hair that seemed to be fashionable now. The lieutenant was tall, angular, Scandinavian-looking. His name was Brett Harriss. Dan shook their hands, haunted by a feeling he'd heard both names before. Pickles. Harriss. But where? "I don't think we've served together," he ventured.

"No sir," said Pickles. Harriss shook his head as well.

"All right, fine . . . How long have you been here?"

They'd arrived three days before and, aside from being assigned the space, had heard nothing. Curiouser and curiouser. He took the third desk, then noticed the yeoman still in the doorway. "Yes?"

"I'm assigned to you too, Captain. YN2 Vigliotti."

"Oh . . . good. You know your way around, then?"

"Been here a month, sir."

"Well, give me a day to settle in, then we'll discuss tasking."

Vigliotti set him up with passwords and a LAN account, then left for a dental appointment. Dan logged in, checked his email, and found eight hundred messages on his navy.mil account. He read the first twenty, then logged out and searched until he found the personnel records.

He leaned back after reading them, fighting anger.

Starting as an aviation ordnanceman in a patrol squadron, Pickles had been accepted into a commissioning program and graduated from U. Miss. with a BS in electrical engineering. She'd served in frigates and done her department head tour as operations officer on *Lewis and Clark*. She'd gone to the Naval Postgraduate School for a master's in information technology, then served in a squadron staff and commanded a minesweeper in the Gulf. After joint professional military education, she'd run enlisted manning at OPNAV before a stand-alone XO tour on a command ship. After a stint at COMNAVSURFOR, she'd been a desk officer at the Joint Staff. She'd then served as exec of an LPD, USS *New York*, the ship with steel from the World Trade Center welded into her bow, then fleeted up to CO aboard that same ship.

An impressive career, especially considering she'd started at the deckplates. To all appearances, Pickles had been slated for higher things. A hot runner, with solid technical and education credentials and glowing evaluations.

Then, a month into her CO tour aboard *New York*, she'd asked to be relieved. For personal reasons, the record read. With no further explanation.

Dan scratched his head, glancing over his screen at her. Her braided head was lowered, showing a white line that centerlined her scalp. What the fuck, over? Family issues? But her DEERS statement showed no dependents.

One didn't just resign from a command tour. Square that, in the middle of a war.

The lieutenant, Harriss, had a shorter career, of course. A Naval

Academy grad, he'd done his division officer tour aboard a Cyclone-class PC, USS *Zephyr*. A junior officer picked up responsibility early aboard a small ship. From there, Harriss had been the navigator aboard USS *Ross*, then been selected for a Burke Scholarship. He held a master's in operations research and had done a thesis in applying AI to ship design.

So far, so good. But during duty in the Gulf before his department head tour, just before the start of the present war, Harriss had led a pair of riverine command boats on a patrol off the Iranian base on Farsi Island. One of his boats' engines had failed, and he was standing by it in the other boat when four much larger Revolutionary Guard Corps patrol craft had surrounded them, trained guns on them, and demanded surrender.

Outgunned and outnumbered, Harriss had ordered the crews not to resist. In custody, separated, and threatened, some of the crew had made statements on Iranian television confessing their mistake. Expressing regret for U.S. violation of territorial waters. Their captors had eventually released them, but kept the boats. The Navy said they'd been in international waters. Tehran disagreed. That was a matter for the international lawyers, but after an investigation, four of Harriss's superior officers had been relieved. The lieutenant himself had been issued a letter of reprimand.

Dan massaged his brow, glancing past the screen at Harriss now. He was kicked back, talking on the phone. They were obviously smart. Had once been front-runners. But after missteps, or just plain being in the wrong place at the wrong time, their futures now were bleak. The Navy seldom granted a second chance. His own checkered career was the exception, and only because he'd been either lucky or unlucky enough to have seen serious combat, and made influential friends.

But it wasn't a good sign, to be assigned two career dead-enders as assistants.

DAN took Pickles and Harriss to lunch at the mess, and the commander quickly got down to business. "Sir, we've been talking to people, trying to get a head start. I don't want to sound negative, but there's going to be serious pushback if we try to get between the SUPSHIPS people and the yards."

"I agree, Kitty. But we don't sit on our cans just to avoid trouble."

"Oh, I agree, sir. That's not what I meant."

"I didn't think so. What's your recommendation?"

"Pick two or three issues we can really impact, especially any having to do with the precom crews, and go to town on those. The nucleus crews always need help. Arranging team training. Preparing for combat systems and propulsion lightoffs. Intermediate post-delivery availability issues. They're always shorthanded, and a big wall of work is gonna hit these guys when they go aboard for the first time. If we can stem the bleeding, they can make their milestones."

Dan nodded. A reasonable line of attack. "Anything specific come to mind?"

Harriss perked up. "Data multiplexing, for the cruisers and Flight V Burkes. And high-pressure air for the weapons, torpedoes especially, for ships that don't have installed HP air systems. But the biggest hard point is going to be propulsion. Half of the new cruisers are nuclear powered. The other half, and all the destroyers, are gas turbines."

"So what's the hitch?" Dan said.

Pickles looked around the mess, then lowered her voice. "The reactor packages are new technology. Half were ordered from B&W/Bechtel. The other half are from NuScale. Unfortunately, they're all behind schedule. Teething problems."

"Well, we still have the gas turbines."

Harriss shook his head. "There are issues with them, too."

Dan shrugged. "We've been putting gas turbines in ships since the seventies. Come on, guys."

"Specifically, sir, the *new* engines," Pickles said.

"The turbine blades are defectively machined," Harriss added.

Dan sucked air between his teeth. "Defective. How?"

The lieutenant reached under the table to a briefcase. He set a chunk of dull-silvery metal between them. Intricately curved, it resembled something organic, rather than a machine part. Perhaps the vertebra of a whale. Dan hefted it; it was as dense as it looked. But the upper part was mangled, obviously torn apart in some violent event. Harriss murmured, "They fail, Captain. Explosively. After about fifty hours."

The lieutenant flicked the tortured metal. "To be perfectly accurate, they weren't machined, per se. They're 3-D printed . . . built up with additive manufacturing. Out of a high-temperature-resistant, polycrystalline nickel/titanium-based superalloy. The manufacturer went to that to save time, since the government gave them an emergency priority.

But somehow the printers left microvoids in the blades. Not cooling channels. Just . . . vacancies. Invisible, even to X-rays during the QA inspections. Until they were PET-scanned at a hospital, to see why they kept failing. The FBI suspects a polymorphic malware."

"Clarify," Dan muttered.

Pickles said, "Cybersabotage. Someone modified the programming for the printers. From outside."

"Holy shit." Dan glanced around to make sure no one was eavesdropping. "Put it . . . put it away. For the *whole class*?"

Harriss straightened from his briefcase again. "Both classes, sir. And if the nukes don't come through either, we're looking at fifty-two new major combatants with dangerous engines."

Dan contemplated this disaster, and how completely a few lines of malicious code could cripple an entire war effort. "Uh, tell me more about these reactors. Can they replace the gas turbines in the other ships in the class? Maybe even in the Burkes?"

Pickles shook her head. "These are small modular units. Nominal forty-five megawatts each. Unfortunately, sir, like we said, the reactor packages are behind schedule too."

"Does SUPSHIPS know?"

"They have the report, but frankly, I get the impression they don't think this is a big problem yet."

Dan grimaced. "Good work, Brett. Kitty. So that's four issues we can address straight out of the blocks. I'd like bulleted lists. Short descriptions of each problem, plus options to address them. In rank order, but it sounds like the engine issue is the most critical."

"I agree, Captain." Pickles smiled at him.

Dan said, "That's great, Commander. But let's get this straight from the start: I don't always expect people to agree with me. If you see me headed for the shoals, say so. That goes for both of you, and Vigliotti, too. I don't think any of us are going to win any more medals in this war, so let's at least try to do some good for the fleet. Understood?"

THAT night he got through to his daughter at last, as he lay on the bed in his BOQ room. The twisted turbine blade gleamed on his bedside table beside the phone. Nan answered on the fifth ring. She sounded tired. *"Dad! They said you were back. I knew it. I never really believed you were, um, gone."*

He hadn't seen much of her after the divorce, which had not been amicable. His ex hadn't exactly encouraged their daughter to feel well disposed toward him. Add to that being deployed, and they hadn't developed much of a relationship. Still, the few times they'd met since the split, they'd gotten along. He was proud of her, that was for sure. She'd completed a tough undergraduate degree, then postgraduate work in biochemistry. *"So where are you now? Out at sea?"*

"No, ashore, San Diego. Sort of . . . on the shelf now."

"They're giving you a vacation?" She laughed. *"About time."*

"Something like that. Anyway, I have evenings free. Maybe even a day off. Any chance we could—"

"From Seattle?" She sighed. *"I couldn't get away, Dad. We're on a high-priority project. And even if I could, the airlines are all shut down. Government flights only."*

"You're still in research? Still with Lukajs?"

"Yes, Dad. Still in research. And still with Dr. Lukajs." The same tone he'd gotten in college, when he tried to ask about her classes. Which had sounded incredibly difficult: "Membrane and Biomolecular Chemistry," "Bioinformatics," "Biotechnology of Microorganisms," "Biochemistry of Stem Cells." He'd opened one of her textbooks once, and quickly closed it, bewildered, realizing how far her world was from his.

"So tell me about it. What're you working on? Anything I could understand?"

Her voice went guarded. He recognized the tone. Christ, was everyone in America on a government payroll now? *"I wouldn't want it to be general knowledge. That I told you this, I mean."*

"I understand. Lips zipped."

"Have you ever heard of H7N9?"

"No. What is it?"

"A virus. Subtype of a pretty common avian influenza, but it never infected humans or mammals before. It drifted and shifted and reemerged in Asia last year. Flu viruses reassort their segments from different strains. Once or twice a century, you get something new. This one's bad. Forty percent mortality rate. We're at a Phase Six alert. That's the highest, if you're not familiar with the alert system."

"Christ," he muttered. "And you're working with this stuff?"

"We have containment protocols. But it might actually be good, that we're at war. The lack of air travel may slow down its spread. It

hasn't gotten to the U.S. yet. But if it does, we could see another pandemic. Like the Spanish flu in 1918."

She sounded breathless. He didn't know a lot about the pandemic she'd mentioned, but had read it had been bad. "Any chance of a vaccine? Isn't that what you'd need, a vaccine?"

"We have a monovalent live attenuated vaccine. It's not great, but we're working to improve it. But Dr. L thinks antivirals will be our best weapon if this breaks out, though. Inhibiting the neuraminidase protein. That's the N in the H7N9. . . . Sure you want to hear all this?"

"If you can keep it Dad simple."

"Viruses produce surface proteins that let them infect your cells. Okay? Then they reprogram the cells, to produce more viruses. Usually your immune system protects you. But this new strain produces a protein that shuts down the normal immune response. That's what makes it so virulent.

"We used reverse genetics to investigate the exact interactions that make this so dangerous. When we characterized the RNA segments we found a unique carboxyl terminus. We've elucidated the structure. Dr. Lukajs and our team are trying to map it out on the molecular level, how it evades immunity and takes over cell biochemistry. Then we might be able to find or create a drug to roadblock it. Either throw a monkey wrench into how it reproduces, inside the cell, or make it visible again to the immune response, so it doesn't get inside at all.

"But we might not have to invent something new. What if we have something that's already passed toxicity tests, that we can pitch in there? I'm looking at some of the new cancer drugs. What we call the EPOCH drugs—etoposide, prednisone, vincristine, cyclophosphamide, and doxorubicin."

Dan cleared his throat. "Uh, okay! Think I got most of that."

"I tried to keep it simple, Dad."

"I'm super proud of you, kid."

"Thanks. But if we can't come up with something effective . . . over a hundred and fifty million died in 1918. From a much smaller global population. It would stop trade, cause famine, more wars—you can't imagine how bad it would be. Like a nuclear war. Only worldwide."

She sounded sobered, even scared. He wanted to comfort her, but could only find fumbling words. "Well, if anyone can find something that works, I know you will."

"Thanks. But we both know you don't know what you're talking about."

"No, I guess not."

"And then . . . if we do find an effective drug, or develop a vaccine . . . there'll be the question of whether to release it."

He frowned into the phone. "Well, of course you would. Why not?"

"And who we should release it to," she added.

"Yeah, I see what you mean. If there's only so much of whatever drug, who should you give it to."

"I didn't exactly mean that, I—Look, I'm in the lab. Gotta go. Really glad you called. And that you made it back safe."

"Good to talk to you, kid. Love you."

"Love you. Bye."

He reset the handset, then leaned back and rubbed his face. A pandemic. Worse than 1918. Millions dead. Maybe . . . billions.

They might not even need a nuclear war to end the world.

He sighed and, after a while, went into the bathroom to get ready for bed.

HALF an hour later he snapped awake. Not fully alert, exactly, but warned by some circuit that something was going on down there, deep in the unconscious. Out of his ken, really, except that it seemed to involve what Nan had said on the phone.

We might not have to invent something new.

What if we have something available already that we can pitch in there, see if it works?

And something else she'd said, earlier in the conversation . . .

It teased in his head, two memes or logic strings that like DNA were trying to combine, twine together, to produce a hybrid.

Maybe, something virulent.

But even as he groped after them they vanished. He lay still, trying to retrace his steps back into the half dream. Chasing the images even as they evanesced back into the vapor of the forgotten. Then gave up at last.

If the clue was that important, sooner or later, the realization would arrive.

9

Dublin

GLANCING out the third-floor window at a bituminous sky looming over Christ Church Cathedral, Blair Titus decided she'd better dress for rain. She and Shira Salyers—the slight, almost frail-looking woman from State, now the official head of the U.S. delegation—had been invited to stay at the ambassador's residence, outside the city. But Salyers had said staying in town would save time going and coming. The VIP Suite at the Radisson Blu St. Helen's was spacious and private, with a separate elevator and discreet access onto a side street, bypassing the lobby. She took one bedroom, Shira the other. The rest of the delegation were staying in the city too, at Jurys in Christchurch.

The conference was at Dublin Castle. The stone fortress hearted the old city, a short uphill stroll from the Liffey. A thousand years before, it had been a Viking stronghold. A century before, center of administration for the Protestant Ascendancy. Blair wanted to walk over from the hotel, but the Garda sergeant assigned to protect them had warned against it. The Irish government provided a black Mercedes, complete with driver and opaque windows.

She decided on a black pencil skirt, white silk high-necked blouse, and gray cashmere jacket. She frowned at her reflection in the full-length mirror. Too austere? Not for an international conference. She no longer wore earrings, because of the missing lobe, but added a vintage silver and green-enamel lapel pin in a Celtic knot pattern, a gift from Dan two birthdays ago.

By the time she and Salyers got to the castle it was raining hard. Shira had been appointed by the secretary of state as a special envoy. The driver escorted them under the stone arch of the main gate, holding an umbrella. They picked their way across the flagstones of a wide court, then though another archway. She recognized it from a recent documentary about the Easter Rising.

In the upper courtyard bereted troops patrolled with rifles and a sniffer dog team, working the perimeters. "Shira, is this usual? All this security."

"Not out of the ordinary." Salyers cocked a wrenlike head. "Think of the bombings in their recent past. Having something go bad here . . . some madman break in and wreak havoc . . . I'm sure they'd rather it didn't happen."

In the Portrait Gallery a pale-blue-and-white ceiling garlanded in eighteenth-century plasterwork lofted far overhead. Eighteenth- and nineteenth-century visages peered down haughtily from gilded frames, resplendently draped in scarlet and ermine robes. A vanished race from a vanished empire. She wondered why the Irish hadn't torn them down, and burned the portraits of their oppressors. Too civilized, probably. Erasing history too often meant repeating it. Low murmurs floated upward, echoing like the imperious voices of vanished viceroys.

As ten o'clock approached, the conferees gathered at a long table. The hall quieted as a dignified woman in her late fifties tapped a gavel.

Blair had met Liz McManus the night before, at the opening drinks reception in the Throne Room. A harpist played Celtic airs as the diplomats picked at canapés. McManus, the "rapporteur" and chairperson, was tall, silver-haired, with elegant cheekbones. A former *teachta dála*, a congresswoman in American parlance, she'd led the Labour Party before retiring. McManus had been gracious but reserved, and Blair had noted her chatting with the Chinese delegates later. A balancing act, no doubt . . .

A man in his seventies, with springy gray tufts sprinkled across an otherwise bare scalp, introduced himself in French. He was from West Africa. Actually, quite a few of the attendees seemed to be African. When McManus began speaking, he excused himself and picked up headphones, as did half the men and women around the table.

"Good morning. Welcome to the initial session of the United Nations conference on possible human rights violations and war crimes by both sides during ongoing military actions in southern Asia and the western Pacific," the chairperson said gravely. "It's worth noting that several possible infringements and infractions have already been reported from this conflict. The Security Council was the initial setting for these charges, and there have been hearings in the council and resolutions proposed, though not agreed on, relating to them.

"In my personal view, no UNSCRs have been adopted because the permanent members are in opposition on this issue.

"Therefore, the UNSC has suggested this special conference. This meeting will not concern itself with specific charges. Instead, we hope for a general exposition of issues. If any charges are brought forward, a separate committee of inquiry can be convened.

"We will consider protocols and staffing for tracking and bringing to public attention possible war crimes resulting from the current hostilities between the Allied Powers, namely the United States, the Socialist Republic of Vietnam, Australia, the Republic of India, and other powers; and the Associated or United Powers, among them the People's Republic of China, the Islamic Republic of Iran, the Democratic People's Republic of Korea, the Islamic Republic of Pakistan, the Lao People's Democratic Republic, and the People's Republic of Miandan."

Blair propped her chin on both hands. "Miandan" was the Chinese puppet state in northern Myanmar. It had been Burma when the men in those portraits had administered the globe. Just another, more distant piece of the British Empire then. Now, conquered territory once more, where a new colonial power was slaughtering thousands who resisted its rule.

The Chinese were seated across the table from the U.S. delegation. A place card in front of the eldest read DEPUTY MINISTER CHEN JIALUO. With pudgy hands folded, Chen returned her stare with a fixed, unblinking gaze through heavy black-framed glasses. All four wore them, as if mimicking their ruthless Leader, President for Life Zhang Zurong.

In measured tones, pausing for the translators, McManus outlined the conference's charter. If they could agree, protocols would be formulated for observation by small teams composed of respected individuals—statespersons, diplomats, military officers, physicians, and attorneys—from nonaligned nations. These teams would not so much gather evidence, as provide unbiased reporting and, perhaps, inhibit by their very existence atrocities and other crimes.

"Our brief is to detect and record any and all violations of international humanitarian and human rights law. We do not, I repeat *not*, intend to inhibit or replace any law of armed conflict investigations or prosecutions carried out internally by the states involved. For obvious reasons, self-policing is the preferred way to prosecute LOAC violations.

But if such states default in their duties and a lack of responsibility becomes evident—as it has in several past conflicts—our reports may constitute the basis for action within the context of the International Criminal Court or ad hoc tribunals like the International Criminal Tribunal for the former Yugoslavia."

She nodded to a bearded, dark-skinned man beside her. "Pursuant to this I have asked Dr. Abir al-Mughrabi, a former appeals division judge, International Criminal Court at The Hague, to outline his proposals for how such oversight might function. Dr. al-Mughrabi has been involved in prosecutions for internal civil wars and genocide in Lebanon, Rwanda, and Syria. He also oversaw the recent investigations into war crimes in Afghanistan. Dr. al-Mughrabi."

Blair fitted the headphones, taking care with her ear, but largely tuned out the translation. Proposals by someone who'd prosecuted the U.S. before? A membership dominated by Africans, when Africa had been penetrated by Chinese companies, their governments bought off with grants and cheap development loans? The rapporteur herself, McManus, seemed determinedly neutral.

But aside from that, just half an hour in, she wasn't getting a good feeling about this.

THE morning was mainly devoted to orienting the members, but many seemed less interested in the mechanics of peacekeeping than in the wines and snacks set out between sessions. Blair kept an eye on the Chinese team. Four of them, all men, in dark suits and with the same bland expressions, the same pale blue ties, the same red-flag lapel pins. Whenever their gazes crossed hers they quickly turned away to mingle with the other attendees. Who often crossed the room to greet said Chinese, whereas she and Shira stood alone under a portrait of Clive. Not one person approached them.

She muttered, "What's your reading on this, Shira? We're lepers?"

"I'm not feeling very comfortable either," the diplomat murmured. "This is quite unusual. Delegations are never intentionally isolated in diplomatic gatherings."

"So why now?"

"I really don't know. But don't take it personally. Remember, we're the ones they're proposing to keep tabs on."

"Granted, but they seem to be chummy enough with China. I feel hostility. Especially from the Europeans." She wanted to say, *And the Africans*, but didn't, since the State rep was black.

Salyers supplied it for her. "I don't like all these Africans. I mean, I *like* Africans, and international oversight's a good thing, overall. But I don't think they can be totally disinterested. Considering all the grants and soft loans the Chinese have been spreading around their continent."

Blair pointed her chin across the room at the bearded diplomat. "This al-Mughrabi. You know him? Where's he from?"

"Morocco. Though his family was originally Lebanese." Salyers sighed, fiddling with a plastic glass of nonalcoholic fruit drink. "They have to signal anti-Americanism. But that doesn't mean they won't give us the benefit of the doubt."

"We have effective courts. The rule of law. A free press. At least, mostly. The Chinese don't. Shouldn't we get more than 'the benefit of the doubt'?"

"Let's rejoin," McManus said just then into the PA system. "Gentlemen, ladies, next on the agenda: the warring powers have requested ten minutes each to make statements. Let's start with Her Excellency Shira Salyers, United States of America, special envoy and head of delegation to this conference. Ms. Salyers, welcome."

Blair tensed. UN meetings, Shira had told her, were carefully choreographed and rigidly scripted. Diplomats adhered religiously to protocols, and surprises weren't welcome. The HOD spoke for his or her entire government. Ill-chosen words could have unpleasant consequences.

They'd drafted this statement together over the last week, passing each iteration back for comments by both State and the White House.

Blair herself had no right to speak. She could sit next to Salyers, assist on points of fact, and whisper discreet advice. But defense and military officials deferred to their diplomatic heads of delegation. All HODs, in turn, reported to their permanent reps to the UN, who reported formally to their heads of state. But informally, and in every meaningful way, to their SecState equivalent.

The Chinese were smiling. Tenting their fingers. Waiting.

All right, Blair thought. Let's see if you're still grinning after this.

Shira stood, meeting not just the stares from the Europeans, the veiled disliking eyes of the Middle Easterners and Africans, but the steady red pilots of television cameras too. Irish TV, or recordings? Blair jotted on a pad. YOU ARE ICY COOL, she scrawled in letters an inch high. The State rep glanced down, smiled faintly, then straightened.

Blair blinked. Suddenly Shira didn't look quite so fragile anymore.

"Madam Chairman, honored delegates, Mr. al-Mughrabi," Salyers began smoothly, voice raised so everyone could hear. "The United States has upheld the rule of international law since its founding, and has supported the United Nations from the beginning.

"Let me recapitulate, to set the stage for a resolution I will move at the end of my statement.

"The current state of hostilities originated after General Zhang Zurong's execution of his rivals in government, consolidating his position as both party general secretary and state president. He now holds all leading titles in what he calls the People's Empire of China.

"Almost two years ago Pakistan and India opened hostilities. China invaded Bhutan, citing a mutual-defense understanding with Pakistan. They also undertook gray-force activities, including the mining of Yokosuka Harbor. Shoot-downs and blinding of observation, communication, and global positioning satellites occurred at the same time as cyberattacks on American banking and financial systems, industrial plants, and power grids.

"The United States retaliated, yes. But our responses were always calibrated to avoid escalation. Again and again, we offered to negotiate our differences.

"However, General Zhang's responses were ultimata and threats. He initiated strikes on American and Japanese defenses in the Pacific. He threatened our allies and our homeland with multiwarhead, long-range missiles developed secretly and in violation of mutually agreed upon strategic arms limitation regimes. He torpedoed Allied shipping, and violently seized islands belonging to regional powers allied with the United States.

"Then, in Operation Sheng Chi, he destroyed the Taiwanese air force and navy and invaded that island. Terrible reprisals have followed, including mass murder, incarceration, and torture of large segments of the population.

"In the most egregious violation of the laws of war, he then carried out an unprovoked nuclear attack on a U.S. carrier group in international waters, destroying the carrier USS *Franklin D. Roosevelt*, destroyer *Elisha Eaker*, destroyer *Richmond P. Hobson*, USS *Gault*, a frigate, and badly damaging another, USS *Crommelin*.

"In all, almost ten thousand sailors, marines, and civilians were killed in this dastardly attack. In comparison, two thousand four hundred soldiers, sailors, and civilians were lost in the Pearl Harbor attack on December 7, 1941, and just under three thousand military and civilian dead on September 11, 2001."

Blair sat riveted as Salyers paused, surveying the inhospitable faces. The State rep took a deep breath. Then lowered her glance to hurl the next sentences across the table, into the round placid visages of the enemy. "The United States has deferred retaliating for these outrages, counting on China to cease its aggression and return to the family of nations without further bloodshed or escalation of this conflict. But other events since, including terror reprisals against China's own minority populations in Hong Kong, Xianjiang, Tibet, and other areas, render it impossible for me to do otherwise than to move that this assembly end its first day in session by *indicting* Zhang Zurong for waging aggressive war and other crimes against humanity. I hereby make a motion to so resolve; and ask for a second."

Beside her, Blair glared across the table at the Chinese. McManus had her head down, concentrating on a tablet computer, though her fingertips had gone white. The murmurs and headshaking had begun as Salyers spoke. As she concluded members rose from their seats, shaking fists and yelling at her. But among the shouts there seemed to be no second to her resolution.

The gavel banged again and again, echoing from the high ceilings, the plaster intaglio far above the angry throng.

THE Chinese had been conferring among themselves while Shira spoke. Now they requested a break before they made their statement. McManus agreed, also noting that as observers to the conference, not members, neither the United States' representatives nor those of the Associated Powers could introduce resolutions. "I'm afraid Ms. Salyers's, therefore, is moot."

Blair and Shira found themselves sitting alone. She got up, wincing at a twisting agony in her hip. Were there chiropractors in Dublin?

No one spoke to her in the restroom. The silence was frigid, faces averted in the spotless mirrors over the marble sinks.

Well, too bad. They'd laid a marker on the table. Pissed against a tree, as Dan's Navy friends might say. She washed her hands, using plenty of lavender-scented soap, then headed back.

After an introduction by the rapporteur, the eldest Chinese, Deputy Minister Chen, lumbered to his feet. A paper shook in his hand as he talked rapidly, round cheeks flushed, head bobbing. Blair closed her eyes to focus on the translation.

"The United States' representative hijacks this solemn gathering to advance outrageous falsehoods. She slanders the good name of the Greater People's Republic and of our revered leader, Premier Zhang Zurong, light of China and standard bearer of the united peoples of greater Asia.

"In fact, it is well known that the actions of the Greater People's Republic were undertaken in self-defense after a long and increasingly dangerous series of adventurist provocations by the criminal and reckless leadership of the United States.

"Miss Ambassador alleges China began this war. In fact America did, with a policy of interfering with universally accepted claims in waters, reefs, and islands our ancient imperial dynasties discovered, explored, and populated over a period of more than four thousand years. Indeed, they themselves refer to the area in question as the 'China' Sea. After many years of threats and provocations, they began overt hostilities with the violent conquest and occupation of our islands in the Mischief Reef area. The U.S. and Indian navies then imposed an illegal blockade, cutting China's billions off from badly needed food, medicines, and oil.

"Next, a U.S. missile cruiser shot down a peaceful communications satellite. Not content with this, American SEAL thugs carried out an armed raid on a peaceful fishing village on Yongxing, or Woody Island, spreading terror among the innocent coastal populace.

"Finally, the United States, along with renegade elements of the disgraced and corrupt former regime of South Korea, inserted itself into China's internal affairs. They attacked civilian passenger ships and hospital ships during the peaceful and mutually agreed upon reunification of Taiwan with the mother country, killing thousands.

"This unprovoked attack, as is well known, forced Premier Zhang to reluctantly order the strike on the American carrier group, which was slinking toward our coast to carry out terror raids on defenseless cities. He regretted this necessity. But after all, can the United States, after

Hiroshima and Nagasaki, protest with a straight face if Asians use nuclear weapons against her, far at sea, when no civilian populations are put at risk?"

Chen stared around belligerently. From the nods around the table, he'd scored a point. He resumed. "Not content with that, they continue to wage aggressive war, threatening China's coasts and interfering with internal production and communications. They damage our nuclear generating stations, endangering large areas with the release of radioactive materials. They derail our high-speed trains. They bomb and strafe our coastal cities, inflicting thousands more civilian casualties. Finally, they foment rebellion by violent extremists within our borders, necessitating stern measures to restore order."

Chen spread his hands, eyes wide, astonished and ingenuous. "All this, despite our respected premier's repeated offers of peace and reconciliation on the basis of mutual respect and resumption of free trade."

One of the younger men passed him a paper. He scanned it, then lifted his head. Slammed his fist on the table.

"I have a further charge to make, and a most grievous one! Not content with causing famine through blockade, the so-called Allies have also released biological agents to decimate crops and livestock. Also, most heinously, this winter they spread infectious viruses among the population, resulting in hundreds of thousands of deaths among the aged, infirm, and those with weak systems.

"This is not merely war! It is conscious genocide against the entire people of China and her gallant Persian and Pakistani allies in this struggle against Western oppression."

The deputy minister looked up at the ceiling, then at his colleagues. He glared at Salyers and Blair. Took a slow, elaborate sip of water, and cleared his throat.

"China respects this distinguished commission and will cooperate fully. At the same time, we will not insult it by introducing spurious resolutions we are not empowered to table.

"Nevertheless, we cannot help rejecting in the strongest terms the lying propaganda of villains such as the woman sitting next to the senior U.S. representative, who no doubt wrote those inflammatory and false words she uttered.

"The 'Honorable' Blair Titus is well known among the peaceful masses as a corrupt tool of the profit-hungry warmongers in the American defense industry. She is a pliable puppet, wife of the notorious war criminal Admiral Daniel V. Lenson, and most likely also the mistress of the insane and irresponsible national security adviser, Dr. Edward Szerenci.

"Truly, this is a woman wise friends of China will avoid. Depraved and malignant, she will be among those standing in the dock when this commission completes its work of documenting America's genocide, war crimes, and other violations of international norms and treaties.

"Thank you." Chen beamed around, scowled at her one last time, and slowly seated himself.

"Ooff," Shira whispered. "Corrupt, pliable, depraved, and malignant. I like the mistress part best, though. Guess I didn't catch that chemistry, when you and Ed were facing off in the Tank."

Blair coolly rearranged her papers, though rage burned like sulfuric acid on her cheeks. Obfuscation, bluster, and lies, but repeat a falsehood often enough, loudly enough, and someone would believe it. Back it up with threats, like the one Chen had just made, and many of the smaller states would fall obediently into line, or at least hesitate to support any Allied charges.

The gavel rapped. The chairwoman admonished both parties, and moved on to the next business.

THE rest of the morning was devoted to procedural discussion, mainly of how delegates to the observation teams would be apportioned among various neutral countries. Blair had her doubts as to how disinterested they would actually be but, after McManus's scolding, kept them to herself. Both the U.S. and China were here only as observers, after all, though as the main combatants, their cooperation would be essential.

This became evident as Dr. al-Mughrabi presented a plan for four teams, three geographic and one for cyberspace issues, to operate across the war zones. Each oversight team would have three members. One would be a physician, one a diplomat or jurist, and one an army officer. A delegate from Chile proposed that the term "army officers" be changed to "military officers," as many of the hostilities so far had been naval. Al-Mughrabi countered politely that as few outrages against civilian populations occurred at sea, it was proper that monitors be army officers, particularly senior ones who'd seen action in such campaigns as that against FARC, in Colombia. After nearly an hour's wrangling, the language stayed as it was.

The next issue was access. Al-Mughrabi asked both combatant representatives if it would be granted. Chen, speaking first this time, said China would grant full and free access, including transport and hosteling, to all oversight teams, guaranteeing them entrée to any portion of any battlefield at any time. He nodded benignantly. "We offer this in the certainty that impartial observers will attest to the scrupulous care the people's armed forces have always taken to avoid collateral damage and civilian casualties."

Shira whispered, "They'll never implement that promise. They'd let them into Taipei? Hong Kong? Miandan, where they're massacring Rohingyas in Rakhine? Near anything that even smells like an atrocity?"

McManus turned to them. "And the representative from the United States."

Blair had discussed this with General Vincenzo during their call the night before. Unfortunately, JCS opposed unhindered access on security grounds. They'd drawn up a précis of his misgivings. Salyers rose, holding a copy. She said carefully, "The United States is prepared to cooperate, but with certain caveats.

"We can provide transport and housing, but subject to the agreement of our theater commanders. Also, we have to keep the personal safety of the monitors in mind. Subject to those limitations, we will host the observer teams."

The old African next to Blair raised a finger. He mumbled, in English, "Why is it that the Chinese have nothing to hide? While you are afraid to offer full access?"

Salyers smiled down at him. "I believe you'll find that American 'limited access' gives them more real opportunity for on-the-ground observation than Chinese 'full access.' Sir."

"We object again to these barefaced lies," Chen snapped from across the table.

At which point it seemed to be time to break for lunch.

MOST of the attendees left, with two hours off before the afternoon session. She and Shira stayed, and hit the remains of the breakfast table. They were standing isolated, as before, nibbling on slightly stale currant-studded scones, when the elderly African ambled up. Blair nodded politely. He inclined his head, smiling, and set a cup and saucer down in front of her. Flicked the saucer with a finger, and wandered away.

"What the hey," Salyers muttered. "He just—"

"Shh," Blair said. When the old diplomat rounded a corner and was out of sight, she set her own cup down. Pushed his aside surreptitiously, and replaced it on the saucer with her own.

Just as she'd suspected, when she picked it up a slip of paper lay under the saucer. She excused herself, went to the restroom again, and locked herself into a stall.

The note read

QUEEN OF TARTS 7 PM

She tore it across. A moment later the toilet flushed, whirling the bits away and out of sight.

THAT night, after a room-service dinner at the hotel, she told Shira, "I'm turning in early. Jet lag, ugh."

Back in her room, instead of going to bed she pulled on a dark gray cable-knit sweater, black pants, and a brown hooded raincoat. She tied a dark green kerchief from the hotel gift shop over her hair, then glanced out into the shared living area. Empty.

She eased the door shut behind her, and took the private elevator down.

The alley was deserted. A wall sconce threw out a greenish glow. It was still raining, with gusts of chilly wind. Pressing the button to unfurl a compact umbrella, she stepped out and quickly left the Radisson behind, walking downhill toward the river, then veering right onto Dame Street, a wide avenue lined with pubs, jewelry stores, and touristy craft shops.

The squared-off steeple of Christ Church Cathedral loomed behind her. Couples she assumed were tourists chatted in German and Dutch and French, strolling past, heads bent under the steady drizzle. The streets glistened like patent leather. A raucous thumping of fiddle and drum accompanied a lively folk tune. Through a pub window she glimpsed people three deep at a long mahogany bar, holding pint glasses and laughing or singing along. Maybe after whatever she was headed for, she'd treat herself to a Guinness, anonymous at last in a happy, rowdy crowd.

The Queen of Tarts, a smartphone search had revealed, was a bakery café opposite the old city hall. It wasn't far from the castle. Tilting the umbrella low over her face, she walked briskly past without looking into the wide front window.

Trying to remember tradecraft from the Graham Greene and Alan Furst novels she'd read, she checked out a window of shoes, then crossed to stroll west on the other side of the street, past the tart shop again. Its facade was painted an eye-catching bright red, punctuated with decorative prize medallions. On neither pass did she spot anyone suspicious, but these days street surveillance cameras could be recording her every step. An indignity James Bond had never had to consider. . . . Finally she took a deep breath, furled her dripping umbrella, and went in.

Four tables were occupied by sodden tourists in jeans and windbreakers in various stages of drying out. The shop smelled of cinnamon and butter and vanilla, with a sharp hint of berries. Across the back, a long glass bakery counter displayed lush-looking pastries, cheesecakes, lattice-topped tarts. She stood gazing down at an enormous raspberry-striped meringue, wondering exactly what she was doing here.

"Help ye, madam?" a red-aproned young woman asked. A smudge of flour dusted one cheek.

"I'm not sure. I was supposed to meet someone here."

"And are ye sure it wasn't at our other location?"

"Your . . . other location?"

"This is our wee bakery shop. The big café is around the corner." She began to give directions with the air of someone who had to do this fifty times a day. Then paused, eyeing Blair sympathetically. "Bleeding awful out, isn't it? We have a way there without going outside." She opened a gate and motioned for her to step behind the counter. "This way. Mind the step down."

Blair hesitated at the worn oak threshold that separated the cheerful bakery from a dim brick passageway. "Go on then," said the girl. "It's a shortcut."

At last she stepped through. It felt ludicrous to suspect this kind, auburn-haired Irish shopgirl of being part of some deep-laid international plot.

The brick-lined, poorly lit corridor, obviously an alleyway in some previous incarnation of this Victorian-era block, zagged and backtracked. At one corner a stir and crackle from a stack of boxes made her flinch. When she peered in, a huge black cat stared up, amber eyes lambent. "Hello. I have a kitty kind of like you," she told him. "His name is Jimbo. What's yours?"

The cat hissed and leapt from the box. He turned disdainfully away and began vigorously washing, as if she'd somehow contaminated his fur.

A few more steps, and a crackle-painted door opened onto a busy, clattering kitchen. Servers pushed past, hefting trays of soups and salads and plates of the same heavenly-smelling pastries and lavishly iced cakes the bakeshop had displayed. She eyed a tray of cherry tarts with fork marks around the edges, the ripe red filling oozing along the darker seams. Yes, one of those, please?. . . . But pulled herself back to the task, whatever that was, and looked around.

The place was packed. Two full floors, every seat occupied. Half a dozen servers in bright red aprons and black pants wove dexterously among tables to deliver orders. Through large plate-glass windows, wire tables and chairs were visible on a patio outside, but they stood empty beneath dripping green awnings. A score of conversations babbled in a dozen languages. She unzipped her overcoat, looking about. Then caught a lifted hand from above.

A stairway led up to three tables set in front of doors that opened, apparently, to the restrooms. They overlooked the organized chaos below. Europeans of various sizes and nationalities occupied two of them.

She almost missed him, he was so unobtrusive. But at the farthest table, against the wall, alone, perched one of the Chinese she'd faced earlier that day. The youngest, perhaps, though she couldn't be sure. Absent, now, the heavy black plastic-rimmed glasses.

"Good evening," he said, half rising. "Ms. Titus. Will you have a seat?"

"I'm not sure. Who are you?"

"My name is Xie Yunlong." He pronounced his family name with a sibilant syllable she knew she wouldn't even try to reproduce. "Please call me Yun."

"All right. Blair."

One of the red-aproned servers appeared, brisk and blond, pencil poised. "Evenin', luvs. Are we startin' with tea today, then?"

Blair ordered Earl Grey and two small tarts, one with cherry, the other with apple filling. Xie quietly asked for cinnamon scones and coffee. When they came, he glanced at the Germans, who were busy with their Guinnesses. Then leaned to her. "I am here without knowledge of deputy minister. Without knowledge of head of mission."

"All on your own?"

"No, not quite. I represent what you might call another faction within the administration."

"I see," she murmured. "A peace faction? One inclined to compromise?"

He pursed his lips. "That would be very premature to discuss."

He spoke with great precision, one sentence at a time, as if reading from some internal script, committee-generated and carefully memorized. "First, I must emphasize that we all, every Chinese, fully agree with everything respected Minister Chen said today. The United States has behaved abominably. Threats and attacks can only be met with resolute defense. Premier Zhang's peace offers are realistic and generous."

"I see. But surely you haven't been sent to meet me—whatever faction, whoever sent you—just to repeat what Chen already said."

"The leadership is united. There is no 'faction.'"

She frowned. Hadn't he used the word first? "All right. I understand that," she said. Thinking: I must tell you again, I am not mad.

Their drinks arrived. Xie sipped coffee. Blair stirred sugar into her tea. At last he murmured, "Still, there are matters best discussed in a way that is not fully public."

"We call those 'back channels.'"

"Back channels; yes. Ever during war, there must be communications between leaders."

She narrowed her gaze, startled. "You're representing *Zhang*?"

"As I said, there are no factions."

She understood less with every exchange. Through the unreality of the setting, the yeasty, fruity kitchen smells, the relaxed gemütlich chatter, a queer unease was bleeding. No factions? Yet he'd started by mentioning one. And if there weren't any, then why an off-line meeting? Even with the Chinese and U.S. embassies withdrawn at the outbreak of war, the UN was still in session in New York.

Still, now that they were here, she should in good conscience try to sound out what he wanted. "The premier is always right. Got it. So what are we here for, Yun?"

He met her gaze for perhaps a tenth of a second before dropping his again. "Today we were arguing over how this war started. It is perhaps more worth inquiring, how it could be ended."

Now they were getting somewhere. She said over the raised teacup, "The first step would be to establish communication."

"That is what we are attempting."

"I see that. And it's encouraging. The second thing, then, the great thing, would be to begin to limit the severity of this very unfortunate war. Your premier has to show good faith. Establish trust. Which, so far, he hasn't shown much interest in, frankly."

The young man whispered, while dissecting his scone with knife and fork, meticulously placing each raisin to one side of the plate, "How could he do that? If he were willing."

Blair thought back to the briefings at JCS. "One way might be . . . let's see . . . for example, let's say he ordered his armies in Vietnam to halt in place. Allow humanitarian corridors to Hanoi, to assist and supply the population. And, perhaps, elsewhere, refrain from further counterforce attacks."

"One-sided concessions. What would you do in return?"

"I'd have to consult with my government. Maybe . . . letting some humanitarian supplies through the blockade. But if fighting died down, maybe both nations could back away from the nuclear brink."

Dark eyes widened. "You are saying the United States is planning to attack us with nuclear weapons?"

She cursed herself. Unfortunately, she was actually privy to the plans for just such a strike. Or at least, the preliminary studies. "I'm not saying that. I don't know. But I do know one thing. China and America are the most powerful countries in the world. If this war goes on, it will end with both exhausted and devastated. Surely your premier can't want that."

A tilt of the head. "It is not always easy for a courtier to know what the emperor desires. But I, in turn, will tell you something. You are using famine as a weapon. Your biological warfare targets our rice and grain crops, threatening millions with starvation."

"I'm sure we're not conducting anything remotely resembling biological warfare. And what about your repeated sabotage of our power plants, our power supplies? With these heat waves, we're losing—"

Yun leaned forward. His voice vibrated, though it was still pitched beneath the clatter of silverware, the chatter of tourists. "Your electricity is a legitimate industrial target. Be quiet and listen! America is carrying out the greatest atrocity of all times. But China will no longer suffer quietly.

"I am here to warn you. We know what you are planning! We are not fools! Your dogs in Washington must know this: if the Party's rule is threatened, we will not go down without turning your entire country into radioactive ashes."

"I'm not sure—"

"I said listen! This is no empty threat. It would be most unwise to push him to that brink you mention. He will not step back from it . . . as the Russian, Khrushchev, once did."

She bought time by starting on the apple tart. She'd hoped he might present a way forward. A message from a splinter group: disenchanted oligarchs frightened of losing their fortunes, generals wary of Zhang's firing squads, disgruntled industrialists. Instead she was getting a declaration that the enemy government was solid. And that, pushed too far, Zhang would unleash catastrophe. "I have to tell you, there are those in my government who feel exactly the same way," she murmured. "We will not retreat. Nor be pushed out of the western Pacific. And we will never abandon our allies. Even if it comes to trading city for city."

"I will take your words back with me," Yun said. He surveyed his raisin-littered plate, patted his lips with the napkin, and rose. He was gone before she realized he'd stuck her with the tab.

In the rain, the darkness, she stood outside, struggling with the folding umbrella in a little pedestrian mall whose slanting concrete slabs were sheeted with gleaming water. The icy rain, halfway to sleet now, pattered down cold and dispiriting and endless. Reflecting the helplessness chilling her heart.

No, it wouldn't end so easily. Both sides would fight relentlessly on.

And many more would die.

10

Eastern Maryland

IT was still raining when the bus pulled in. The windows were streaked and the sky was gray in the early morning. Hector was home at last, though for a while it hadn't seemed like he'd make it. No flights, even for military members on leave. No way to rent a car, even if he could afford twenty-dollar-a-gallon gas. Which had left the bus.

But gradually the plains had climbed to the rolling Appalachians, then smoothed again. He'd changed at Washington, where a young white woman had spat on his uniform outside the terminal. Changed again at Baltimore, and headed south.

Now, three days into his week's leave, the bus pulled off Route 13. It halted, groaning like a weary mammoth, at the Exxon station where, centuries ago, he'd boarded for boot camp.

The pile of worn used tires for sale looked exactly the same. All that had changed was the price, five times higher than when he'd left. He waited, sweating in the early heat, as the driver dragged his duffel out of the luggage compartment, and thanked him.

"Hey, thank *you*, soldier."

"Marine," Hector said, then wondered why he'd bothered.

Oh yeah. That was what one of his dead friends had said, when someone had called her a soldier.

No telling when he'd get in, so he hadn't let anyone know he was coming. He shouldered his duffel and headed down the road. The rain was easing off. It looked like it was clearing. Not a hundred yards on, a grizzled black man in a battered pickup pulled over for him. Hector started to refuse, noting a faded bumper sticker that read MI CASA NO ES SU CASA. But he was dead on his feet. He'd tried to sleep on the bus, but the coughing and wheezing had gone on all night long. So he grabbed the door handle, dragged it open, and climbed in.

He settled in, looking out the cranked-down window. The Shore smelled like it always did in spring. Turned earth. Soybeans. A gold-and-lavender frost of pollen and petals gilded the old truck's hood. A vile, low-hanging stench blew in through the windows on the hot wind: a ramshackle chicken house, half hidden behind a row of scraggy pines.

There were hardly any cars on the road. In the distance rows of people in wide-brimmed hats and kerchiefs stretched across a wide field, bent low over plowed ground. Men on horses cradled shotguns.

The old man didn't say much, just puttered along at thirty-five. Hector leaned to inspect a yellow ticket pasted inside the windshield. "Five gallon a month," the old man muttered. He pulled out to the left, lifting a hand as he passed a small cart pulled by two panting pit bulls. The cart driver nodded.

When the old man turned back Hector saw that the left side of his face was melted, burned, distorted. He wore a black eye patch on that side.

"See you got the Heart," the old man said at last.

Hector touched the ribbon. "Yeah."

"China?"

"Aren't there yet. On an island."

"Uh-huh. Vietnam, m'self."

"That right? What branch?"

"Eleventh Cav."

"Tanks?"

"ACAVs—M113s. There in sixty-seven and sixty-eight."

Hector looked at his seamed half-horrible face. "Wounded?"

"In the Iron Triangle. RPG come through that aluminum armor. I's the only crew got out."

Hector glanced at him again. "Does it . . . go away?"

They drove for a mile before the old man muttered, single-eyed gaze fixed sternly on the road ahead, "It don't never go away, my man. It don't never."

THE veteran dropped him at the shell drive to his mom's house. He contemplated the battered mailbox. Remembering the time his dad had come home, and they'd mixed concrete and dug in the post for it. Finally he shouldered his duffel and trudged on, boots scuffing up bleached broken shells and dead leaves. A horse was tethered in Mrs. Figueroa's yard. It snorted and eyed him as he shuffled past. God, it was hot here.

The key was under the mat. "Mom," he called, inside. No answer. Maybe they were all at work. He dropped his gear in front of the TV and flicked a light switch. No power.

He wandered through the little house. The kitchen was a stench of garbage and buzzing flies. Dirty dishes piled the sink. Up the narrow creaking stairs to his old room. The heat was thick up here. A second bed had been crammed into it, and someone had taken down his posters. An extra mattress lay on the floor in his mom's room too.

Back downstairs he found farm eggs in the fridge, chilled with a half-melted bag of ice from the Shore Stop, and made himself eggs and toast. He ate at the kitchen table, then washed up in the bathroom from a pitcher of water and shaved. He threw his uniform in the washer and turned it on before remembering the power was out. He pulled it out again and draped it on a hanger.

Upstairs again, after some rooting around he found his clothes in a plastic storage box under his mom's bed. He put on jeans, a T-shirt, and running shoes and went downstairs again. Stood motionless, looking in the mirror over the sideboard. Then turned abruptly and went out the back door.

His old car was there, but up on blocks. Leaves and pine needles covered the hood halfway up the windshield. A chesty brown dog he didn't know was tied up by it. It barked at him, but when he held out a hand it sniffed it, then let him approach. He shook the red plastic gas can they used for the lawn mower, but it was empty.

He unlatched the door carefully and slid into the battered Kia. The seat felt damp and squishy. The interior stank of mold. A dusty pink plastic rosary hung from the rearview. He twisted the key, in the ignition. Not even a chatter. "You were always a piece of shit anyway," he told it. He touched the rosary, then dropped it into his pocket.

He pulled his old bike out of the garage, inflated the cracked, mud-caked tires with a hand pump, oiled the chain, and pedaled down the drive. He cycled slowly through the neighborhood, then out onto the main road. Not one car passed him all the way into town. Most of the stores were closed there too. Even the Dollar General. A ghost town, like in a Stephen King movie.

All too soon he was at the plant. It was running, though, with plumes of steam and smoke coming off the stacks and cooling towers, and the usual horde of seagulls wheeling and screaming above, or strutting stiffly about the parking lot as if protesting what was happening to their fellow birds inside. The smell was the same too, a dense eye-watering stench of manure, burnt feathers, and ammonia. Diesels droned: generators, back by the loading dock. He kicked the stand down and leaned the bike against the chain link, where a sign read

DEFENSE ESSENTIAL PLANT.
AUTHORIZED PERSONNEL ONLY.
DEFENSA ESENCIAL INSTALACIÓN.
SOLO PERSONAL AUTORIZADO.

The guard in the shack glanced up from a magazine. "Ramos?"

"Hey, Jessup."

"Thought you was in the service."

"Home on leave. Thought I'd stop in and say hi to the guys."

"Go on in," the guard said. "Prob'ly not too many left from your time though. Been a lot of turnover."

The trucks squatted by the loading dock, engines off. There weren't any drivers lounging around talking where they used to either. A forklift was shuttling cells onto the conveyor. The operator, a short black woman, waved him impatiently out of her way.

As he climbed the steps he could hear it. A familiar metallic crashing, underlain by the hum of electric motors.

He had to stop and breathe for a few seconds before he could stick his head into the Hook Room.

Stainless hooks marched steadily along, dangling from a polished I beam. From them hung upside-down U's of heavy, polished metal, just long enough to trap a hand. The endless chain passed through a slot in the concrete-block wall. The concrete floor was spattered with a brownish-black crust inches thick.

The birds were fighting and pecking as four workers pulled them out of their modules. The women wore goggles, thin rubber gloves, and heavy boots. They flipped bird after bird upside down, spun, and hooked the claws into the wire loops. Inverted, the birds stopped struggling. And with a musical jingle, an electric hum, the Line carried them on, out of sight, through the slot in the wall.

A heavyset fortyish woman in a blood- and shit-spattered canvas apron lifted an arm to shield her eyes. She peered, blinked, then gestured furiously for him to close the door.

Hector had to sit on the concrete steps to the loading dock for a while, breathing hard and holding his head. At last he got up slowly, and walked back down the road.

"HEY, 'f it idn't fucking Heck-tor Ray-mose. Back from the wars."

Hector tensed. He was sitting at the bar at Porky's, nursing a beer. Early, but who cared. A chill prickled his back despite the heat. Grasping the bottle, he spun around on the stool.

To face . . . Mahmou'.

His old enemy from the plant had gained weight. He looked older, but better dressed than when they'd worked in the Hanging Room. He was even wearing a tie. Hector stared, surprised less at his former adversary's appearance than at his own lack of terror. The other had stolen money from him, bullied him, made fun of his slowness at arithmetic. Hector had always dreaded meeting up with him.

Confronted with his silence, the Arab seemed taken aback. "So . . . um I read something 'bout you in the paper. Some kinda medal."

"Yeah." Hector held his gaze.

"Well, uh-huh. You back for good?"

"Week's leave. Before we ship out again." Hector looked him up and down, from the new dress loafers to the slicked-back black hair. "I didn't see you at the plant."

"I work in the Zone now." Mahmou' glanced at the bartender. "A beer. And another for my old friend."

"The Zone," Hector repeated. "What's that?"

"Used to be the prison. They moved all the old convicts out and brought the others in."

"What others?"

"You know, the slants . . . Pakis . . . Jehovah's Witnesses. Antiwar woollies. Enemy symps. All women, this facility." Mahmou' shrugged and smiled as he pushed a bill across the bar. "A two-week school, and now I'm Cat One, in charge of thirty guards." He smirked. "And since you ask, yeah, I been porkin' 'em all. Plus half the inmates. Any that's worth bonin', I mean. Give 'em some store, a day off fieldwork . . . they're real grateful, if you know what I mean."

"Cat One. Exempt, right?"

"Reserved occupation, amigo. Vital to the war effort. As important as whatever they got you doing. Maybe not so dangerous. But maybe, yeah, maybe it's just as dangerous. In other ways." Mahmou' grinned, his upper lip lifting the same way it used to when he'd call Hector a dumbass, a wetback, dumber than chickenshit. "We both come a long way from the Kill Room, din't we? Hey, you wanna come by the camp, I can like, hook you up. A little recreation for the big hero. There's this brunette, hey, I think you know her. Mirielle. She gives the best—"

Hector's head lifted so fast a muscle protested in his neck. "Mirielle works for you?"

"Hell yeah, out at the camp."

"Huh. Let's go someplace we can talk." Hector nodded at the bartender. "Like, out back."

A few minutes later he was wheeling away on his bike, sucking skinned knuckles. He hadn't killed the fucker. Just reminded him of all the times he'd stolen from him, played tricks on him. Halfway through Mahmou' had begged, on his knees. Offered whatever he wanted, just to stop. But Hector hadn't stopped. Until the *chingado* wasn't begging anymore.

He swerved to the side of the road, where it crossed a culvert, and threw Mahmou's car keys and wallet into the scummy water. Then pedaled on.

HE was waiting on her porch, on the glider, feet propped on a pillar, when she let herself down off the bus and trudged up the drive. Mirielle was in a blue pants uniform like nurse's scrubs. Her long hair was trapped in a net. Her shoulders drooped and she was thinner than he remembered. She halted when she looked up at the porch. Then came on. Her confident stride was gone. She limped as if her feet hurt.

"Hector, ¿eres tú?"

He stood and stretched. *"Sí, claro.* It's me."

"What happened? Last time you wrote, you were in California."

"On leave. Before we ship out again."

She climbed the steps and stood there uncertainly, biting her lip and not looking at him. Hector almost took her in his arms, but her expression stopped him. Instead he looked around. "How's your mom and dad?"

She raised her arms to take the hairnet off, revealing sweat stains at her armpits, food stains on her smock. She caught his glance and lowered them, flushing. "They're all right. How's your mom?"

"I guess okay. Haven't seen her yet. Just got back this morning."

She shook her hair out and sighed. Crossed her arms, hugging herself. She kept lifting her gaze to his, then quickly dropping it. She used to do that in math class. When he would be hunched over his paper, staring hopelessly at the equations. "I'm glad you're okay. I was worried, when you wrote from that hospital."

"I'm okay now. I guess."

"Well, you want to sit out here? I'll get some tea. We don't have no ice, but there's well water. It's nice, in the shade of the camellias."

He said sure. She went inside, and came out again with tall glasses of tea with mint syrup. She'd changed her top and combed her hair. He shoved over on the glider to make room.

She apologized again that there was no ice. "They used to turn the electricity on for a couple hours in the evening, so people could make dinner and maybe watch TV. But now it's out, all over the Shore. No lights. No air-conditioning. Everybody says the old people are just going to die, if we get another heat wave like last summer. But they need all the power for the Victory Plan, they say."

"Yeah, looks like everybody's working hard."

"Everybody's got a job, sure. But you have to go where they say, and take what they offer. There's no union or strikes or walkouts anymore." She cast a frightened glance toward the main road. "The Loyalty Leaguers keep track of everybody. You can't say anything against the war, or you end up in the camp. They burned down Mr. Wilson's house, for saying things about the president. Anyway . . . you were in the fighting. Was it bad?"

"It was pretty bad."

"You lost friends?"

"Yeah."

They rocked for a while in silence. Finally Hector asked her where her folks' carport was. She said it had gone during a scrap drive.

He thought about not asking, then about asking; and finally did. "I heard you work in the Zone."

She looked away. "In the kitchen. I just, you know, cook. Everybody's got to eat. . . . How'd you know that?"

"I ran into somebody who works there."

"I just work in the kitchen, Hector."

He put out a hand at last and let it rest on her shoulder. The long shining hair he'd stared at for hours in high school, in the days when he'd sat behind her in class, was lank and dirty now. The hands in her lap looked chapped, the fingernails broken or bitten. "Mir . . . I thought about you a lot. While I was over there."

She blinked into her tea. "I thought about you too, Hector."

"You need anything? Money, or anything?"

"We have what we need. Anyway, it wouldn't be right."

"They pay us, but there's nothing to spend it on. So you might as well have it."

"I won't take your money, Hector. And that's all I'm going to say about it."

They rocked for a while more. The old glider creaked and squealed. "You need some oil on this thing," he said. Then, "It was Mahmou' who told me you were working there."

She didn't say anything. So after a while he added, "He was saying some evil shit about you."

"Oh, I can guess." She laughed dully. "He's an asshole. Always hitting on us."

"He always was a dick, back at the plant. I didn't believe anything he said. But I don't think he'll be bothering you anymore."

She rocked, and maybe she was smiling, just a little. "Should I thank you?"

"Up to you."

She said, not looking at him, "Hector, there was never anything agreed between us."

"I know that."

"It's not like we were in love or anything."

"I know . . . but I always sort of felt . . ." He trailed off, then tried again. "I carried your picture, the one you gave me in school. Still got it." He slipped out his wallet. The plastic lamination was cracked.

"That old thing," she said, laughing. "I look so fat. You carried that around? Over there, in the war?"

"Uh-huh. I always sort of felt you liked me."

"I did. Back then, I mean."

"How about now?"

"I don't know, Hector."

He waited, but she didn't say anything more.

"I can't make any promises, Mir. I don't know if I'm going to come back. If I don't, I don't want you to be unhappy. Or if I'll be worth anything if I do. After all this is over." He remembered what the old vet in the pickup had said. "If it's ever over."

She looked uneasy. "The war? It's got to be over sometime."

"Maybe, but . . . The slants are tough. They're gonna hold on to what they got."

He reached over and turned her face to his. When he kissed her, she smelled of tomato sauce. He didn't mind that. Didn't mind it at all.

She whispered, "Do you really have to go back, Hector?"

"I got to. Yeah."

"What happens if you don't? They say some soldiers don't. Would they put you in the Zone, or what?"

He thought about the squads he was training. The helpless, babyish faces. He said slowly, "It don't matter, what happens to me. Yeah, it'd be the Zone. Or Leavenworth. But that ain't it. It's the new kids. They don't know yet what they're in for."

"Who doesn't? I don't understand."

"The recruits. Something big's coming. I got to train them right, or they're all gonna fucking die." He pulled her closer. "Mir. I want you to wait for me."

"*¿A dónde voy?* Where else am I gonna go?" she said softly. "I'm sorry, I don't mean to sound bitter. But I don't know what to do, or what's going to happen. To me. To us. To anybody, now. So maybe you're right. Maybe we shouldn't make any promises."

After he left, coasting down the drive toward the road, shells crackling and popping under his bike tires like distant rifle fire, he looked back. She was still staring after him, hugging herself.

11

USS *The Sage Brothers* Honolulu

THE noise was like a thunderstorm crammed inside a shipping container. A bellow of acoustic energy no mortal ear could have withstood unattenuated. Even separated from it by a foot of dense insulation sandwiched between layers of steel, Dan's guts quivered from the subsonics as he peered through a Perspex window two inches thick.

He stood deep in the ship, between boxlike enclosures painted cream white. Windows permitted a close-up view of the machines suspended inside, braced and strutted by heavy steel. Not much larger than a refrigerator, each General Electric gas turbine produced twenty-five thousand horsepower at full throttle. They were shafted to Curtiss-Wright generators, which supplied power to huge superconducting electric motors housed farther aft.

All in all this engine room, plus another staggered aft of it and separated by watertight bulkheads, generated over a hundred thousand horsepower.

But they weren't new engines.

He'd woken up after his chat with his daughter with his course clear in his mind.

We might not have to invent something new.

What if we have something available already that we can pitch in there, see if it works?

Wielding a wartime priority, Kitty and Brett had scoured the planet. Some units had come from other navies. The Spanish, Italian, and South African fleets were now operating on half their former power. Two turbines had come from *Queen Mary 2*, and two from Celebrity cruise liners. Others were en route from generator stations in Iceland.

But by far the majority of the two hundred–plus main propulsion engines the Navy was installing in the new-construction cruisers, the Flight V destroyers, and the SBX-2 class of seaborne early-warning radars, had come from the idled American civilian air fleet. The LM2500 had been derived from a high-bypass turbofan aircraft engine, the CF6. Though there'd been changes through the years to fit them for marine use, the cores, with their arrays of finely machined blades, were still so similar that minor work-arounds made them one-for-one replacements.

Nearly six hundred commercial airliners stagnating in hangars across the country because of fuel restrictions had suddenly become an engine mine. The core roaring at his elbow had come from a Delta Air Lines Boeing 767. The one next to it, also thundering in a full-power test, had been sourced from a pumping station in Saudi Arabia, originally used to compress natural gas. The two in the After Engine Room of USS *The Sage Brothers*—named after three brothers who'd died off Vietnam in USS *Evans*—came from a FedEx DC-10.

The engines had hours on them. And they came in different variants, so installation kits for each version had to be fabricated. But they would serve. Meanwhile, GE and Rolls-Royce had scrubbed down their 3-D printer drivers and were producing new blades and cores. As the used units reached the ends of their service lives, they'd be replaced with uprated cores, producing more power with lower fuel consumption.

But by then, Dan hoped, the war would be over. One way or another.

The NCIS and FBI had found the production flaw. It had been a Trojan horse exploit. Someone had slithered past all the safeguards and inserted a surreptitious alteration deep in the code. When the printer hit a certain point in the metal-deposition process, instead of spraying alloy the printer head stuttered, inserting air-filled microvoids deep in the blades.

How wasn't his concern, though it was worrying. The really unsettling question was what other malicious code might have been inserted into the other weapons the Navy, the Air Force, and the Army depended on to take the battle to the enemy. And what about the ABM systems that were supposed to keep Seattle, Los Angeles, San Diego, and the other cities Zhang threatened safe in case of a major attack?

"Sir?" The destroyer's skipper leaned in, shouting over the din. Dan lifted his ear protection. "That's hour two at fifty percent. Going up to one hundred percent now. You might want to step back."

Dan nodded and retreated a few steps, glancing around.

He remembered crawling rusting, flaking, oil-crusted bilges as a midshipman, grease-stained qualification book in hand. In those days, destroyers had burned bunker oil so thick it had to be heated before it would flow. Asbestos-padded overheads had dripped like triple-canopy jungle. Hissing steam from leaky joints waved white plumes in air so hot it scorched your throat when you breathed, unless you were standing directly beneath the huge intakes that whooshed outside air into the faces of the sweating men who tended the boilers. The boilers themselves had towered like the furnaces of Moloch, from massive keel footings up level after level. The air had been solid noise, solid heat, thick with the smells of fuel and steam, sweat and corrosion.

The Sage Brothers' white-painted Engine Room was clean as a hospital cafeteria. There wasn't even a control booth anymore. Coveralled men and women stood studying readouts on handhelds for the tests, but when the destroyer was under way, everything would be controlled from the bridge. The helmsman would press a button on a touch screen, and an engine would start itself. Generators, pumps, and motors would adjust themselves, and in case of damage would shift the load to maximize the ship's fighting efficiency.

Or so the theory went. But when fuel fires raged, when shaped charges penetrated with jets of fire, when the shock of a detonating torpedo or warhead or mine or bomb whiplashed equipment on their isolation mounts and the sea poured in through split hulls . . .

He remembered those times. Had lived them. Aboard USS *Reynolds Ryan, Barrett, Turner Van Zandt, Horn, K-79, Savo Island.* When crews had saved their ship and fought on. When they'd coped, made do, sacrificed themselves for their shipmates, and overcome.

How would the hidden processes of digital intelligence respond? It was a new world. An antiseptic, inhuman, depersonalized world of metal and electrons. But still, one of savage struggle. From a wielder of weapons, the warrior had become the director of machines that wielded themselves; launching on their own, changing course, varying tactics, needing only to have their targets designated. And soon they would no longer require human direction even for that.

He shivered. Then nodded again to the skipper, and headed for the ladder up.

CAMP H. M. Smith was perched high above the harbor. He'd been here before. The CNO had personally pinned on his stars here, before the opening strike on the Chinese mainland. "Thanks, I won't need you for the rest of the day," Dan told his driver, getting out in front of Building 700.

Nipa palms nodded, fronds clashing in the cool breeze from the sea. The Nimitz-MacArthur Pacific Command Center overlooked the harbor and shipyard. To the north, ridge after ridge of forested green hills receded into the distance, the valleys hazy with mist. To the east, more hills surged like a stormy sea. To the west spread the city, glittering and vulnerable.

The fronds clashed again, clattering like colliding bayonets. He took off his cap and ran a hand over sweat-soaked hair. He stood for a moment more looking down at the sea. Then headed for a concrete entranceway.

He told the guards he was scheduled to meet with General Faulcon. They checked his ID against a list, rifled through his briefcase, wanded him, and took custody of his phone. The elevator dropped fast. He swallowed to clear his ears, fighting a claustrophobia that threatened whenever he went underground. Ever since the Signal Mirror mission into Baghdad . . .

Still fighting that memory, he stepped out into a coldly lit, low-overheaded, air-conditioned passageway that felt like some W. A. Harbinson fantasy, below the ice cap of Antarctica. Officers and enlisted scurried along, abstracted as ants, avoiding his gaze. Situation rooms and intel spaces opened off the passageway. Every fifty yards the tunnel made a right angle, walls slanting away at each corner. It looked like feng shui, but it was meant to confine blast, in case a bunker penetrator made it this deep.

The corridor gave way to a higher-ceilinged office space that wouldn't have looked out of place in the Pentagon. "Captain Lenson, for General Faulcon," he told a digital assistant on the table, and waited.

"*Captain? The general will see you now,*" it said several seconds later.

Dan had worked for Randall Faulcon when the latter had been the joint special operations commander north of Kandahar and west of the White Mountains. Planning black missions into Pakistan. Never admitted, never acknowledged.

The general was so gaunt now his face looked vacuum-sealed. They said he had only one good eye, but Dan couldn't tell which. Both, as he inspected Dan, were totally emotionless. Just as in Bagram, his office here was walled with maps, though now they were up on vertical large-screen displays. Callouts from active drones crept across seas and mountains. Comm channels murmured. It was less office than tactical operations center.

Faulcon saluted Dan's Medal of Honor, though they were both bareheaded and deep below ground. Feeling foolish, Dan returned it.

The general's skeletal fingers gripped his like Death seizing a reluctant soul. "Lenson. We've met before, haven't we?"

"Yes, sir. Afghanistan. With Tony Provanzano."

"With Tony, yeah. You were running the CIRCE program. And I saw your wife not that long ago. In Washington."

"Yes sir."

"She knows what she's talking about. But let's get to business. I hear you reengined our new naval construction with parts stolen from civilian airliners."

"Basically true, sir. But I didn't do it alone."

"Welcome to my world." Faulcon crossed to a screen. It showed the western Pacific. "I understand you left your flagship after she was hit."

Dan pushed down anger. Would that canard ever stop dogging him? Would that imputed dishonor always stain his name? "I left, correct. In order to shift my—"

"Transferring your command, I know. There are still questions being raised. But Jim Yangerhans is willing to look past that, at least for now. He wants to know if you're ready to go back on full duty."

"I think so, sir."

"Medical?"

"I'm recovered enough for desk work. As for going back to sea—it might be wise to take a few more weeks."

"That's honest. To be honest right back, there won't be any sea commands for you. Not until certain political elements get distracted by something else."

He forced a nod. "Copy that, General."

"All right, here's where we're going. There's not a hell of a lot of strategic guidance coming out of the Chiefs. They're giving us intermediate objectives, but not defining what could constitute an acceptable end state. It's up to us to develop the operational approach. So we're more or less running strategic guidance, concept development, plan development, and plan assessment simultaneously. Just remember, SecDef can reenter the process at any time."

Faulcon positioned two hands on the wall display of the Pacific. "The ten-thousand-feet overview: We're preparing for a two-pronged offensive. The northern prong will begin with filtering-in operations by special ops, to take the islets bracketing Taiwan. They'll be supported by air strikes from Itbayat. If they succeed, we'll follow up with a multidivision assault, link up with the resistance, and fight it out with Lieutenant General Pei and the Chinese army we've trapped there."

Dan nodded, and the general spun the map to show the South China Sea. "The southern prong's less clearly envisioned so far. You won't see this on the news, but the Vietnamese are being hammered. They've lost Hanoi. The Chinese are still advancing. We're not ready to put major land forces ashore, but we have to do something or see one of our toughest allies forced out of the war. Planning's under way for several options. One is landing a tank brigade in the rear of the advancing Chinese forces. Cutting their logistics lines."

"Like Inchon," Dan said.

"Exactly, like MacArthur's landing. I have to say the Army chief of staff's not happy with that idea. But at minimum, we need a demonstration. A major carrier strike, at least. Like the one you vanguarded in Recoil."

Dan nodded, and Faulcon spread his fingers on the screen, zooming in on the southern coast. "Another option is a strike against the naval, air, and submarine base at Yulin, on Hainan Island. An attack there should force them to pull back forces from Vietnam. That effort would leapfrog from our joint Vietnamese-Indian-U.S. base facilities in the Spratlys."

"A strike, a raid, or a landing, General?" A strike was a quick blow from the air or the sea. A raid meant commitment of ground forces, but with only temporary occupation in mind. A landing would be fought for tenaciously, with the idea of permanent occupation.

Faulcon shrugged. He slid behind his desk and pointed to a chair for Dan. "Not sure yet. At the least, as I said, a major strike. Maybe also, factor in consideration of a tactical nuke. Though that might be outside the political box."

Dan took the chair. "Outside how, sir? They wiped out a carrier strike group. They went nuclear first. No one I know understands why we didn't retaliate."

The general bobbled his head. "True, and the Chiefs are game, but NCA's hanging back. Grand strategy? Fear of the next escalatory step? I can only speculate why."

"Uh, I understand the Chinese have problems too. Famine. Reduced production. Unrest. And disease."

Faulcon frowned. "We can't depend on a virus to win for us." He slid open the drawer and plopped a fat red-and-white-striped folder on the desktop. "I'd like you to head up one of our planning cells. Develop courses of action, campaign and contingency plans against the requirements identified in the planning directive. You'll have forty people. In the second-level basement. With Indian and Vietnamese liaisons. Relieve the colonel in charge. Or keep him as your deputy, if you want. We need these as soon as you can produce them."

Dan wondered why the incumbent was being relieved of command, and then, why *he* was being slotted in. "Yes, sir. Can you give me a readout on his uh, or her, performance?"

"Osterhaut's a good man. Just not plugged in enough to naval aspects of the operation. PACOM wants your ass in the chair."

Dan nodded. "I had some sharp folks on the engine project. They're at loose ends now."

"Pull them in. See the J-1 to cut orders. You'll report to J-3, of course."

Someone tapped on the door. Faulcon blanked the screen and stood. Dan got up too. "That's about it. My aide has your access codes, passwords, and the key card to a room at the Ala Moana. Though I doubt you'll be there much. I don't have to remind you to keep a lid on this."

"No, sir."

"Report to the J-3 daily. Admiral Verstegen. You're familiar with the RATE process."

"Refine, Adapt, Terminate, or Execute."

"Correct. Admiral Yangerhans will be assessing your progress. He'll make decisions as events work forward. See the J-2 for intel, enemy intentions, force levels . . . you know the drill."

Dan nodded, and followed Faulcon out.

THE "basement" was Level 2, two flights down from the ground floor. Fifty feet by a hundred, its raw concrete still embossed with the shapes of its molds, it had been equipped with gray-blue padded partitions and battered desks that looked like they'd come from a bankruptcy sale.

Cables snaked the concrete floor. Pipes zigzagged the ceiling. A guard with a sidearm was posted on a folding chair by the stairwell.

Dan shook hands with the colonel he was relieving. Balding, studious-looking, with ribbons from Afghanistan and Syria, Sy Osterhaut explained that the partitions separated their cell from those planning other operations. Dan wondered if those others were working the alternate options Faulcon had mentioned—the demonstration against northern Vietnam, the landing of the tank brigade—but knew better than to ask.

HE caught up over the next twenty-four hours. The base-plan package Faulcon had turned over described the concept of operations, the major forces, the concepts of support, and anticipated timelines. His cell's job was to add annexes, time-phased force and deployment data, and other detail to arrive at three COAs—concepts of operations.

These would be briefed to J-3, then PACOM personally, after which one or more COAs would be further developed as a conplan. Conplans weren't operations orders yet, but they were getting closer. The final joint op plan would be massive, with a full discussion of the concept of operations, all applicable annexes, and force-deployment tables identifying the specific forces, functional support, and resources needed to execute through to completion.

Working with Osterhaut, Dan met with the liaisons, revised the work teams, and added bodies, including Pickles and Harriss. The enemy order of battle needed updating too, and he asked for more Intel help.

Computers and screens were in short supply, so a big map covered with acetate went up on one wall. It gradually filled with symbology: missile batteries, radars, troop concentrations, military installations. He spent hours standing in front of it, memorizing bays and capes and beaches, mountain ranges, rivers, cities, roads, and airfields. Getting a feel for the operational environment.

Hainan Island lay off China's southern coast, separated by a twelve-mile strait. A hundred miles wide by a hundred across, population nine million, it was only a little smaller than Taiwan. Its southern interior was mountainous, with the largest cities, Haikou and Hainan, opposite the mainland on the north.

The main targets lay near the city of Sanya, in the south. Over the past decades, several small ex-Japanese naval bases and airfields—Japan had occupied the island during World War II—had been expanded, and new facilities had been built, to support China's gradual takeover of the resource-rich South China Sea.

One of Dan's reserve officers, in civilian life a history professor at the University of Hawaii, had researched the last seizure of the island. The Japanese had landed in Tsinghai Bay, on the north end, in 1939, followed by a second landing near Sanya. The native Li people had fought, but the invaders crushed them ruthlessly, killing over a third of the male population. They'd used their bases to blockade China and as a stepping-stone to the invasion of French Indochina. The Japanese had left only after the overall surrender in 1945.

Studying the map, Dan contemplated a restaging of some of that history, though without the mass executions. Seizure of Sanya not only could cut off the last remnants of sea commerce and fisheries; it might also establish command of the air over south China. Hong Kong and Macao lay to the east; unrest and resistance had been reported from both former colonies, despite savage repression by Beijing.

No one was planning an invasion of the mainland, to his knowledge. The Allies had no forces large enough to contemplate that. Only the Vietnamese had enough divisions in the line to confront even part of the Chinese army.

But if the war had to be fought to a conclusion, a landing on Hainan would be a giant stride forward.

On the other hand . . . Zhang had made it clear that any attack on China proper would lead to savage reprisals, including nuclear strikes on the American homeland.

But that wasn't Dan's remit. He was to flesh out the plans and present options. Yangerhans would make the decisions, and pass them down to the fleet and Air Force components for execution.

Back at his desk, calling up info on the southern coast on the top secret LAN, he came to a first conclusion. Hainan should be only one of several plausible targets. That was how Operation Overlord had succeeded. British and American deception plans had divided German attention among multiple possible invasion points, from Norway down to the Mediterranean coast of France. That had forced Hitler to scatter his forces, while Eisenhower could concentrate his, and strike with overwhelming power in Normandy.

He read intel summaries. A classified source called Night Light said the Chinese expected the Allies to renew the from-the-south drive that so far had removed the Spratlys, the Paracel/Xisha Islands, and Scarborough Shoal from the People's Empire. The enemy was deploying to counter raids or landings at various points, but no further information was available as to where.

When he was ready, he called Pickles over. "Okay, Kitty," he told her. "We have some work to do."

SEVERAL days later he convened the analysts, plus Osterhaut and his top intel guy, an Army major, in a swept, secure area on the fifth floor. They all looked close to nodding off, rumpled, squinting in the unaccustomed sunlight slanting through the windows. He was tired too, but had tried to pace himself. At least five hours' sleep a night, and he'd spent that Sunday afternoon dozing and baking by the pool at the Ala Moana, in trunks, sunglasses, and a slather of sunscreen.

This afternoon, they would present their conclusions to the military chief of half the planet's surface.

A tap at the door. An aiguilletted aide looked in. "Captain? We're ready."

The brightly lit room had antieavesdropping curtains over the windows, a large screen display on the wall, and four men ranged around a polished table. Jim Yangerhans, bony and awkward in khakis, in his habitual slump. Randall Faulcon, taut and expressionless in Army greens. The J-3, Bren Verstegen, a small, thatch-haired admiral in trop whites, whom Dan had briefed several times already during the development of the COAs. Jack Byrne, in sunglasses as usual, waved from a chair by the wall; the former ONI officer, now civilian adviser to the Pacific Command, was an old friend.

And a familiar round, beaming face atop a stocky khakied barrel chest. Dan stepped into a cigarette-infused bear hug. "Admiral Jung," he muttered into the Korean's shoulder.

"Dan." Min Jun Jung clapped his back, hard, then released him as reluctantly as a teenager on a first date. "It is very good to see you again. Thought we lost you, after our epic fight together in the Western Sea."

"I'm back in battery now, sir. And Min Su, he's doing okay? Is he back on your staff?"

"Oh, yes, your fellow castaway is quite recovered. His new front teeth are beautiful. Captain Hwang smiles much more often now, to show them off."

"Are you with us for this operation? I didn't think we had a Korean component."

Yangerhans cleared his throat. "The admiral's come for another briefing. He heard you were here, and asked to see you. You might be interested to know, he's just been officially recognized as the legitimate representative of a country under domination by the Opposed Powers."

Dan hesitated, unsure whether to congratulate or commiserate. He finally decided on the former. "They couldn't have chosen anyone better." He shook Jung's hand again.

"We will fight side by side, until the end. No matter how far or how long that road may be," Jung said pontifically, gaze searching heavenward.

Yeah, Dan thought, he'll make a great politician.

"Also," his old shipmate went on, "it is a little late for a formal presentation, but then, it was originally posthumous. This is for you."

Dan blinked down at the gold-toned box the Korean extended. Inside was an elaborately crafted but somehow somber medal, a cross and wreath of subdued red stones, white enamel, and dull bronze.

"The First-Class Cordon of the Order of Military Merit," Jung intoned. "The highest decoration for military valor the Republic of Korea can award."

"Thank you, sir. I'm deeply honored." Dan let Jung pin it on, then stood fidgeting as the others applauded.

But not for long. Yangerhans cut it off with a brisk "Okay, thank you, now we really need to get down to business. Min, let's get together again before you leave Hawaii."

Jung nodded enthusiastically, shook hands all around, including with the Vietnamese and Indian liaisons but not the U.S. staffers, then left. Yangerhans pointed to the Korean's vacated chair, lifting his chin at Byrne; the policy adviser joined them.

When the door closed, Dan kicked off with four minutes of memorized remarks. After thanking his staffers, he described the three COAs J353 had developed. Option one: land the tank brigade on the coast of Vietnam, behind the Chinese. Two: attack Hainan Island, either a strike or a raid. Three: a strike or a raid on the Hong Kong/Macao area.

He passed out a matrix. Printed in four colors, it graphically presented a multi-attribute utility function scoring each COA on surprise, risk, flexibility, possible retaliation, impact on Allied partners, legality, external support, force protection, and operational security.

Each of his analysts, and each of the liaisons now seated along the wall, had had an input. Each had lobbied hard for his or her own option. But the time for arguing was over.

The principals studied it in silence. Until Yangerhans bobbed his head. "All right. Discussion? Recommendations?"

Dan said carefully, "Option one and the other two are mutually exclusive. We can't generate adequate force levels to both project a brigade and supporting elements onto the Vietnamese coast, protect the landing afterward, and strike at China proper. For the same reason, an operation has to be limited to a strike or at most a raid. We won't have enough special operations forces and ground forces left for a second full-on landing once Army and Marine expeditionary elements are committed to Operation Causeway, against Taiwan.

"Also arguing against option one is the continued activity of the Hainan airfields behind where the Army might like to land. The only ports suitable for offloading heavy armor and resupply are Haiphong, Da Nang, and Ho Chi Minh City. Haiphong is too far north. Da Nang we could cover from the captured airfields in the Spratlys, but it's a long way south of the front line. Saigon is even farther.

"Also, note the very high risk factor associated with option one. This reflects the massive Chinese army currently engaged south of Hanoi. It's also consistent with the Army chief of staff's opinion, that any force we put ashore on the mainland could be a total loss."

Faulcon nodded, expressionless. "Noted. Go on."

Dan clicked up another slide, wondering why he was enjoying this. Weird. "On the other hand, options two and three might be combined. That is, a four-carrier strike group, augmented by Allied forces, could approach on such a bearing that it could be headed for either the Hong Kong/Macao area, or Hainan.

"Diversions, communications misinformation, and other operational deception activities could further mislead the enemy as to our target. At the last moment, we swing west and hit the Hainan air defenses, then the Yulin base. A sustained three-day strike package should knock the whole island out of the war, leaving it open for a later invasion, should NCA decide that's the next step."

Yangerhans sat back, massaging a prognathous jaw as if his teeth hurt. Faulcon, beside him, just looked icy. No one said anything for a while. Finally PACOM murmured, "I also asked you to evaluate a tactical nuclear strike."

Dan took a deep breath. "We called that option four. We could combine four with other options, depending on which archer we choose for the weapon."

He flicked up another matrix, trying to ignore the roiling unease in his gut. An aftereffect of the parasitic infection, or of contemplating nuclear escalation? "Uh, after studying various delivery methods, we suggest substituting a Tomahawk-borne warhead from a submarine for the penetrating conventional bomb strike subheaded in option three. As you see here, delivery via a cruise has two advantages. It looks less like a ballistic strike, lessening the risk of triggering a retaliatory response. Second, it can actually fly into the covered pens before detonating. This reduces blast and fallout effects on the nearby city."

"Which largely consists of support industries and personnel housing for the sub and air bases," the Air Force general pointed out.

"Could be, General." There was really no best answer. In World War II, the U-boat pens at Brest had survived dozens of attacks with the heaviest bombs the Allies could lift, obliterating the city around them. The Chinese installations were even more thoroughly hardened, burrowed under millions of tons of rock and concrete. A nuke might be the only way to take them out. In that case, collateral damage would be unavoidable.

"Jack, any input?" Yangerhans asked Byrne. The intel officer pulled on a lip, then shook his head.

The Air Force general spoke next. He advocated a standoff weapon from a bomber instead of the sea-launched missile, but said he'd worked with the planning cell during option development, had his subordinates check the calculations, and the choices seemed clear.

"Randy?"

Faulcon leaned to mutter something inaudible. The theater commander nodded. Braced both palms on the table, and unfolded from behind it like some long-limbed stick insect. The others got to their feet. He angled that massive jaw around, and said, "I'll review your products and make some calls. I understand our forces are limited, but we have to help the Vietnamese. Take the pressure off them. Or at least look like we're trying." He nodded again, and turned for the door.

Dan was thinking about finding a head when Byrne sidled up. "Good presentation."

"Thanks, Jack." Dan shook hands, wondering, as he always did, how Byrne managed to keep that bone-deep tan. Well, maybe in Hawaii it wasn't that hard.

The retired ONI officer placed a finger on the Korean medal, still on Dan's chest. "Real glitzy piece of tin. I'm jealous. Too bad you lost the stars."

Dan grinned. "They were only temporary, Jack. I'll retire as a captain, same as you."

"Hey, I'll be happy if we make it through this without everybody getting turned into toasted cheese sandwiches." Byrne slipped his sunglasses down and peered over them. "Daughter still in Seattle?"

"Yeah. At Archipelago."

"Christ. I'll warn you again, Dan. She's sitting right on the bull's-eye. So's Blair, in DC."

"They're adults, Jack. And both in the war effort. I can't order grown women to jump ship. Especially those two. Where's Rosemary, by the way?"

"In a safe place. But all I can do is warn people." The tone was joking but the intel officer wasn't smiling. Considering he was the senior intel rep on Yangerhans's staff, Dan didn't think he was blowing smoke.

Blowing smoke . . . toasted cheese sandwiches . . . neither a reassuring image. Especially when juxtaposed with Nan and Blair.

Byrne clapped his shoulder and wandered off, leaving Dan with Osterhaut and his analysts. He stood irresolute, but definitely not at ease.

Neither of the main antagonists was attacking the other's homeland yet. They were targeting cyber infrastructure, their armed forces, and peripheral allies. Locked in a desperate wrestling match, still with weapons in reserve.

But gradually, inexorably, the war was creeping closer to both homelands. Each escalatory step increased the danger. Edged both sides closer to an apocalyptic thermonuclear precipice.

He wished he could talk it out with Blair. But this wasn't the kind of thing you discussed via electrons. Not unless you had the high-security, quantum-entangled channels that linked the combatant commanders with JCS.

His gut rumbled again, and a stabbing cramp made him wince.

Yeah. A restroom. And the sooner, the better.

12

Pearl Harbor, Hawaii

THINGS are heating up, Captain."

Reading the message again, Cheryl Staurulakis could see that. The spare lines of text conveyed it in terse dry sentences.

The comm officer was standing with her on the quarterdeck. "This backs up what we've been hearing," Dave Branscombe said.

Savo Island was tucked deep into the inner harbor, starboard side to Sierra Pier, her bow pointed generally west. The only ship at Sierra. A few others, less damaged, lay along the other piers closer to the harbor exit.

The largest Navy base in the Pacific was emptier than Cheryl had ever seen it. The strike groups had departed. Across the turning basin, off Ford Island, the gray upperworks of USS *Missouri*, the moored museum ship, were just visible. Between them lay the maintenance and shop buildings that lined the piers and dry docks.

She passed a hand over her hair. She was in civvies: casual, shorts and a loose, cool blouse, a gym bag at her feet. After so many weeks aboard, she'd awarded herself an afternoon off. Her arm still hurt, but it was healing. The air was warm, with a breeze from seaward. "From Shanghai Sue?"

"Her, yeah, but from intel too. Zhang's promised a violent response to a landing on Taiwan. Or any violation of China's territory."

Chief Quincoches stepped onto the quarterdeck. His eyes widened as he took in her shorts, dropped to her sandals, then rose again. He coughed into a fist, averting his gaze. "Um, loadout's complete, Skipper."

Cheryl nodded to return his salute. "Very well. How are the tests going?"

"In progress now, ma'am. Uh, you headed ashore? Captain."

"Just for a couple of hours." She turned back to Branscombe. "Taiwan, which they took by force."

"It's still a warning. If we attack Chinese soil, we can expect the worst."

"But we already did. Right? Operation Recoil, the strike on Ningbo. But he hasn't retaliated for that."

"Yet." Branscombe scowled.

Crossing to the lifelines, she looked down at the small colorful wrasses that milled in the clear water between the hull and the pier. Then aft, at a yard tug moored astern of the cruiser. "If he does, where? Honolulu? LA? San Diego?"

"They're starting to evacuate. There are demonstrations, riots against the war in San Francisco, Chicago—"

"They can't expect us to make peace now. After *Roosevelt*, and the way they've wrecked our economy." She contemplated the pier, where a lift crane was backing away. It had spent the morning loading newly arrived missiles into *Savo*'s magazine, aligning each carefully vertical before lowering it into the cell. Technicians tested its connections; then the cell door was sealed, hiving it belowdecks.

Retiring from the strike on Ningbo, the cruiser had barely avoided sinking. Deliberately grounding on a submerged seamount, Cheryl had let her rest on the bottom for a night and a day while the Damage Control teams feverishly localized the flooding, built temporary shoring, dewatered flooded spaces, and welded hasty patches over the holes. The next night she'd ballasted up, gotten under way again, and ghosted through the Ryukyus, seeking radar shadows and staying as far from the Chinese airfields as she could.

And the luck of the damned had been with them. On her rendezvous with USS *Megan McClung* east of the Ryukyus, Fleet had given Cheryl a choice. Transfer her crew to the destroyer, and let *McClung* sink the battle-damaged cruiser with a torpedo. Or debark all nonessential personnel and try to make it home.

Cheryl had chosen the second alternative, and *McClung* had stood by her during the excruciatingly slow voyage back.

Now USS *Savo Island* lay nestled deep in port, too crippled to venture back to sea. Or so the Tiger Team flown out from Pearl had judged. Too much topside fire and blast damage. The port engines and reduction gears too wrecked by blast, fragments, and flooding to repair. Damage to the main hull girder. Compromised watertight integrity. It would be impossible to replace the aft radar arrays without a major shipyard availability, and no spares were available anyway.

Cheryl had fought for funding, for priority, but it was denied. Instead all but fifty crew members had been ordered back to the States. Most of *Savo*'s remaining ordnance had been transferred to other hulls. Leaving the ship with only small-arms ammunition, some Standard SM-2 antiaircraft rounds, and the SM-X rounds they'd just loaded.

Making a total of six antiballistic rounds in her forward magazine, and the two forward phased array radars still operational.

"Pretty obvious what they've got planned for us," Branscombe said, after a pause. "I wasn't sure at first what you wanted the safe room for."

"Now you know?"

He nodded grimly.

After the shipyard teams had left, and she'd accepted, reluctantly, that *Savo* wasn't going to be repaired, she'd gone to DC Central to study the ship's plans with Lieutenant (jg) Jiminiz and Senior Chief McMottie.

Chemical, Bacteriological, Radiation—CBR-designed—warships had a "citadel" deep in the hull. Armored, and with charcoal-filtered air, it could be isolated from the outside environment. But Ticonderoga-class ships had never had CBR protection beyond the usual Circle William and washdown systems.

After considerable discussion, they'd selected air-conditioning machinery room #2. A Spartan compartment with only a few pieces of machinery and a gray-painted steel deck, it was far aft and two decks down. Protected by several thicknesses of steel from blast and fragments, it was also flanked by fuel storage. The tanks, which she'd topped off, would give them neutron shielding.

The engineers installed ventilation and jury-rigged filters. They led in air lines from the high-pressure tanks, and stocked the compartment with self-contained breathing apparatuses, MREs, water, battle lanterns, protective suits, and buckets to crap in. Finally, she had paracord strung down from the topside accesses, so anyone could reach the safe room in total darkness, fire, or smoke, just by following the nylon strand. Even if *Savo* sank alongside the pier, she couldn't settle far before coming to rest on the harbor bottom. When the attack was over, the crew could regain the main deck through an overhead hatch and escape trunk.

A direct hit, of course, would vaporize everything: steel, fuel, and flesh. But short of a thermonuclear warhead landing within a kilometer, she hoped they could survive.

In fact, thinking it over, she'd done just about all she could do to get ready. The ship wasn't going anywhere, so it didn't really need much in the way of warm bodies. Those she had left, mainly to run the hotel functions, power system, Aegis, and the forward magazine, knew their jobs. She had total confidence in them.

"Well, I'm going ashore," she told the comm officer. "We've got local cell, right? Call me if anything changes. I won't be too long."

A warm breeze blew steady and clean off the Pacific. She felt guilty, but after so long, she just had to get off the fucking ship for a few hours. It felt strange to be out of uniform. Curious to be walking on grass, or even asphalt, instead of steel.

She caught the shuttle (the only person in it) to the base pool. After a short swim, taking it easy on her arm, she luxuriated in a long, hot shower, lathering, rinsing, and conditioning, not caring for once about saving water. She dressed again, and decided to hit the Exchange.

The parking lot was almost empty, as was the store. Many of the employees, military dependents, had been evacuated early in the war, or had left of their own accord. Large sections were closed off with metal security screens: the optometrist's, the flower shop, the cosmetics counter. Unfortunately, that was where she'd hoped to find shampoo and soap without the sulfiates that made her itch and flake.

She scratched between her fingers nervously. Maybe in the drugstore section? She walked the aisles of clothing and computers, liquor and magazines, noting the empty shelves. Where a colorful cornucopia of Chinese- and Korean-made products had once beckoned . . . She paused at a mannequin in a bathing suit. At the pool, her flowered two-piece had felt loose. She'd lost even more weight than she'd thought.

Where had she bought that one? Oh . . . wait. Damn.

Their honeymoon, in Tahiti. On the beach in front of their hotel, Eddie had dared her to take off her top, when the Danish tourists were strolling around without theirs. Reluctantly, she'd tried it, and to her surprise enjoyed the sun on her breasts. Though she'd drawn the line at him taking pictures.

Now she wished she'd let him snap all the fucking photos he wanted. If it would have given him pleasure . . .

How would she ever get used to being a widow? A "widow." It sounded so nineteenth-century. There were going to be a lot of widows after this war. Widowers, too. But she and Eddie had spent so much time apart, deployed, it didn't really feel as if he was gone now. Not dead, so much as just . . . somewhere else.

She closed her eyes. *—Eddie, are you there? I wish I'd let you take that picture.*

—Maybe I did, babe, when you weren't looking.

But that was what he would have said, not what he'd actually . . .

She shook her head furiously. Fuck! Stuff it down, Cheryl. Just like everything else you don't want to feel.

The jewelry store's steel-chain shutters were drawn. She hooked her fingers on the links, staring through like a captive ape. Christ, she couldn't escape the past. They'd bought their rings here. Haggled a little, though there was never much room for haggling at the NEX.

That had been, what, two years ago. Then . . .

She clenched her fists. So many warnings. China could not have risen without American know-how, financing, and technical support. But gradually it had turned from a client, a friend evolving toward democracy and openness, to a glowering rival. Crushing dissent. Stealing intellectual property. Penetrating American databases and defense networks. Carrying out a long-term, cunningly plotted succession of salami-sliced aggressions.

But administration after administration had looked away. Borrowed Chinese money. Fought with the opposing party. While a huge, ancient, and intensely proud nation had gathered strength for the final contest.

And turned, at last, from rival to enemy.

"Hey there," said someone behind her.

She flinched, jerked from angry thoughts. It was a marine, a second lieutenant, in uniform. He looked startled, then a bit disappointed. As if not expecting her, when she turned, to be older than he was. "Sorry, ma'am," he muttered. "Didn't mean to startle you."

Ma'am. She compressed her lips in what might just pass as a smile. Though she didn't feel like smiling. "No problem."

Still, he didn't leave. "Lot of echoes in here. Since all the dependents left."

"Uh-huh."

He glanced at her hands. She didn't have her ring on. She'd taken it off, since it seemed to exacerbate the red eruptions. She thrust both hands into her pockets.

"I'm from the garrison," he said. "You?"

"The cruiser in the harbor," she muttered.

"Yeah? Say . . . the Starbucks is open. Maybe if you wanted to—"

"No thank you."

"Just be nice to have somebody to talk to—"

"See you later." She turned and walked away. Feeling his eyes on her back, but not caring.

BUT Starbucks didn't actually seem like a bad idea. She ordered a green tea latte. Grande. With a red velvet cake pop, yeah. Amazing, that they were still shipping cake pops to Hawaii. Or maybe they made them here. Life went on. Even when some people lost husbands, wives, children . . .

She sipped the hot comforting liquid, revisiting what had just happened. Someone had found her attractive. From the back, which wasn't quite as complimentary. But still, the first time anyone had seen her as anything but "the skipper" for months.

But how had *she* felt? Insulted? Interested? Hostile?

Or maybe some mixture of all three . . .

More honey might be good. She was stirring it in when her phone went off. She snatched it up. "CO here."

"Officer of the deck. Base just announced attack conditions. They're going to close the gates."

"What?" She frowned. "Fuck . . . Any idea what for?"

"Flash message coming in now, Radio says."

The PA system came on. It crackled, then someone said, in Filipino-accented English, *"Attention, Navy Exchange patrons. Attack condition red. Attack condition red. All personnel take ready shelter until you are told it is safe to leave. While in shelter, tune in to local radio stations for further information."*

She rolled her eyes. Had to be a drill. No way the Chinese would attack Hawaii. Still, she ought to get back. "On my way."

She tucked the phone into her bag and rushed outside. Maybe the shuttle would be at the stop. But of course it wasn't. Carrying the latte, she oriented by *Missouri*'s masts and began walking rapidly downhill, toward the highway overpass that led back to the harbor.

A moment later sirens started to wail. Her phone pinged with another warning. She cursed and broke into a run, two-pointing the cup into a trash can.

She ran more than half a mile, over the overpass, through the gate, flashing her ID, then pelting down the pier. By the time she reached the brow she was sucking wind. She hauled herself aboard, yelling at the petty officer, "I left my Hydra on charge. Do you—"

He handed it to her. Danenhower answered at the first call. "Tell me this is a drill," she gasped out.

"I don't think so, Skipper. We got a flash," he said. *"Not sure about what yet."*

She still couldn't quite believe it, but no one sent flash messages without good reason. "Air attack?" She scanned the sky, though any strike would still be far out.

"Doubtful. We sank one of their carriers, and the other's damaged, in port. They don't have the shore-based range to hit us here."

"Where are you?"

"CIC."

"See you in a sec."

THE Combat Information Center was chilly and dark as usual, though only a few consoles were manned. The Air Control and ASW teams had flown back to San Diego. Chief Wenck was still here, though, and Petty Officer Terranova—Donnie and the Terror were bent over the radar console. And Matt Mills was still with them, thank God. As Cheryl slid into the command seat a staccato note sounded. The all-too-familiar musical tone was the cuing bell for a missile-launch detection.

So this was no drill.

But it was still possible it wasn't headed their way.

Mills slipped headphones off and unlooped the beaded chain with the launch keys. "Captain? We're getting cuing from Japanese Air Control fusion center."

When she draped the steel around her neck it was still warm. "Japan, good."

"But it's going to lag. They bounce it up from Kyushu to whatever nanosatellite's overhead, then it relays and downlinks."

"Copy. Got a launch point?"

He tapped the keyboard, and the center screen zoomed while the rightmost remained steady. Cheryl studied them, chin propped on fist.

The right screen, ALIS's view of the world, was extremely constricted. The ballistic missile defense mode sucked down so much computer and radar power that instead of an all-around view, they now had a cone of awareness maybe 5 degrees wide.

But the center screen showed Asia. The launch point was over *Savo*'s radar horizon, of course, far out of range. The callouts were in Japanese characters. They cycled on and off inland from the coast. *Far* inland.

"Way north," Mills noted. "That's got to be close to the North Korean border."

"Look at that boost rate," Wenck called. "It's solid fueled, but heavy."

The Chinese had expended most of their road-portable IRBMs to soften up Taiwan and Okinawa before invading. It seemed unlikely they'd been able to build many since, considering the famine and power interruptions the intel summaries kept saying were endemic.

But they still had a powerful ICBM force, larger and more accurate than the Allies had suspected before the war.

A chill ran up her spine. This was it. The nightmare.

Folding her arms, she sat back. Forcing herself to concentrate. Not to give way to emotion. She had to play this out by the book.

Fortunately, they'd rehearsed a scenario like this. But there was bad news too. Pearl had originally been protected by three Army THAAD batteries, one at the Pacific Missile Range Facility at Kauai, the other two at Hickam Air Force Base. All had been directed by separate AN/TPY-2 tracking radars. But under intense public pressure, Washington had pulled all fixed antimissile defenses back to California and Alaska. A move protested by the Joint Chiefs, but in vain.

Now *Savo Island*, moored with her remaining radars facing northwest, owned the Defense of Honolulu mission. The only protection the base, and Oahu's population, had.

And most Hawaiians had stayed put. Over half a million U.S. citizens, not counting those on the less populated islands scattered like an unstrung lei across the blue Pacific.

"First-stage burnout. Separation," Wenck murmured from the console.

"Watch for more," she told him. "They're not going to fire just one.

Not if this is a major attack." She reached for the red phone, still with that sense of near dream. This could not be happening . . . yet it was. "Matt, did you inform Washington? And the base commander?"

"Seventh Fleet did, via nanochat. I called Base Ops. They're putting it out to civil defense, Hickam, and the other bases."

"Where's that first incomer targeted?"

Terranova said, "Can't say for sure until pitchover, ma'am. But we're the most likely target."

"I agree," Mills said. "They're still boosting. So this is a long-range shot. And the initial azimuth's pointed right down our throat."

Two minutes later the missile's boost phase ended. ALIS had developed a track, computed intercept trajectories, and was initializing the SM-Xs.

The target was Oahu. The lit circle of the area of uncertainty lay over the island, jerking this way and that as Aegis recalculated. In roughly twenty minutes, as the missile began to drill down through the mesosphere, the AOU would contract down to the IPP, the point of predicted impact.

Cheryl sat back, scratching between her fingers. The lead missile, and so far the only one, was still far out of range. It was entering midphase, coasting in a great arc through near space. Despite its tremendous speed, there was no friction heating. It was head-on, too, so not only was it infrared-dim, its radar cross section was at a minimum. "Focus on where we expect to pick it up," she muttered, though she figured Wenck had the reentry window already locked on.

Several minutes passed, during which she called the state civil defense authorities, at the command center on Diamond Head. They confirmed receipt of the warning, said they were getting instructions out to the citizenry, but sounded as if there wasn't much they could do but advise everyone to shelter in place. "*We can't evacuate the city. Not with twenty minutes' warning. We'd just expose everyone, out in the open. Won't you be able to shoot it down?*" the woman asked anxiously. But Cheryl couldn't give her much reassurance.

A subdued bong sounded as she hung up. "ALIS has lock-on," Terranova announced. She never sounded upset, stressed, or even all that interested. Cheryl wished she had the petty officer's sangfroid.

The screen jerked. The "gate," the automatically generated hook of ALIS's acquisition function, was represented by a pair of rapidly occulting bright green brackets. It darted in, circling a blurry contact. Slid past it, corrected, and locked on.

"We have track," Terranova announced.

Mills said, "Very well. Manually engage."

Cheryl sat forward, intent. The green brackets vibrated around the white dot. "Profile plot, Meteor Alfa," Terranova announced. "ID as hostile. No IPP or intercept angle yet."

"Good solid lock-on," Mills murmured. "But Jesus, look at that speed."

The callout wasn't just incredibly high, fifteen thousand miles an hour; it also didn't vary much from second to second. Its velocity would remain constant until it hit the atmosphere. Then it would start to burn, growing an ionization trail as its sheathing ablated. The electrically charged plume would present a huge radar blip.

But if this was an advanced weapon, a DF-41, and she was pretty sure now it was, the payload would be accompanied by decoys. She'd have to decide which to engage, based on the threat and the probability of kill, and gauge the intercept point. Once ALIS had those instructions, it could launch.

"Clear the forward deck," she murmured. "Launch warning bell."

Unlike earlier versions, which carried explosives and were limited to low-altitude interceptions, the wartime-developed SM-X had a steerable kinetic warhead and was designed for midphase intercept. Boosted to near space by two solid-fuel stages, its three-band infrared seeker could steer to intercept an evasively maneuvering warhead. Instead of explosives, a head-on collision added the velocity of the kill vehicle to the momentum of the incoming warhead, using the target's own kinetic energy to blast it apart.

Unfortunately, neither the SM-X nor ALIS had been designed to counter ICBMs. The intermediate-range weapons the system was optimized against flew lower profiles at lower speeds. Intercontinental missiles flew higher, and far faster, tearing down through the atmosphere at almost five miles a second.

She tapped her fingers, evaluating the decision. Where to intercept? Midphase, or terminal? If she waited until reentry, the targets would glow more brightly, present bigger radar returns. It would be easier to sort decoys from live warheads. But that gave up her chance to refire, in case of a miss.

On the other hand, if she launched early, that would allow her Standards to climb for an exoatmospheric intercept. But in the cold of space, the incoming warheads would be harder for them to lock on to. And her interceptors would be at the outer envelope of their design parameters, nearly out of fuel, with more stringent demands on the maneuvering thrusters.

The documentation didn't offer much guidance as to which choice was better. *Savo* had fired earlier mods of her antimissile weapons several times, but there were significant differences with the SM-X. In fact, though their kill probabilities were decent against slower missiles, as far as she knew no SM-X had ever been tested against an ICBM.

All this raced through her brain as she reviewed the checklist in the notebook. She needed to isolate any variables that might affect interception of a higher-velocity, higher-altitude target. "Donnie," she muttered, "I'm thinking, hold fire until we see reentry heating."

"Concur, Skipper. Gives us an extra thirty seconds to sort things out."

"Um, yes. What've we got on this? There's still only one, right?"

The chief said, "Yes, ma'am. Still only one. But . . . this is the big-league bad boy. Like the old Peacekeeper we used to deploy in silos. Eighty tons at launch. Three solid-fuel stages. Can carry eight to ten independently targeted MIRVs. And probably steerable decoys too."

She sat back, scratching her head instead of her fingers now. These were the weapons Zhang had been threatening the U.S. with since the beginning of the war. Built secretly, and emplaced deep in the mountains of Northern China. The Dong Feng ("East Wind")-41 was both heavier and longer-ranged than anything in the current U.S. arsenal. She told Mills to toggle back to the picture from Kyushu. But it came up still showing no callouts for follow-on launches.

"He's firing *one* missile?" she murmured to Mills.

"Well, makes sense, sort of."

"How so?"

The TAO shrugged. "Another warning. If he figures we're going to hit the mainland again, or maybe invade Taiwan?"

"But a thermonuclear, on U.S. soil? That's a major escalation."

"If he figures we won't hit back, sure. And we haven't yet. So . . . why not?"

She huffed, and twisted in her chair. Think all that out later. Right now Death was bearing down on her, and a hell of a lot of other people, at five miles a second. "Terror, got an IPP yet? I need one. Yesterday, if possible." They wouldn't get an intercept angle until they had the impact point prediction, but she was hoping for no more than 5 degrees. That would make the "basket"—the imaginary circle in space their interceptor had to go through to hit its target—as wide as possible. "And a regional view too. We can't see shit in ALIS mode."

Hawaii bloomed on the left screen. A fourteen-hundred-mile scimitar, sweeping up in a counterclockwise arc from the Big Island to Kauai. Beyond that, the emptiness of the central Pacific stretched away toward Asia. "Matt, where are we pulling that picture from? It isn't Japan."

"It's a fusion. From the Army radar site up in the hills, the AN/TPY-2 at Hickam, and whatever MOUSE satellite's in range," he muttered. "Not gonna be great detail. But it should pop a flare on anything else major going on out there. Like an invasion, or an air strike."

She sighed. Doubtful that the enemy had enough remaining long-range forces for invasion. What worried her most was those "eight to ten" maneuverable warheads the thing was supposed to carry. If all ten were thermonuclear, cloned from the U.S. W87 . . . the plans for which the Chinese had stolen from Los Alamos . . . then each would be about half a megaton.

She flipped through a reference notebook and interpolated. Ships were designed to accept a certain level of blast overpressure, but not an infinite amount. The table said a half-megaton air burst would wreck any ship within two kilometers of ground zero.

So where *were* they targeted? "I need intercept angles and IPP, Terror!" she said, more urgently. Once she flipped that Launch Enable switch, the weapons would run through a built-in system test, match parameters with the computer, and fire at the optimal moment.

From there on, it was out of her hands.

"Intercept angle, four point two degrees," Terranova murmured, at the same time Wenck said, "Captain, look."

She blinked at the screen. The single blip on the center display had separated into two, one larger, the other smaller. As she frowned, another smaller contact separated from the main body.

The chief called, "That's the post-boost vehicle system. The 'bus,' they call it. It's dropping off the reentry vehicles."

"Can you distinguish decoys from warheads?"

"Can try . . . stand by." Seconds dragged, during which yet a third contact fissioned off the bus. The chief lifted his voice again. "No . . . I can't really tell. Thought if there was a weight difference, we could identify the lighter vehicles by the velocity differential as they hit atmosphere.

But they're all flying pretty much the same profile. If we could do some kind of neutron emission test . . ."

"But we can't," Mills said tightly, and Cheryl glanced at him, surprised. This was the first time she'd seen any sign of stress from the blond TAO.

Terror said, "No, sir."

"We've only got six rounds. If they throw ten targets at us—"

"Gonna miss some. Yep." Wenck nodded vigorously. "But we could get lucky. Pick the ones that're live."

Cheryl thought the odds were against it, but no point in saying so. Instead, she keyed the 1MC. *"All nonessential hands to citadel. I say again, all nonessential hands to the citadel, on the double,"* echoed in the passageway.

"That doesn't mean us," she added, to their inquiring looks. "We'll fire, then duck and cover. Donnie, I need to know what these vehicles are doing."

Wenck tapped keys, and the rightmost display, from *Savo*'s own radar, changed. Now a whole small constellation of contacts was burning down through the high thin air of the troposphere, each growing a cometlike ball of ionized air. "I'm seeing six contacts now. That pulsation on the bus means it's rotating. Dispensing one vehicle with each revolution. That imparts an outward velocity vector. I'm not seeing independent maneuvering from the smaller contacts."

Cheryl forced herself to concentrate, though her nails itched to dig holes in the desk. A seventh contact separated from the slowly revolving main body. Now she could make out a horizontal spread, left to right, with the bus in the center. "Anyone else see a pattern here?" she breathed.

Mills said, "I'm gonna guess the first ones it shits out are the decoys. That way we waste our rounds on them, and the real warheads get through."

"Those are the ones it dispensed to the left of the main body. Donnie, Terror, what's your take?"

Wenck toggled the screen to show the IPPs ALIS was calculating. They overlay Oahu from north to south, with two centered on Pearl Harbor.

Cheryl frowned. "Why are there six IPPs, when we have seven radar contacts?"

Mills said, "The bus will break up as it hits atmosphere. They wouldn't leave a live warhead in it. Those have to be oriented base down to reenter."

That made sense. "Okay, so we're dealing with six reentry bodies. We can't tell which are decoys and which aren't. We have six Standard Xs. How do we allocate?"

"There's another," Terranova said in a quiet voice. "Number eight separating, to the right . . . and something just flew off the bus. . . . It's decaying."

On the rightmost screen, the nimbus of the largest contact seethed and boiled. Bits tumbled off, and the corona pulsated more and more swiftly.

It suddenly disintegrated into hundreds of small glowing bits of debris, artificial meteors, incandescing and then flashing into plasma as they hit atmosphere. Leaving only the seven smaller contacts, more compact, glowing more and more fiercely as they burned downward through the steadily thickening air.

Mills said, "I'm seeing something out to the west. Not sure what it is yet."

Cheryl squinted up at the left-hand screen, the one with the fused display. Two hundred miles out. Small contacts. "What are they?"

"Not sure yet. Speed's fifty knots. Too fast for surface ships. But too slow for aircraft."

"IFF?"

"No identification, and EW reports no emissions."

Cheryl dismissed them for the moment, reconcentrating on the AOUs. The predicted impact areas were ovals half a mile across. She scratched viciously between her fingers, ignoring the bloody furrows her nails left. Seven incomers. But only six missiles to take them with.

Seven quivering ovals. Two were centered more or less on the naval base, and two more over Hickam Field, the Air Force installation south of where *Savo* lay pierside. The Air Force had pulled most of its bombers out months ago. She hoped any personnel who remained had shelters. Another oval vibrated to the north, over Kunia, up in the hills. Probably earmarked for the tracking radar that was giving her the wide-angle view to the west.

But it was the last two, aimed some distance east of the harbor, that made her blood run cold.

Those IPPs vibrated above Honolulu, spaced three miles apart down the coast. Assuming they were thermonuclear, the blast areas would cover most of the city.

She swallowed, disbelieving once more. Could the Chinese really intend this as a countervalue strike? To wipe out tens of thousands, no, *hundreds* of thousands, of civilian noncombatants?

Unless, of course, the reentry bodies aimed at the city were the decoys, and the ones targeted against military installations the live warheads.

Should she assume they were? And take under fire only the five aimed at the harbor and the bases?

She froze in her seat, still as stone. Unable to breathe. Or speak.

Yet she had to decide.

She had to decide *now*.

But even as she reached for the switch, she knew what her decision had to be.

She'd studied under the best. Under Daniel V. Lenson. And he'd taught her two things. Two, above all.

A commander in battle always worked with inadequate information. Clues, fragmentary reports, undependable intel, guesses as to enemy vulnerabilities and intent. The CO's duty was to make the best estimate possible, as coolly and rationally as possible . . . then act, boldly and without hesitation.

And second, when you faced that ultimate decision, you put yourself aside. Not just your own ego, or sense of fitness. Not even just your own career.

In the military, you had to substitute other priorities: the mission. Your crew.

Just as he had, over and over. Charging forward in the Taiwan Strait. Retiring in the face of torpedo attack, when it might be taken for cowardice. Protecting the carrier, when he'd directed her to emulate it, attracting the weapons that had wrecked their ship.

"The contacts to the west," Mills reported. "Ten of 'em now. EW identifies as Zubr-class hovercraft. They have air cover. Probably UAVs they launched themselves."

Cheryl frowned. Hovercraft? She studied the leftmost screen, then called up a tool. The system-generated track led to the Pearl Harbor entrance.

"An invasion force?" Mills said.

"Pfft. With ten units? More likely a raid. What do those things carry?"

The keyboard rattled. "Four tanks. Up to a dozen AFVs. Plus up to four hundred troops each. I'm passing that to Hickam now."

She was impressed despite her fear. Before the war, the Chinese had invested heavily in hovercraft, surface effect ships. But usually these were short-ranged, due to high fuel consumption. Somehow Admiral Lianfeng had managed either to extend their range, or to refuel them en route. From submarines, perhaps.

No matter how, it was an amazing achievement. A rabbit punch back at America, for the Allied raids on the Chinese homeland. Unfortunately for those aboard the craft, it was also a major overreach. She said slowly, "So it's not just a one-missile strike. But they're going to lose those troops."

The TAO said, "Probably. Yeah. Tactically, a long shot. Maybe he figured, use 'em or lose 'em. But if they can get ashore, four thousand troops with light armor could do a lot of damage. Like I said, I passed them to the Air Force. But I can take with our SM-2s, antisurface mode, when they get in range?"

"Okay, but first things first." The ALIS feed was flicking from contact to contact, switching among the incoming reentry bodies. The system could track and execute, but it couldn't make the ultimate decisions. She muttered to Mills, "TAO, your opinion?"

"Doctrine says self-defense comes first. Second, we defend military assets. Third, populated areas."

She felt as if they were onstage, in a play, and nearing the dramatic climax. But these were probably the last few seconds any of them would live. "So?"

"As far as self-defense . . . Once we fire, we're off the board no matter what happens. And Pearl, the air base . . ."

"They're military assets," she reminded him gently.

"Yeah, but." He swallowed, not meeting her eyes. "TAO recommends . . . we take out the ones aimed at the city. Two-round salvo each."

"That leaves one round each on the two aimed for us." But she nodded nonetheless. Doctrine, versus letting a hundred thousand civilians die? No contest. She glanced at the operators. "Terror, Donnie. Concur?"

"Shoo-eh, whatever," Terranova said softly, as if it didn't really matter to her.

"Same here, Skip," Wenck said.

Back to the screen. The jellyfish ovals were contracting to points. The last few items on the checklist, then. "Wind direction, speed, five knots from the southwest."

The memory of a sea breeze thrashing the nodding palms. Creamy sand crunching between her bare toes.

"Check."

"Close vent dampers. Pass Circle William throughout the ship. Launch warning bell forward . . . roll FIS to green."

A thousand drills, and then a world war.

Eddie's arms around her. For the last time.

She fitted the key and twisted it. "You have permission to engage. Shift fire gate selection. Launchers into operate mode. Set up to take Meteor Delta, two-round salvo. Next salvo, Meteor Echo, two-round salvo. Meteor Bravo, one-round salvo. Meteor Charlie, one-round salvo. Total six rounds. Then fire out all the SM-2s on the Zubrs. Empty the magazines."

"Warning alarm forward. Deselect safeties and interlocks. Stand by to fire. On CO's command."

On CO's command.

She. Cheryl. The last commanding officer of USS *Savo Island*.

She flicked up the red metal cover over the Fire Auth switch. Deep in its integrated circuits, the ship's artificial mind was running ranges, speeds, probabilities, recalculating everything ten times a second. When she removed the last logic barrier, the computers would fire at the instant P-sub-K peaked.

"Released," she muttered, and flicked the switch over. And looked up to face the others, staring at her.

"Now get the hell out of here," she barked.

THEY'D barely reached the mess decks when the bellow of departing boosters shook the ship. She didn't pause, just kept running. Reaching a ladder, she vaulted down it after Wenck, braking with her hands on the rails, slamming her boots into steel grating at the bottom. Terranova was right behind her, Mills bringing up the rear. A second roar and rattle, more distant, with thick steel between them and the igniting booster.

She wished there was a lot more of it. Metal would boil away like water in the unimaginable heat of a nuclear detonation.

At least they wouldn't suffer. Just be obliterated, instantaneously vaporized to hot gas.

Fainter roars, behind and above. The ship was carrying out its last instructions. Emptying its magazines. Aegis would die fighting.

Could a computer recognize the end of its own existence? Become conscious, in the last microseconds?

The door to the citadel was closed. Wenck hammered at it. "Open the fuck up!" he shouted. She and Terranova exchanged glances. What if the others didn't let them in? Well, it probably wouldn't make any difference.

It swung open at last. The remainder of the crew huddled inside. They stared up, blinking, pale, cheeks shining with sweat. Mills slammed the door behind them, twisting the dogs home with the wrench.

Cheryl checked her watch, drawing each breath slowly, savoring that single bite of air as if it were her last. The second hand was clicking from numeral to numeral. "Brace for shock," she called, two seconds before the IPP time for the warheads targeted on the base.

The second hand clicked forward. Again.

A reddish-ocher flash flickered in her head, not behind her eyes, but so deep in her brain that it seemed for a moment more like her inmost soul, illuminated suddenly and brutally, from within and without alike, by a deep, all-encompassing russet-ruby light.

A moment later the steel around them whiplashed. It knocked those who were standing into power cabinets, fuel transfer pumps, and air-conditioning units, and jerked those who'd been sitting off their chairs. The lights cut off, plunging them into absolute darkness. The sound was beyond sound, a sharp solid cone that penetrated her eardrums like a steel spike. The compartment shook again, from side to side and up and down. It seemed to reel around them in the darkness.

The shock wave bass-drummed away, succeeded by silence. Ringing, earsplitting, eerie silence.

A beam cut the darkness. It flickered, went out, glowed on again.

The emergency lighting revealed pallid faces, some streaked with blood, others with tears. Bodies were sprawled around the compartment like rats tossed by a terrier.

Cheryl found herself on hands and knees on the starboard bulkhead, which seemed now to be the deck. It was still vibrating beneath her palms, thrumming like a huge taut string. But the compartment was totally silent.

Someone was shaking her. A young woman's face above her, mouth open.

The corpsman, Duncanna Ryan. Cheryl shook her head, pointed to her ears. Then caught the tail of the shout as one ear, at least, returned to operation. ". . . *okay?*"

"Yeah. Yeah, I'm all right, Dunkie."

Another voice was sobbing in the far corner, by the air-conditioning unit. "Somebody's hurt."

"Doc's taking care of him. Can you get up?—Skipper's okay!" Ryan yelled across the space.

Cheryl peered around, disoriented and dizzied. Was the compartment really on its side? A huge machine loomed ominously above her. The #2 fuel transfer pump, but at a crazy angle. Wrenched halfway off the shockproof mountings.

She felt weak, shaky, but when she kneaded her arm, it seemed no worse. Then she noticed that water was rolling this way and that across the deck. And that a stench of burning was penetrating the closed, quickly heating air of the compartment.

Bart Danenhower helped her to her feet. The big engineer didn't look as if he was going to crack any jokes today. "We're blown over. Nearly on our beam ends. Shock wave hit us on the port side."

"Will we come back upright?"

"I'd need to be in DC Central to answer that." He reached for his gas mask.

"Bart . . ."

"I'll just stay out long enough to counterflood."

"No. I mean, I'm going too. I have to get topside."

"It's gonna be bad up there."

"Well, at least we know where one warhead was targeted."

She wondered briefly if *Savo*'s weapons had connected, if Honolulu's population still lived. Then pushed it from her mind. All that remained was to lead her people to safety. If she could.

If, indeed, it was safe outside the skin of the ship. Usually warheads were set for airburst, but there would still be fallout. Sleeted with neutrons already, though partially protected by fuel and steel and plastic, none of *Savo*'s crew needed more exposure. Not to mention whatever other horrors lurked up there: fire, spilled fuel . . .

The door clanked open, silhouetting Danenhower against the glow of the battle lanterns; then it closed again. She rapped out orders. Commence emergency destruction. Prepare to abandon ship. She clanged open the locker and rummaged for a protective suit. Bent, and began pulling it up over her coveralls.

SHE climbed toward the main deck, planting the heavy floppy rubber overboots clumsily on the ladder treads, peering through the curved plastic of the mask. The hood of the nuclear-bacteriological-chemical suit was drawstringed tight around the one-piece lens. She felt breathless in the Joint Service mask, but not as severely as in the old MCU-2. This mask was better balanced, too, with filters that stuck out on both sides. The thick rubber gloves cushioned the handrails she grabbed to pull herself up. She felt as if she were being controlled from a distance. By herself, or some other entity? That was the question.

At the main deck level she turned left for the door. She had to hammer the dogs to get it open. They groaned open reluctantly, meaning the superstructure was distorted by blast.

When she stepped outside she saw why.

The whole side of the ship was smoking, its paint blistered down to bare metal. The liferails were twisted inward. The heavy doubled lines holding *Savo* to the pier were charred, burning, dancing with bluish flame.

She surveyed smashed buildings, fiercely burning rubble. The cranes were toppled into acres of burning fuel. Beyond that she couldn't see much for the smoke, but ground zero of at least one burst had been west of the harbor, perhaps over the old naval airstrip on Ford Island. Bracketing the base, for maximum damage.

Lifting each boot was an exertion. She plodded toward the brow. The metal gangway was buckled, crumpled up into the quarterdeck. It creaked and rocked alarmingly as she pulled herself onto it. Behind her the remaining crew edged out onto the main deck, then backtracked to head forward along the less-damaged starboard side.

Mills and McMottie accompanied her, as slow as she was in overboots and protective gear. Like large green grubs with insectile faces, they inchwormed over the groaning, rickety brow to the pier.

Here, concrete smoldered. The pier itself looked mostly whole, though cracks ran through it, but black puddles of liquid asphalt burned where the roadway had been patched. The darker surfaces had absorbed more heat from the fireball's flash, torching anything that would burn. Then the overpressure, shock wave, blast, had knocked down every building and blown apart any structure that offered resistance.

Shading her gaze, she twisted to peer eastward. Expecting more smoke, fire, disaster. But though huge pyramids of flame and great black billows rose from the fuel facility, she didn't see any smoke in the direction of the city. Had her missiles knocked down those warheads? Or had those only been decoys, cunningly aimed to force her to waste ordnance?

No answer suggested itself, so she turned back and plodded aft again, toward the little civilian-contractor tug that had been moored astern. As she'd hoped, it was still afloat, though listing. The black-painted hull was scorched and the rubber-tire fenders were still gouting yellow flame and thick inky smoke, but apparently the cruiser's bulk had shielded it from the worst of the flash. The gangway had been blown into the water, leaving only shreds of aluminum, but the *Savo* sailors were able to clamber down to the deck. Cheryl and Mills headed for the pilothouse; McMottie found a main deck door and disappeared below.

Cheryl's Hydra clicked on shortly after. "*We're in luck,*" McMottie said. "*One of the crew was sleeping aboard. Feels sick, but he says he can turn the engines over.*"

"Good, Senior Chief. Get a mask on him. If you have any of those radiation pills left, give him a dose." She peered through the glassless, blown-out window openings, the smoke from the burning rubber. If he felt sick already, the neutron flux up here must have been horrendous. So high that her own crew would be feeling the effects soon, though they'd been more sheltered.

She studied the controls. Z-drive, with twin joysticks to manage thrust, and nearly the same bollard pull in any direction. Ticos had no thrusters to control the bow, so they usually used two tugs to moor, one fast to the bow, the other standing by astern to call in as needed. She had only this one, and unfortunately, with all the topside damage, no idea now how the wind would take the ship.

They'd just have to cope. "Matt, get those lines cast off. Chief, let me know when we have propulsion." Was she feeling nauseated too? She wasn't sure if it was the mask, the horror all around, or the beginning of radiation sickness.

And it probably didn't matter.

She just had one last thing to do.

A pair of Engine Ready lights illuminated on the panel. *"Can only start two,"* McMottie crackled over the Hydra.

"No problem, Senior Chief. That'll be adequate."

"Ready to answer all bells," the engineer said, with a firm certainty in his tone. The pride of all the engineers who had propelled Navy ships through almost two centuries.

She punched the horn, but it didn't work. Sheared off, probably. And slowly advanced the throttle, cautiously, listening in case any debris had ended up on the bottom near the screws.

The last charred, still-burning line to the pier parted in puffs of soot and sparks. The tug edged sideways out of its berth. She nudged the thrusters around, and it straightened and headed up *Savo*'s side. She hugged the cruiser's hull, and when she bumped it, the tug's still-smoldering fenders smeared off a black smoking smudge.

She halted at the bow, idling while the ad hoc line-handling party dropped a mooring line to Mills, standing on the tug's broad rounded stern.

It didn't have to be the towing hawser. They didn't need to go far.

Mills stepped back from the bitts and flashed her a thumbs-up. She waved him clear and advanced the throttle again. The line came taut, but nothing happened. She examined the controls, then advanced them to 100 percent power. With a squeak and a tortured writhe, the heavy hawser went rigid-taut.

After several seconds, the cruiser lurched. The pier wall fell back a few feet, then stalled again. She backed off, letting them all recover, then applied full-ahead power once more. This time when the hawser came taut the tug shuddered, then slowly moved ahead.

Glancing back, she saw ten thousand tons of cruiser slow-marching after her. *Savo*'s upperworks were wrecked. The phased arrays had been blasted into junk. The pilothouse, all its glass blasted out, its paint scorched black, was visibly bent to starboard.

Once the pride of the fleet, USS *Savo Island* had taken her crew around the world. Fought in the Med, the Gulf, the Indian Ocean, the

China Sea. Now she was a hopeless wreck, magazines empty, on fire, headed to her grave.

But even there, she could still serve.

With the tug's engines pounding at full power, Cheryl steered out of the Southeast Loch, past the destroyer piers, into the turning basin. Ahead of her smoke boiled off USS *Missouri*. Aside from having her antennas sheared off, the old battleship seemed largely undamaged. Only her paint was on fire. The white concrete arch of the Arizona Memorial lay toppled and broken, smashed down into the sunken wreck below in a second, even more perfidious act of infamy.

Aiming the tug's bow to port, she made for the channel out. Past Ford Island, off Hospital Point, the way to the sea pinched in. If she could scuttle athwart that narrowing entryway, *Savo*'s dying hulk, nearly six hundred feet long, would block the channel. If the raiding force managed to land, they'd have to debark across an open beach. She would deny any invader the harbor, the naval and ship repair facilities, the airfields . . . or what was left of them.

Mills stepped over the wreckage of the door to stand behind her. Squinting ahead, she picked out where best to ground the bow, east of the channel. But how to get the stern around? She squinted aft at the burning cruiser, trying to judge if the wind would help or hinder.

Mills's glove on her shoulder. "What are we planning here, CO?"

"Trying to figure out where the stern's going."

Well, if she rammed the bow in hard enough, the inertia of thousands of tons of steel should swing the stern outward. If it didn't stop where she wanted it, she'd just have to reposition the tug, and hold the ship in place as it settled.

She glanced at the Fathometer, but of course it was dead. Burned out by the electromagnetic pulse. The queer maroon flash she'd sensed even through closed eyelids. Staring through the shattered window, she nudged the thrusters left, overcorrected, corrected back.

A few minutes more, and she'd no longer be the skipper. Once *Savo* was in position, the engineers would trigger the demo charges and blow the bottom out.

Cheryl doubled over, gagging inside the mask. Bile rose in her throat. No question, her hands were shaking. "Eddie," she whispered. "It won't be long now."

The *second* nuclear attack. And this time on an American base, a helpless city. Surely America would strike back after this. Surely China would pay.

But what about her crew? Perhaps they could straggle ashore, find shelter, a way to help fight off the approaching enemy. Or else just drag themselves to some dark corner, like a perishing animal, to lie down and die.

They would just have to see.

III

MY SHIP HAS NO RUDDER

13

The Karakoram Mountains

HE is here, Lingxiù." Guldulla loomed in the cave's portal, blocking the light.

Teddy had been squatting on his haunches, mind empty, watching the clouds go by.

A month had passed since the raid on the pipeline. They'd taken even more losses on the march back. Drones tracked them night and day. Gunships struck each time they crossed a stream, a valley, the smallest patch of open ground. Mountain troops hit them twice, inserted by helo overlooking pinch points. At last Teddy had confiscated a herd of goats, and split the party up. Posing as locals moving their flocks to pasturage, they'd filtered back.

But only sixty-one fighters had stumbled in, out of two hundred. They'd lost dozens of weapons. All the donkeys, broken down, shot, or starved. No one had kept a count on the bearers, mostly slave women, at all.

The upside: Akhmad had been uphill during the battle, videotaping. Dubbed with stirring music and a running commentary of hate, they had a propaganda masterpiece. The Han controlled the internet. But copied and passed from bazaar to madrassa, hamlet to city by friendly truckers, the video brought in a flood of new recruits. He'd bloodied them with raids on police stations and wind generators, targeted assassinations of local officials and Uighur collaborators.

Some of the new arrivals, of course, had been spies. These Guldulla took down into the canyon. They did not return.

Now it was time to render an account.

* * *

INSTEAD of a greatcoat, on this visit their field officer wore a camo field jacket. Under it, though, was the same maroon turtleneck. And the shoulder rig, of course. A duffel lay at his feet. Reflective sunglasses hid his eyes. His stubbled cheeks were altitude-burned. Three others stood with him: shorter, swarthier, in local dress and sandals. They looked uncomfortable with the Uighurs' rifles pointed at them.

"Vladimir" shook hands. "Ted. I saw the video. Great optics! Congratulations!"

Teddy had to retwist his brain into English. At last he managed, "We took a lot of losses."

The Agency liaison eyed him curiously. "How's the leg?"

"It's not too bad."

"Doing okay, up here all alone?"

"I'm not alone. Yeah, I'm doing fine."

"Okay, if you're sure . . . Some good news. First, congratulations. You're the million-dollar man."

Teddy just stared at him.

"The Chinese put a bounty on you. A million dollars." The guy seemed to reflect, then, that Obie might not see that as good news. He added, "And, well, that shopping list you gave me? I think you'll like what you're getting. Two truckfuls."

"Trucks?"

"Well, they're forty miles away. Parked, camo'd, and guarded. Back roads from India. The slants have beefed up their recon. Drops are getting risky; thought we'd better find an alternate supply route." Vlad stripped off his gloves, looking around. "So . . . we go inside?"

"Maybe. Who're your friends?" Teddy nodded at the others, liking neither the news of a price on his head, which around here meant literally, nor the fact the CIA officer had brought strangers along. Once the Han knew where the caves were, raids by their special ops teams wouldn't be far behind.

Vladimir introduced "Pancho" and "Leonardo," obviously code names. They muttered greetings in what he was pretty sure was Burushaski while extending limp handshakes.

Vlad said, "The Hunza operate on the other side of the border, in Azad Kashmir. Antigovernment, so they're on our side. Sort of. Upstairs thought it'd be good for them to link up with you ITIM guys, since what we brought had to come through their territory. And, to be frank, they got a hefty cut."

Teddy had had to put some sort of name on the video credits. ITIM—the Independent Turkistan Islamic Movement—harked back to an earlier resistance the Han had crushed. But also forward, to the promise of a union of all the Turkic peoples from Azerbaijan, Kazakhstan, Kyrgyzstan, Turkmenistan, and Uzbekistan. And of course, above all, "Chinese" Turkistan. Teddy shook hands with them. Then turned to the third, who hadn't been introduced yet. An older man with a grizzled beard. Squat, smiling, he hesitated before accepting Teddy's handshake.

"And who's this?"

"Call me Qurban," the guy said in Uighur, still grinning. He and Guldulla eyed each other.

"Abu-Hamid al-Nashiri's been a guest of the U.S. government for a while," Vlad explained breezily. "In a warmer location. Now he wants to fight on our side."

Teddy gimlet-eyed the guy. "A warm location. Where?"

"Guantánamo," the CIA man said reluctantly. "But he's tame now. Wants to cooperate. Higher thought you could use him."

Teddy gripped his rifle, hardly believing what he was hearing. "You brought *al-Qaeda*? From *Gitmo*?"

"Well, he was once. But like I said—"

"I have reformed my allegiance," the man said, in English. He met Teddy's gaze. "I wish only to fight our common enemy."

Teddy bit down on a curse. This dude was going to be trouble. But instead of protesting more just then, he introduced Guldulla, and sent a boy to find Akhmad. Any question of linking up with the Hunza had to be blessed by the old imam. He shouted for Dandan, and ordered food and tea. Pancho asked for his rifle back. "Later," Teddy told him in Uighur. "You are our guest now." Then led them inside.

TEDDY attended prayers, during which Vlad stood by the cave entrance, observing. The guy from Gitmo joined the other worshippers, quietly sliding into the back row.

Now they were alone at last, Teddy and the CIA officer, in his sleeping cell. Dandan had brought in tea and rice, then bowed and retreated, backing out.

"I see you aren't happy about al-Nashiri." Vlad removed his sunglasses and started picking at his food. "Or with me bringing in the Hunza. But you're not the only team on the field. We support Tibetan resistance. Pakistani, like Leonardo's guys. A group in Hong Kong. Manchurians. Mongolians. Yunnanese, in the south. Sunnis in Iran. The more angst we stir up, the better."

"Zhang's got a shitload of troops," Teddy said.

"A lot, but not an infinite number. And insurrections soak up security forces like you wouldn't believe. Five to one, troops to rebels. If we can coordinate, things might really break loose." The liaison seemed to recall something, and reached into his vest. "Oh, and this might brighten your day."

He unsnapped a case, and Teddy stared at unfamiliar bars of blue, white, and red on a scrap of ribbon. A bronze medal, a five-pointed star, an eagle's head. FOR VALOR, the engraving read.

"Fuck's this?" he muttered, frowning.

"This is the Intelligence Star, Ted." He pinned it on Teddy's shalwar kameez. "At the direction of the director, Central Intelligence. For extraordinary heroism under conditions of grave risk. I also have something for your assistants." He laid smaller cases on the worn carpet. "If you think it's advisable."

Teddy sipped tea. "I'd like to hold off on that. They're starting to accept me. Why remind them I'm not really one of them? Also, take this 'Qurban' dude back with you. Al-Qaeda, seriously? Find that fucker a billet shoveling shit in Ceylon. No, better yet, a bullet in the back of the head."

"Can't, unfortunately," Vladimir said. "Nobody else would take him. But the guy's got an interesting history. At one time, he was the highest-ranking ALQ in custody. Veteran of Afghanistan. Bosnia. The Yemenis had him, and reported him dead in his cell. But somehow he turned up again in Mosul. That's where we picked him up. He could be useful. Bin Laden used to have a pretty good network here, all the way into Afghanistan. Gray Wolf can organize the villages for you."

"What's that mean, 'organize the villages'? I don't want to reactivate fucking al-Qaeda."

"You're not. He promised."

"Ha-ha. With what? A pinkie swear?"

"All he's gonna do is lend you credibility, and get you a lot of popular participation."

Obie muttered, "Until after the war."

"Let's worry about that bridge later, Ted. Right now our priority's gotta be to win this thing somehow." Vladimir stirred his rice. "You do know Zhang nuked Hawaii?"

"No. I didn't." Teddy banged the teacup down. "Nuked it . . . holy Christ. Where'd we hit back?"

The agent looked away. "We haven't. Not yet."

"What the . . . ! First the *Roosevelt*, then Pearl? And we do jack shit? What the fuck's going on?"

"We're losing the cyberwar, too. Unless we can pull something out of our ass, worst case, we could get disarmed and occupied. It's that serious." Vladimir let that hang a moment, then pulled the duffel toward them. "But there may be a way to turn it around. How many effectives you got now?"

Teddy tried to refocus. But a nuclear strike on Hawaii was a shocker. . . . "Uh, we're back up to about four hundred, all told."

"I don't see that many."

"Most of them aren't here. We whistle, they muster. Hit a patrol. Blow a power line. Take over a police station, kill the cops, steal everything that's not nailed down. Then turn back into peasants and shopkeepers. Fish in the sea."

"Huh. I'll take your word for it." The field operative opened the duffel and took out several small boxes. "These are the crown jewels, so guard them. The first one, this is Swiss technology. An early-warning system. It picks up the video signals the drones emit. Mount them on your mountain peaks.

"This second system." Vladimir extracted several long rods, a triangular antenna, and what looked like the buttstock to a FAL rifle. Teddy raised his eyebrows as the operative assembled it into what was obviously a weapon, but like nothing he'd ever seen. "I know, *Star Wars*, right? This is a beam gun. It's for if you have to go where the drones live, or one makes it past the stakeout. You can disable a flyer two ways. Either cut the connection between the pilot and the UAV, or else, if the thing's autonomous, jam its altitude radar and navigation. It either crashes, or just wanders away."

The field officer shouldered it and pressed a button. A hornet whine permeated the cave. "Powers up in half a second. Reflex sight, you're familiar with those. It detects, decodes, and puts out a coned twenty-degree beam. Jams the target's control frequencies."

Teddy accepted it. Hefted it. "What's my range? And how about power?"

"Range depends on the make of the drone, but at least a thousand feet. For power, rechargeable lithium batteries. They're compatible with the solar panels you got on the second drop." The officer sat back. "I brought night vision, too. Plus more of the usual: ammo, boots, antibiotics, Serb-surplus body armor."

"That'll help," Teddy murmured, still not happy about the new join, but figuring he could take care of him somehow. Maybe send him down a ravine with Guldulla.

Vladimir sighed and stood. "Good. Hey, love to stay, but like I said, we need to turn this around fast. Give me ten guys and twenty donkeys. We need to head down to the trucks tonight."

"Tonight's gonna be difficult," Teddy told him. "This is Lailat al Miraj, you know? They're gonna be up all night praying."

"Shit . . . You can't break me out ten guys?"

"I'll see what Akhmad says," Teddy told him reluctantly. He yelled for Dandan as Vladimir broke down the beam gun.

THE cave was bright with hundreds of candles, glowing from the scarred mouths and empty eye sockets of the broken Buddhas. In wall niches, and scattered across the floors. Gas lanterns hissed. A black blanket was drawn across the entrance, with a guard outside to check for light leaks.

Within, the assembled rebels sat cross-legged in rows as the old imam intoned, in his weirdly accented Arabic, the story of Muhammad's night journey. The women were gathered separately in a side cave. Teddy sat at the back, cross-legged like the rest, though his mangled foot throbbed, listening to the story. Which by now he could sort of follow, more or less.

The Prophet's ascent started in Mecca, when he was halfway between sleep and wakefulness. After the archangel Gibreel greeted him, he mounted Al-Buraq, a magical flying horse, which took him to the farthest mosque in the world. Then God raised him up through the seven heavens, until he reached Allah himself. There he was told the Faithful must pray fifty times a day. But on Moses' suggestion, Muhammad asked for a break, and got the obligation down to five.

Teddy caught himself nodding off, and straightened. Halfway between sleep and wakefulness . . . that was how his own night journey had started. On the mountain, freezing, starving, spooned against the other escaped POWs for warmth. There hadn't been any talking horse, but hadn't there been something like an ascent . . . like being washed clean . . . and finally, a Presence.

But then it had let him go. And he'd hurtled down, toward the black mountains opening below like gulping mouths. Himself screaming, flailing, wanting to dwell forever in the timelessness he'd known so fleetingly.

Had that been a visitation of God? Or just the misfiring of a starved, dying brain?

He had the uncomfortable feeling that he wasn't ever going to know. Not in this life, anyway.

Up front, Akhmad was winding up. The old imam began the final prayer when one of the men stood. Bowing to the imam, he asked humbly if he could say a few words.

Teddy tensed. It was the newbie, the squat bearded man Vlad had called Gray Wolf. Another bow, and he was standing in front of the congregation. Stroking his beard, smiling, he began in Arabic, much purer and clearer than the old imam's, then switched to Uighur.

"Praise be to Allah! Most compassionate, most merciful. Who created humanity for his worship and commanded them to be just.

"But he also permitted one who was wronged to retaliate.

"My name is Qurban, meaning 'the Sacrifice.' For that very many years ago I offered myself as a living offering, to oppose all those who oppress the Faithful. I have fought on many battlefields. Endured long years in prison. I greet you now in the Holy Name and praise you as brave warriors who stand up against the godless empire of the Han.

"Peace forever be upon he who follows the guidance of Allah! But to him who oppresses the Faithful, it is lawful to lay waste to him and to his lands and families. It is said that the Chinese are powerful. That opposing them and their killing machines of the air is futile. That for a man to defend himself and his people, as you are doing, is terrorism and rebellion.

"Well, if it is, we must accept whatever follows. Yet I remind you that nothing is impossible for Allah.

"Please accept me as one of yourselves. Not as a leader, for you have wise leadership in your respected imam Sheykh Akhmad, in brave Guldulla, in canny Nasrullah, and in your war chief, the battle-scarred

Lingxiù Oberg al-Amriki. In all humility will I carry a rifle by your side, and stand or fall beside my brothers as Allah wills."

Qurban bowed again, even lower, to them all. "That Allah is our guardian and helper, I say again. All peace be upon him who follows His wise guidance. *Amin*."

Leaving Teddy gritting his teeth and scowling as he wended his way, smiling, back to his self-effacing seat in the rearmost row.

THEY stood together at dawn, watching as the last crates were carried up from the valley below.

"Can't do it, Ted," Vladimir said again. "Direct orders. Let him build a mass movement. He's got the track record."

"A record of fighting guys like me." Oberg growled. "I was starting to get them used to my leadership. Now he's given me a new name. Al-Amriki—'the American.'"

"Which you *are*—right? He's onside, Ted. Six years in Gitmo, he's learned his lesson!" The officer sighed. "Put him in charge of the resistance cadre. Let him grow the insurgency. Meanwhile, you focus on tactical objectives. Take the warm bodies he pulls in and deploy 'em where they'll do us the most good."

Teddy said nothing. The guy was mouthing unconventional-warfare doctrine, without getting the picture on the ground. Obviously he'd have to solve this problem on his own. Okay, he could do that. One way or another.

"Cool." The CIA man nodded. "And now you've got all the shiny new toys, we have a new tasking for you. Ready to copy?"

"I'm listening," Teddy muttered.

"Raids and ambushes are great. But it's time to amp up your game. Still got that phone I gave you?" The contact touched his to Teddy's. "I'm transmitting a task order, a map, and your risk assessment. There's a facility east of here. In the Taklimakan. We need you to penetrate and destroy it."

"Oh yeah? What are we calling this op?"

"Checkmate." Vladimir hesitated. "I understand you were part of the first TA-3 mission."

Teddy blinked, studying the map on his screen. Vladimir was referring to Echo One's assault on Woody Island at the start of the war. A raid, as far as most SEALs knew. Only he and the lieutenant had been trusted with the real mission. "Uh-huh," he said tentatively. "Where exactly is this?"

"Northern edge of the desert basin. South of the Tien Shan mountains."

He nodded, remembering one night during the escape from Camp 576. On the far side of miles of sand hills, a long line of saffron lights had sparkled and wavered. Smaller blue lights had circled beneath the black bowl of a starry sky. The fugitives hadn't gone any closer, but it had seemed like a hell of a lot of activity for the middle of nowhere. "I might know where you're talking about," he said slowly. "It's a long way east of here."

"But you made it. During your escape. We'll arrange a drop halfway, if you stay in the mountains."

"Yeah, we made it, but we lost guys on the way," Teddy said. "Taking a couple hundred troops through high-relief terrain like that is gonna be rough. We'd need bearers, guides. . . ."

Vladimir unbuttoned his jacket and pulled out a heavy-sagging belt. "This should help."

Teddy accepted, and almost dropped it. "Christ. What the fuck you got in here, lead?"

"Close."

He peered inside, to see . . . shining disks of yellow metal.

"Gold Krugerrands," Vladimir murmured. "Should help you find bearers."

"Okay, good. Sure, that'll help. But that's a big fucking installation, judging by the lights we saw. Even if we make it there, how are we going to take out something that size?"

The CIA man strolled a few yards away. He unzipped, and hosed down the side of a boulder. "You emplaced these units on Woody. So you know what they're supposed to do."

"I know what they *told* us it was supposed to do. Which—" He'd been about to say *Which it didn't*, but remembered in the nick of time how classified that little factoid was. And compartmented meant *compartmented*. "Uh, yeah. I know."

"It's an electromagnetic-pulse generator. The TA-4's smaller than what you had to carry before, but Sandia's doubled the range. Enough to fry any circuitry for a quarter mile. And the facility you're hitting is mainly computers."

"Double the range, that's eight times the power. In a smaller package? How'd they manage that?"

Vladimir raised his eyebrows. "Smart guy, eh?"

"Don't think SEALs are dumb just because we're handsome."

"Uh-huh. Then you might as well know. It isn't a conventional explosive."

Teddy had unbuttoned and was sprinkling the rock too, but the relevant muscles tightened so suddenly he doused the toes of his boots. He sucked air. "It's nuclear?"

"The gloves are coming off, Ted. The Chinese crossed a red line attacking Hawaii."

"So we're taking down this facility. What is it, exactly?"

"You have no need to know that. If any of your guys get captured, this was a simple raid by a bunch of rebels with Klacks."

"My guys know better than to get captured."

"This is going to be a hard one, Ted. You'll lose people just getting there. Maybe a lot more in the assault."

He shrugged. "Failing to plan means planning to fail."

Pancho and Leonardo sauntered out of the cave and joined them. Teddy nodded to the guard, who handed their rifles back. After handshakes and embraces all around, they and Vladimir set off downhill.

Shading his eyes, Teddy watched them shrink, until they were lost in the wilderness of tumbled rock that spread down the valley for mile on mile, from the Karakoram to the borders of Tajikistan, Pakistan, Afghanistan, India. The roof of the world. The perfect base area for a guerrilla war. A hundred thousand ridges and canyons and caves, where a million rebels could hide forever.

Unlike the desert. Flat. Exposed to the sky. No cover. Waterless.

You'll lose people just getting there. Maybe a lot more . . .

Operation Checkmate. He was beginning to identify with his rebels . . . eat with them . . . even pray with them.

Now he had to lead them into the Valley of the Shadow. With a price on his head, in case any of them cared more about cash than the Cause. Oh yeah—and with a charismatic ex–bin Ladenist asshole, who was already working to undermine him.

Guldulla climbed up to stand beside him, hand resting on the butt of his signature automatic pistol. "Lingxiù. What was the spy saying to you?"

"We have a new mission."

"What?"

"I'll tell you about it later."

"I see. But he is gone now? We can resume training?"

"He is gone, Tokarev." Teddy took a deep breath, looking into the rising sun, and let it out. "And as far as training . . . we're going to have to add some serious mountaineering."

14

USS *Rafael Peralta,* DDG-115 The South China Sea

THE Combat Information Center was darkened, its frigid air underscored with a solid grumble of noise. It leaned as the destroyer sliced through the night sea. Screens glowed with frosty light, as if the world outside could be viewed only through panes of ice.

Dan hadn't fully grasped the layout yet. Unlike the cruisers and destroyers he'd served on before, the functions here seemed fragmented. Antisubmarine here. Antiair, there. Antisurface, in yet a different place. Strike, ditto. Antiballistic defense, all the way across the compartment.

Oh, he understood. They were linked digitally, rather than by proximity. No one had to shout to another console to pass a command. Even a comment into a throat mike was rare. But seated in front of the large-screen displays at the command desk, he missed the sense of stovepiped support backing him up. He couldn't trade glances with the operator at the SPY-1 console, the way he'd done so often aboard *Savo Island.*

Savo. A mangled wreck at the bottom of Pearl Harbor. When he'd read that, something had wrenched inside his chest. As if his heart had been popped into another shape, like a protein flipping into a prion.

A nuclear strike on U.S. territory. Apparently the city center itself had been spared, protected by the old cruiser's last salvos, but still there'd been thousands of injuries and hundreds of deaths, both shipyard workers and civilians. While he'd been arguing with the Air Force about collateral damage.

But now, at long last, the Allies were punching back.

He slouched, rubbing his mouth. The screens showed only the baseline geographic plots, and feeds from mast-top infrared cameras. Deep night, deep war, and the strike group was running dark and quiet. The last enemy recon assets had been wiped from the sky, including the gauze-winged insectile spy drones he'd identified during hunter-killer operations in the central Pacific.

In retaliation for the attack on Hawaii, the strike on Hainan he'd planned in the PACOM basement had become Operation Uppercut. Surface and submarine assets were gradually enveloping the coast in a distributed-lethality filtering-in operation, spreading out the enemy's remaining surveillance and strike assets and complicating his targeting. SEAL teams were landing on outlying islands. U.S., Indian, and Australian submarines were clearing the lanes in, then laying mines to isolate the battlespace.

Massive as the movement was, he still suspected this was only a diversion. Part of a long-prepared combined offensive.

And he had to admit, since the Chinese had counted nuclear coup twice now, it was long overdue.

He'd heard rumors, and read the tea leaves. The Allies would apply pressure at multiple points. Squeezing the Associated Powers like a ball of plutonium, until fission occurred. Without much doubt, the main event would be the long-discussed assault on Taiwan. At the same time, the Indians were carrying out an offensive with three motorized divisions, to take the Pakistani-Chinese port of Gwadar.

He shivered in the frigid air, and reached for the foul-weather jacket he'd brought down from the bridge. Resistance would be stiff. As Allied forces closed the mainland, they'd come into range of a robust layering of defensive systems built up over decades. Some elements would be obsolescent—Soviet-era missiles, short-range diesel boats and fast missile craft—but still dangerous. Even a modern fleet could be overwhelmed by carefully timed mass attacks.

Not that he'd be in command. He was still attached to the PACOM staff, and as such, more or less a supernumerary aboard *Peralta*. Verstegen, the J-3, had wanted him here to help coordinate the mission.

"Prep going okay?"

It was Tim Simko, in charge of the raid. Short, dark-haired, round-headed, the strike group commander had gained weight over the years since Dan had played lacrosse with him at the Academy. But his classmate had bulked up even more since they'd last met, aboard USS *Vinson*, as the war started. His chubby face was pale, yet mottled with red patches. His gut strained at his web belt.

"Hot, straight, and normal," Dan told him.

Simko settled into the command seat with a sigh. He called up a formation diagram and meditated, head bent. Riffled through other screens fast as a card shark, fingers clicking busily. Then touched his throat mike. "EW, Simko. I don't see any lock-ons yet."

Dan started to shift to that circuit too, then didn't. Oversee the strike package, that was his job. Though all that remained, in the next few minutes, was launch.

Simko settled a bulky helmet-headset to rest on his shoulders. An armored-cable-and-hose tail trailed from it. Black goggles covered his eyes. Tiny optical phased-array cameras were mounted around the helmet, so the wearer could toggle back and forth from virtual reality to a 360-degree physical line of sight as well. It looked ominous, as if the ship's computers were consuming him, starting at the head.

Dan took a deep breath, lifted his own helmet, and settled it onto his shoulders. Ventilation spun up with a whisper, blowing cool air onto his forehead as the displays lit, read the curve of his eyeballs, and refocused. He toggled through them, quickly evaluating the internal ships' statuses, and booted up level after level.

Until at last he floated next to another male figure, to his right. Hovering together in space, they gazed out over an immense flat blue tabletop scored with latitude and longitude lines and layered with altitude readouts. With a click of his controller, radar emanations appeared in shades of yellow and green and red: neutral, friendly, and hostile.

Genderless and uninflected, the tactical AI spoke in a monotone. *"Surface contacts. Range, two hundred forty-seven nautical miles, sortieing from Hong Kong Harbor,"* it intoned. Then, *"Correlates with Luyang 2, Type 52D destroyer. Accompanied by . . . two Houbei-class missile catamarans. And four UAVs. Course one-niner-zero. Speed just increased to twenty-seven knots. Destination uncertain, but seventy percent probability intercept course, Pack Charlie."*

"Armament?" he muttered.

"Type 052D destroyer armament, AESA radar, 130mm main gun, torpedoes, 64-cell VLS with CY-5, CJ-10, YJ-83 antiship missiles, HHQ long-range SAM, quad-packed medium-range SAM."

"Range on the YJ-83s."

"YJ-83 has one-hundred-fifty-kilometer range at Mach point nine. Two-hundred-kilogram HE frag warhead. Active radar terminal guidance, secondary infrared. Peralta *P-sub-K ranges from point six*

to point eight. Optimal system is SM-2. Optimal intercept between fifty and one hundred kilometers. Optimal—"

"Enough."

The voice acknowledged the command. Simko's avatar issued another instruction, and glowing golden lines appeared. Weaving complexly, the computations converged on a solution, knitting together the advanced tracks of the moving forces to highlight nodes where they could engage the oncoming enemy with the lowest probability of loss.

Dan lifted his chin and ascended. The horizon receded, bowing into a curve. The enemy coast, seven hundred miles ahead, pushed up over it. Flung across scores of miles in a random-looking scattering, the advancing fleet was connected not by proximity, but by quantum-linked comms squirted up into a busy lace of low-orbit microsatellites, then down again to recipients. The baud rate was low, but adequate to coordinate movements and pass warnings.

Far ahead, over the enemy coast, blue contacts zigzagged and circled. Some of the emulators were Gremlins, air-launched UAVs dropped from mother ships. Others had come from submarines close in to the coast. They weren't just decoys. Some detected enemy radars. Others kamikaze'd in to detonate in fiery explosions. They milled in knots over bases and cities, coordinating their jamming. A few winked out as they were destroyed, but the cloud, like a roiling swarm of stinging midges, did not seem to thin.

Beside him again, hovering, Simko's avatar, in a green flight suit and without the bubble helmet, turned its head. "We have to make a choice," it said. "Go active, or see if we can get closer before we break EMCON."

"If you emit, you can be hit," Dan murmured.

It was hard to hide a fleet, even if it was communicating by vertical bursts. The answer Kitty Pickles had evolved, over dozens of game runs, had been to emulate *hundreds* of ships. They were converging on the coast in four separate "packs," only one of which consisted of actual ships and aircraft. If it worked, instead of the massive air and sea defenses the enemy could still muster, they would face only a quarter of them.

If, that is, the Chinese took the bait. And didn't have some sensor or leak, some key to their real intentions, that the Allies didn't know about.

* * *

FOUR days earlier, he'd stood sweating in the heat, observing tensely as marines cordoned off the pier and a crane slowly lowered thirteen slim gray switchblade shapes into cells aboard the destroyer.

The last nuclear-armed Tomahawks had been pulled from service years before, but the Air Force had kept the kits to retrofit them. And Sandia had stockpiled the physics packages.

The subsonic BGM-109G was considered slow these days, but its small cross section and extreme low-altitude profile should get it through the Chinese defenses. The old, laboriously programmed navigation system had been replaced with GPS-independent inertial guidance, mediated and updated by terrain-reading AI.

The cell had modeled the approach over and over. The Tomahawks would travel in three flights, separated by thirty seconds. Once air defenses had been suppressed by the Gremlins and Air Force standoff missiles, the Tomahawks would drill in from seaward, accelerating and reducing altitude as they neared the beach. The lead wave of eight, with conventional high-explosive warheads, would pass the submarine piers and the demagnetization facility six feet above the surface at low tide, below the tops of the piers. They would splay out to strike administrative buildings, repair facilities, the gates of the dry dock, and ammunition storage bunkers.

The second wave of three would proceed up the bay to the underground submarine facility. An autonomous probe had revealed a steel net draped across the entrance, as well as batteries of ten-barreled close-in guns. The second wave would target the emplacements and the netting, blowing both off the mountain and into the water.

The last ten simulation runs had ended with the two missiles of the final wave vanishing under the overhanging concrete brows, into the gaping maw of the access tunnels. Their warheads were the unglamorous but dependable W84. A two-stage thermonuclear package, a foot in diameter and a little less than a yard long, it could be dial-selected for yields up to 150 kilotons, ten times the destructive capacity of the Hiroshima burst. One hundred yards inside, they would trigger. The geologist they'd called in to predict weapon effects had said it would probably cave the whole mountain in, burying most of the residual radioactivity.

It would be as close to a surgical strike as was possible with nuclear weapons. Certainly it would be less savage and indiscriminate than Zhang's bombardment of Hawaii. Followed by additional waves of air-

and surface-launched strikes from the surface group, Uppercut should end with the effective destruction of both the island naval bases, Yulin and Longpo, as well as the Southern Fleet headquarters on the mainland opposite.

A time readout flickered into existence in his field of view. A countdown began flashing, numeral by numeral.

They had four minutes to launch.

SOMEONE was tapping his shoulder. He glanced to his left, but saw no one. And frowned, confused, before he understood, and separated his virtual self from his physical one.

He sighed, reached up, and lifted the helmet. Blinking, startled at finding himself back in the dark whirring confines of the CIC.

It was Harriss, who'd come up behind him. "Brett? What is it? I'm kind of occupied here."

The lieutenant bent in to call up something on Dan's keyboard. "A YouTube clip you need to see. Admiral Simko, too."

"YouTube?" Dan muttered.

Harriss tapped the Play icon, and a lovely familiar face came up. No one was sure if Shanghai Sue was one woman, or several, who looked and sounded so much alike they couldn't be distinguished. There were also those who said she wasn't human at all, but a computer animation. "We know your plans for China," she was saying, with only the trace of an accent. "And must warn those warmongers who seek to return the Middle Kingdom to the weakness and submission that the West has always desired.

"Marshal Zhang Zurong has promised a violent response to any violation of China's sacred sovereignty. He says again, with the most grave seriousness, that if the soil of the People's Empire is attacked, American soil will not remain inviolate. Anyone who has relatives in U.S. cities should tell them to escape to the countryside. For their health."

The smooth, high-cheekboned face's expression was so calm, its inflections and the movements of lips and arched eyebrows so symmetrical, that for a moment he wondered if it could be true, that she was an artificial visage projected by some intelligence greater than human. "As for the American flotilla advancing from their illegal and temporary lodgments in the eternally Chinese Xisha Islands," she added, "I speak of the task force centered at eighteen degrees, fifteen point four minutes north, one hundred thirteen degrees, eleven point nine minutes east. We are aware not only of your location, but of your intent. If you are wise, you will turn back now."

She paused to consult a note. "We speak directly to Admiral Timothy Simko, United States Navy. My dear Tim: Save yourself and the lives of your shipmates. Turn back now. Otherwise, you will all be destroyed within the next twenty minutes."

The clip ended. Harriss hovered, as if ready to receive an order. But Dan didn't have any.

Beside him Simko had taken off his helmet too. He looked shaken, even more flushed than before. "That's our latitude and longitude," he muttered. "To the fucking minute. WTF, over."

"I don't get it." Dan called across to the TAO, "Are we emitting, Commander?"

"No sir. EMCON Charlie on all circuits."

He fought a sinking feeling, searching desperately to understand. Detection at some point had been inevitable, but he'd hoped to get closer before launching. The shorter the flight, the less time the enemy had to react. Finally he said, "If they know where we are . . . there's no reason for us not to go active."

After a moment's hesitation Simko said, "I don't agree. They have to be tracking all four packs."

"Then how do they know we're the real strike force?"

"A guess. A bluff. Based on the centroid of whatever they've detected."

"Okay . . . Still, they can target based on that fix, however they got it."

"I'm going to pull left and go to flank speed. Get off the bull's-eye."

Dan wanted to say it didn't sound like a guess, but kept silent. He wasn't in command here, after all.

Seconds after the task force commander passed the new course, the seat slanted beneath him, though the artificial horizon in the VR stayed level. The effect was nauseating. A distant siren screamed. Around them men and women hastily donned flash hoods and pulled out masks and emergency breathing devices.

Burkes were sealed and pressurized against nuclear, bacteriological, and chemical attacks. Air locks protected each penetration of the skin of the ship. *Peralta* had heavier, more effective armor than earlier destroyers. But once that was penetrated, and toxic smoke or gas or radioactive particles filled one or more of the interior zones . . . He settled a flak jacket over his uniform. Pulled on flash gloves over control gauntlets, tucked trouser and sleeve cuffs, and settled the helmet back on, this time pulling out the weighted neckpieces to seal it to his shoulders. The helmets had their own filtration system, though they wouldn't supply oxygen. Worst case, he'd have to ditch it and don an escape breathing device.

But if that happened, they wouldn't be fighting anymore. Only scrambling desperately to escape a flaming hell.

He couldn't help remembering last year. The shaped-charge warhead that had blasted through the armored hull of USS *Hornet.* The fiery jet of incandescent metal had caught three watchstanders at their stations. Their lower torsos remained seated, cauterized black. Above the belt line, everything had been vaporized.

"We still launching?" he asked the avatar floating next to him. It turned its crewcut head, gaze aimed past him, and nodded.

"Two minutes," the sexless voice intoned. *"Preparing for thirteen-round engagement."*

He barely registered the litany as the strike team counted down the seconds, checked off switches and cutouts. He was white-knuckling it, trying not to let fear master him.

He wasn't afraid for himself. And not even for the men and women around him, within the skin of this ship, and aboard the dozen others flung out across miles of sea. Rushing into battle. It was what they'd signed on for, trained for, after all.

He was worrying about Nan, and Blair.

In World War II, Korea I, Vietnam, Afghanistan, Iraq, the civilians at home had been safe.

Now no one was. Zhang, along with his fellow dictators in Iran and North Korea, had made good on every threat they'd uttered in this war. The crackdowns in Tibet and Xinjiang and Mongolia, the mass shootings and concentration camps in Taiwan and Hong Kong had made his ruthlessness perfectly plain. He'd carried out reprisals against his own population.

If he threatened to incinerate Seattle . . . neither Nan nor Blair, nor millions of other Americans, were even remotely safe.

Yet this war had to be ended. Somehow.

A warning note gonged. The tactical AI advised that additional enemy forces had been detected. Gesturing his avatar higher, he saw them appearing, seemingly from nowhere. Not from the coast, but from the west, from the left flank.

But no surface units had been detected there. Aircraft? Angling out around Hainan to avoid detection? No, these new threats were emerging from a patch of empty sea. Circling, as if orienting themselves . . . then appearing to gain direction, intent, purposefulness.

A wave of contacts that even as he watched accelerated, settling into courses that led inexorably to the strike group.

The tactical AI's flat voice stated, *"Fifteen air contacts bearing two-eight-zero correlate with CM-709 submarine-launched antiship cruise missile. Range two hundred miles. Inertial guidance, millimeter wave homing. One-hundred-and-fifty-kilogram warhead."*

"There are no fucking submarines there," Simko observed. "We cleared that area."

"It's shallow enough you don't need a sub," Dan hissed. "They laid them in pods, on the seabed. Waiting for us to come in range."

"In *pods*?" The admiral's voice climbed, nearly broke.

"One minute to thirteen-round engagement."

"Launch early, launch *now*," Simko's avatar said. "Shift Aegis to self-defense mode. All units, go active. I say again, all sensors released."

The harsh chatter of a launch buzzer chiseled Dan's eardrums. He toggled to his helmet cameras. The large-screen display went from nighttime dark to glary, then blanked from smoke. Nine seconds later another star lifted from the foredeck. It rose, rose, canted, then shrank to a departing comet as the booster separated and the sustainer turbojet ignited.

"Missile two away," the 1MC announced. *"Three away . . . four away . . ."*

"The die is cast," Simko murmured.

Miles above the night sea, Dan rotated in space. Golden lines crisscrossed the scarlet reticulations of electromagnetic signals. Data beams were vertical lavender pillars, each marking a task force unit. Satellites twinkled above. Reports from secure chat scrolled up to the left of his vision. Callouts winked on and off. There seemed to be fewer blue ones over the coast.

The soft, agendered voice directed his attention to a second group of aircraft approaching from the east. From the airfields on Taiwan. *"Correlates to YJ-12 air-launched antiship missile,"* it observed.

"Range two hundred and fifty kilometers. Two-hundred-and-fifty-kilogram warhead. Supersonic sprint final approach. P-sub-K over eighty percent."

Dan hadn't expected this, either. The range was too great. But obviously the Chinese air force had refueled in midair. And the Allied diversions had been flimsy. Penetrable. Brushed aside like the first morning web of a summer spider.

A vibrating red dome of radar coverage wheeled into position overhead. He twisted in midair, but couldn't make out its source.

"Find this radar," Simko said in his ear, whether from headphones or his natural voice Dan could no longer distinguish. The real and virtual worlds were merging. But he couldn't get disoriented, or both would come crashing down. "EW, find it for me. Take it down, or we're going to get nailed by a ballistic homer."

Dan spun helplessly, turning in the air.

In a very few minutes, they could all be dead.

The Tomahawks would avenge them. They'd carry out the mission. Deliver the message.

But none of them would live to see that.

To the west, the red inverted carets of the CM-709s jumped ahead with each update. To the east, the air-launched YJ-12s drew quickly closer to the inverted boxes that meant friendly surface.

At twenty miles out, they accelerated to burst speed and streaked inward.

To contact. One after the other, elements of the strike group reported engaging. *Emerson Martin. Michael Kuklenski. McFaul. O'Kane. Detroit. Wichita. Fort Worth.*

The frigates went down first. Their symbols blinking dark on the displays. Then the destroyers.

Dan couldn't watch. He had his own mission to track. He toggled out of the high-altitude overview and dropped, dropped, until he was low to the sea, south of Hainan.

The Tomahawks inched ahead, creeping like snails compared to the hypersonic enemy weapons. But they flew below radar coverage, only a few feet above the surface. Spread out. Only as they approached the twin islets that guarded the entrance to Longpo Bay did they converge, joining up, falling into step in the triple waves he'd planned.

He tensed, zooming low to observe as the first flight threaded the needle.

They turned onto their courses for the piers, the ammunition storage, the administration buildings.

Then they began tracking around.

The lead missiles wheeled, making 90-degree turns to the left. They headed west, flashing over a long walkway connecting two of the islands.

Still powering westward, they crossed the empty bay, and, one after another, their callouts winked out as they slammed harmlessly into a bare rocky cape, fully five miles from any of their intended targets.

Thirty seconds behind, the second wave followed them. Instead of heading for the tunnel opening, blasting apart the gun batteries and steel nets that blocked it, they too made a hard left turn. Crossed the bay, and immolated themselves on the deserted cape, just as the first flight had.

He hovered, unable to draw breath, as the final two BGM-109Gs tracked in. They passed the outlying islands, running hot, straight, and normal. Jinking, to throw off any gun-radar tracking. Aiming straight for the tunnel entrance.

But at the last second, they too turned away, as if suddenly given a "by the left flank, march" order. Making the same 90-degree turn to port as the preceding flights, they angled away from the base, crossing the bay, heading for the cape.

But before they reached it, they leaned into another 90-degree turn. To port.

Now they were headed back out to sea.

A Priority message glowed on his helmet screen.

SHRAPNEL: STRIKE, THIS IS SHRAPNEL.

Shrapnel was *Peralta*'s call sign. For some reason, "Bluebeard" had been assigned to Dan.

Dan typed, without looking at his physical fingers.

BLUEBEARD: STRIKE, OVER.
SHRAPNEL: ARE YOU MONITORING OUR SPECIAL WEAPONS? THEY'VE BEEN CYBERJACKED. HEADING BACK OUT TO SEA.
BLUEBEARD: ARE THE WARHEADS STILL LIVE?

"What's happening, Captain?" Simko's avatar asked him.

Dan felt sick. "Someone's taken control of our 109Gs."

"Are they still live?"

He had to force out the words. "As far as we know."

"Fuck. *Fuck,*" Simko cursed softly.

Dan lifted, ascended, rising like Elijah until he could make out both the outlines of the bay and his surface group itself, 120 miles out. The pulsing blue extended tracks of the remaining Tomahawks intersected the Allied force.

Three hundred kilotons of thermonuclear hell was headed their way.

The picture wavered, swam, dissolved. It blanked, then regenerated. Wavered again.

"Cyber intrusion detected," the sexless voice said. *"Outside entity attempting to crash Aegis. Attempting to lock out our defensive systems. Virus intrusion alert! Rebooting. Regenerating. Re—"*

The virtual universe went black, and the voice cut off.

When he doffed his helmet, the ship's officers were snapping out orders, assigning weapons to incoming threats. Long-range Standards to the incoming Tomahawks and the lead elements of the incoming CM-709s. Shorter-range but supersonic Evolved Sea Sparrows, quad-packed in the vertical cells fore and aft, to the faster weapons arriving from the east.

The command screen in front of him, the large-screen displays, the radar picture, all wavered and blanked, then lit again as the ship's computers dueled the invisible intruder. Hollow thuds sounded from overhead as chaff mortars flung infrared flares and millions of millimeter-wave reflective dipoles into the air.

But the jaws were closing, east and west. Clamping down on the ships like a snacker on sweet morsels. On nuts, destined for crunching.

"We don't have enough to take down both strikes," Simko grated. "I've got three units in mission kill status already. Even if we can stop our own nukes, we need air support. We need more defensive weapons. Shit. Shit! They're going to decimate us."

Dan balanced the helmet in his lap. Pondering.

Then a choking noise, a harsh rapid panting, snapped his head around.

A rictus contorted Simko's face, which had gone purple. He clutched at his left arm, then his chest. Dan stared, then grabbed his hand. Their eyes met. "Admiral—you okay?"

"Chest . . ." Simko blinked rapidly, panted four rasping, laborious breaths. "Crap," he whispered. "Not again. Feels like my fucking . . ."

His eyes rolled upward, and he sagged back in the command chair.

"Holy crap," the staff TAO gulped.

"Corpsman—get a corpsman up here," Dan ordered. "ASAP. Right now."

The TAO hit a lever. *"Corpsman to CIC, on the double,"* boomed out over the 1MC.

Dan stared for one more second at the motionless form slumped beside him. He was still breathing, but barely. He didn't want to accept that Simko wasn't going to open his eyes again. That he wasn't going to resume command.

Then *Peralta*'s CO was bending over the admiral. "What happened?"

"He's out of action. Looks like a heart attack."

Their gazes crossed, and the CO's dropped. "Where's his number two?"

"His deputy's on the bridge," the TAO said.

Dan glanced back at the vertical displays. They flickered again, then steadied.

"Get the word to Higher," he told the CO, who looked startled, but nodded. He spoke rapidly to the TAO, who relayed the news. But Higher was a hundred miles astern.

Dan typed rapidly, addressing the group's air coordinator. The only thing he could think of to do. But if that action was to succeed, it couldn't wait for the admiral's chief of staff to get to CIC, get read in to, and be convinced to give the order.

He'd just have to give the command himself, and own up after the fact.

If they survived.

Seconds later, someone touched his arm. "Helmet's back up, sir," a female petty officer said.

When he lowered it over his head again, a blue haze fogged the northern horizon. "Come on," he muttered. "Come *on*."

The inverted carets of friendly air marched forward. But they weren't fighters. They were Gremlins, plus the UAVs the ships had launched earlier. Scores of the autonomous vehicles, called back from their orbits over the coastal bases. Angling seaward again, but not back to their mother-ship C-130s, or to the strike force, for recovery on their flight decks.

He'd ordered the UAVs, guided by their own synthetic intelligences, to head between the oncoming missiles and the Allied strike force.

Directed, now, to take out the attacking weapons. By any means, including their own destruction.

He turned his head to the right and toggled to the goggle cameras. Two corpsmen were hauling Simko out of his chair, laying him out on a litter. Fitting an oxygen mask. Administering an injection. The chief of staff was hovering, apparently more wrapped up in the admiral's condition than in the tactical emergency. The helmet display, the large screens, the radar pictures, blanked, regenerated, blanked as they crashed again. In the brief intervals they steadied, Dan noted more and more strike group units fading to black. Sweat prickled his forehead. Chatter resounded in the darkened space as human voices, nearly silent until now, shifted to voice circuits to pass targeting commands.

"Leaker. Leaker. Bearing two-seven-two."

"Engage with five-inch, Sea Whiz, Bushmaster."

"I say again, all topside personnel, take cover within the skin of the ship. Launch warning bell forward and aft."

"Activate CID. Activate decoys."

A flash of imagery from a flight deck camera showed self-defense drones leaping skyward from popped-open casings lining the helicopter nets. The bass *BRRR* of the Phalanxes filtered through the superstructure, with heavier jolts as the five-inch/62 and 25 mm Bushmasters opened fire.

The cameras cut in and out, a bewildering montage of strobe-rapid flashes on a dark horizon. The black dots of incoming weapons. A glimpse of surging flank-speed wake lit white-orange by gunflashes. A crazily canted quadcopter as it sped to intercept something beyond the camera's view. The combat system regenerated, then crashed again, jittering and blanking in tenths of a second. The ship's brain lightninged with epileptoid flashes as internal code clashed with the malignant interloper. The computer status display over the LSDs flickered madly, green-orange-red-green again, then back to red.

The chief of staff loomed over him, fists clenched, shouting, "You had no right. You had no right!"

Gripping the edge of the table, fingers tensed within the thick gauntlets, hunched and sweating under the heavy cowl and gloves and flak jacket, Dan Lenson ignored him. Squinting into the flicker, he waited for fate to decide the battle.

15

The Western Pacific

THE marines waited bowed under their loads, stacked in the slanted passageway. The night illuminations glowed like radioactive rubies. Engines bellowed down the ramp from the flight deck, funneled by slanted steel until their reverberation obliterated thought.

Hector Ramos pressed the switch on his intrasquad radio with his tongue. "Take a knee," he told his people.

Second Battalion, Third Marines, the same unit he'd landed on Itbayat with. But the only ones left from those days were a couple of lifers in the head shed.

And of course Hector. He walked the squad, looking into each man's or woman's face. Then went back to the head of the line and took a knee, fingering, in a pocket, the rosary Mirielle had once given him.

He hadn't lasted at Pendleton. The second time he'd slapped a recruit after coming back from leave, they'd shipped him back to his battalion. Not putting it in his record, since he wore the Heart and the Pacific Ribbon, but the Top had said he wasn't cut out to be an instructor. The good thing was, he'd gotten to go through predeployment with the platoon.

Now he was a squad leader, and for this operation, a heliteam leader as well. Tactical dispositions had been reorganized. New equipment and weapons had come through. A Marine rifle squad still had eighteen men and women, organized into three fire teams of six, and each team was still led by a corporal or lance corporal. But the teams were built around an M240B now instead of a light machine gun, increasing both firepower and basic load. All their weapons had suppressors. Their comms and logistics were secure against intrusion. Their jelly armor was tougher and lighter than steel. Their new goggles incorporated both night vision and BattleGlass data, and opaqued instantly when brushed by a laser. Their helmets protected them from explosive shock as well as projectile impact.

The platoon also had new members. The Chads were lined up on the other side of the ramp. These were different from the ones he'd trained with at Pendleton. The smaller-headed, thick-bodied C models stood motionless, shifting their "feet" only a bit as the ship rolled, multilensed oculars glinting in the red light.

Hector wondered why they always stood together. Wouldn't it make more sense to stand with the rest of the team? But whenever there were two or more, they clustered. Not under fire—they spaced out to combat distance then, like the human troops—but they seemed to prefer one another's company to that of flesh and blood.

Lieutenant Ffoulk jogged up the ramp as if surfacing through a deep crimson sea. Staff Sergeant Clay strode behind her. Ffoulk, radio call "Rampart," was short and African-American. Clay was white and six five. They stopped to talk to Glasscock, in Third Squad, then moved up to Hector. "Just so you're clear," the platoon commander shouted over the engines, her voice slightly too high. Hector glanced past her to Clay. "The platoon will land as second wave. Assault, seize, and defend the LZ. Link up to left and right, then push toward the terminal. That's your first objective. Try to limit damage in the terminal, especially to antennas and control equipment. Clay here will set up a CP, direct the tactical interaction between your squads, and coordinate with the other platoons. I'll be right behind you."

"Yeah, we pretty much got all that, ma'am," Hector told her. "Just like we drilled at Pohakuloa." He wondered if he should add *And don't feel like you got to be a hero, 'cause I sure don't*, but finally didn't.

"All right then." Ffoulk patted Hector's arm, punched his gut through the jelly armor, and marched on up the ramp.

Clay hung back. "Just keep talkin' to me," he asided, flicking Hector's mike so it popped in his ears. "Long as we got comms, rounds, and water, all gonna be okay. We been here before, Ramos. *Claro*?"

"Yeah, I got it." Hector looked after the officer. "Just don't let Lieutenant Fuck ffoulk us."

"Ha. I won't." Clay squinted the nearest troop up and down. He about-faced and stared at the Chads. Then wheeled again and hiked away, marching up the ramp after the lieutenant.

The illumination deepened to violet and began pulsing. Hector waited until the platoon ahead cleared, then extended an arm aft and swung it forward, palm down. The marines struggled to their feet and followed him.

Up, up, into the open night. A dark wind staggered them as they labored forward under assault packs, weapons and ammo, chow and water. The night flickered with invisible light, bellowing with the heavy *SHUMP SHUMP SHUMP* of huge rotors powering around. Navy flight deck crew in colored vests pointed light wands, shepherding them to the pickup point and warning them to stand clear of turbine danger areas.

Hector slapped the manifest into the loading assistant's palm, gripping it tight against the propwash, then pivoted to face the rear ramp of the MV-22. He bent to each man or woman as he or she boarded, rifle in hand, reminding each, "Strap in and signal when ready." The Chads came next, after the marines, but he didn't say anything to them.

When he had everyone accounted for, he gave the assistant the windup signal, and boarded.

THE sickeningly fast vertical takeoff squeezed his skull down into his shoulders. Vertigo reeled the narrow night-filled tube around him. The marines were lap-belted into fold-down canvas seats facing one another. The Chads sat on the deck, spaced out fore and aft. They'd bunched together during the rehearsal and nearly crashed the aircraft, making it tail-heavy. The interior bulkheads and overhead were lined with pipes and cables laced tight with white zip ties. Except for the bulkhead behind the pilots, which was one big switch panel, like the light console for a rock concert. Oxygen bottles and fire extinguishers vibrated above the seats. The whole fuselage shook. Everything rattled, boomed, or whined. No windows, but even after the rear ramp came up the back was still open. Though all there was to see was darkness.

Hector didn't want to look out anyway. He hunched, rifle clamped between his knees, trying to forget the last time he'd done this. In an amtrac, with his battle buddy Troy Whipkey, just before they'd been hit and most of the troops in the 'track had been killed.

This time it was the big one. The big island. Taking on the People's Liberation Army itself.

Taiwan.

A heavy impact from beneath the fuselage quivered the seats. But the crew chief, back by the ramp, didn't react. Hector couldn't see his face for the goggles and helmet, but apparently the bump and noise were normal. He hoped.

The briefers had said Guam was out of action, which complicated things, but there was a major airfield on Itbayat now, with heavy missile batteries, and the Philippines were letting supplies through even though they told the Chinese they weren't. Recon marines and SEALs had filtered over in small detachments to seize three small islands just off the coast. Enemy reinforcements were being cut off by U.S. and Japanese drones and submarines.

Operation Causeway would begin with the seizure of an airhead. The concept of operations, as briefed to the troops, had the first waves seizing an airfield and one of the few ports on the east coast, at Taitung. Once a perimeter was secure, air defense was in place, armor was landed, and logistics was coming in, they'd drive inland to link up with the local resistance on their right and the Army forces, landing at the southern tip of the island, to their left. It would be a hard slog through bad terrain, but when they broke out into the western plains, the armor could maneuver to pin down, surround, and destroy whatever was left of the occupation forces.

Hector hoped they could do it. The Marines had fought Chinese in the mountains before, at Chosin Reservoir, and barely managed to get out more or less intact. Every single briefer had warned it would be rough.

But that was was O-level stuff. He just needed to get his guys through today. He pushed it out of his mind as the aircraft pitched and rattled like an old pickup on a rough road.

A pickup. A rough road. The old veteran with the burned face . . . *It don't never go away, my man. It don't never.*

If this thing crashed, they'd all burn too.

He was checking the seating of his magazine when the dulcet-voiced tactical AI cooed in his earbuds, *"Rampart 1-2, Iron Dream, Five mikes."* He click-hissed to roger, tongued the button, and transmitted the heads-up to his squad.

He smacked a dry mouth, sucked a sip out of his CamelBak, and said a Hail Mary, squeezing his eyes shut. Afraid to the deepest pit of his gut. Not that he'd die, because he didn't actually give a shit anymore, but that he'd fuck up and get his people killed.

When he opened his eyes one of the Chads was watching him, tiny head cocked, its buglike, multilensed oculars glittering in the gloom as if lit from within. Its identifier, stenciled on its chest, read 323. They stared at each other for several seconds, both in silence, machine and man.

Something detonated outside, or maybe it was just flares being deployed. The airframe jolted, then rolled so far he grabbed for the seat frame. *"One mike,"* said Iron Dream in his earbuds. Then another voice, male. *"Heliteam leader, crew chief. You'll exit the aircraft facing south. The terminal will be to your right front. The fighter revetments, behind you. The ferry harbor will be on your left."*

"This is Rampart 1-2, roger. Thanks for the lift."

"Give 'em hell, Rampart."

They'd practiced fast roping during the rehearsal, but Higher had changed their minds about that when one of the Chads broke the rope. Seconds later the airframe jolted, hard, and Dream added, *"On deck."*

"This is crew chief: On deck, dropping ramp."

Hector popped his lap belt and hoisted to his feet. "Rampart 1-2, load and lock. Deplane, deplane!" he yelled.

THE first thing he saw as he jogged heavily down the rear ramp, burdened but jacked to the max, was the fires. They spread up the hillsides like lava eruptions. Bombs or heavy shells were going off to the west, so close together it was a long unending rumble, *BRUMPBRUMPBRUMP.* Bomb-lightning flickered above hills that poked up like black turrets to the north. He risked a quick glance back toward the harbor. Only a narrow strip of beach was sloped enough for the air-cushioned landing craft that would follow the Ospreys in and disgorge tanks, artillery, antiair. In his night vision hot green points circled above it. He hoped they were friendly. . . . Facing front . . . Fires glared along the runway, too. Tracers drifted up from around it, the red Chinese tracers crossing the green Allied ones in a dreamlike slow interleaving that was strangely beautiful. Weirdly entrancing . . . before they zipped earthward, abruptly gathering speed toward him. A circling aircraft darted down a solid-looking beam of white fire, searching out the emplacements. Wherever it touched, explosions flickered, erupting in artistic displays of fireworks.

He tore his attention back to the squad. They'd drilled LZ Bandit with three landing sites. The first wave had set up an initial perimeter on Orange Site, where he'd just landed. "On me," he transmitted, and followed it with a hand signal.

The Brooklyn-accented voice of Dolan, the First Squad leader: *"1-2, this is Rampart 1-1. See me? Over here. Guide on my right."* Bent low as bullets whacked down into the tarmac, Hector double-timed toward him. He passed Clay and the lieutenant, both down on a knee, speaking into their mikes. When he caught up, he angled to the right and set his men out in a defensive position.

But they couldn't stay here. They had to get off the runway. Several bodies from the first wave sprawled scattered around the strip already, though they'd only been on the ground a few seconds. A corpsman knelt beside one. He stood and a Chad stenciled with the Red Cross eased down to a squat. It lifted the body in its arms, rose smoothly, and walked after the medic with that queer gliding step.

Hector spoke rapidly on the net. Getting his fire teams out, lagging them by about twenty yards, so he could coordinate if they hit opposition. He linked up with the rest of the platoon, leapfrogging the teams forward so they could cover the point.

Another burst of fire came down on them from the side of the runway. A heavy machine gun. A helicopter roared low overhead and took it out with rockets. Fiery white disks cartwheeled into the air, shedding crackling scarlet sparks before crashing back to earth.

A tremendous noise came behind them, so loud it was almost solid. He twisted his head. An Osprey was falling from the sky, slowly, spinning as it fell. Figures scattered from beneath it. But not all could clear the impact area before they were wiped out by a massive orange blossom of flame. A dense cloud of smoke swept down on the platoon, layering them with choking oblivion and the stink of explosive and burned fuel. A crackle of rifle fire beyond it from the harbor meant those units were hitting resistance too. The bomb-flickers in the hills built, intensifying, until it seemed the earth itself must be coming apart out there, shivering loose and roaring down into the abyss between worlds.

A row of concrete barriers barred their way, before an open patch of grass. Beyond it stood the terminal, hangar buildings, the round white sphere of a radar dome. Hector radioed, "Hold up at the barriers. Chads: Advance in direction two-two-zero. Sweep for mines. Open fire on the building ahead." The mechanical forms separated from the humans, who took a knee to rest while the robots plodded ahead, zigzagging heavily across the open field like aging linemen. They lifted rifles and aimed, firing as they advanced.

The smoke thinned. When the skirmish line was halfway to the terminal, a three-story white concrete structure, fire lanced out at the advancing figures. Two blew apart in massive detonations as their power supplies triggered. The booms rolled across the open strip. The marines opened up at the gunflashes. The laser-ranged rounds lashed out, arching over the advancing robots, blowing out the second-floor windows as they detonated inside.

"Contact right, seven o'clock." Hector wheeled, snap firing as his IR sight picked up blurry warm shapes in front of a hangar opening. The flash of automatic weapons. Then a distinctive crack: the high-velocity Chinese DB 95 round going past.

A 64-grain bullet with a muzzle velocity of three thousand feet per second . . .

Taking him back to boot camp, the Hat leaning into his face . . .

"When fired from what?"

"Sir! When fired from a Type 95 rifle with a rate of 650 rounds per minute in full automatic fire. Sir!"

"What is the cost of the standard Chinese rifle round?"

A hoarse, tired bark. "Sir! Uh . . . This . . . recruit . . . does not know the cost of the Chinese, uh, whatever you said. Sir."

"You dumbass bullet stopper . . . The Chinese rifle round costs a yuan and a half. A yuan is worth ten cents. It costs the Marine Corps a million dollars to train each of you meatheads. It costs the People's Liberation Army fifteen cents to kill you. How in the name of Christ are we going to win this fucking war? Ramos, tell me the answer."

"Sir, this recruit is going to have to kill a shitload of Chinese, sir!"

He ran dry, swapped magazines, and tongued the mike. "Rampart 1, 1-2. Taking fire from right flank. Danger close. Two hundred meters. Request support."

Clay's voice, deliberate, reassuring. *"On it, 1-2. Continue toward terminal. Assault through objective and clear the building. Stand clear of the hangar area."*

A motion at the edge of his vision, and something exploded directly above his right-flank fire team. Figures reeled and collapsed. Another MG opened up, bullets sizzling past. A new explosion overhead sent fragments whickering down, boiling chips and spitting powder off the tops of the concrete barrier. The chips stung his face below the goggles. They were taking too much fire. Nobody was hitting the emplacements on his flank. What was Clay doing? Where was the lieutenant? They couldn't stay here.

He tongued the mike. "1-1, 1-3, this is 1-2. Cover us, we're going in."

Along the barrier, muzzles spat flame in a continuous stream. Hector vaulted the concrete, hoping the Chads hadn't missed any mines, and pounded awkwardly across the slick yielding grass toward the terminal. His lead fire team followed, with his other two echeloned out covering the flanks, the right-hand team firing steadily at the flashes from the MG position.

They were halfway across when a stream of blazing fire fell from the heavens and precessed along their flank two hundred meters out. The flashes blanked his goggles. The noise, like a million grinder wheels cutting steel, deafened him. He tripped and rolled as hostile fire ripped up the ground around him. A perfectly aimed burst, but to his surprise he didn't seem to be hit. He lurched the last few yards to the terminal and heaved a grenade through a shattered window.

Oculars glittered on the other side of the entrance. "Chad, clear the room!" he shouted. The robot nodded. It stepped forward, squared on the door, and took five long strides, gathering speed.

It hit the door like a battering ram, head tucked, shoulder down. The door folded and the robot rolled in like a wrecking ball. Hector pitched a second grenade after it. His assistant squad leader followed it with another.

When they exploded he stepped inside, crouched against the possibility of a bullet, and swept the room with his sights. A wide dark interior. Shining-slanted metal. Green carts set haphazard. Overhead signs in three languages. Oh yeah. The baggage area.

Gunflashes flickered from behind one of the carousels. Hector lasered and fired. The shell burst above the carousel, too high to do any good.

Another burst, from farther away. At least two shooters, covering each other as they fell back. Bullets caromed off the deck and ripped through the stacked carts. The lead Chad, the one that had jacked the door, hydraulic'd down to a bent-knee crouch. It looked painful, but it seemed to be a stable position for them. It fired three rounds. The lead fire team was putting out lead too, covering flanking moves by the others.

"Clear," the starboard team leader shouted over the net. *"Two Charlies down. Weapons clear. Moving on. Over."*

Pushing on, boots echoing in the empty concourse, they passed signs for restrooms and an abandoned serving cart to reach a wide flight of escalators. The power was off, so they weren't running. The level above was brighter. The waiting area.

Hector took out a foot-long tube, unsafed it, pointed it toward the steps, and squeezed the activator. The spring-loaded little drone popped out, unfurled its wings with a snap, and tumbled to the concrete, where it buzzed and spun like a dying cicada. "Fuck," Hector muttered, and stamped on it with a boot heel until the buzzing faded and it stopped twitching.

"Want mine?" said the assistant squad leader, Corporal Karamete. She held out another tube.

"No. I'm gonna send the Chads up. Stack your guys, get ready to follow." He backed into a corner by the baggage cart line, to avoid being surprised, and switched the lead robot to teleoperate.

With his goggles on remote, he was looking through its "eyes," listening through its "ears." The head position was locked to sensors on his exoskeleton, so when he turned his own head, the Chad's moved in sync. When he raised an arm, the robot raised one too. Hector hadn't done this often, and it felt disorienting, but he was surprised at how quickly he could merge his own reactions with what he was controlling. Like being in two bodies at once.

Hector/the Chad raised his rifle and swept the open, dark space. Above him the great panoramic windows were shattered, glassless, blind. Through them the explosions in the mountains flickered dimly and fitfully, with deep throbs of wavering sound he recognized as thermobarics. Somebody was bombing the shit out of whoever was out there.

The thing came out of the dark at him fast and quiet, its steps cushioned by soft footgear. He got the rifle half up before it had him . . . *swaddled.* He couldn't see exactly how, but when he went to lift the weapon the rest of the way, he couldn't move. A heavy web or net dragged at his arms. A dreamlike sensation, this silent, twilit struggle.

Then another motion drew his attention down, to where a metal disk was clinging to his breast armor.

The goggles seared, then died to black. Simultaneously a heavy detonation echoed down the stairwell. Hector crouched. So this was death. . . .

No. Not *his*. His puppet's, his other self's.

But what had attacked it? He tongued the intrasquad, then changed his mind. "Rampart, Rampart 2. Over."

"Rampart Actual, over. Where are you, 2?"

"Terminal. Foot of the stairs to the second deck."

"We're at the far end. Uh, the north end. Assault up the steps. We'll be on your right. Tell your guys. Ensure no blue on blue. Over."

Hector clicked his goggles back to IR mode and hand-signaled his teams toward the stairs. But he didn't give the go-ahead yet. "Rampart Actual, this is Rampart 2. One of our Chads got taken out by something weird. It ran up, immobilized him somehow, and stuck a shaped charge on his chest. He's DIA."

DIA was disabled in action, what they used for the Chads instead of KIA. The lieutenant wanted to know where the assailant was now. Hector said he didn't know.

Ffoulk sounded uncertain, but told them to push on up the steps while Glasscock's squad assaulted from the north end and Dolan's continued on up and took the second-floor balcony. *"Let's sew this up. I want this place secure by plus five."*

Hector rogered, but with a bad feeling. He took the lead on the right side of the escalators and went up totally slow. One foot in front of the other, sliding up a step, waiting, then another. On the far side, Karamete mimicked him. At the top Hector straightened, peering over the sights, searching the dark for motion. But even the enhanced goggles gave back nothing. He took a step and stumbled over a body. Not the Chad. A Chinese, a civilian, it looked like. But where was the disabled robot? What the fuck was a civvie doing here? Oh yeah. It was a civilian terminal, or had been before the mainlanders landed.

"Clear," his fire teams reported. *"Clear at this end." "Clear on the balcony."* He relayed that to Ffoulk, but got Clay instead. The platoon sergeant wanted casualty and ammo reports. The 81 mortar platoon, the antiarmor platoon, and a heavy MG platoon were moving in behind them. When they showed, he was to orient them and cover them as they set up for defense, then push out OPs in the fields beyond.

They seemed to have a breathing space. Hector sagged into a plastic chair facing the smashed-out window, happy that no one, except that single unlucky robot, had been lost. One guy had a twisted knee, there were a few fragment wounds and armor hits, but considering the storm of fire they'd had to sprint through, they'd been lucky.

Flashlights and voices. A uniformed team came striding up, pistols drawn, carrying drab green cases. "Sergeant? We need to get to the roof," their leader shouted. "Air Force combat controllers. Can you give us force protection?"

Hector checked with Clay, and detached Niegowski's team to escort them up to the roof. When they were gone he stretched out across the seats, propping his head on an armrest. The flutter-beat of helicopters pulsed though the windows. The follow-on waves. Once they had artillery, he'd feel a lot safer.

He couldn't believe they'd gotten off this easy. Maybe the slants were weaker than everybody thought? More likely they were being sucked in. Set up for a counterattack. Allowed to put a foot on the ground, so tanks could chop it off.

Shanghai Sue had threatened the Marines by name. Said they'd be wiped out. How were the Army landings going, down south? Maybe that was where all the enemy tanks had gone. Leaving the Marines in the Hanging Room, to be taken care of once the Chinese chewed up the Army.

Way above his pay grade. He pushed up the goggles and massaged his face. Until his earbuds crackled, *"Rampart, this is Actual. NCOs to me. By the coffee bar."*

Ffoulk, Clay, and a lance corporal with an antidrone rifle were accompanied by a figure that Hector recognized after a moment as the company commander. The captain beckoned him in. He and Glasscock and Dolan took a knee with him. Clay and Ffoulk were there too. "Anybody see an Air Force spotter team?" were the captain's first words.

Hector told him they were on the roof, with one of his fire teams. The company commander nodded. "Good. The 155s and Hawks are coming in. Resistance is light. We surprised them. Plus, we got Shucheng's people to carry out attacks up north, to draw their mobile forces."

Glasscock coughed into a fist. "Who's that, sir?"

The captain said, "Good question, Sergeant. General Luong Shucheng is the senior Taiwanese general still at large. Not all Chinese are going to be hostile, so don't assume that. The Taiwanese have sustained an insurgency in the mountains. They'll be our guides, our translators, and deal with the civil population for us.

"Our next objective will be the road north. Simultaneously, the rest of the force will secure our rear." He sketched on his pad, sending the map to their Glasses. The main road paralleled the beach a couple of miles in. "Depending on how the Army does, we can either push south to link up, or head north. If we're directed north, we'll probably hook west here—at Chishang—and punch inland along this canyon road. Which way we turn depends on how the southern landing goes. That's the main push, from the Army. We're out here on their flank more or less as a diversion."

The commander grinned. "At least, that's what they think. But Division suspects we can punch through those valleys and come out farther west. Maybe even get behind the enemy. Cut them off, plaster them with air, the Army pushes from the south, and we secure the whole island by D plus ten or so.

"That's it so far. Set up your perimeter where I'm indicating." A red line ignited in Hector's Glasses. "Implant sensors half a mile out and confirm they work. Then get some shuteye. Two on, two off. We'll shoot a resupply up on carts. Expect a movement order by dawn. Oorah?"

"Oorah," the squad leaders echoed. The echoes died away in the empty terminal, and over them rolled again the sodden endless surf-rumble of distant bombing.

As they broke Hector fumbled out the tube to his CamelBak. Suddenly, now that it was over, his hands shook. His mouth was parched. He gulped water, and followed it with a pill.

It was a plan. Yeah. The generals probably thought they were pretty fucking smart. Had it all figured out.

But he'd learned one thing, at least, from being in combat.

Nothing ever went like it was supposed to, once you met the enemy.

16

Long Beach, California

THE spring sunlight seemed concentrated down here, though they were far belowground. It shimmered from the concrete bottom of the dry dock. Commander Cheryl Staurulakis shaded her eyes, squinting up at where a series of thin flexible rods projected from the turn of the bilge.

The rods were the sensors of a new passive sonar system modeled on the whiskers of seals. The Naval Undersea Warfare Center had promised it would furnish as much information as the old active sonars, without putting sound in the water to reveal the listener's location.

She fought a sudden, disorienting déjà vu. Hadn't she been here before? In coveralls, boots, and hard hat, looking up as sparks coruscated down, and sunlight gleamed far above?

Yeah. When the message had come in giving her command of the old *Savo Island*.

Now another hull wedged the sky above her. But this was much larger, and its form was different, longer, squared off where the old cruiser's bottom had been round. She paced its length, examining the small, evenly spaced screwpods.

Then halted and bent over, resting her forearms on her knees. Fighting nausea, and memories.

As *Savo Island*, her bottom blown out by demolition charges, had settled into the mud of Pearl Harbor, the remaining crew had climbed down onto the tug's foredeck. Cheryl had headed them west, making for the Coast Guard air station at Barbers Point. Mooring at a barge access there, she'd led her crew ashore and reported in.

Some were still with her, busy aboard Hull #CGA-91, as the not-yet-commissioned ship looming overhead was still officially termed. Matt Mills was a lieutenant commander now. Bart Danenhower had gone to other new construction. Chief Wenck had gone elsewhere as well, but Master Chief McMottie and Lieutenant Jiminiz were here, overseeing the propulsion plant installation.

Everyone was being promoted these days. Beth Terranova was a chief. "The Terror" and Petty Officers Eastwood and Redmond were at the Missile Defense Agency, training on the new upgraded Aegis known as ALISE, with quantum processors. Hull 91 would carry the anti-ICBM upgrade of the Standard, the "Alliance," as well as new autonomous hypersonic strike missiles.

Cheryl hauled herself up the ladder toward the sunlight. *If* they could get to sea in time. After the nuclear attack on Hawaii, the war had taken a long stride deeper into night with the strike on Hainan and the invasion of Taiwan. No one seemed to know what the next step would be.

Or whether it would take them all over a cliff.

She emerged into a bustle of front loaders and a harsh cacophony. Cables and high-pressure air hoses serpentined across the concrete. Contractors' trucks packed the waterfront. Lines of men and women in hard hats and coveralls queued at the brow, toting test equipment and toolboxes. Grinders whined. A yellow yard crane suspended a massive generator above a gaping hole above which the flight deck would soon be installed.

Blinking in the sudden sunlight, Cheryl shaded her eyes, surveying her ship from stem to stern. Mills was walking the deck, carrying a clipboard. He raised a hand; she waved back. He pointed to the quarterdeck and raised his eyebrows. She nodded. Who needed the Hydra on her belt? She and her new XO could communicate without words.

The Savo Island–class cruisers were based on Zumwalt hulls, but with more seaworthy bows. The hangar was belowdecks, as in the Virginia-class nuclear cruisers. They could launch swarm attack drones as well as manned helicopters. Radiating forty megawatts from a twenty-foot ICBM-intercept-capable radar made hiding impossible, so the ships were designed to survive heavy damage. Their all-steel superstructures sloped like pyramids. Beneath the steel, graphene/Kevlar armor protected CIC, the magazines, and the machinery spaces. The blast-hardened panels of the dual-band radars could operate with as few as 10 percent of their radiating elements remaining.

Missiles were still the main weapons, and they had double the magazine capacity of Ticonderogas. But the new cruisers also carried electrically powered railguns fore and aft, plus hundred-kilowatt combined-fiber lasers, to take down incoming targets quickly and in almost unlimited numbers.

But the biggest changes were belowdecks. Extra command and control spaces and comms. No shafts or reduction gears, but electric propulsion motors directly coupled to propellers. A through-hull access well that let them deploy undersea vehicles. The crew not only had a citadel deep in her guts, but could fight from there; CIC was encapsulated, NBC-proofed, and armored.

Powering it all were turbogenerators that would run the entire weapons and sensor suites while pushing the ship at forty knots. The computing architecture was run on glass, not copper wire. It was EMP-hardened and isolated against cyberhacking.

And of course the ship could fight on her own. Her combat system was directed by a Watson-derived tactical AI. Some of her designers had questioned the need for a human presence at all.

The new Alliance missile was forty inches in diameter, instead of the old Standard's twenty-one inches . . . one reason why the new cruisers had to be so much larger. The whole ship was double the displacement of the old *Savo*, but manned by a crew half as large. They were almost all ashore now, at the class training facility in Norfolk. Cheryl had split her own time since returning to the States between there and the yard, overseeing construction.

Which unfortunately was running into snags. Most of the modules had already been assembled when she was released from the hospital after the stem cell replenishment. But a lot remained to be done, and it wasn't going smoothly. The new turbogenerators didn't seem to be testing out. Which was why the #2 generator dangled now motionless above the ship, instead of being lowered into position and bolted down.

And not only that . . .

Four bongs sounded as she wheeled onto the gangway and began climbing. *"Precom det 91, arriving,"* said the ship's 1MC.

The ship wasn't commissioned yet, so there was no ensign to salute. She nodded at the security watch as Mills approached. "Disturbing rumor, Skipper."

"What've we got, XO?"

"A work stoppage. Or rumor of one."

"From whom?"

"Electrical workers."

She considered this as they walked forward. "I thought strikes were outlawed. You know, the Defense of Freedom Act."

"It definitely outlaws a lot of things we used to take for granted."

"Down, boy. We need to get this ship to sea."

Mills lifted his head, and the breeze ruffled blond hair that glittered in the sun. She stared, fascinated. So much like Eddie's . . . "I know, Skipper. I just think we're getting more like the People's Empire the longer we fight them."

"Off the record, I agree. But . . . this rumor?"

"I was talking to the lead shipfitter. They're getting paid barely enough to get by, with inflation. Can't buy food for their families. But that apparently isn't the real reason."

They stepped over cables on the foredeck. She forced her gaze away from his profile. "What's the real reason?"

"LA's the bull's-eye, the guy said. Ground zero. But if they leave their jobs, their cards get pulled and they go straight to camp. Not exactly how you motivate people. Maybe why we're seeing so many piping welds failing inspection."

"All right, I'll see what I can do," she murmured, though she didn't see what. She couldn't change how Washington was organizing the home front. The only person she could even think of asking was Captain Lenson's wife. Blair was apparently some mucky-muck high in the administration now.

They went over the day's to-do list, then parted. She tracked his easy saunter between the massive armored hatches of the missile cells. They yawned empty now, festooned with test cabling, but soon the massive long missiles would be lowered slowly into them. Lowered . . . then withdrawn, oh so slowly . . .

She shook her head. It didn't take Sigmund Freud to interpret that image.

THAT afternoon, at the shipyard commander's office. It overlooked the dry docks where the cruisers were being built. Other ships, including one of the new escort carriers, were moored along the outer seawall, being completed or in for repair of battle damage.

The gray-haired black man tented his fingers. "I understand you're not happy with the rate of progress on 91."

"Not unhappy, no. Just . . . I don't understand why we're the lead ship of the class, but *Itbayat Island* seems to have priority. I know you're doing all you can, Captain. I'm just eager to get back to sea. You can understand that?"

The shipyard commander rubbed his eyes. Benjamin Cadden was a retread, a reactivated thirty-year retiree. He had peacetime ribbons on his service dress blues: Meritorious Service, Navy Commendation, the Achievement Medal, and the Armed Forces Service Medal, along with the new yellow-and-brown Pacific War Service Medal, awarded to anyone in uniform during the current unpleasantness.

"We owe you a lot, Captain," he began. "You saved thousands of lives. Prevented the invasion of Hawaii."

She relaxed a little. Maybe this would go her way. "We're not sure exactly what we contributed, sir."

"You shot down six warheads. Only bad luck two got through."

She contemplated setting him straight. There was no way to tell how many live warheads the DF-41 had carried, and thus, how effective her salvo had been. Her team had been locked down during the intercept, and the terminal bodies in question had been knocked off course and gone into the sea. Except, of course, for the ones that had wrecked Pearl Harbor and Hickam Air Force Base.

On the other hand, since fighters had made it into the air before the nuclear strike, the Air Force had been able to intercept and annihilate the Chinese raiding force. She finally compromised with, "We did the best we could."

Cadden smiled. "I mention it only to preface that if there was anything I could do for you, I would. But my orders are to get the first hull to sea ASAP. SUPSHIPS direction: Better one ship now than three next year. I have limited manpower, especially machinists and welders. And components . . . well, our supply chain has withered. Which is one reason those are Tesla truck motors in your pods."

"I thought that was for quieting."

"That too, but we can't forge a shaft for a major combatant anymore. We had one supplier, in Erie. A ten-thousand-ton hydraulic press with computer controls. It woke up one night and hammered itself to pieces. Anyway, that's why I've reallocated work hours."

She turned on a smile. "I understand that, Captain. What can I do to lighten your load?"

His frown read *You could start by getting off my desk*, but his next glance, at her decorations, which included the Navy Cross and now the Silver Star for Hawaii, apparently silenced his actually saying it.

Well, so be it. She'd argued her case. Heck, maybe try a little charm? She wasn't above that. She laid a hand on his. "My crew's eager to get back in the war, sir. I'd so appreciate it if you could do anything at all to advance our schedule. Without impacting *Itbayat Island*'s, of course."

Cadden glanced at her hand, and she removed it. Added, "Um, also . . . I heard a rumor about a slowdown. By the electricians?"

His gaze narrowed. "Where'd you hear that?"

"Waterfront scuttlebutt. Among the yardbirds."

"Not 'yardbirds,' Captain. They're shipyard personnel, doing the best they can under a wartime workload. And a lot of other challenges."

"Sorry. I didn't mean . . . but . . . what *are* their other challenges?"

He sat back, looking cunning. Then innocent. Then cunning again. He tapped a pen on the desk. "You know, it might be a good idea . . . might be, to talk to them yourself."

"Happy to, if you think it would help. Is there a point of contact?"

"That would be Teju Yeiyah. Organizer for Local 40. I think you know him."

"I don't believe I do, but I'll find him. . . . So, next issue. My generators. I understand they didn't pass acceptance tests."

The yard commander sighed. "I'll explain this all to you again, Captain. . . ."

THE afternoon shadows lay velvety deep behind warehouses and workshops. She snatched off her hard hat as soon as she was outside the wire, and blotted sweat from her hairline with her old *Savo* shemagh. It was getting ragged, worn from too many shipboard launderings. The olive and black were both fading to gray. Only a few crew members still had them. They were a badge of honor now. Lenson had bought them in Dubai, after the clash with the Iranian Revolutionary Guard. . . . Why was it so fucking *hot* here? She wiped her face again. No breeze from the sea. And no air-conditioning inside the ship, since too many accesses were open for work.

She really didn't feel well. Nauseated. Weak. Actually, she hadn't been herself since the stem cell replacement. She'd have died, of course, without it. After the neutron flux from the close-in burst, then the exposure to fallout on the tug. But she still didn't feel normal.

Not to mention fighting depression, and mourning Eddie . . .

The man hopped nimbly down from his perch on a lube oil drum as she approached the pier. "Good to see you again, Captain," he called.

When he held out a hand, a tattoo of a dragon decorated his bare forearm. Yeah, she *had* seen this guy, at the work-progress conferences. His skin was so smooth she wanted to touch it, like a fine light brown leather. His black hair was cut short in front, longer in back. Muscle threaded his arms, and those tanned fingers gripped like iron. But not as if he was trying to intimidate. Just that . . . he was strong. Blue jeans and a leather tool belt were slung low on his hips. "Teju Yeiyah. Organizer for IFPTE Local 40. You wanted a chance to talk?"

"Thank you. I understand you're contemplating a slowdown. At least, that's what I heard."

The organizer shook his head. His eyes were a deep warm brown, the lashes long and dark enough to make any woman envious. "I can't comment on that."

"Sorry, I don't understand." Cheryl forced her attention back to the conversation. "You can't comment?"

"Advocating a stoppage, that's treason. So it's best if I just don't say anything."

She rubbed her chin, nonplussed. "So you're *not* contemplating one?"

Yeiyah looked away. "You brought it up. Not me."

"Because I heard a rumor. If there's no grounds for it, neither of us needs to waste our time. Don't worry about me turning you in to Homeland Security. I would never do that. I need your folks here."

He said reluctantly, "There might be some basis in fact."

"Thanks. If there is, what's driving it? A pay issue? What're you guys paid, anyway? Guess I should know that already."

"No reason why. Base rate's sixty-five an hour blue-collar, more for brazers, welders, electricians, shipfitters, fiber fitters, et cetera et cetera. That's for six days a week, ten hours a day. We protested that, no overtime, I mean, and got shut down. Fact, our legislative liaison got threatened with prison."

"Who by? Captain Cadden?"

Yeiyah relaxed back onto his perch on the barrel. He cocked one leg up, holding it with interlocked fingers. "Benny? He's not a bad guy. It's the Homeland cops. Actually, we're lucky we still have a union at all."

Cheryl glanced around, making sure no one was in earshot. It felt strange to fear other Americans, but the new security agencies didn't limit themselves to running the detention centers in Indiana and Oklahoma where enemy nationals had been confined, or to hunting down actual spies. Digital public information signs, TV ads, and Twitter posts gave email addresses where Associated Powers sympathizers, or "asssymps," peace activists or "antiwas," and other opponents of the state could be denounced. After drumhead hearings they went to the Zones, and delators got half the value of their confiscated belongings.

But she and Yeiyah seemed to be alone here, except for gangs of workers coming off the brows and trudging for the gate. Who didn't so much as look their way. "So this isn't a pay issue?"

"Ten years ago sixty-five an hour would have been great. But now a loaf of bread's twenty bucks, and forget about a Big Mac with fries and a supersize shake. They pay you on a chip card. After taxes, surtaxes, and the bank's ten percent cybersecurity fee, there's not much left.

"But the main problem is, a lot of our guys are missing family. They're immigrants, single, and a lot of those that aren't, they've moved their families back to wherever home was. But Honolulu scared everybody. They listen to Shanghai Sue, about what Zhang's threatening to do to LA next. And there's not enough calories in the individual ration to keep working for ten hours. They get here hungry, they work hungry, they get back to the barracks late and miss chow."

"I agree, that's not right." She felt guilty. The first thing they taught you at OCS: Take care of your people. Okay, maybe these weren't *hers*. They were Cadden's, if anyone's. But they were building her ship, and she hadn't even realized that the workers lived isolated in barracks. Much less that they were malnourished. She said tentatively, "Would it help if we provided some messing?"

"Could you do that?"

"I have a discretionary budget. For incidentals, and commissioning. But we don't need an expensive ceremony. How much would it be? How many guys, I mean people, are we talking about?"

"I'd have to get back to you on that. Around three hundred? Ballpark."

She did a quick calculation on her phone. "We'll do breakfast and lunch. Starting Friday. Nothing fancy. Oatmeal. Pancakes. Wraps and tacos, for lunch. With an apple for roughage, or salad."

"Roughage, huh." He smirked. "Rabbit chow."

"Don't give me that look. Everybody needs it. Um, would that be enough? To keep everybody fed and working?"

"It'd sure help. It's not that we're not patriotic, but . . . shit, you know what I'm sayin'. That would be appreciated. If it happens. We get a crapload of promises, you know?"

"I keep mine," she told him firmly.

"Uh-huh. Okay."

"Are there stoppages planned for *Itbayat*?"

He bent a sharp glance on her then. Oh, no, she thought, I've made him suspicious again.

"I don't know," he said coldly. "I told you that. Look, we didn't have this conversation, okay? And I don't want my name mentioned."

"Of course. Sorry I asked."

"No problem. I just might trust you." He hopped down again, stretched like a cat, and thrust out his hand. "Till later, Captain."

She couldn't help eyeing his blue-jeaned behind as he loped away. The guy had to be ten years younger than she was. Well . . . maybe eight. Or even just six? He'd seemed interested, too. She hadn't seen a ring. Though they might take them off during work hours, to avoid accidents.

She scratched absently between her fingers, although there was no rash there now. It had become a habit. Noticing only then that she wasn't wearing her own gold band either. She hadn't for several days.

"Yeah," she muttered. "I keep my promises."

She couldn't help imagining what Eddie would have come back with, though.

Sure you do, babe.

Sure you do.

17

Jet Propulsion Laboratory, California Institute of Technology

THE huge open bay was dazzlingly lit, but in a curious rum-butterscotchy hue. Blair's Louboutin heels grated and slid on grit the color of dried blood as she neared a patch of rocks and heaped dirt under a high-arching dome.

The center administrator said, "It's what the sky on Mars would look like. Varying from a deep brown to a sand-tinged blue, especially at dawn and dusk. We tested the Curiosity rovers here."

The JPL at Caltech had been lead for robotic exploration of the planets, asteroids, and outer solar system, including Voyager, Cassini, Juno, Rover, Dawn, and others. But NASA had been redirected to war projects for two years. Now a dozen congressmen, staffers, and military officers were getting a classified introduction to the results, not just from JPL, but from Glenn, Goddard, Langley, Johnson, Ames, Kennedy, and other federal research facilities.

As their footsteps crunched onward, the director said, "As you may imagine, our work with orbiters, rovers, and landers has given us the ability to build near-autonomous probes capable of withstanding the cold of space and the heat of the sun. They can operate for years, if not decades, without repair or recharging.

"This project began with a Venus flier we started five years ago. Trugon—the Greek name of the turtledove, Aphrodite's sacred bird—had to withstand both the vacuum and cold of space and the enormous heat and pressure of the planetary surface. It had to self-charge and self-deploy, since it takes several minutes for external commands to reach Venus. We kept the name for the mission, but redirected our efforts. As you'll see.

"Ladies and gentlemen, meet Trugon Beta."

Something buzzed softly. For a moment, she couldn't tell from where. Then part of the red soil shrugged aside. A machine, perhaps the size of an adult hawk, or a rather oversized Frisbee, slowly rose, propelled by some invisible-to-her means of levitation. It hovered at head level, eyeing the group with turreted lenses from atop a curved carapace. They clicked from one to the next, as if memorizing their faces. Then it glided to one side. As it crossed a patch of shadow, it changed color and shade to mimic the new background. Shadows chased themselves across its surface. Even from fifteen feet away, it was hard to focus on the machine. Its outline seemed to waver as it blended chameleon-like with the backdrop.

She slowly realized it wasn't alone. From under the soil, under the rocks—indeed, from the tiled floor around them—other shapes were lifting, surrounding them with a whirring, insectlike chitter. A chill harrowed her spine; she couldn't help shivering at an unnerving impression of malevolent observation, of cold, evaluating intelligence.

"Are they armed?" one of the congresswomen asked, arms crossed over her chest. She sounded as uneasy as Blair felt.

"We're working on weapons mounts, but the primary mission is observation. As you know, we have few humint assets inside China, Iran, Korea, Tajikistan, Pakistan, and the other zones of conflict. Our observation satellites were shot down or blinded at the opening of hostilities. We have Mice up now, but the Chinese are using smoke obscuration and camouflage to screen their sensitive areas from above."

Responding to some collective decision, the individual units drifted together, interlocked with echoing clicks, and ascended as a single mass toward the far-above ceiling. "DARPA tasked us with changing that."

Blair lifted a hand. "How will you deploy these . . . machines?"

"Trugon is self-deploying. We can release it from outside the borders, or air-drop it as close to sites of interest as possible. The upper carapace is not only active camouflage and impact protection, it's also a highly efficient solar panel. Recharging by day, flying at low altitude by night, these units can cover four hundred kilometers in a diurnal cycle. Reaching their assigned overwatch points, they select discreet positions with good fields of view. Then land, dig in, and hide."

Another lifted hand. "How do they transmit their—pictures?—back?"

"Scrambled burst transmissions, at very low power. Undetectable, unless you're right on top of them. And it's not just images they'll send."

A general cleared his throat. "I'm assuming these will go in near airfields, major roads, missile bases."

"Correct, but also within industrial installations and near command points—their sensors can pick up computer data transmissions. In tests, we've decoded keystrokes from three hundred and fifty meters, and Bluetooth-frequency transmissions from much farther.

"As to follow-on development . . . You've seen an example of early cooperative behavior." He waved at the hovering, humming swarm above them. "Trugon Gamma will be capable of true intelligent thought: selecting patrol routes, identifying targets, plotting approaches, and autonomous mass attack. A self-directing weapon, cheap, easy to deploy, and capable of hiding until conditions are ripe for assault.

"We'll have the first two hundred production units operational within weeks. The first run's being built by 3D Robotics. Mattel will deliver a thousand more a month later. General Atomics and AeroVironment, the legacy drone makers, are fully tasked. We needed mass production and wanted it cheap. That's why we went with the toymakers."

"What happens if they're discovered?" a staffer asked. "Couldn't the enemy turn them, transmit back misleading information?"

"Excellent question. Which leads us into a demonstration. Those of you off to the right, there, you might want to move back a few yards."

A unit detached from the swarm still hovering ominously overhead. It dropped to the soil, burrowed under a wheelbarrow-sized rock, and vanished, except for a glint of lens and a stub antenna, which repainted itself rust-red. "This is one of our prototypes. Outmoded, but useful as a demonstrator. Let's see what happens if it's noticed."

Across the dome, a tracked robot, some kind of rover, whirred into life. As it ground forward the turret focused on its approach. Almost fearfully, Blair thought. The turret retracted, as did the antenna, leaving only a curved surface the same color and granularity as the soil around it. It seemed to stir once, shifting slightly under the friable red sand around it.

But the rover kept boring in. It oriented clumsily, whining, then telescoped a steel grasper arm.

With an earsplitting crack, a smoke of fragments and gray blast gas enveloped the rover, which staggered back, rocking on its tracks. When the smoke cleared, dozens of silvery gashes gleamed on its paint.

The director said, "An antipersonnel charge, focused toward the disturbing agent. The blast not only destroys our probe, but acts to discourage further attempts to find or investigate others."

And what if a curious child finds one? she wanted to ask. But merely questioning the war effort in public was treason. She compressed her lips.

The director announced their next demonstration, in an adjoining lab. No one spoke as they left the whirring swarm behind, dozens of lenses still tracking them as they somewhat nervously strolled away.

Instinctively, Blair tried not to limp.

THE tour had begun with the Naval Research Laboratory, then moved on to the Lockheed plants in Alabama, the revitalized land-based strategic deterrent forces in Wyoming, Montana, and North Dakota, the huge Archipelago campus just outside Seattle, and the Defense Innovation Unit in San Francisco. Finally, they headed back to Pasadena.

There were a few bright spots in the generally dark overall picture of the war. Zhang had made the mistake of thinking this would be a short conflict. Of course so had the U.S., but the Chinese response had been to halt research that wouldn't produce short-term results. Their leading facilities had been closed or cut back, the personnel drafted. And some, such as the research campuses in Shenzhen, had been targeted in Allied raids and cyberattacks, though it was difficult to gauge if significant damage had been inflicted.

The NRL had showcased autonomous submarines and mine-torpedoes that penetrated harbors on their own. Lockheed, the new F-40 and AAF-X fighters, and soft-kill antimissile systems. Other companies had demonstrated armored battle robots, to make up for Allied shortfalls in fighting manpower, and a line-of-sight weapon that combined fusion and X-ray lasers to generate a lethal beam.

The only area where the enemy seemed clearly to be ahead was in cyberwar. But that might, in the end, be enough to decide the battle.

Jade Emperor, wherever and whatever it was, had outmaneuvered its American digital adversary, Battle Eagle, again and again. It had taken down power grids, crippled financial markets, melted routers, ATMs, and air traffic control computers with malware, deleted medical and payment records, ransacked databases and corrupted their contents, and siphoned billions of digital dollars from Vanguard, Schwab, and Fidelity into shadowland accounts. A DEA report said half the Chinese weapons purchases from Russia had been paid for in stolen U.S. dollars. Of late it had sucker punched American cyberteams, fabricating dummy sites that consumed enormous effort to penetrate . . . to reveal even more cunningly designed viruses lurking within.

The shell game left the U.S. players staggering away, computers riddled with code so virulent they had to junk the useless, hopelessly compromised machines.

Worst of all, evidence showed, over and over, that the repositories of advanced Allied weapons technology had been Trojan-horsed, and cyberdrained of the most advanced specs, tests, and production data.

Jade Emperor, which seemed to be growing more cunning and stealthier by the week, was turning the whole U.S. research effort into a free resource for China.

She wondered if Zhang had been right, after all, to dismantle his own scientific infrastructure. Clever . . . and thrifty.

Why feed the cow, when you can steal all the milk you want?

THAT evening she flopped into a chair at an executive inn on Colorado Boulevard. The room smelled musty and the carpets felt matted and sticky underfoot. The clerk had seemed absurdly grateful to accept her government housing voucher. Without air travel except for government flights, and few trustworthy means of buying goods or services other than cash, a lot of businesses had gone under. Defense hiring had taken up some of that slack, but not all.

So many were hurting . . . and now the combatants were about to field a whole new generation of weapons. Driven by the inevitable spur of war . . . The bed creaked as she sat on it. She rubbed her face with both hands, wishing Dan were there. Sometimes you could have fun even on a lumpy mattress, in a creaky bed.

But even more than that, she missed having someone she could trust to be on her side. No matter what.

She sighed. Glanced toward the bathroom. Maybe a shower . . . Instead she got up to check the minibar, conscious of a sudden overwhelming anxiety. A gin and tonic . . . but the bar was nearly bare. No gin, but an off-brand vodka that might do the trick.

She built a stiff drink and flipped through tomorrow's schedule. Up early, 0400, to head back to Washington. She opened her notebook and started typing notes for her trip report.

The hotel landline rang. She almost didn't answer, but picked up unwillingly on the sixth ring. "Hello?"

"Ms. Blair Titus?" An unfamiliar female voice, the accent Indian? Bangladeshi?

"Mmm . . . Who's this?"

"Can you hold for the honorable Liz McManus?"

The chairperson of the UN conference she'd attended in Dublin. But why was McManus calling her? And how had she even gotten the number? "Yes, I can hold."

McManus was on the line almost at once. "Blair? Your office said you were in California. This isn't a bad time?"

"No, no, I was just putting my feet up . . . it's ten at night. What time is it there? Where are you, anyway?"

"In Bruges. It's early morning here."

"What can I do for you, Ms. McManus?"

"Liz, please. I was asked to relay a message. From . . . the young gentleman you met in Dublin."

For a moment she stared at the dusty drapes, groping. Did Liz mean some illicit rendezvous? She almost laughed. With her schedule these days, how could she fit one in, even if she wanted to. "Um, I'm not following. Young gentleman?"

"He says you met at Queen of Tarts. And had quite a fascinating conversation."

She nodded, suddenly grasping what was going on. McManus, no doubt assuming this phone conversation might be bugged, was casting it as a personal call, a heads-up between girls. "Uh, oh. Oh, yes. The one with dark hair, right? Yeah, he's a serious, um, hunk." Good grief; she sounded so dated. What did twenty-somethings say now?

"I wish I were in your shoes. He sounds eager to see you again."

"Um, that may be difficult. But he's . . . What else did he say? Anything about me?"

"Just that he wanted to get in touch again. He left a Gmail address."

She pulled a hotel notepad over, biting her lip as she scribbled. Fucking hotel pens . . . Gmail was totally unsecure, but maybe Xie Yunlong thought that out in the open was the best way to conduct a sub-rosa negotiation. But their exchange at the pastry shop hadn't left her with the impression there was any air between whomever he represented and the Zhang regime.

On the other hand, she shouldn't have expected anything major to be revealed or discussed at a first contact. Maybe Yun had needed time to assemble a peace offer. Or to consult with whoever in the Chinese state, party, or army had asked him to set up a back channel.

A third possibility was that this was a trap. Laid either by the enemy, to draw in and then destroy her, or by someone on her own side, to see if she could be tempted to divulge confidential information. A sting operation. She slowly drew a honeybee on the corner of the pad, then added a smiling face. Her second bee, fatter, wore a truculent scowl and dark-framed glasses. "Any idea what he has in mind?"

A chuckle. "What do all the lads always have in mind?"

"Good point. But I'm a little older than guys his age usually go for."

"You're a good-looking woman, Blair. I still get offers myself. You might be astonished. But let's not go into that!"

She chuckled, though it felt forced. "I take it he wants to meet up?"

"I'm not sure he's able to. He said his . . . wife is jealous. So don't tell anyone else. The woman keeps close tabs on him. And she may have a friend, someone you know as well. Which is why he's getting in touch via me. A go-between, you might say."

Blair licked her lips. An *extremely* unsettling piece of information, that about the "wife" knowing someone *she* knew. "Um, understandable. I'll think about getting back to him. If he calls you again, um, for the record, I really liked his—I liked his cologne. Okay? You can say that. And see if there's another way to talk. Other than email. And thank you for passing on the, uh, the pass, I guess." She tried for a breathless giggle, but it didn't sound convincing.

McManus said that was what friends were for, that she hoped they would meet again someday, and after a few more neutral words they hung up.

She topped off her drink with a shaking hand, and propped bare feet up again. The ice in her glass was actually clattering.

Obviously the Irish diplomat had passed her the approach in the hope of at least getting the opposing sides talking. Which *might* be good.

But she, Blair, wasn't about to open an email exchange with the Chinese, in any way, shape, or form. The draconian penalties of the Defense of Freedom Act aside, both the Chinese and the Russians had doxed Allied cable and email exchanges . . . hacked and then altered them, then released them on WikiLeaks and alt–fake news sites: all part of a separate propaganda war that took place in another sphere than the real war, but that many overseas (and some in the U.S., too) took for gospel.

Play in tar, and some will always stick.

On the other hand, if someone in the other side's command structure was actually reaching out, looking for a way to end hostilities short of mutual catastrophe, shouldn't she pursue it? Szerenci wanted war to the knife, total carnage. Judging by some of the national security adviser's remarks, he seemed to regard a nuclear exchange with optimism. But she'd read about the German generals' attempts to reach out to the Allies, both in 1939 and later, as the war turned dark for the Axis. Both times the Allies had looked away, or treated the feelers with such suspicion they'd never yielded any benefit.

Resulting, perhaps, in millions of unnecessary deaths.

If Zhang's generals were getting disenchanted, the way Saddam's generals had, she couldn't ignore this.

There was only one thing to do. It was risky. But it was the only way she could both pursue this outstretched hand, and defuse any suspicion of treachery on her part.

Setting up the notebook, she logged on to the hotel's Wi-Fi. These days the internet went up and down like a carousel horse, but at the moment, she had bars.

But she hesitated, fingers poised trembling above the keys.

Nothing online was safe. Never type anything you didn't want read. Even her DoD quasi-quantum scrambler might theoretically be penetrated, given enough computing power. Which Jade Emperor seemed to have.

And not only that. What if she *did* message Szerenci? He'd be mistrustful. Would grill her. Grow angry she hadn't reported the approach in Dublin. Grow suspicious of her? Perfectly possible, given their history. And if she asked, Should I respond? He'd just say, Have to get back to you on that. Leaving her in exactly the same place, but degrading their working relationship.

Could she bypass him? Take it to Ricardo Vincenzo? The JCS chair seemed less eager to prosecute this war to the bitter end. Maybe, more open to a negotiated solution. If one was possible.

She slowly lowered her poised hands. Then after a moment, closed the notebook.

No. She had to tell Szerenci.

But it would be better to do so face-to-face.

THE next morning, 0400. Stumbling around, groggy. Never having been a morning person. Throwing things together, only slightly fortified by bitter brew from the room's coffeemaker, so acidic it almost made her throw up. She grabbed a Danish in the lobby as she whisked past, toward the car waiting outside.

The roads were empty, and not just because of the early hour. Fuel rationing kept most people home, or close to work. From a devolving-to-1957 economy, the United States was now regressing toward 1912. Some in the rural areas were hitching horses to trailers, reinventing the pony cart.

This war had to end. Soon, or both Asia and North America would suffer for generations.

The Air Force plant shared with a regional airport. The plant side was busy; the civilian side, deserted. The car stopped at a two-engine business jet. Two others, men who'd attended the briefings with her, were waiting to board. She nodded to the Air Force general who'd asked about the Trugon reconnaissance positioning the day before, and a scientist who consulted for Lockheed. A Jeep Wrangler was parked a few yards away, and a pair of paunchy and graying "M&Ms"—Mobilized Militia—with red-white-blue armbands and hunting rifles stood between a fuel truck and the air terminal.

A pilot in uniform came back from examining the forward landing gear, saluted the general, nodded to her, and ushered them aboard. Her roll-on bumped painfully against her bad hip as she maneuvered it into an overhead bin. She sank gratefully into a seat, snapped on a reading light, and flipped her notebook open.

"This is your pilot speaking. Madam Undersecretary, General, Dr. Pirrell, welcome to the U.S. Air Force, 89th Squadron, out of Joint Base Andrews, from Pasadena to Joint Base Andrews."

The engines spooled upward. The wheels bumped over seams in the concrete. Then she was pressed back in her seat. Out of habit, she glanced at her watch. 0537.

They hurtled, climbing. Outside her window, the city's gridded streets so queerly resembled the 3-D microcircuits she'd been shown in briefing after briefing it gave rise to uneasy musings. Which one truly held more intelligence? And how easily a single nuclear airburst could erase the millions spread helplessly below. The city scrolled aft, replaced by blue tormented mountains, glazed here and there with what looked like late snow, though that was hard to believe, warm as Pasadena had been.

An hour droned past. Each time she glanced out, the landscape below looked drier and more mountainous. They must be over Arizona. Cowboy country. She opened her notebook, and was soon deep into a report on the effectiveness of six hundred Israeli top-attack fire-and-forget antitank weapons that had been placed in the hands of the Vietnamese People's Army.

WHEN it happened she felt nothing. Or perhaps the tiniest jolt, a slight bump of turbulence. No shock wave, and no blow to the airframe. But after several seconds they started a gentle bank, pressing her against the side of the seat. Her glass walked toward the edge of her tray. She grabbed, but too late; it tipped, spilling soda over her stocking, and bounced away. "Crap," she muttered, mopping with a napkin.

"Can I help you with that?" said the general. She accepted his napkin as well.

The plane steadied on what seemed to be a new course.

The general was frowning. He seemed to be listening to something she couldn't hear, like a dog picking up a silent whistle. After a moment he unbuckled and went forward. Tapped at the bulkhead door. It opened, and he slipped inside.

"This is the pilot . . . a little glitch up here. Autopilot disengaged for a sec. Regaining control now."

She called up another document and began reading.

SOME minutes later the general came back. He settled into his seat again. "Problem up front?" she muttered, still absorbed in a report on influenza viruses.

"Glitch in the autopilot, like he said. A transient."

"Serious?"

"Not really. No."

But when she glanced out, noting the position of the sun again, something didn't seem right. "Uh . . . weren't we headed east?"

The general frowned. "Should be."

"I agree. Yet Mr. Sun says we aren't."

He peered out, brow furrowed. "Damn. Good eye, ma'am."

"Call me Blair, please."

"Rick Ackert. Air Force Strategic Development Planning & Experimentation Office, out of Wright-Pat." They shook hands. "Excuse me, I'll go see what's happening."

This time he was gone longer. Blair glanced across the aisle at the scientist. He seemed to be sleeping, head back, eyes closed.

When she looked out again they were still headed north. A worm writhed under the surface of her calm.

Ackert came back looking worried. He stood in the aisle, gripping a seat back. "Uh, guys?" The other passenger looked up. "Got a problem up forward. As the undersecretary noted, we're off course. Thought at first we had a missed input in our flight computers. However, our navigation systems are involved too."

The civilian said, "An EMP pulse?"

"Um, considered that, Dr. Pirrell, but rejected it. A strong EMP shock would do more damage. Not just the computers but the electrical system . . . popping circuit breakers, frying our other electronics."

"Solar activity? Lightning?"

"Solar might cause radio interference, but not loss of control. And it's pretty dramatic, when you're struck by lightning. We'd know that. The charge is conducted through the exterior skin and exits. Usually leaves a burn hole."

Blair stirred in her seat. "*Loss of control?* What exactly is happening, Rick?"

"Well . . . to be perfectly frank . . . we don't seem to be flying the aircraft anymore."

She and the scientist exchanged glances. "How about manual control?" Pirrell asked.

Ackert glanced toward the cockpit, as if longing to be back there, but turned to face them again. "Navigation and autoflight computers help the pilots fly. With the older models, pilots make direct inputs to the flight surfaces—the ailerons, elevators, rudder. Worst that can happen then is hydraulic failure, losing the amplification of the control inputs."

She nodded. "And?"

"But with newer aircraft, like this"—he glanced forward again—"they're fly-by-wire. The pilots input commands to a computer, which then moves the control surfaces. We fly it, but indirectly."

"Then it could be EMP," Pirrell insisted.

"Again, we didn't see any evidence." Ackert scowled. "And, actually, everything seems to be running perfectly. Except that the nav system says we're going east, while the autoflight computer's taking us north."

"Reboot the autopilot," Pirrell suggested.

"Getting ready to try that," the general said, but his lips tightened after he said it.

"What's your data source?" Pirrell asked.

"Our databases? Uh, well, our nav computers are periodically, routinely, reloaded with updated data as that information changes."

"How often?"

"Usually on a bimonthly schedule."

"When was it done last?"

"I'm not sure."

"Well, could be corrupted. I could see that."

"Corrupted, how?" Blair put in.

"Reloading the flight logic computer with a rogue program. One that allows the autoflight to take over and fly a preprogrammed route."

"So, essentially, we've been hijacked?" Blair said. "Like 9/11? Only without a live terrorist in the cockpit?"

Neither man disagreed. She rubbed suddenly damp palms on her skirt. She'd been in the South Tower that day. Had watched the first airliner approach, then plunge into the World Trade Center, shooting bodies and flame out the other side. Had been burned and broken, as the South Tower too was hit and collapsed. Had nearly died.

She carried the scars to this day. Burn-scars, her shattered hip, her ear . . . She forced words past something hard in her throat. "And where's it taking us?"

"Nav still shows our final destination as Andrews. As per the original flight plan."

The cabin audio clicked on. *"This is your pilot. General Ackert is explaining the situation to you. There's no need to feel anxious. We're initiating a reboot of the flight system. May be some turbulence. But after that, we'll regain control. Please make sure your seat restraints are fastened, and secure any drinks or loose objects about the cabin."*

She was already belted in, but tightened the restraints. Then looked anxiously out the window. At green-and-brown mountains, veined by rivers, far below.

"Coming up on reboot . . . now."

A jolt. The nose rotated slightly, then settled back down.

With a shudder, something clunked above her. The sound was succeeded by a faint whistle. Her ears popped. Then again, more forcefully.

A bit of gas wormed out before she could stop it. A barely audible fart. Neither man seemed to notice, though, and she almost giggled. Actually she felt quite euphoric now. What had she been so worried about? Silly to think anything could go wrong.

When she lifted her hand, her fingernails looked odd. Darker at their root. She frowned. When she glanced up, the atmosphere in the cabin seemed to have gone misty. Foggy.

A compartment popped open above her. An orange plastic mask jangled on a transparent coil. But her vision was blurring. Still feeling happy, she groped for the mask. It evaded her hand as the aircraft sideslipped. Ha-ha. Like her cat Jimbo chasing the spot from his laser mouse.

She finally got hold of it, still chuckling, and clumsily strapped it on. The euphoria disappeared instantly, leaving her terrified. Her vision cleared, though her heart was still doing fast laps and she was hiccuping, close to puking. She twisted in the seat. Ackert, his own mask already on, was fitting one to the scientist, whose face was going blue. . . . "Rick. Rick! What's happened?"

"This is your pilot . . . just experienced decompression at altitude. Please don masks. And stay in your seats, firmly belted in."

"That shouldn't have happened," the general muttered. He looked apprehensive. "We need to descend below ten thousand. Cabin oxygen only lasts for fifteen minutes."

"Or what?" Though she was pretty sure she knew.

He looked grim. "Hypoxia. You start losing higher brain functions. Reasoning. Eventually, brain death. If they can't repressurize."

"Which is under the plane's control, right? So you're basically saying it's trying to kill us?"

He looked away, taking several deep breaths. Then heaved himself up, removed his mask, and went forward again.

She hesitated, then unbuckled and leaned across the aisle. The plastic tube reached just far enough for her to make sure Pirrell's mask was sealed, that he was getting oxygen. His skin was shading toward pink from the near blue of moments ago, but he still didn't respond to a yell, or even a sharp pinch.

The plane jolted. She floated up off her feet, then crashed down again. She hauled herself quickly down beside the civilian, and belted in again.

She was trying her cell, but of course without success, when Ackert returned. "The reboot didn't help. It's something in the software."

"A Trojan horse? A back door?"

He reattached his mask. "Whoever put it there, it's deep in the basic software. Even after the reboot, we go back to the same course."

"Do we know where?"

"Jack plotted it on a lap board. We're headed toward Albuquerque." He hesitated. "About a hundred miles off our flight path."

"Albuquerque," she echoed. "Sandia?"

"Or Los Alamos." He nodded. "Sandia makes the guidance chips, actuators, for the new strategic missiles. Los Alamos assembles the warheads on the mesa. Even if that's it, we won't know which is the actual target until the last couple of minutes out."

By which time it would be too late to do anything to save either themselves, or whoever was at the intended point of impact. She tried to put her own danger out of her mind. "We have to warn them. We declared an emergency, right?"

"No can do. Remember, we don't have air traffic control anymore. ATC lost their radar at the beginning of the war."

"But if this is a zero day virus . . . more planes may be headed for the same target. Or others. A mass attack. We have to get someone to . . . to shoot them down."

"I hope it won't come to that," Ackert said grimly. "But—"

"But if it does, they have to be warned. Somehow." She tapped her phone again, but again got no signal. "Is there any way to—"

"Jack's trying to raise someone on the emergency transmitter. So far, no joy."

The airframe juddered as if tormented by parasites. Probably the pilot was trying to take back control. Something whined from aft. But the nose always swung back to the same heading, a compass needle inexorably returning to its predetermined goal.

She couldn't believe how quickly a routine flight had turned them into unwilling suicide bombers. Imprisoned in an out-of-control weapon, bound for its own destruction—and theirs. On one level, she had to admire it. The plan was masterful. Someone, whether Chinese, Russian, or an internal turncoat, had filtered or dodged level after level of security and protection and buried the programming—most likely during a routine update. Penetrated the Air Force's systems and the builder's, without setting off any alarms.

Until the plane was in the air, in range of its intended target.

Incredibly clever, and chillingly inhuman.

The question was: who?

Maybe . . . Jade Emperor?

Oxygen still hissed into her mask, but for how long? She took a deep breath, then regretted it. How many more minutes of conscious life did she own? "We have to end this flight, Rick. Before we pass out. Crash it, if we have to. Like the passengers did on United 93, at Shanksville."

Ackert rolled his eyes. "We've discussed that in the cockpit. Believe me. Unfortunately, we don't have control of any of the automatic systems. Just lucky the oxygen sensor for the masks was hardwired, or we'd be dead already. Jack's trying to dump fuel. If he can do that, at least we won't reach the target. Maybe we can regain control at a lower altitude."

But he didn't sound hopeful. And that solution, even to her, didn't sound very likely. Whoever had designed this virus had anticipated how they would react, and forestalled it.

Beside her in the seat, the civilian twitched. His eyelids fluttered, then flew open. He flailed about. A fist caught her on the eyebrow. Ackert bent over him, pinning his arms and shouting in a high, strange-sounding voice. The cabin pressure was still dropping. But when she looked out the window, the ground was closer, more imminent. Shouldn't the air be growing thicker as they descended?

The general patted her shoulder. "Stay with him, okay? I'm going to see if I can help out somehow."

"What else can I do? Look, do we even have parachutes?" Even as she asked, she saw the answer in his averted gaze. A shake of his head confirmed it.

"What's goin' on? A hijacking?" Pirrell muttered woozily.

"Sort of," she told him. "But the pilots have it under control."

No good would come of his freaking out, even if these were the last seconds of their lives.

* * *

OVER the next few minutes she tried to make peace with . . . whatever. It didn't take all that long. Really, she'd done what she wanted to do with her life. Except maybe Congress. And frankly, her work now at DoD was more vital to the war than holding down a plush seat in the House. Her mom would miss her. Dan too, of course. For that matter, so would her cat. As for the rest . . . well, she'd done the best she could.

But she couldn't just sit still. Finally she unbelted and went forward. The cockpit door was unlocked. When she peered in, Ackert and the two pilots were deep in discussion over a paperbound manual. "What's going on?" she asked.

The general looked up. "Might be a solution. It's off-the-wall, but . . ."

"Hey, I get it. What?"

"If we have corrupted flight-control logic . . . we're going to have to completely depower in flight."

"And that will—?"

"Conceivably, that might let us regain control."

"But you already tried to reboot," she pointed out.

The pilot nodded. "But that just reinitialized the bad code. This time, we'll disconnect the engine-driven generators. Turn off the control breakers. Then cycle the battery switch off momentarily."

"That should depower all systems," Ackert said.

"Yes, sir. We pull out the breakers for the computers. Then, flip the battery and the generator control breakers back on. That might repower the flight controls, while leaving the computers out of the loop."

The engines spooled downward just then. Both men glanced out the window, as if looking at the turbines might restart them. "Out of fuel," the pilot sighed.

She couldn't believe it. "We're *out of fuel*?"

The copilot kept flicking switches. He mumbled, "We dumped it, remember?"

"But will we even fly without the computer?" Blair feared it was a dumb question, but she had to ask.

"That's what we don't know," Ackert said. "How 'bout it, Jack?"

"Sometimes we electrically depower on the ground."

"And do you have control then? When you do that?"

"We don't try the control surfaces then. I'm just gonna hope they left some residual control built in." The pilot was flicking switches again.

The engines had stopped, leaving only a whistling, rushing roar from outside the skin of the falling plane.

She clung to the back of the copilot's seat, staring past him at the onrushing ground. At mountains. Canyons. Mesas. At tan-and-russet rock, revealing itself now in all-too-high-resolution detail.

"You two better get belted back in," the pilot said, not looking away from his controls. "I'm looking for somewhere flat. You know the drill, General. Head down, and if we make it in one piece, exit the aircraft as soon as you can." He reached overhead and pulled a block of black plastic out of the overhead. The breakers, she assumed.

Back in her seat, she assumed the position. Belted in, head down, folded forward. Clutching her knees. The aircraft shuddering, still nose down, still headed for the now terrifyingly close arid-looking surface rushing toward them.

At the last moment the nose lifted. She felt suddenly heavy, then light, then heavy again. The right wing came up. Something tan and brown and frighteningly close flashed by at incredible speed.

They slammed down with a bang. She screamed, shaken like a battered child as the belt all but cut her in two. The interior blurred. The window burst apart. The last thing she registered was the piercing, never-ending scream of metal being ripped apart like rotten cloth by hurtling rock. Then it all went black.

18

In the Tien Shan Mountains

THE dark was impenetrable at the bottom of the valley. At fourteen thousand feet Teddy gasped for breath at each uphill. His head swam.

The younger men around him plodded on, chattering among themselves. They'd grown up at altitude. But he had to keep up. To lead.

He was the Lingxiù, after all. Lingxiù Oberg al-Amriki, as they called him now.

He grunted, hoisting one boot after the other, leaning into the climb. Little more than a goat trail, the valley-bottom route the locals were leading them on wound along a rushing nullah, a snowmelt-fed stream, between boulders and over the sloped rubble-piles of landslides. Each step had to be studied before he took it, while the locals scampered along as if living under a different regime of gravity.

The stars were emerald pinpoints in the optics of the night vision. The mountains, obsidian shadow. The men were blobby amoebas with legs, their packs and rifles showing up darker, colder, in the infrared. At night it was below freezing this high up. In the daytime, men fell out from sunstroke, and the rock valleys trapped the heat until it was like an oven set on Bake.

He was retracing his steps, in a way. He, Ragger Fierros, and the two Vietnamese, the aged, blinded Major Trinh and Sergeant Vu, had marched this way in their epic escape from POW Camp 576. Though not over these exact trails, which were much higher and deeper in the mountains. They'd lost Magpie, the Australian, getting through the wire. Then left Vu crumpled in a crevasse after a failed traverse.

His bones were still out here somewhere, probably picked white by the vultures.

Teddy halted and bent, trying to catch his breath. In four days they'd made only fifty miles, led by local guides paid with Vladimir's gold Krugerrands. Marching at night, holing up by day in the caves and clefts that rived these precipitous steepnesses. The most energetic outflankers carried the drone detectors, setting them up on peaks ahead of their progress. They carried short-range radios, too, to serve as outer security.

The main body stuck to the valleys, unless they had to cross a ridgeline. A hundred men, with MANPADs, light machine guns, and RPGs. They traveled in column, twenty meters between each squad, Teddy up with the first fire team.

Slung on his back, adding to the load, he toted the beam gun. He glanced back at a thin short form burdened with gear as well. Dandan climbed ten steps behind, carrying his rice, their blankets, and his rifle. Behind her came two of his sturdiest rebels, with the Package slung between them. The sleek black ovoid was wrapped in heavy canvas and padded with dried grass. In case the worst happened, on some perpendicular incline.

The line halted. Teddy looked up. "Oh, crap," he muttered.

The cliffside was studded with wooden pegs and flattish rocks hammered into crevices. A blurry blob swung from one to the next, like a sailor up a ratline. One of the guides. But they weren't burdened the way his men were.

The column waited while the lead man belayed a climbing rope. Teddy squatted, chewing on a piece of corn-and-apple bread. The line moved up a few yards, then halted again.

Finally it was his turn. He shrugged his burden higher and searched with his fingers for a hold. A splintery balk of wood, already worn slick by many hands and feet. His boot started to slide off, and he grabbed for the rope. Balanced there, clinging like a baby opossum to its mother's fur, he swore and groped for the next step.

Up, and up. The chuckle of the nullah grew distant. He panted, wheezing, and almost fell again. Hands reached down to help him along. After a hundred feet the vertical climb gave way to a two-foot-wide shelf that led upward at a steep angle, but that at least meant he could dangle his hands. The gulf to his left seemed to call to him. It exerted a magnetic force. All he'd need to do would be lean out from the rock face, let the drop take him . . . Gazing into the abyss, it gazes into you. . . . He couldn't remember where he'd read that. A bumper sticker? This would make a hell of a movie. Once, he'd wanted to make movies.

Once upon a time, a lifetime ago.

A chasm opened between two peaks. The green shadows of the goggles showed dizzying cliffs thirty meters deep. A storming river was wedged between, foaming and leaping in a long stone-punctured ladder down the mountain. A chilly mist wetted his face like cold sweat. A flashlight-flicker outlined a figure ahead, kneeling seemingly in midair, swaying between the craggy faces of rock.

"You got to be kidding me," he muttered.

When he reached the spanning, he had to take deep breaths. It was barely recognizable as a bridge. Just three ropes. A hemp cable, maybe two inches in diameter, where the men ahead of him were placing their feet. To each side, smaller lines were strung for handholds. Thin lashings of braided leather every couple of yards connected the side-ropes to the central cable. But there was more empty air than actual bridge, and from the lip of the cliff the cable headed almost straight down before leveling out halfway across, then climbing again. The guides danced over it, crooning some native song that merged with the clashing roar of the waterfall below. The rebels followed more cautiously, gripping the handropes, halting occasionally to stare down.

Behind him Dandan squeaked, "*Obe, wo hàipà.*"

"*Jin jin zhua zhù shéngzi,*" Teddy told her, pulling her after him. "*Rúguo ni diào xiàlái wo huì jie zhù ni.*" Then thought: Why in the heck am I reassuring her? She's gotta cross it anyway.

His troops were watching. He couldn't hesitate. Grabbing the ropes on either side, he forced himself out. The first couple of steps were okay, but then his boot slipped again.

"Fuck," he muttered, realizing it was because the mist was freezing on the foot-cable. Not only was he swaying a hundred yards above a river full of rocks, he was walking on ice. Dandan, behind, was crowding him, almost hugging him. "Back off," he snapped over his shoulder.

A low moan behind him. "*Wwo hàipà . . . wo hàipà.*" Her little voice, already high, was shaking.

"I know you're fucking scared. Just suck it up, bitch." He caught a back-turned grin; one of the guerrillas. "Or you're gonna get yourself a beating tonight," he told her.

Facing front again, he hauled himself another few paces forward. Midway? Nearly midway? Maybe this wouldn't be too bad.

Then, under his boots, the bridge started to sway.

He leaned the other way, but somehow that made it worse. He caught a glimpse of the men ahead leaning in the opposite direction. The bridge swung out, hesitated, then headed back. It apexed, then reversed its swing with a whiplashing, violent twist. Someone was retching so violently it was audible over the roar of the rock-echoing river.

"Give me a break," Teddy muttered. "Don't barf on the fucking cable." The bridge swayed back, gathering momentum for another wild crack-the-whip. Crouching, he gripped the handropes so hard his fists cramped, cursing desperately as he rose, floated sickeningly, then plunged downward again. Even if it didn't snap under them, this thing was going to dump them all into the gorge.

Behind him Dandan whimpered something about him not caring, about no one ever caring. A rebel behind them laughed. Jesus, it was as bad as being married! Enraged, he twisted on the swaying ropes, and aimed a vicious backhand. His flattened hand slammed into something soft, and she gave a short scream just as his boots slipped again on the icy hemp, almost sending him into the roaring chasm below.

When he recovered his balance and looked back again, she was gone. Just that quickly. Leaving only the echo of her scream, a wider than usual gap in the lashings, and her cap, fluttering away, being sucked down into the boiling mist.

As if pacified, the rope-span lost its rhythm, gentling again to something resembling navigability. The men carrying the Package were looking down, into the thundering emptiness from which fresh eddies of chill moisture eddied up. "Where'd she go?" Teddy asked them.

A white-eyed glance was his only answer.

TWO hours on, he was still thinking about Dandan. Guilty, a little, but angry, too. The stupid bitch had taken his rifle, ammo, food, batteries, his prayer rug, and his bedroll down into the river with her. When all she'd had to do was keep her fucking mouth shut and follow him. He'd treated her well, considering. If it hadn't been for him, she'd have been a slave for somebody really nasty.

His stewing was interrupted by the crackle of his short-range radio. He crouched against an icy boulder on slanting slippery scree. "This is Lingxiù. Go."

"Forward outpost. Drone signal detected. Signal strength weak."

He considered. Signal strength should be at least medium before the drone was close enough to pick them up. On the other hand, the mountains barriered electronic signals. Meaning that if the detector wasn't absolutely on the highest point around, the incoming machine could suddenly pop over a ridge and have them in its sights before they could react.

Well, at least it hadn't come by when they were on the cliffside, or even worse, pinned to that fucking bridge. Reluctantly, because they were already behind schedule, he raised his voice. "Drone detection. All hands take cover."

A scuffling in the dark, mutters and the scrape and clack of rock. He made sure the TA-4's bearers were well concealed, then bent and crawled beneath a shelf of icy stone. He switched off his optics—he'd have to conserve charge now, since the spare batteries were gone—and lay staring up into total blackness.

Some minutes later a faint bee-hum, a distant whine mingled with the sigh of the wind. One of the motorized, longer-ranged UAVs. They seemed to comb the mountains on a schedule he hadn't yet figured out, or maybe run on a random search pattern.

Regardless, it was up there. Stripping off the goggles, wriggling until his eyes just cleared the ledge, he peered upward.

A dim light pulsed high above. Red and green, alternating flashes that stood out even amid the glaring stars, which shone fiercely and unwinking this high in the mountains. It drifted very slowly across the sky, tracking east to west.

Fortunately he'd carried the beam gun himself. His fingers crept around the stock, then paused. Dropping a drone might signal its operators there was something of interest at, or near, the point where it went down. In the morning the gunships would arrive, or heavier UAVs with air-to-surface missiles.

He flexed his finger, then edged it away from the trigger. The lights above circled lazily, leisurely, then continued their drift westward.

He waited until they were out of sight, and the rear guard reported no emissions. Then slid out, brushed off, and called to the others that it was time, once more, to get on the trail.

THE cliff, the bridge, then waiting out the drone, put them behind where he'd hoped to get tonight. Dawn caught them still descending the mountain face. But as the sky paled and gneisses and schist and bands of darker rock took shape around them, he shoved apprehension aside. Tightening bleeding fingers on sharp rock, he hustled downward, as fast as he could without losing his footing, intent on the cave-mouth looming ahead.

Qurban's squat form pirouetted there, with the new joins all gathered around him. 'Gray Wolf' was older, but he didn't look as tired as Teddy felt. The new guys were jumping around in place, chanting. He caught the chorus: *"Take up your guns. Take up your guns, and kill. The evil Han, and all* kafirs *and* mulhids." He'd heard the tune before, on the march.

"Inside," Teddy told them. "Get out of sight."

The dancing petered out, the men looking unhappy about it. The short man said calmly, "Lingxiù. Why did we not march farther today?"

Teddy gave him a SEAL master chief glare that would have wilted any enlisted man in the Navy, or any officer up to at least O-3, but Qurban didn't seem to register it. His seamed, leathery, gray-bearded visage maintained its gentle smile. He spread his hands. "It would not harm anyone if we marched for another hour. In the daylight, we can make better progress."

"In the daylight, they'll fucking spot us in a second," Teddy said. "We hole up. Just like I said."

But instead of inclining his head, as the rebels typically did in response to an order, this one turned to his clique. Younger men, wildly bearded, the recruits Qurban had brought in from mountain fastnesses and madrassas, Islamic schools. "What do my friends think? Trust Allah, and go on? Or follow al-Amriki? True warriors do not cower like frightened dogs. They advance, in the knowledge they are following His will."

Teddy gripped the thin-blade in his loose trousers. But suppressed the urge. Not the time to take down this fucker. Not with so many witnesses, anyway. Use reason first. Only if that didn't work, go to the knife. Past them he caught sight of Nasrullah, inside the cave, holding an AK muzzle-down, watching.

"I remind you of your honor," he told them. "You are sworn to me and to your imam, Akhmad. But above all, sworn to obey the orders of those who lead you. Is this not what you agreed to, when you joined us in resisting the godless ones who oppress the Uighur?"

The young men glanced at one another. Qurban waited, arms crossed, a patient smile curling his lips. Finally one youngster, no more than fifteen, mumbled, "Hiding is not the way to win battles. And you have the magic rifle, for the ghost-eyes, do you not, Lingxiù-Sahib."

Teddy stared him down. "You want to fight gunships in the open, like mice before the hawk? Wasting your life is not the way to defeat the Han. Use your fucking head, *ahmoq maymun*, that's what I'm trying to get you people to do." He caught himself; never diss your troops as a group. "Forgive my harsh words. I was angry. I find no fault; you have marched well. Hajji Qurban and I must confer. The rest of you, into the cave. Get dal and chapatis, then sleep. We will rise early, before the dark comes again, and march even harder tonight."

They all got the glare this time, and after a moment even the most sullen gazes dropped. They shuffled their feet, and finally filed inside.

"Over here," Teddy snapped to the ex–al Qaeda soldier. Still smiling, the squat man accompanied him into a niche in the rock. "We're on our way to battle. In enemy territory. Is that the time to question the leadership?"

"I merely hoped we could make more progress. I did not mean to contradict you," the man said in his strangely accented, oddly formal English. Which he must have learned, Teddy figured, at Gitmo. Picking it up the same way he himself had learned Han Chinese: from his jailers.

"These aren't your men, Hajji. They're ITIM, not whatever off-brand of al-Qaeda or Daesh you're trying to push."

"It does not matter what we are called. We are fighting the same enemy," the smiling man observed. "That makes us all of one heart. Does it not, al-Amriki?"

Teddy poked him in the chest, hard, knowing he was pushing it, but with the knife gripped in his pocketed hand. "Fall in line, mac, or you'll be standing in front of the imam yourself."

Qurban coughed into a fist. Or was it a chuckle? "What is the worst you can do? You can beat me, I suppose. But is it done, to beat one who has already sacrificed so much for jihad? I think it is not. The worst would be to murder me, American. But I do not think you or I is fated to die just yet."

Teddy gritted his teeth. He almost said *try me* but didn't. Never warn a man you intend to kill. "Right now, we're going inside. You'll apologize to me in front of the squad leaders, then again in front of the rest."

"It is as Allah wills," said the bearded muj, spreading his hands. "Is it not written: 'You should listen to and obey your ruler even if he is a black slave whose head looks like a raisin'?"

Teddy scowled. "Are you insulting me . . . comrade?"

"Far from it. I am praising you," Qurban said. "But truly, al-Amriki, you are a puzzle. You pray with us. Fight alongside us. But have you fully opened your heart to God? That is what I do not understand, Mr. Oberg. Perhaps you do not see this clearly yet yourself.

"But the end of days is coming. The final battle. Soon you will have to choose, between your corrupt and murderous masters in Washington and the one Master in Heaven. But for now, let us shake hands. Then say a *dhikr* together and make peace between us, and I will do even as you say and apologize before the assembly."

He bowed deeply, and stayed that way until Teddy, though still steamed, judged this not the time to press the point. He nodded curtly, and stepped away.

TRUE to his word, the guy apologized, at length, first in classical Arabic, with many flowery quotations from the Koran. Then in Uighur, stroking his beard and smiling beatifically. Even in apology, he seemed to be conveying something rebellious to those silent young men who stood at the back of the cave, separate from the others. Even when it was time for prayers they prostrated themselves with everyone else, but remained apart.

Teddy prayed too, but kept an eye on them. Oh yeah, Qurban had apologized.

But he still wouldn't turn his back on this guy.

IV

THE REMOTEST REGIONS OF DEATH

19

Laguna Beach, California

LYING in bed before dawn, staring at his face as he slept, Cheryl wondered: What is this? What the hell am I doing?

Maybe the answer was simple.

Or perhaps more complicated than she'd ever dreamed.

The resort must have been super expensive before the war. Nestled deep in a green-forested canyon, it faced a golden beach and a lapis sea. Their two-story creekside cottage's floor-to-ceiling windows looked up along the nature trail on one side. On the other, down onto the heated saline pool, and beyond that the golf course and riding stables. Morale, Welfare, and Rec had gotten her a special rate. Though now most of the cottages were empty, and they'd been almost alone out on the links, where she'd given Teju his first lesson.

Two days of freedom, before she had to be back. Forty-eight hours of pleasure, larded with guilt.

She hovered a finger five millimeters above black stubble on cocoa skin. His mother was Thai, his father Nigerian. "All my father's family was tall," he'd said. He'd grown up in Echo Park, in a family of six. He slept perfectly quietly. Unlike Eddie, who'd snored.

The minutes ebbed as the big room they lay in slowly became visible. A modernistic chandelier of twisted, tinted glass. High beamed ceilings. A gigantic bed, sized for newlyweds.

But this felt less like a honeymoon than an assignation. Not quite adulterous. But different from anything she'd ever done. At least, since college.

And definitely something that couldn't last.

She got up quietly. In the bathroom she washed her face and gazed into her eyes.

I look every minute of thirty-six, she thought.

He was twenty-five.

She'd explained about Eddie, and Teju, in turn, had come clean about his wife. She'd been evacuated, he told her. No kids yet, though his older brothers both had large families. "You must have had lots of girlfriends," she'd teased him over the dinner she'd ordered from room service. California cuisine. Lobster. In their cottage, brought by a silent black-uniformed woman who'd glanced at him as he lounged bare-chested in swim trunks, then had met Cheryl's look with a collusive, eyebrow-arched half-smile. As if they were sisters, sharing some shameful but juicy secret.

Maybe it was just that clandestinity, that feeling she had to keep this under the radar, that made it so delicious. It wasn't exactly against regs. The peacetime purges of commanding officers for extramarital affairs had been forgotten with the coming of war. And she wasn't sure a union official who worked at the yard could really be considered in her chain of command, anyhow.

But it was definitely . . . out of the ordinary.

Was it about race? Or class? No, that was Oldthink. But no question, it would shock the wardroom if they saw their all-business, tightly wound skipper shacked up with a yardbird. No, a "shipyard worker."

And Eddie . . . she just had to change her mind to another channel whenever something reminded her of him.

This was their first time, and probably the only one, so she'd wanted to make it special. Thus, the resort. They saw each other now and then during the day, on the ship. Teju seemed to spend more time aboard supervising now, and she suspected he was the main reason they'd retaken the lead from *Itbayat Island.* Now Hull #91 would be commissioned first.

In fact, today. She rubbed her face, noting, in the mirror, the sunburn flush on her cheeks. They'd thought about sea kayaking, but she wanted to walk the woods instead. Feel the pull of a hill in thighs and calves. So they'd taken the nature trail yesterday, holding hands, and on the canyonside had found a secluded bed of maidenhair fern shaded by live oak. The half-pain, half-heaven so wringing-sharp she'd cried out, staring up through the shifting patterns of light falling through the leaves.

Then wended their way back down, fingers entwined. No need for words, after what they'd just shared.

Then the pool, and the session on the links, where he'd been so abysmally bad they'd both collapsed in laughter.

Feeling each minute bleed away . . .

She shook her head, then lifted a monitory finger to herself in the mirror. But it had to end. Today. She sighed, brushed her teeth, sketched on light makeup, then padded back in. Changed silently, so as not to wake him. But midway through fastening her bra she felt his arms slide around her waist, his breath warm on her nape.

"You don't need to do that just yet," he whispered. And led her, once again, to the bed.

THE day would be hot. Already, as she headed toward the ship from the CO's parking space, heat shimmered up from the concrete. Damn, she was sore. But she didn't regret a minute of it. For the first time in months, she didn't feel anxious. She checked her phone: an hour until the ceremony. Decent timing. She climbed the brow, which had been decorated with red, white, and blue bunting. Changed into whites in her stateroom.

The wardroom of the new *Savo Island* was no larger than that of the old, but she was glad to see they had the old silver out. Lenson had sent it ashore for storage early in the war, and back it would go to some obscure Navy vault for safekeeping after today, but now it sparkled, freshly polished, set out on spotless white tablecloths. Pastries. Coffee. Tea. Excellent.

"Good morning, Captain." Mills, looking handsome indeed in short-sleeved trop whites.

She nodded. "Morning, Matt. What have we got today? Any issues?"

"We trimmed down the ceremony, like you wanted. No band, no bandstand. Just a short ceremony, remarks, then we break the pennant and come alive. Coffee and cake in the wardroom after."

"Is Mrs. Calvin here yet?"

A gray-haired woman peeked in the door. "I'm Mrs. Calvin."

Cheryl took a soft, frail-boned hand. Jeanne Moore Calvin was the granddaughter of Samuel Nobre Moore, last commanding officer of USS *Quincy*. Moore had been killed on the bridge by a direct hit during the 1942 battle for which Cheryl's ship was named. Calvin would be the ship's sponsor. "I'm so glad you could make it," Cheryl said. "What with the crashes."

"They sent me a priority pass. I was able to take the train." They exchanged a few more polite words before Cheryl excused herself.

"Matt, we've got the music, I hope?"

"You said no band."

She tensed. "We need the national anthem, XO!"

He patted her shoulder, a quarter inch short of patronizing. "Got it covered, Skipper. I have a recording. And a backup."

She frowned. "Don't pat my shoulder, Lieutenant."

"Sorry. Just meant . . . I apologize."

"Forget it," she muttered. "Backups, good." Christ, she was getting wound up again, just when she'd been congratulating herself on being relaxed.

Following the ceremony, the crew would get one day's liberty, after which they'd get under way for shakedown exercises with air and submarine services in the Southern California oparea. A shipyard availability would correct anything the workup revealed. They'd head to Hawaii for fleet exercises, then ballistic missile defense qualification and certification with the Afloat Training Group.

From there, if they passed their final exam, *Savo* would be assigned to one of the new strike groups being formed for the counteroffensive.

Then it would be back to war. . . .

COMMISSIONING gave a ship her name. Until the ceremony, she belonged to the yard. Afterward, she was officially in the Navy. Part of history forever, though her battered fabric might lie fathoms deep in a distant sea, or be recycled into something new. Or like a very few, enough to count on the fingers of one's hands, be preserved as a historic ship.

The proceedings today, in wartime, would be truncated. But still, not brief. She sat with ankles demurely crossed on the bunting-draped podium with Captain Cadden, the local congressman, the deputy commander, Third Fleet, and the other notables. Eddie would have been with her, if . . . if only. And Teju, well, he wouldn't really fit in up here, though he was in the audience, five rows back.

They sweltered through remarks by the mayor of Long Beach, the congressman, then the shipyard commander. Mrs. Calvin gave a speech about the sacrifices her grandfather, and so many others, had made to stop the Japanese in World War II. At the end of her remarks, Cadden turned the hull over to Fleet, who accepted on behalf of the CNO and the Navy.

By then Cheryl was sitting in a pool of sweat. She hoped it wouldn't show on the back of her skirt when she got up. Finally the admiral turned to her. "Now we'll hear from the first commanding officer of the new USS *Savo Island*, and the last commanding officer of her namesake. Commander Cheryl Staurulakis, United States Navy.

"But first, a sidebar. As the skipper of a cruiser, is the rank of O-5 really appropriate? Cheryl, what do you think? Wouldn't it be better if her CO was a full captain?"

A scatter of surprised laughter. She had to smile and nod, and pretend this was all a big surprise. She stood at attention as he replaced the shoulder boards on her trop whites with the four gold stripes of a captain. She stepped back, saluted, then shook his perspiring palm. So he was feeling the heat too. Wasn't there any way she could cut this even shorter? Unfortunately, she didn't think so.

Smoothing her pages out atop the podium, she looked out across the faces, over the heat-wavering pier, to the great flat slab of gray-painted steel that in moments would officially become a warship. Mills caught her eye and gave a nod. Apparently that meant the flag-hoisting party was standing by.

"Good afternoon. Congressman, Mr. Mayor, Mrs. Calvin. Admiral, Captain. The heads of teams for our major contractors. It's very hot today, so I may abbreviate my remarks somewhat. But let me say first how happy I am to stand here today, and how proud.

"As others have mentioned, USS *Savo Island*, CGA-91, represents our newest class of surface combatant. It carries the latest antisubmarine, antiair, antisurface, and antiballistic missile armament of any ship of any country. Its new Alliance missile, with multiple kinetic kill vehicles, is AI-enabled to discriminate between decoys and live warheads. It offers a robust defense against heavy ICBMs in the midcourse phase.

"Our railgun and advanced beam weapons are game-changers. They will extend the reach and lethality of any force *Savo Island* accompanies. New survivability features will enable us to operate in the most hostile environments. As a multimission platform, with advanced command and control and intelligence fusion, the ship is designed to operate in many mission sets. With surface strike groups, carrier strike groups, other adaptive force packages, or on our own in tailored anti-ballistic missile protective missions. A new dynamic access network will provide high-bandwidth data exchange among air-, surface-, sub-surface-, and ground-based tactical data systems, both U.S. and Allied.

"As the admiral said, ships of this class truly represent the best our country can produce."

She took a breath and scanned the crowd. Skip the next part? No, it was tradition. "Our name commemorates a deadly naval battle fought north of Guadalcanal on August 9, 1942, an action in which our sponsor's grandfather gave his life as a hero . . . which she has so vividly recalled for us.

"The first USS *Savo Island*, CVE-78, was a Casablanca-class escort carrier built in Vancouver, Washington. Commissioned in February 1944, she received four battle stars during World War II. She also received a Presidential Unit Citation for her service in the Western Carolines, the Philippines, and Okinawa between September 1944 and April 1945. This first ship to bear the name was struck from the Navy list in 1959.

"The second *Savo*, a Ticonderoga-class cruiser, was built at Bath Iron Works. She served with the Atlantic Fleet until transferred via the Med Sea and Indian Ocean as part of the rebalance to the Pacific. She received numerous commendations during her career, including the Presidential Unit Citation for her actions at the opening of the present war. I had the honor of commanding her."

She looked to the sky, blinking to avoid tearing up. "That second *Savo Island* . . . after receiving battle stars for actions in the Taiwan Strait, the Battle of the Central Pacific, and Operation Recoil in the East China Sea, was lost in action during the nuclear attack on Hawaii. Many of the current complement, whom you see before you, are former members of her crew."

She went through the obligatory thank-yous: the prime agencies and contractors, the subcontractors. "And especially, the yard personnel who worked alongside our deckplate sailors to install and test hundreds of systems, many brand-new to the fleet. It has been extremely beneficial for us to learn from and work beside them.

"Mr. Mayor, Congressman, we've been treated well by Long Beach and California. This city, too, will always be in our hearts."

She took a breath. "To my sailors: You've met all the challenges presented by a first-of-class ship, with flying colors. I'm proud of you. I know you'll bring the same expertise, teamwork, and toughness to working up with other elements of the fleet. Together we will sharpen USS *Savo Island* into the shining tip of America's spear. We will give battle to our country's enemies, and liberation to our allies in Asia."

She gave it a pause, meeting their expectant gazes, then lowered her eyes again. "I will now read my orders.

"'From: Chief of Naval Operations. To: Captain Cheryl F. Staurulakis USN.

"'Effective immediately, proceed to the port wherein USS *Savo Island* may be and upon her commissioning, report to your immediate superior in command, if present, otherwise by message, for duty as commanding officer of USS *Savo Island*.'"

She turned to the admiral. "Sir: I am ready to take command."

He saluted her gravely. "Carry out your orders, Captain."

She turned to the waiting ranks of white-uniformed men and women. So few, really, to run such a massive ship. But they were ready. Mills turned, lifted a sword—crap, she hadn't expected that—and boomed out, "Ship's complement: atten-*hut*."

The national anthem, from the topside speakers of the ship's 1MC. Good.

"And the home . . . of the brave."

"Ready . . . two."

She dropped her salute, and stepped back to the mike. But remembered at the last second that traditionally the ship's sponsor gave this first order. She gestured Mrs. Calvin forward. Bending to the microphone, the old lady intoned, "Officers and crew of USS *Savo Island*, man our ship and bring her to life!"

Atop the vestigial mast, the whiplike commissioning pennant broke. At the same moment, the ensign climbed into view on the fantail.

The rearmost rank of the crew stepped back, right-faced, and double-timed for the brow. They broke step as they crossed the long gangway. Disappeared for a time, then reappeared, lining up along the main deck, aft, the foredeck, and high on the bridge. Reaching position, each faced the pier and snapped to a crisp parade rest.

Mrs. Calvin was dabbing at her cheeks with a lace-edged handkerchief. Cheryl gave her an impulsive hug. "Thank you so much for coming," she told her. Then drew herself up, turned to the admiral, and saluted.

He regarded her impassively, returned the salute, then dropped it and shook her hand. "Congratulations, Captain."

"Thank you, sir."

"Don't give up the ship."

"No sir. Never."

"I guess you've proven that. Now take charge. Always do the right thing. And may God be with you."

THAT evening, after cake and tea in the wardroom, and the formal dinner the city put on for them, she drove back to the resort.

He was there already, in their room.

They went to the beach bonfire, almost the only guests there. The wind-whipped flames blazed in the darkness. Sparks snapped and whirled up into the dark. Surf crashed with a long, dull, withdrawing roar. Slow, long-period waves, born deep in the far Pacific.

She and Teju stole away into the night. He drew the blanket over them, and she dug her head back into the sand, gasping as they drove together to the blazing hearts of the stars far above.

When they lay apart, yet with legs still entwined, he murmured, "So. What happens now?"

The question she'd been dreading. "Now? I have to go to sea," she whispered. "To war. There's just no way around that."

"Yeah. I know. You're the fucking captain. So, this is it? We just . . . say so long?"

"You're married. After the war, you'll be back with your family."

"If there is an 'after the war.' If the Chinese don't nuke us all."

She couldn't say anything to that. Because it was all too possible.

"And you?" he murmured.

"I don't know," she confessed. "But I don't think I'll still be in your life then, Tej."

He turned his face away. "Do you want children?"

Thank God, she didn't chuckle. "I don't know. I did once. But the war . . . my husband . . . I might've with Eddie. Now, I just don't know."

"So I'm a gap filler. No . . . I didn't mean that the way it sounded—"

She couldn't help snorting, but quickly sobered. "It was great, Tej. I'll always remember you. But we're, you know, ships in the night. We both understood that, right? That's what war does. Makes it . . . hard to plan anything."

"But if you could, if we could . . . if we didn't have commitments . . ."

What the hell? There was only one possible answer. Whether she felt it herself, or not. She mustered a white lie. "Then I'd be yours. Heart and soul. You know that. Forever."

She wrapped her arms around him, and drew him down, in the sandy darkness, once more. He was so cute. And at this moment, so very hard. She caught her breath again. Ow. Ow. The sand . . . But she let him press on with what he so obviously wanted.

After all, it was the last time.

20

Central Intelligence Agency, Langley, Virginia

ONCE, again, a meeting. But not in the National Military Command Center. Nor with the Chiefs, but with a small ad hoc working group. Addressing a single topic.

Blair took a seat near Denson Hui, of the Missile Defense Agency, and nodded to those she knew. Haverford Tomlin, from SAIC, Strategic Plans and Policy Division. Rick Ackert, the general from Wright-Pat who'd nearly crashed into Los Alamos with her. Shira Salyers, she noted, had not been invited, nor anyone else from State.

Most of the rest of the men and women gathered in the second-floor office were young, in casual dress, even T-shirts, except for one man. Dark hair was slicked back from a sharp-chinned face. He wore gray slacks, a button-down shirt, and a blue blazer with a U OF MARYLAND crest on the pocket. When he sauntered over to shake hands, she glanced down at high-arched, hand-tooled cowboy boots. Well, he needed the extra height.

"Blair Titus? Charles Anthony Provanzano. With the Directorate of Operations. Old friend of your husband."

"Good to meet you. But I don't think he's mentioned you."

"I'm glad we've finally met." He uncapped a white tube and stuck it into one nostril, half turning away. She smelled koala bears. "Vicks, in case you're wondering." He sniffed, then did the other nostril. Coughed. "Habit I picked up in Afghanistan. From the dust. Sorry."

"No offense taken."

"Dan and I were orcs there together. He helped us with CIRCE." She must have looked puzzled, because he added, "A stochastic modeling agent reasoning framework. Which, actually, it's good he never told you about."

"There's a lot we don't share."

"I hope that includes what we're going to talk about today." Provanzano waved to the younger people, who fell silent. "All here? T team? Let's get started."

The first slide up quieted everyone. Smoke and fire streamed from a mesa crest. The next slide showed collapsed buildings, flames, fire trucks playing hoses over the wreckage of some large machine. Then bodies laid out in rows, with radiological-suited, masked responders rolling more onto litters.

"The attack on Los Alamos," Provanzano said, tone steely. "Where the warheads were being assembled for the long-range standoff cruise. The fallout plume reached Amarillo. Two million people are being evacuated.

"The next pictures are from Sandia Laboratories, in Albuquerque."

Buildings on fire.

Wrecked factories.

More bodies, many still in white smocks or the hoods and cleanroom suits used to work on microchips.

One of the T team, whatever that stood for, summarized the damage. He concluded, "Only fifteen percent of the emergency modernization program was complete. Essentially, the attack denies us achievement of nuclear parity. For at least a year, we continue to operate from a position of strategic weakness."

She lifted her head. "You're not counting the sea-based deterrent?"

Denson Hui said soberly, "The submarine-based leg of the triad may be essentially all we have left, Dr. Titus. With the heavy throw weights and tight CEPs of Zhang's new missiles, even our hardened silos are vulnerable to a first strike. That's one reason why we were so constrained in responding to their attack on Hawaii. And their air defenses deny access to our bombers. That was why we accelerated deployment of the enhanced-range standoff Gorgon."

"Which we now have no warheads for," someone else put in.

The CIA officer nodded and the projector went dark. "Correct, and their guidance was one of the other projects Sandia had in hand: the GPS-independent, firewalled navigation system for the hypersonic standoff. Fortunately, they missed the assembly building for the boosted penetrator."

The T-team briefer resumed. "Here's what we know. First, this hijacking occurred simultaneously across eight airborne platform types. Second, the enemy attacked our strategic center of gravity—our nuclear development and strategic missile sites.

"They obviously knew our programs in intimate detail. Assembly points. Airframe and rocket engine factories. Chip fabricators. That's what they targeted."

Provanzano said, "I know the tech types think this is a digital war, and the military types think it's a military war. But it's really an intelligence war."

He spread his hands. "Fifteen aircraft cyberjacked. Eight hit their targets. One that didn't was Dr. Titus's." He nodded to Blair. "Who barely escaped. She's also read into what we know about the enemy's main cyberweapon. Which is why she's at this briefing."

He sat back. "All right . . . Dr. Nadine Oberfoell is from the Office of Cyber Security. Doctor, what do we know about Jade Emperor?"

A small, bent, rotund woman, almost a dwarf, stood with evident difficulty. "More than we did last year. But not much more."

"Start at the beginning. Not everybody here's read in."

Blair expected her to start with the origin of the name. The "Jade Emperor" was a legendary figure in Chinese history. Overthrowing an army of evil demons through his great wisdom, he had become the supreme overlord of both men and gods.

Instead, Oberfoell began with the technology. She described a massively capable artificial intelligence somewhere in the Chinese interior. Even before completion, it had been able to infiltrate internet data packets anywhere in the world. It had been behind the takedowns of the financial markets, the brownouts in the U.S. West and Midwest, thermal and nuclear power plant failures, remote industrial sabotage, cell service disruption, and breakdowns in satellite communications.

"We gradually learned it could penetrate our most secure high-side command networks. Our NATO allies confirmed this during the Ukraine campaign, when they discovered Beijing was sharing their internal deliberations with the Russians. We feared that when fully operational, Emperor would become even more dangerous. Able to not just interfere with, but reroute and control industrial processes, financial networks, communications, and power. Invisibly to us, working deep within the codes that control these highly digitized systems."

Oberfoell bent at the waist, as if easing a pain in her spine. "That fear is now coming true."

"But we have a counterweapon," Blair put in.

"Ma'am, we did. A DARPA-chartered project by Archipelago Systems, a merger of the blue-sky departments of Alphabet, Facebook, Intel, and Amazon. It too was a massive self-programming neural network, intended to dominate the digital battlespace. It showed early promise. We were able to degrade North Korean missile guidance, and decode encrypted Chinese submarine cable traffic."

Blair remembered the first time she'd heard about Battle Eagle. She'd almost laughed. But every war brought new technologies forward. Bombing aircraft had been a fantasy in 1913. Atomic weapons had been science fiction in 1939. Now, instead of teams of human hackers, two titanic programs were locked in mortal combat, deep in the stygian labyrinths of cyberspace.

"Unfortunately," Oberfoell was saying, "our AI seems to have been penetrated and taken over by theirs very early in the development process. We had to shut down large portions to seal off the infection. This reduced Battle Eagle's power to see through its opponent's stratagems.

"Plus, in many ways, the Chinese economy is still not as digitally dependent as ours. Making us more vulnerable to sophisticated hacking."

Provanzano flickered his fingers in the air. "The bottom line, Nadine."

"Of course. Which is, that in instances such as the takeover of the airliners, we thought we had safeguards in place. But not only couldn't we prevent it, we actually—our human teams—don't understand how it was done even now."

Oberfoell looked down. "The first stage of AI was to assess and integrate information to help humans make decisions. The second, to make those decisions on its own, replacing a human, though humans could still understand its processes.

"Jade Emperor is third-generation. It's too fast and too intelligent for us even to understand what it did, or how. And it's moving beyond our capabilities to protect ourselves.

"That's what this aircraft takeover is really telling us."

For a few moments, no one spoke.

At last Provanzano said, "Thank you, Doctor. Not encouraging news.

We're being dominated in cyberspace. And now, relegated to second place in strategic weapons." He looked at a younger man in a PROTESTANTS AGAINST POTPOURRI T-shirt, who had squirmed and fidgeted during the briefings. "But I think the T team has something positive for us. Art?"

"Yes, sir. There's one bit of good news."

When the T-shirted man rose, a new slide came up: a sharp, detailed overhead shot. Desert. Mountains at the top of the picture. Amid miles of undulating brown sand hills, a single arrow-straight road led to a sprawling construction site.

The T-shirted guy said, "This was taken before the war started. This is the Taklimakan Desert, in western China. At first we thought it was a brine evaporation facility. Then we noticed solar arrays." The picture vanished; a fuzzy, canted one replaced it. "This is from a MICE overfly three days ago. Unfortunately, we don't get great imagery from their tiny cameras. But you can see the difference."

The photo showed nearly pristine desert. Blair frowned. Ackert said, "Where'd it go?"

Provanzano nodded, clicking a laser pointer. "Good question, General. Where indeed? You can just see, here"—an arrow appeared, tracing a faint line—"where the road used to run. Or may still, beneath the sand. But as you can see, the solar arrays have vanished. Construction, parking, cooling ponds, all gone."

Art said, "We think the facility's been buried. Probably just bulldozers pushing the dunes over it, sculpting them to look like their previous conformations. If the wind didn't do it naturally.

"Here's the same area, in infrared, on the next pass."

An even fuzzier picture, but dotted with blobs of glow beneath the dunes. "There's something giving off a lot of heat down there. Fortunately, just now it's winter, or it might not show at all. One more thing: there's a lot of drone activity over that area. In fact, it's the largest concentration of UAVs in China."

Provanzano thanked the analyst and pointed him back to his seat. "All right, let's cost out our options. Their system has a robust instinct for self-preservation. Archipelago tried to run a virus in. It came back out improved, and targeted at us. We lost ten percent more of Battle Eagle before we blocked it. The Army and NSA's cyberteams both had a go. The Army came away with fifty ruined routers. NSA blocked the counterpunch, but had no success penetrating the defenses. Essentially, we've exhausted our nonkinetics."

"But there's a kinetic solution." Ackert said. "Now we've located it."

"We're on the same page, General. Unfortunately, it won't involve the U.S. Air Force. With the demise of the Gorgon, and the concentric rings of Russian-contracted air defenses, the only way we can reach that deep into Asia would be a ballistic strike."

"Which would bring on massive retaliation," Blair said.

"Correct. So: what assets could penetrate a hidden facility, deep in the desert interior?" Provanzano turned to the techs and support personnel. "Principals only from here on, please."

When the room was cleared one man remained sitting along the wall. Up to now, he'd said nothing. Had barely moved, though he'd followed the discussions with rapt attention. Provanzano beckoned him to the central table. "Let me introduce Andres Korzenowski," he said.

"Mr. Korzenowski is a former Ranger, now with the Special Operations Group, Special Activities Division. As a paramilitary operations officer he specializes in raids, sabotage, ambushes, unconventional warfare behind enemy lines. Andres."

Blair examined high Slavic cheekbones, dark stubble, and a receding hairline, though the operative couldn't be more than thirty. Deeply hooded eyes. A straight, thin nose. Jeans, combat boots, and a maroon turtleneck under a tactical vest. His interlocked hands rested on the table in front of him.

Korzenowski inclined his head and stood. "Thank you, sir.

"For the past months, we've been in contact with a guerrilla group operating in the fringes of the Tien Shan. The rebel force is small but growing. We were supplying arms and equipment. Mainly, to harass the enemy's interior security, and provide a focus for Islamist discontent with Han rule in Xinjiang. Eventually, we hoped to mature it into a significant resistance movement.

"However, we've recently redirected it to a more narrowly focused mission."

He explained, and the attendees shifted in their seats. When he was done no one spoke for a few seconds.

Ackert shifted in his chair. "It sounds . . . risky for these, um, rebels."

"We expect it to be, yes sir," Korzenowski said quietly. "They will be outnumbered and outgunned."

"Losses?" Blair said, though she already knew the answer.

Korzenowski turned to her. "Probably heavy, ma'am. But bear in mind, they're not U.S. nationals, or even Allied troops. We have very little investment in them, except for their weapons and one noncommissioned U.S. liaison."

"And what do we need to do here?" the Missile Defense Agency director asked. "Are we approving this operation, or what? Because it seems to me—"

Provanzano stood, pushing back his chair. "No sir, Mr. Hui," he said quietly. Respectfully, but with utter implacability. "You are not required to approve. This is an Agency operation. And it is already under way. It may win the war for us. Or not. This is for your information only. So we all can prepare for the next step. In case we fail."

AN hour later she stood outside waiting for her car, reading the printed-out daily intelligence summary, the same one the CIA had provided for the president that morning. More strikes in the defense factories. Draft riots in Detroit, Boston, and New York.

But though no one had mentioned it in the meeting, there was good news too. Israeli antitank weapons and U.S. air support from Da Nang had finally stiffened the Vietnamese People's Army enough to halt the Chinese advance.

Also, Hong Kong was in revolt. An all-too-brief treatment speculated it had been triggered by hope of a U.S. landing after the strike on Hainan.

The final item on the brief described new rumors out of China, about some form of sonic operations on rebels' brains to render them more pliable.

She grimaced. That was all the enemy needed, a way to turn human beings into obedient robots. It would make Zhang's control unshakable. And the Party's philosophy had long ago discarded any "bourgeois" ethical restraints.

The gray Lincoln pulled up and she slid into the back.

The streets were deserted. If people still had jobs, they slept at work, bicycled, or walked. Many had left for less threatened areas, deep in the country or high in the hills.

Alone in the backseat, staring at the shaven skull of the driver, she worried. Everyone had expected a short war. But after years, it still hung in the balance. The Allies had made progress in the South China

Sea and in space. Maintained the blockade, and raided the enemy mainland. But with the loss of nuclear and cyberspace dominance, the alliance was in mortal danger.

The radio was on. The Liberty Broadcasting System, the only network still on the air, though now with censored news. No one would hear about strikes or draft riots there. As far as the public knew, the Allies were winning on all fronts.

But the truth was, destruction was creeping nearer both homelands.

And no one could yet envision how this war could be won, or even terminated, before it escalated into a massive thermonuclear exchange.

Feeling her chest tighten, she counted her breaths in and out, slowly, trying to stave off a panic attack.

HALF an hour later the car eased through the security cordon on Lafayette Square.

At the West Wing portico once more. Marine guards, then a retina scan. She left her phone and computer at a desk, and headed in.

The Roosevelt Conference Room. She'd been here so many times before. The atmosphere now, though, was tenser than ever.

She glanced at her watch. They were due to see the president. But the national security adviser was supposed to be here. Where was Szerenci?

Then there he was, gray-suited, natty, but looking exhausted. His security team stood like a brick wall behind him. "Blair," he said, smiling, and took her elbow. "So glad you made it through that horrible crash. I'd have hated to lose you. Who else keeps me on my toes, the way you do?"

She managed a tight smile in return. "Thank you. Ed."

"Sorry I'm late. What did they decide, at Langley?"

"They think they found it. And CIA says there might be a way to get to it. At least, to degrade it." She gathered her courage, glancing at the still-closed door. "I have to say . . . now that we've lost escalation dominance . . . this might be the time to make peace. Let me get back to the guy who contacted me in Dublin. Find a compromise. A modus vivendi."

Szerenci massaged his eyes with finger and thumb. "Not you, too. I just had this argument with the SecState."

"It's not an 'argument.' It may be our last chance to avoid a catastrophe."

"This isn't the time to weaken. It's time to finish the job. Destroy this aggressive, criminal regime, and defang China for the next hundred years."

She sucked a breath, horrified. They'd been skirting the precipice. Looking over it. Drawing closer and closer to the abyss. And now, he sounded almost eager to jump. To still think that, knowing what he did . . . "You still think we can win a nuclear war."

He looked away. "We may not be able to avoid one. Not this time." His shoulders rose, then fell.

She gripped his sleeve. "What are you saying? Ed? What are you really saying here? Just between us. It won't go any further. But I deserve to know. For planning purposes. If for nothing else."

He murmured, still not meeting her gaze, "It's not a question of winning anymore, Blair. If their forces are superior . . . and central nuclear war is inevitable . . . that leaves us no choice but to launch first. We'll suffer damage. But less than if we cede the strategic initiative. It'll be our only chance to even survive."

The door opened. A young woman leaned out. She too looked tired, harried. "Dr. Szerenci? Ms. Titus? The president will see you now."

21

The Taklimakan Desert

ONCE more, Teddy lay overwatching a target. Only this time it wasn't a road, a gas line, a transmission station, or a police outpost.

In fact, he wasn't sure what it was.

He scratched his leg, remembering what he'd seen over a year before, looking down from these same foothills, across this same desert.

He and Trinh and Fierros had been trekking west after their escape from the POW camp. Back then, across these undulating miles of sand hills, they'd stared at the sparkle and waver of a long line of orange lights. High above had circled smaller, bluish lights, busily patrolling the black bowl of starry sky.

But now, though it was night once more, he didn't see any of the orange lights at all.

His men had felt their way down out of the last mountain pass the night before, completing the approach phase of Operation Checkmate. He lay now motionless, studying the ceaseless lazy weaving of the little blue lights through his field glasses. He still couldn't figure what they fucking were. He didn't think they were drones. The Chinese lit their drones with red and green, or flew without running lights when they thought they were being covert, though you could still hear them for miles.

His second in command, Guldulla, was lying beside him. "What are those blue things?" he muttered.

"I don't know, Tok."

"Can they see us?"

"Might could if they were drones. But I don't think they are. There, see that red-and-green flash? *That* one's a drone."

They both studied the sky for some minutes longer. "Hell of a lot of churn," Teddy muttered at last.

"What?"

"Nothing . . . But we can't wait for them to go away. 'Cause obviously they won't."

Tokarev stroked his mustache. "Attack despite them?" He sounded doubtful.

"No choice." Teddy shrugged. "Get the assault element suited up. And make sure they have plenty of sand on that wool."

He'd anticipated overhead infrared sensors, either on the drones or on masts, to detect any infil by night. To lessen their signatures now, the two platoons he'd told off for the assault—eighty men out of the hundreds of rebels and porters that had made the march—began unpacking the gear they'd carried all the way from the Pamirs.

A sniper was trained to stalk his target deliberately, slowly, while camouflaged to blend with the surroundings. As a SEAL sniper Teddy had built his own ghillie suit, laboriously gluing netting and garnish onto a set of inside-out BDUs.

But the sand hills ahead were vacant of vegetation. Over open, wind-sculpted sand, a conventional ghillie would stand out like a red velvet ant on a billiard table, and warm bodies would glare against the cool sand.

So he'd run some experiments. The most effective used raw wool, or better yet, lambs' hides. Nasrullah had put the word out to the villages, and eventually they had enough hides to cover each man's head, back, and lower body down to his feet. Stuffed under their kameez and loose pants, or pulled over their heads, the result looked horrible and smelled worse. The raw, heavy, matted mountain wool hadn't even been washed. But when he checked with his night vision, it reduced the heat signature significantly. Their drag bags, with their weapons and explosives, were sand-colored canvas.

They wouldn't be undetectable, but it would take a sharp eye to pick them up, if they followed the topo contours, took their time, and above all, got lucky.

Of course, once they engaged, concealment would be out the window. After firing ten rounds, the barrel of an AK would glow like the strobe of a state police car at 2 a.m.

For night after night, he'd studied topo maps and imagery from earth-probing radar that Vlad had downloaded, together with the Agency's guesses as to what lay below the smooth sand in the pictures.

The Checkmate installation lay in open desert, with one road in from the east. That two-lane had probably been marked by the orange lights, though now they'd been taken down. The road itself, according to the imagery, was all but covered, blown over by wind-driven sand.

His demo guys were headed out there now, circling wide to the east. Once they struck the pavement, they'd emplace mines, sealing off the target from reinforcement by road.

After long examination, he'd noticed that the overheads showed a shallow arroyo or dry streambed leading down from the foothills. The gully veered this way and that, following the contours of the gradually declining land, then bent away four miles northwest of the target installation.

A four-mile crawl would be pushing it even for SEALs. But these mountain peasants came tough. He'd selected out the fittest into two assault platoons, one led by Nasrullah and the other by Qurban, and drilled them in low crawls back and forth through a patch of sand near the base camp for days, until their shalwar kameez were worn through at the knees and elbows and they were close to mutiny. It was then he'd introduced them to the old SEAL mantra. "If it didn't suck, they wouldn't need us to do it."

It had been touch and go there for a second, but at last they'd laughed. Nodded, then all dropped to the sand together, demanding to do it all again.

He would keep the remaining platoons in the arroyo as a quick reaction force, ready to cover the assault element's withdrawal, or if things went to shit, to try to extract them. The ravine would also be the rally point after the strike, though he doubted extraction would work out too well, against whatever QRF and security the Chinese had to have around this thing.

Whatever it was. The CIA man had never said. Only that it was electronics-heavy, computer-heavy, and so the main point of the mission was to emplace and trigger the Package.

Casualties, yeah, they were going to take them. But it had been made abundantly clear that this was important enough to waste the whole outfit, if that was the price.

Not that he'd shared that nugget of information with the Uighurs.

* * *

TWO hours on, they crouched in the ravine as Teddy took a cross bearing with his compass. The blue lights still circled. Still no orange ones, though. He binoculared the sand hills ahead for observation posts or lookout towers, but saw only rippled sand.

He lowered the glasses, puzzled. Beside him Guldulla whispered, "If it is this important, shouldn't there be guards? Razor wire?"

Teddy didn't answer, but felt doubtful too. Maybe this wasn't what the Agency thought. It wouldn't be the first time they'd committed friendly insurgents to a deadly boondoggle. Or worse yet, an ambush.

But the overhead imagery had shown a camouflaged entrance. From penetrating radar, intel predicted a corridor or vestibule just inside, probably a logistic area. Then a T-shaped intersection, with branches leading northeast and southwest. Judging by the infrared signatures, Vlad had said, the left branch serviced living quarters, while the right one led to their main target.

Emplacing the Package there, and executing the trigger protocol, would accomplish the mission.

After which, they'd have fifteen minutes to get clear.

Their contact hadn't said what would happen after that.

THE sand was heavier than he'd expected, grittier, denser. Not like crawling the beach at BUD/S. This stuff was gray, dead dry, and disintegrated into a choking dust at the first touch. The wind quickly coated his throat and nose with it despite the cloth around his face and the goggles over his eyes. It itched in his crotch and armpits and burned in his groin.

He low-crawled on, belly to the ground, dragging the beam gun in a bag beneath him. Which didn't help, since its protrusions kept jabbing his balls. When he neared the crest of a sand hill he halted. Waited for a gust, to skip small whirls of powder along the top of the dune. Then, head down, pushed himself up and over with the toes of his one good foot, half an inch at a time. When he had cover he rose slightly and scrabbled ahead, like some half-evolved reptile, not yet fully a quadruped.

Pausing to swill out his mouth with a swallow of water, he relived the long crawl in Ashaara, toward the high-value target. Over a mile of upward rocky slope, with only a few rocks and bunches of dried grass for cover. He'd oozed from gully to gully like a torpid snake, despite a fractured collarbone. No one could see him. No one could stop him. He'd been Invisible Death, inching closer to the one whose time on earth was ticking away.

But he'd been younger then. Harder. Taking orders, not giving them. To his left and right now other forms inchwormed across the blowing sand, each covered, in the green wavering of infrared, with a shapeless blur of the wool-and-hide insulation. He could make his men out from the side, but hoped they weren't that visible from above.

He was still thinking that when the drone buzzed toward them. Scarlet and green pulsing lights, like the ones that had searched for them in the mountains. The thin whine of a high-compression engine. He froze, digging bare fingers into the grit. Facedown, motionless, breathing the warm plume of his breath directly down into the squeaking sand. Hoping the others, around him, were following the drill too.

HE'D mustered them before the attack, where the arroyo left the foothills. Gone over what each squad had to accomplish, what might go wrong, and how to adapt in case it did. Asked for questions, and answered them. Then, after a blessing from old Akhmad, they'd prayed together.

Finally, he'd taken a knee in front of them.

"I, your Lingxiù, will be at the forefront of the attack. Follow me, and you will not go far wrong. But if I fall, follow Guldulla, the one you know as Tokarev. And if he falls, Nasrullah and Hajji Qurban.

"And if we all fall, press on and do what we came to do. Kill Han, yes. But above all, leave the black egg our friends have prepared. It will do even more damage than we shall with our arms, as God wills."

"As God wills," they'd muttered back, shifting on their haunches.

He'd looked to the sky then, and back down at them. Trying to summarize what twenty years in the SEALs and some desperate situations had taught him. Some of what they'd shouted together at BUD/S. Some from his own experience. All of it, translated into what the anxious men in front of him might understand.

"I will leave you with this," he said. "I was trained by men of war, and myself have taken part in many battles. My beard has had time to turn gray because I took these words to heart. Listen well, that you may become better fighters.

"First: The enemy is more frightened of you than you are of him. For you will go to paradise, and the godless Han will not. Let the enemy feel fear, not you.

"But do not run blindly to your death. Inspect the terrain and the number of cartridges in your magazine before you move forward. Let your friends cover you with fire, and cover them when they are ready to advance.

"Press on with the attack once you start. More men get killed running away than ever die fighting. Never give the enemy your back as a target.

"The true battle starts once you get wounded. Any man who can pull a trigger can still fight. If you can wield a knife, cut a throat. We will not take prisoners, nor leave wounded behind for the Han to torture. Do you all understand this?"

The seated men exchanged glances. They nodded, and murmured agreement.

Teddy went on. "No plan survives contact with the enemy. The enemy will fight back. They will not all be cowards. That will not matter! Resolve now that you will accomplish the mission or accept your death.

"Don't think about your fear. It is a demon companion, sent by Shaitan to tempt you from courage. Just do what we drilled, and follow me and your other leaders."

He'd taken a deep breath, and looked around at them. "These are my words of wisdom. With God's help, tomorrow we will be victorious. *Hooyah!*"

"Hooyah! Hooyah! *Allahu Akhbar!* God is great!" they'd shouted back. And leapt to their feet, shaking their rifles above their heads, wailing and chanting as they began a stamping, whirling dance.

NOW he lay totally motionless, breathing down into a hollow scraped in the gritty sand with his chin, as the drone circled above them. His back prickled. Were these fliers armed? He'd never live to know it. Even a small frag warhead detonating from above would take out everyone within a sixty-meter circle.

He counted seconds. Three . . . four . . . at ten, if it was still up there, he'd roll over, pull out the beam gun, and take the thing down.

The whine waxed, held, and then, gradually, waned. He didn't dare look up. Just waited, until he judged the thing was headed away.

That was close . . . He checked his compass again. Then reached out and pulled more of the desert toward him, pushing himself forward with the toes of his boots.

AN hour later he was exhausted. The sand had worn through his gloves and now was abrading the skin off his fingers. He gritted his teeth as his damaged leg flared. The beam gun, under him, was wearing a hole through his belly.

"If you don't mind, it doesn't matter," the BUD/S instructors had yelled. "The only easy day was yesterday." "Embrace the suck." "All in, all the time." "Pain is weakness leaving the body."

And in mission after mission, from Afghanistan to Iraq to Ashaara to Woody, he'd managed to bull through. To accomplish the mission.

At some point, though, even the sturdiest steel failed. Maybe he'd broken already, in the torture session on Woody Island. He couldn't remember. They'd come so close to starving in the camp that he'd lost it, after he'd killed the girl guard, and started to carve out a piece of fatty meat. Until an appalled Ragger had stopped him.

The long hungry march through the mountains, skirting cliffs in the dark, climbing snow-covered slopes of unstable scree. Another test.

But then, the thing he still couldn't figure. That . . . *experience* . . . he'd had. Did God, or Allah, or whatever you called Him, still speak to men? Had he spoken to Teddy Oberg? Raised in Hollywood privilege, but fallen. Brought low, to killer, man of violence, failed filmmaker?

"Fuck it," he muttered. Don't think. Just execute.

He dug into the sand and pushed with his toes.

Until his head broke the top of a dune, and he froze.

He blinked at distant lights. No. Not so distant.

About two hundred meters away, two very faint illuminations. He reached up and adjusted his goggles, passive only, so he didn't set off any alarms.

Two slits glowed low to the ground. Guardhouses, made of what looked like local sand but was probably sand-frosted concrete. In the green seethe of night vision, bright beams glared from them like searchlights. He ducked quickly. IR illuminators. And above those, a flat panel that looked like some kind of directed-energy or plasma weapon.

Overhead imagery had scoped out a cunningly concealed entrance between the bunkers. But to reach it, they had to neutralize the guard posts.

Unfortunately, if the insurgents crawled any closer, they'd be lit up like deer on a superhighway. With that flood of infrared even their woolly coats wouldn't shield them. There'd be machine guns in those bunkers. And phones, to a reaction force based inside.

He could shoot the lights out, but that would warn whoever manned the bunkers. There might be external sensors, too. Something as high-tech as this, that wouldn't be out of place.

He checked his watch, then the sky. The first gray of dawn would be here all too soon. Enough starlight, though, to catch a back-turned face wrapped in black cloth. He lifted his head, very slightly, and nodded.

Two dark forms rose from the sand, shaking it off. They were slight, smaller even than the other insurgents, but bulky under heavy black burkas. They trudged up and over the crest of the dune toward the guard posts, bent under heavy packs.

Teddy slid back into cover. With hand signals, he maneuvered the demo squad into position, then aligned the assault teams behind them.

The stars wheeled as the women trudged slowly toward the bunkers. The rebels lay motionless, faces buried in the sand, fleeces pulled over them. Teddy lay listening for drones. Then raised his head an inch, squinted, and pulsed the goggles again.

A rectangular opening glowed, silhouetting one of the women. Then it occulted, a door closing.

A flash flickered at the observation slit. A *thump* trembled away through the sand. When he pulsed the goggles again the door hung awkwardly athwartships in its jamb.

The suicide vests had been Qurban's idea. Teddy had agreed, when he couldn't come up with a better way to deal with the guard posts. Now one was out of action. The occupants of the other had been too suspicious to let in a woman approaching alone from the desert, crying that she was lost, to be let in, to be given water.

Regardless, he couldn't lie here any longer. Pushing to his feet, throwing off the sheepskin, he shouted, "RPG teams, attack!"

Yells and screams as the command was repeated down the line.

Among the stars, along the top of the hill, silhouettes rose out of the desert like the sandworms of Dune. They waded downslope, then paused, reorganizing into fire teams, just as he'd taught them. They started forward.

But suddenly they wavered. Some halted in place. Others bent as if into a high wind, covering their faces with their arms. Teddy frowned, and started forward himself.

Then he too halted, pinned in place as heat seared his face and the exposed backs of his hands. It felt exactly like holding his skin against a fired-up hot plate. Scorching, burning. He could feel the blisters rising. But after a moment in hell the scorching faded. The beam, whatever it was, had moved on.

To his right, lances of bright fire as rocket-propelled grenades lashed out toward the observation slit of the remaining post. The heat cut off abruptly. When he pulsed the goggles again the flat plate was gone. Blown off, leaving only a rotating stub.

Time to act. He went to one knee and pushed the Initiate stud on the beam gun. Its awkward "barrel" wavered as it whined, charging up. The green diode winked on, and he swept it along the top of the dune.

The drone dropped straight from the dawning sky, rotating as it fell. Fifty feet above the sand it suddenly snapped out of the descent, stabilized, and came whirring in at them. Teddy twisted his upper body to track it, got it in the reflex sight, and pressed the trigger. The red Engage LED came on. Then began blinking, as the circuitry identified the command signal and began jamming.

The drone fired six rounds, *brrrp*, then seemed to decide that was a bad idea. It shuddered and rotated slightly, as if distracted.

Then it lost its grip on the air. Tumbling end over end, it dove violently into the sand, throwing up a spray of gray dust as it crumpled.

Releasing the stud—Vlad had warned battery life was limited—Teddy got up and half sprinted, half limped toward the entrance, which his demo team was hoofing it back from. He took a knee again fifty meters off and scanned the sky once more. A distant speck wavered, but did not approach.

The doors flashed. The blast thumped his chest. Twelve pounds of C-4, divided between the hinges and the centerline of the doors, blew thick steel chunks out cartwheeling into the desert. One door came down square on an insurgent, whose scream was cut short. Teddy rose again and limped on past, bending to pick up the dead man's AK, but still carrying the beam gun too, tucked under his arm.

A cloud of choking smoke. Teddy pointed to Nasrullah and waved him on in. The platoon leader screamed to his men, beckoning them on. They swarmed into the entrance, firing down the corridor inside.

Teddy had to stop and blow, bent over, resting the two weapons on his knees. Just too fucking tired . . . hard to keep up with twenty-year-olds. Especially guys who'd grown up scampering over mountains eleven thousand feet up.

That was when the second quadcopter popped over the rise, bearing directly down on him. The machine gun, slung on a pod beneath speed-blurred rotors, winked as it came. The *brrrrrp* of a long burst stitched up the sand leading to Teddy's boots. He hesitated for perhaps a tenth of a second. Then dropped the drone gun, charged the AK, and set the butt to his shoulder, ignoring the sand-spray of a second burst from the rapidly nearing, canted-forward drone.

Something whined past: small-caliber, high-velocity, the kind that made little holes going in and gaping ones on the way out, after the bullets tumbled and fragmented, blasting apart meat and bone. The drone canted left, then right, hosing the bullet-spray past him in one direction, then the other. He was just starting to think he was invulnerable when a fist slammed into his side, the impact jerking his sights off the oncoming target.

The battle starts once you get wounded.

He pulled back onto the jinking drone, muttered, "Fuck you, machine," and pressed the trigger.

FOUR minutes later, inside the complex. Blood soaked his side, but it was still numb. He didn't have time to stop and bandage it. Anyway, not much you could do with an in-and-out other than patch it. He'd slung the beamer over his shoulder at the entrance, aiming the Kalashnikov now as he stepped over bodies, both Han and Uighur, some dead, others moaning and writhing. The Kalash had never been his favorite, but at squash-court range it delivered the mail. The tunnel was twenty yards wide with an arched overhead of corrugated metal and drop lighting. The floor was raw concrete. He limped past parked sedans and something that looked like an olive-drab Chinese version of the Wrangler, but with an extra axle at the rear. None looked to have been driven recently.

Up ahead, flashes, reports, and battle cries. Zigzagging forward, using the vehicles and pallets of boxed supplies labeled in Mandarin for cover, Teddy caught the full-auto chatter of at least three different calibers clamoring down the tunnel. Behind him trotted the litter team, toting a wooden pole. Swaying beneath it like a captured tiger was a black torpedo-shape.

The TA-4. Get it down this corridor, hang a right, find a place to park it; then they could withdraw. Now was when seconds counted. There goddamn had to be a major reaction force on its way, to back up whoever pulled security within the complex.

He was thinking this when a door slammed open and four Chinese in helmets and black tac gear emerged from a side corridor. They moved in urban assault stacking, obviously practiced. He admired the way each pivoted to cover a different threat axis even as he shot the first two down while they were still in the fatal funnel, giving each a burst in the groin and belly, in case they were wearing armor.

The remaining two ducked away behind one of the jeeps. As Teddy signaled his bearers to take cover, the Chinese split up, popping up to mask each other's rushes with fire as they worked forward, obviously intending to pincer him between them.

This was decent. Unfortunately for them, they made two mistakes: not moving fast enough, and expecting him to retreat. Instead Teddy rolled behind a stack of pallets, and crawled rapidly along on one hand and both knees until he figured he was flanking the Chinese closest to him. He popped up above the boxes lined up where he expected the guy would go. And there he was, side profile. Before he could react Teddy double-tapped him in the head. The trooper went down, hard.

Except that after Teddy's second round the rifle clicked empty. "Fuck," he muttered. He dropped the magazine and yeah, it was dry. Should've picked up the rest of the dead rebel's load, but sucking wind and already carrying the beamer, he'd let it go. A bad decision.

But one he could fix. He ducked back as a burst blasted apart the boxes he'd just fired from, filling the air with rice flour. Surprise, speed, and violence won in close quarters. This lone survivor would already be rattled, from having his buddies dropped.

A thud, a rolling clank, off to his right, but no pop of a grenade spoon.

A can or something, thrown to make him reveal his position. Instead, bent double, Teddy limped rapidly around the line of pallets to where the third Han, the one he'd just double-tapped, had gone down.

The guy was still dying. Bleeding out, convulsing, eyeballs rolled back, out of it. Teddy stamped a boot on his throat to make sure, crushing the windpipe. He picked up the trooper's rifle—a QBZ-95, the carbine model—and racked it. A live cartridge flew out. The guy had grenades, too. Creeping to his left, Teddy popped up and triggered a short burst toward where he'd started from.

A head jerked up from the pallets ahead, looking downtunnel. As he'd expected, hearing his buddy's rifle behind him had made the guy complacent. Teddy stitched a burst across the back of his skull, enjoying the low recoil impulse of the little high-velocity rounds. Then shot him again in the upper back as the black-clad soldier twisted and sagged, disappearing amid the stores. As soon as he triggered the last round Teddy dropped again, in time to let another burst from uptunnel pass harmlessly overhead.

Ears ringing—he liked this carbine, but firing it in an enclosed space blew your eardrums in—he yelled to the guys with the litter, who'd taken cover while he dealt with the defenders, "Follow me!" He closed the side door, lived one of the grenades, and wedged it under the handle, in case somebody else decided to make an entrance, stage right. Then wheeled and limped on, waving the guys with the Package after him.

He touched his side. Sopping wet now, and the numbness was wearing off. It was gonna hurt, all right.

When he reached the crossbar of the T more bodies lay about, some in dull green uniforms, others in the shalwar kameez of the insurgents. Here and there, too, a few in white lab coats. Some fights had gone hand to hand, judging from the way the corpses were interlocked, and the blood and guts congealing on the concrete.

Teddy swept left and caught Nasrullah's glance. The platoon leader had his remaining men in cover, ready to hold against any assault from the living areas that lay that way. He swept right, but saw no one in the right-hand tunnel. There were no pallets here, no cover, just concrete, overhead lighting, and doors opening to both sides. And through the singing of his ears, a low, susurrant hum. Each door was labeled, but he couldn't read Chinese.

Where the fuck was Qurban? Had the big tough al-Qaeda dude chickened out? Then he noticed that each door's window had been bashed in.

Fire crackled suddenly from ahead. Squinting through the carbine's optic, Teddy kicked open one of the doors and peered in.

Into an antiseptic, humanless world, inhabited only by that unending hum, now so deep it vibrated his teeth. The room was floored with white, ceilinged with cream acoustic tile, and only dimly lit by widely spaced overhead fixtures, as if sight were not really necessary here. The converging rows of servers, computers, whatever they were, breathed a continuing sigh through hundreds of fans. Perhaps that was the singing hum he'd been hearing. It was mesmerizing, and he sucked a breath. Blue LEDs glowed at each cabinet, spaced every few meters down a receding length, fading into darkness so far away he couldn't actually even guess at how far under the desert the space extended.

"What the fuck *is* this," he muttered. Obviously computers, but he'd never seen banks of them like this. He crossed the corridor and poked his head into another door, to be confronted by the exact same sight, as if he were wandering a house of mirrors.

If every one of these doors opened onto a corridor like this, there had to be thousands of these ominously blinking machines.

Okay, Obie, Teddy, Scarface, Lingxiù Oberg al-Amriki—whoever you are now—better focus. The litter bearers had been hanging back. He waved them forward. They looked cowed, bent under the weight of their burden, but intimidated, too. He gave them a smile and clapped a skinny kid on the back. "*Ni shi haoren*," he told them, but got only frightened glances in return.

Okay, they were spooked, too. Odd, there didn't seem to be many people around. Just the security force, which had actually been fairly light, and the few white-coats he'd stepped over.

Where was everybody?

What *was* this place?

"The mission," he grunted, and limped rapidly along until he figured he'd gone about two hundred meters down the right hand of the T. He couldn't shake the creepy suspicion he'd missed something and was screwing up. Generally when he felt that way, he'd discover later he was right, but just now he couldn't see where he was going wrong. Just that this all seemed too easy. He'd lost maybe twenty out of his assault force, serious losses, sure, but still, it should have been harder than this, penetrating a high-security installation that obviously meant a lot to the enemy.

But hell, when you catch a break . . . He pointed the bearers into one of the side rooms. They slid the Package out of its sling, easing it to the floor between the purring ranks of cabinets. The tiles sagged under the weight; for a second Teddy wondered if they'd hold. But they did, and he signaled the littermen out to establish a perimeter while he bent to the weapon.

Two ways to initialize the thing. The simplest was with an app on his phone. He called it up, entered the access code, and hit Confirm.

FIFTEEN MINUTES TO GET CLEAR the screen read. ALLOW AT LEAST 1000 METERS BETWEEN PERSONNEL AND GROUND ZERO.

Okay, a klick in fifteen, they could do that. If they weren't carrying wounded, a decision he'd already gotten the Uighurs' buy-in for. He fingered his side, which was really hurting now. A slow seep of sticky blood, but he could still walk. Hell, yeah. If the alternative was getting fried.

He slid the green circle sideways until it winked and turned red. 15:00 came up on the screen. Then 14:59. 14:58. 14:57 . . .

"Time to scoot, Teddy boy," he muttered. He straightened and pointed his guys toward the exit. Out the door, down the corridor, to the left. "*Women zhai zeli wancheng. Ran women likai zheli.*" Let's get the hell out of Dodge, or as close as he could manage in pidgin Han.

But as they emerged into the corridor again something loomed out of the dimness ahead. Teddy braked, puzzled. What the fuck, over.

At first he thought it was a guy. Huge, but still a human silhouette.

Then he realized it wasn't.

He froze, staring at the thing.

It towered from the concrete nearly to the curved overhead. Two-legged, but it seemed to glide forward rather than walk. A head with three cameras swiveled this way and that as it advanced. From there on down it presented solid-looking green-painted metal.

Beside him Qurban was taking aim. Bullets sparked off the thing's head. But each time he fired, one of the cameras seemed to . . . *blink*. A steel shutter, snapping closed over the optic when microwave radar or lidar detected the possibility of damage.

So it could sense as well as see. Probably had infrared too.

Astonishing him even more, it spoke. In a computerized voice, not monotone, but the singsong inflection of Han made it sound even stranger. "*Tóuxiáng, ni huì shòudào haopíng.*" He wasn't completely sure, but it seemed to be inviting them to surrender.

Well, fuck that. Teddy rolled behind a stack of palleted supplies as the thing skated forward, its head inclined. Motors whirred. Steel wheels grated on concrete. The cameras moved independently both of the head and of one another, mounted on stalks, like the prehensile eyes of a lobster. One locked on Teddy. An arm lifted, steadied, locked, and fired a ripping short burst of heavy slugs. They tore through the bags in front of him in a spray of rice to spin bronzeglittering on the concrete. One hit his thigh, but robbed of velocity by the rice, the impact only made him grunt.

"Fire together. One, two, *three*!" Teddy yelled. He and the hajji both popped up simultaneously. Teddy hosed the chest area. His bullets didn't seem to do much more than scar the paint.

As they continued firing, a litter bearer scurried forward, doubled over. It was the skinny kid. Before the towering machine could react he tucked a grenade beneath its left foot. Then straightened and turned. But before he could escape the left arm rotated backward, in a way no human limb could have flexed, gripped him at the waist, and whirred shut.

With a choked scream, the insurgent came apart. His chest and head fell in one direction, his legs in another. They kicked, then went still, gushing blood.

A short, sharp bang and the left foot lifted slightly from the concrete. The robot held it aloft. Shook it. Then set it back down, rebalancing in an elephantine fashion that gave the impression it must weigh many tons. The upper half of the bisected rebel went on screaming, covering his face with his hands, until his cries ebbed and he too fell silent.

The robot took a tentative stride forward. It favored its foot at first, then seemed to sense it wasn't seriously damaged and took another, firmer step.

Teddy fired out his magazine until the carbine clicked empty. He dropped it and rolled from cover, another burst following him, and scrambled into a side corridor. Not the one with the Package, though they all looked identical. A hall of mirrors . . . With Qurban and his remaining littermen close behind, he limped rapidly down the passage. When he glanced back the robot was peering in the door. It looked far too large to fit through it, though.

A pincer gripped the jamb. It levered, and motors whirred.

It tore the jamb upward. Its other arm gripped the far side, and tore that apart as well.

"Fuck," Teddy muttered, scrambling away across the smooth plastic floor. Searching for a shortcut between corridors, or a way out.

Actually, he wasn't sure what he was doing. Scooting like a scared rabbit seemed to about sum it up.

The thing stepped through. It set a foot gingerly on the floor, as if testing it. The tiles groaned and bent.

It lifted its foot, ducked, and peered through the torn-open door. Aiming carefully, it fired a burst after them. A rebel spun and fell, dead before he hit the floor. But the other projectiles whined harmlessly past, centerlined between the parallel rows of consoles.

Teddy got the idea. It was programmed to avoid harming the computers. It couldn't even enter the computing area, since apparently there were cable runs under the thin flooring. The thing was dangerous as hell, but could only navigate on the concrete pavement of the main tunnels, or maybe outside on firm ground.

But what was directing it? The monster was big, but not large enough to have a man inside. So it was either self-directed or remotely controlled.

If the latter, who was at the controls?

Or . . . what?

He had no idea what all these computers were doing, but they were *active.* The omnipresent hum, the dancing LEDs, told him that.

Could they be piloting their guardian? Obviously that wasn't all they were here for, but could that be part of it?

If so, there might be a way around this thing.

At last, a door. He motioned the others back and went through first, sweeping the muzzle of the carbine left, then right. But encountering only chill air, the queer diffuse light, the same acoustic tile overhead, the same smooth, perfectly clean plastic underfoot.

Another door. He took that one fast but cautious, and emerged into what looked to be a maintenance area. Grounded stainless-steel workbenches. Racks of test equipment. Boxes of spare cards, ready to plug in when a blade failed. The air was cold and still here, too, and no one, white-coated or otherwise, was in sight.

Staying low, he crab-walked back toward the main tunnel. Best guess, they were abreast of where the access and logistics tunnel intersected the crossbar of the T. Depending on how smart this thing was, it either would be waiting for them there, or had left for the bunking area to clear out Nasrullah's platoon.

He didn't want to think about how many casualties his insurgents might have taken. He hadn't heard any firing for a couple of minutes now.

A couple of minutes . . . oh shit. He checked his phone. The glowing numerals nearly stopped his heart. *11:29 . . . 11:28 . . . 11:27.*

If he didn't get cracking, they'd still be bottled up in here when the Package went off.

Behind him, Qurban gripped his shoulder. "Lingxiù al-Amriki . . . where are you going?"

Sucking a breath, Teddy handed him the carbine. "Just follow me. And stay out of the way."

A shattered window and a wash of white light told him the corridor lay ahead. He shifted left and right, but couldn't spot the robot. To the left, right, or downtunnel, between them and escape? He'd have chosen the latter course, but did a machine think like a human?

No way to tell. Seizing one of the steel rolling worktables, he pushed it forward, ready to topple it for cover if the monster suddenly lurched into sight, and unslung the beam gun. It whined softly as it powered up.

When the LED went to orange he kicked the table rolling out the door, took four quick steps, yelled "Hooyah!" and leaned around the jamb, pointing the antennaed muzzle.

The Iron Monster was facing him forty meters away, slightly crouched, as if waiting to spring. Bodies lay at its feet like sacrifices to some terrible juggernaut. As the table rolled out the oculars rotated, locking onto it, then onto him.

It straightened, striding forward as it raised its weapons.

Teddy caught the spinning oculars in the reflex sight and pressed the Fire stud. The LED went from orange to red, then began blinking. The circuitry had identified a command signal and was jamming. But the thing was still moving. The machine gun steadied its aim on him. The robot leaned forward, bracing itself against recoil. Teddy stared into the multiple open mouths of the Gatling gun, waiting for the flash, the impact of the slugs.

Instead the beast halted. The oculars kept spinning, but the joints seemed to lock. It seemed to relax slightly, to settle, as if it had suddenly grown even heavier.

He waited another second, but it didn't move. Just squatted there, immobile, as if paralyzed.

Which the fucking thing might just be, if its control system was jammed and there was no onboard intelligence. He kicked the heavy table over and took a knee, resting the forestock of the beamer on the folded steel edge, and thumbed the power stud to Off for a second.

The huge green machine flinched, and tried to stand again. Teddy rethumbed the stud. Green, to orange, to blinking red.

The thing stood immobile, its uncanny mechanical simulacrum of life processes halted, in abeyance.

Then his gun's Battery Low light came on.

At the same moment, from down the main hallway a second gigantic form came striding forward. It hulked between his men and the exit, nearly filling the arched space of the corridor. And this second monster was if anything even larger than the first. "Fuck," he muttered. "What is this, Grendel's fucking mother?"

Nasrullah and six other insurgents—Christ, was that all that was left of his platoon?—rolled out from cover and began firing. As Teddy had already discovered, though, small-arms projectiles just irritated the things, like honeybees stinging a grizzly bear. This one wasn't even firing back. It just came rolling forward, intent on ripping them to pieces with the hydraulically driven, pincerlike appendages it extended in front of itself.

Teddy wavered. He could jam one or the other, but not both. The smaller one was to his left, uptunnel; the larger to his right, blocking their escape.

The Battery Low light began to blink.

He was still paralyzed himself, as indecisive and immobilized as the machine he held entranced, when the snarl of a diesel at high revs echoed from downtunnel. It neared rapidly, the transmission shifting gears higher as it accelerated.

The hulking machine dipped a shoulder, glancing backward. It started to twist around.

So it was momentarily off balance when the uparmored Wrangler slammed into it from behind at full speed. The momentum instantly transferred to the inelastic steel of the guardian like a cue ball to a billiard ball, catapulting it headfirst past Teddy, missing him by inches, to slam through the flimsy partition of the computer bay. The monster immediately crashed through the flooring, which parted under its weight. It fell through first one level, to judge by the fade of heavy crashing and banging. Then another. And perhaps even a third.

Teddy marveled. *Other* floors of computers, deep below this one? Then glanced at his phone.

3:14. 3:13 . 3:12 . . .

They weren't going to get out of here. Not in time.

But he still had to try.

He sprint-limped past the crumpled hood of the Wrangler, peered inside, then reached in. Qurban and the others gave him a hand, and together they extracted a dazed Guldulla, mouth and face bloody, from the driver's seat and through the window. His second in command was mumbling something incoherent.

Teddy squeezed his shoulder. "You done good," he told him in Uighur.

But the exit was still two hundred meters away. Nope, we ain't gonna make it, he thought.

Then he frowned. Looking at the line of dusty vehicles.

THEY followed their headlights, tearing down the road at a hundred kilometers an hour, the other jeeps and sedans slewing wildly behind them. Weird, taking the wheel after so long. A moment of nostalgia for his old Shelby Mustang . . . then he concentrated on driving.

Excited chatter broke out in the backseat. The car was crammed with the remaining insurgents, some bloody, all smeared with burned powder and gabbling with excitement. Then he remembered, too. Somewhere along here, his boys had planted mines in the road. They had to get away from the Package, but he didn't want to blow them all up doing it.

He twisted to look back, and asked if any demo guys had made it out. One guy raised his hand. "Okay, great. Where'd you put the mine?"

The rebel shrugged. "It was at night, Lingxiù. Somewhere along here?"

"Just . . . fucking . . . great," Teddy growled. He glanced at his watch, did a quick calculation, and took his foot off the accelerator. When the speedometer dropped he pulled off onto the berm. The surface here was firmer than the surrounding sand, but still the tires slipped, the car sideskidded. He checked the timer again. *0:21 . . . 0:20.*

"Debark!" he yelled, and braked so hard the Wrangler spun, coming to rest in a cloud of dust. They piled out and dropped to the sand, digging in, pushing up small hillocks between them and whatever cataclysm was going to happen behind them. At the last possible moment, he turned off his phone and buried it, too.

The ground quaked. Not heavily, but a chilling shiver that disquieted his genitals, which were pressed into the sand. A queer crisp squeak or crackle, maybe individual grains of sand shifting. Head down, he didn't see a flash. Maybe there hadn't been one.

When he came up for air the desert was dark. Then, as he blinked, the stars came out. Passionless and remote, barely twinkling in the fine high desert air. They watched his men as they crawled out from their nests and brushed sand from their weapons.

Teddy didn't get up. He lay shaking, and couldn't stop. Rolling onto his back, he stared up at the silent constellations.

Remembering another night, high in the Tien Shan. When Something had spoken to him.

Beside him Qurban muttered, "Lingxiù . . . you all right?"

Teddy tongued gritty sand from his mouth and spat. The constellations lurched above him. "Yeah . . . yeah, I'm . . . fucking great," he rasped.

"Is it done? What we came for?"

He panted fast and hard and finally got back a little control. He rolled to his knees. His head reeled. He coughed out more dust and spat, long drooling strands, noticing vaguely only now that the eastern desert was graying. Light was revisiting the world. They had to get out of here, off the road and under cover from the air. . . .

"Is it done?" The squat scarred man beside him repeated, shaking Teddy's shoulder.

"Fuck, get off me. . . . It went off. That's all we had to do, get it there and set it off."

He dug out the phone, but didn't turn it on. Touching his side gingerly, he winced. The wound had clotted. He felt dizzy, feverish. Well, they had antibiotics, no problemo.

He forced himself up and gazed around, tottering, knees shaking. All too few other forms were shaking themselves off, staring around as he was doing. And probably counting the survivors, like he was. They'd gone in with eighty men. Fewer than a score stood around him, and many sagged or sat down again in the sand, exhausted, wounded, bleeding.

Mission accomplishment, check. But with 75 percent casualties.

He hoped whatever they'd destroyed was worth the cost.

Beside him the old hajji was kneeling. Teddy glanced down. The others knelt too, in a neat line on the sand. Most had spread scraps of carpet, or their shemaghs. They faced Mecca, all together.

"Dawn is coming. Time for morning prayer." Qurban smiled up at him, face smeared with black blood and sand. "You fight beside us. You are one of us, in all but faith. Will you not surrender, at last, al-Amriki ?

And gain the peace you have always sought. Your very name, you know. Theo-dore. It means gift of God, does it not?"

Teddy's world lurched. The sky tilted again. He jackknifed, holding his stomach, shaking, recollecting not the desert before his eyes but something beyond description, beyond reality, beyond Time. A revelation, when he'd expected only more suffering. A Presence, where through his whole life he'd assumed there was nothing.

All things were of Him.

All things were foreordained.

There was no chance. Choice was an illusion.

You have always done My will. . . .

A sensation, inside his chest, of many small parts long locked but now unlocking . . . dropping out of alignment, then rotating minutely and rising again to reengage. Remeshing into a different combination. One that changed not the outside world but the process, the eye, the I, that perceived it.

And in so doing, altered all Creation.

Teddy Oberg fell to his knees among his men as Qurban led the prayers in a loud voice, exultant, triumphant. He didn't know the words, but he could follow the prostrations.

One among others now, the Lingxiù rose to his feet, bowed, then knelt again. "Allah," he murmured, when he could not follow the words. "Allah. Allah. Allah."

Yes, a voice whispered in his inmost ear in reply, a word more intimate by far than any he'd heard in mortal life.

Whatever you do is right. This has all been written by Me.

"God is great," the Lingxiù whispered.

Then he shouted it aloud, dancing, yelling up into the rosy dawn over and over as the others chuckled, patting his back. They joined in the chorus, firing their weapons into the air in long ripping bursts that floated away across the desert. *"Allahu akhbar! Allahu akhbar!"*

God is great.

God is great.

22

Taiwan

HECTOR Ramos huddled mute and motionless in the mud at the bottom of his fighting hole, gripping the plastic rosary in his cargo pocket. The barrage had been going on so long he could no longer formulate thoughts. Descended into the mute suffering no-self of a tormented animal, he lay with head tucked, helmet locked under his other arm.

Rain pelted him. The ground quaked. The soft dirt when it burst apart was orange, like the guts of a broken melon. Under that was rock. Fragments of steel hissed overhead. Shattered stone and the red soil clattered down, half burying him and Corporal Karamete. They lay curled together like twins before birth in six inches of slime and splintered rock from entrenching explosive and then the bombardment. He wheezed into the gas mask, hoping dully that the filter would take out the explosive residue that blew over them in invisible clouds, but no longer caring if it didn't.

The other guy in the hole with them was a replacement. Hector didn't remember his name. Fresh out of boot camp, without even School of Infantry. The assistant squad leader was holding him down, making sure he didn't lose it and jump up during the barrage. On the boot's other side, also holding him, was the last Chad, C323.

Tall stolid Sergeant Clay was dead, killed by a creeping mine that had guided on his body heat west of Chishang. Little Lieutenant Ffoulk was gone, blown over a cliff and missing, presumed lost. Four of Hector's squad were out of action, one KIA in a barrage, one blinded by a laser dazzler, and two others wounded. The Chads had broken down one by one—the C models were smarter, but didn't seem as durable as the Bs—or gotten wasted in one way or another. All except for 323, which just kept going. He hoped he'd expended the others in ways that had kept down the Marine body count.

The load-bearing exoskeletons were pretty much useless too, after the first couple of days. The platoon had quietly surveyed them, just leaving them behind as they'd advanced, along with a lot of other gear that hadn't worked out.

They were a week into the campaign, with no end in sight. It had started low-key, with only the lightly opposed securing of the airhead. The assault grew bloodier as the Marines pushed north along the beach road. They'd fought an encounter battle near Chishang with elements of a second-line Chinese infantry division. After demolishing that unit, the general had wanted to keep pushing north, toward Taipei. But the Army needed help. Higher had turned the axis of advance left and started them slogging up along the mountain road, intending to break through and emerge behind the enemy line of resistance.

But there was no room to maneuver in the mountains of central Taiwan. Highway 20 led west across the island, following the river. The division had managed to link up with the Nationalists, though Ramos hadn't seen any yet. The insurgents, hastily reequipped with U.S. weapons and stiffened by Force Recon teams and close air support, had driven slowly up the right side of the valley, taking hill after hill. Meanwhile the grunts advanced on the left, in rough step, along ridges that built higher and higher until only this single pass remained.

These mountains were rugged, wild, scabbed with jungle. The maps showed only one village. The armored columns had dueled in the pass for three days, the largest tank battle in Marine history. Until losses got too high, and word had come down to wait for the Army to chew up more enemy before the Marines mounted another push.

The next day both flanks had shouldered forward, to gain the high ground on both sides of the valley. If they got lucky and locked the enemy into a defensive position, the Air Force could drop MOABs on them. But within a day and a night that advance had stalled too. The narrow, switchbacked two-laner was more difficult than anyone had expected for heavy American vehicles to negotiate. The Chinese blew bridges and toppled a cliff. As the lead elements left naval gunfire support behind, and exhausted the fleet's land attack missile inventory, they'd had to depend on organic artillery and air. Both used up ammunition and fuel far faster than anyone had expected. After a couple of miles, this had stopped the flank advances, too.

Now the Marine Third and the Nationalist 905th were hammering away toe to toe with the Chinese First Amphibious Mechanized and the 45th Airborne Mechanized divisions. The battle had gone on day and night, with only brief pauses of mutual exhaustion. Both allies were in contact, fighting to hold the heights to either side. If they buckled, the enemy could break through the middle, and overrun the battered forces holding the valley.

Only Charlie had heavier artillery than the Marines and a lot more of it than Intel had predicted. Right now they were hurling shells as if they had freight trains running right back to the mainland. Probably, the captain said, to soften them up for a renewed assault.

It would be head-to-head butting, a ground game in the mud. So now, huddled in his hole with tac gloves locked over his helmet, Hector lay empty as a seashell while the earth jolted and earthquaked around him. His ragged Cameleons displayed only brief swatches of color, since the dirt was so ground in by now that the men were the color of the dirt. He lay atop an M240, the new lightweight model printed out of titanium. Trained as a machine gunner, he felt safer behind it than with a rifle.

A heavy blast blew more rock and dirt over them. The recruit groaned loudly. The assistant squad leader was talking to him in a slow calming monotone, hugging his waist. Hector pushed his head up. Shuddering, he tried his Glasses again. They were dead, though the opticals still worked. No calm dulcet voice advised him now. To pass orders he had to use hand signals or yell. After the first couple of days hardly anything digital had worked at all. Both sides were jamming and EMPing from the Ka-band on down. The clouds of hand-launched drones had vanished, sucked up by the rain, the mountains, and the raptor UAVs that soon fell in their turn.

Until they cowered in the mud under a furious barrage. Just like World War I.

He figured that in the end it was still going to be human against human, mediated by lead.

SOME interminable time later the ground ceased vibrating. It was still raining hard, but the shelling lifted, rumbling away into the distance.

He kept his head down, trying to quiet his shaking. One more minute until he had to get up. Ten more seconds . . .

A sliding rush of wet dirt and pebbles, and a hand gripped his shoulder. Hector pulled down his mask and rolled over.

The company runner was a gracile, ironhearted Pfc. In civilian life Patterson was a girls' soccer coach. She broken-field sprinted through the barrages while others cowered, wearing two sets of jelly armor and carrying nothing but a pistol and supplies for the corpsmen. Her face was orange dirt streaked by rain, and her pale eyebrows quizzical. "Hey, Sergeant. Another day in Marine paradise."

Hector spat out grit. "Fuck you, Wombat."

"Need a report. Battalion wants to know effectives remaining."

"Fuck. Don't know."

"You're Rampart now, Sergeant. Till they send another O."

"I don't know. Don't know!"

"Secret Squirrels expect an assault. Ten to fifteen vehicles moving up the road. Heavies. Self-propelled mortars. Major wants ammo count. Effective rifles. Tac says, move up to the edge of the cliff. Don't let them push you off 298. You're the point up here. You gotta hold."

That was their position. Hill 298. They were dug in on a terraced ridge, with only the hilltop above them. He muttered, "The edge? Where they're fucking shelling?"

"They're not shelling us now," she pointed out.

"They will be in a minute. An assault . . . we need reinforcements. We need counterbattery. Comms. Ammo. Tell 'em that."

"I heard something about a team coming up to help you."

Hector didn't want to get out of the hole. He wanted to cower in the mud. Away from the hydraulic knives that whickered the air. Away from the Kill Room, which was everyplace above ground level.

But he was responsible for the platoon now. A fucking E-5, and he had the platoon. "Fuck," he grunted again, and pushed himself up.

The hill had been tangled jungle two days before. Now it was blasted-down matchstick trees and exposed rock with a coat of raw wet harrowed soil. The orange mud glittered with steel fragments and ammo casings. They were dug in on a level bench above the valley, with a fifty-meter rise behind them, then a saddle to the rear of that. Hector trudged his line, fighting hole to fighting hole. Patterson tagged behind, underhanding med packs to the corpsmen.

At Milliron's fire team Ramos stood over a hole in the ground pasted around with a pinkish doughnut of body parts, unidentifiable except for an incredibly long spiral of intestine, glistening with moisture, and a boot with the lower leg still in it, and a skull fragment upside down like a bowl of gray goo. No, wait, there was a spinal cord, too. The air smelled of burnt explosive and boiled blood. "Direct hit," the fire team leader said, tone dead, eyes small dark holes. He rubbed a stubbled chin over and over, like a madman locked in a trance. "No point callin' the doc."

"Who was it?"

"Salacia. Flynn."

Hector remembered their faces, and where they were from, all of them. Kansas, Indiana, New Mexico, Pennsylvania. The names of their girls and guys on the Wall of Shame. But he felt nothing yet. Just numb detachment. Another shell crumped upslope, blowing rocks to patter down around them. He crouched, ready to dive for the grisly hole, but the barrage he'd expected didn't follow.

Yet. Still trailed by the runner, he crawled to the edge of the cliff. Sprawled full length, and peered over.

Not really a cliff, just a slope steep enough that no trees had grown on it, leaving bare earth and rock and bushes. Smoke blew over them from down in the valley. It was more like a canyon there, precipices combed by waterfalls. Before the war the view might have been beautiful. Two hundred meters below, a switchback was blocked with wrecked tanks and APCs. The dead lay in rows where the right flank had dug in. Some of the vehicles were still burning, and the stenches of scorched rubber, explosive, and roasting bodies seethed and marinated like the wind from hell's mess hall.

Hector scribbled on Patterson's pad, adding the sums with tongue clamped between his teeth, and jerked his thumb rearward. "We need comms, ammo, reinforcements," he said again. "Tell them."

She nodded and sprinted off into the murk. Dropping into the shell hole, he felt around in his assault pack, found one last MRE, and tore it open, staring blankly at the pieces plastered into the dirt.

Even chewing exhausted him. His jaw seemed to have lost the ability to close. Finally he gave up on the meal, since he couldn't taste it anyway. He rolled out and snatched another peer over the edge, keeping his head low. The enemy's snipers were dangerous out to a mile or more. They'd had their own scout sniper team until the night before, when one of the creeping mines had scrabbled up the cliff somehow and homed in on them. Hector hated the six-legged things. They moved slowly, like ticks, but never stopped. They snuggled up to you as you slept. Then chirped, so they startled you awake a quarter second before they detonated.

The chirp, that was what Hector couldn't figure out. Unless it was just to scare the fuck out of everybody before it blew some unlucky bastard apart.

Some minutes ticked past. He kept expecting the shelling to resume, but instead it tapered off, then stopped entirely.

Around seven H&S sent up chow and ammo on a robo mule. Eggs, toast, and the nasty sausages everyone called "dicks of death." Hector got the ammo out to the line first, then chow. The food was cold, and watery with rain, but a private brewed quadruple-strength MRE coffees. Black smoke rose in the distance, and the *whump* of distant explosions. But only an occasional shot echoed from the valley.

He didn't like the silence. He kept checking his sensors. A few still worked. But nothing seemed to be coming their way yet.

NOT too much later, Patterson scampered up again to say his reinforcements were here. She brought a heavy brick of a radio, too. One of the old PRC-117s. He accepted it doubtfully, looking it over. Then got up. Leaving his Pig with the Chad, he walked to the rear to meet the new arrivals, keeping an eye out for cover on the way in case the shelling resumed. The rain had finally stopped, though. That was a plus, though it meant the smoke was heavier.

The team was in spotless Cameleons. The guy in the lead even had a crease in his trou. Their helmets looked new. Even their boots were clean. They stood erect, not crouched, and frowned down at Hector as if at a leper. He felt like one: wet, dirt-smeared, filthy, stinking, with shit staining his pants and ripped gear and hands that only stopped shaking when he held a machine gun.

Marines didn't wear insignia in combat. "Platoon commander?" the creased guy asked, pulling a bottle of water out and extending it.

Hector uncapped it and chugged it. "Am now." He wiped his mouth with a filthy sleeve.

"Charlie's gearing up to hit you. Fortunately, they can't get armor up here. We're from Division, and we're here to help."

Hector nodded. He picked out a rock he could dive behind and squatted, watching. They jabbed jointed rods into the soil and stretched an IR tent, for overhead concealment, then snapped open crates. Finally they gestured him back, and the lead guy—Hector figured him for staff brass—fingered a controller.

Something buzzed, and a disk the size of a turkey platter jumped into the air. It stopped at eye level, hovering with a buzz. A camera topped a curved carapace like a horseshoe crab's. Its lens clicked from one jarhead to the next, as if memorizing their faces. Then the thing wheeled and circled them, dipping to search each fighting hole. The grunts stared at it dully, as if nothing surprised them anymore. The flying plate seemed to wink in and out of visibility as it crossed a patch of tumbled rock and plowed-up ground.

"The fuck's that?" muttered Karamete.

"NASA developed it," the Crease said loftily. "The Gamma. Charlie won't even get in rifle range."

"They're what, killer drones?"

"Like your Chads. Only you don't have to give them permission. You got OPs out?"

Hector told him they didn't, since they were at the edge of a cliff. He shot the thing a distrustful look as it scouted their perimeter, then dipped below the dropoff. The rest of the team were deploying more. Three dozen of the things lifted into the wind, oriented themselves, and sped off. "Up and away, my pretties," Crease said. Then, to Hector, "They look for avenues of approach that give the enemy cover. Patrol in short hops until they sense movement."

"Then what?"

"Home and destroy. Twenty Gammas, we've seen them get twenty kills."

"In combat?"

Crease looked away. "Well, not yet. Those are test and evaluation's numbers."

Hector wished they'd have sent up another infantry platoon instead, but maybe the things would work. He needed to walk the line again, make super sure his fire teams were set in right and what linked 7.62 he had left was redistributed. "They won't go for us, will they?"

"They won't hit an American."

"How do they know?"

"They integrate uniform, weapon, facial recognition, and query your chip. No ID, facial features Asian, carrying a weapon, they take you out."

Before Hector could object he added, "I know, we've got friendlies without chips on the right flank. There's an inhibit-fire line halfway down the valley. All taken care of, Lieutenant."

"Sergeant," Hector said.

"You kidding? Where's your commander?"

"Out of action. So's the platoon sergeant. That leaves me."

The officer looked doubtful. "Well, warn your guys these things are friendly. And very expensive. We don't want them shot down by mistake."

Karamete said, "Will they return fire if we do?" She'd been taking a breather on a rock, listening. His assistant did that a lot, just listened. Hector didn't mind. Shit, she'd probably get the squad next. Once he got his legs blown off like Clay, or took a shell hit, like the guys spread like birthday frosting around the rim of their fighting hole.

The staff officer said they wouldn't, in a tone that made it clear he got a lot of stupid questions and that had been one. He handed Hector a controller, and demonstrated various screens that showed the things' locations and how to tap into each unit's video. Hector nodded and tucked it into his blouse.

The rain had resumed while they talked, pinging with random drops on the IR netting. Now, with a breath of cold air, it fell in earnest, quickly increasing to a downpour.

Then he heard it. "Incoming!" he yelled, and rolled for the rock he'd scoped out.

The mortars ripped across the hill from one end to the other, then back again. Deadened by the roar of the rain, the blasts sounded like the mountain was huffing deep breaths. They squeezed his lungs as he lay flat, fingers digging into the soil. Probably the self-propelled 120mm's Tac had seen moving up. Hector fumbled with the radio, then yelled to the staff officer, who was flat on the ground, to let Higher know they were under fire. They needed counterbattery, approximate bearing two-nine-zero.

But the techs were pulling out, leaving the equipment cases littering the ridge, the gauzelike tent fluttering in the smoky breeze. Its edge dipped as it shed torrents of rain, then collapsed into a heap as the spindly rods gave way.

The shelling shifted to their flank. Hector scuttled back on hands and knees through the mud and rain, and dropped into the fighting hole in the center of his line.

The last Chad, C323, turned its oculars from the M240 to check him out, but said nothing. Rain danced on its shoulders, on its hatchet-shaped gray metal head, sparkled silver off the machine gun. Hector nodded approval. The bipod was dug in right. 323 was holding a "hand" over the open feed tray, to keep water and grit from fouling the action. The belt was laid in clear to feed. Hector tongued his tac radio, on the off chance, but all he got was the roar of multiband jamming. He tried the older radio next, but the slants were jamming that, too.

The mortars walked back toward them and he cowered. The world staggered. Curled in the mud, he hugged the robot's curved shell. It shifted to shelter him with its torso.

A blast pressed him down in the hole and shattered the eroding mud sliding down around him. Fragments whanged off metal.

A blackness . . .

When he came to, water covered his face. He clawed at his mouth, but more mud filled it. He screamed into the slick cold. Then a powerful arm reached under him and pulled him up. He scrabbled at his face, scraping mud off.

From down the ridge machine-gun fire clattered. Then, amid deeper explosions, engines growled. They didn't sound like tanks or fighting vehicles. These were higher pitched, like the dune buggies the scout snipers roared around in. He needed to see. He needed video. "We got any switchblades left?" he yelled to Karamete.

"All expended."

He remembered then, pulled out the controller. The screen was cracked. Water slid around a blank screen. He threw it away and hunkered again as mortars thundered and lightninged behind him on the saddle. Softening up their rear, interdicting any more reinforcements and supplies.

But they weren't getting reinforcements. Just the disks, which he hadn't seen hide nor hair of since they'd scooted off.

The growl of motors grew, straining, revving. He hesitated, glancing at the assistant squad leader.

I'll go, she mouthed, tilting her helmet toward the drop.

Hector hand-signaled her to stay put. He jumped up and dashed forward. The wet fabric dragged at his legs. His mud-caked boots squished at each stride. He collapsed at the edge, coughing, and clawed his way forward to peer over.

Behind him something grabbed his boot in an iron grip. When he looked back the C was right behind him, lying full length with its belly in the mud. Its oculars eyed him expressionlessly. The nictitating covers blinked every couple of seconds, wiping its lenses clear from the rain.

Between the treetops below, through streaming billows of white anti-targeting smoke that filtered through the shattered forest like hair through a comb, something was moving. No, several somethings. Then, as one reared up to roll over a shell-toppled bole, he saw it clearly.

Only he wasn't quite sure *what* he was seeing. He squinted through the mist and rain and smoke. Why was it that in every battle it seemed to rain? Then another of the sluglike shapes crossed an open patch, approaching the hill. The smoke blew aside for a second and he finally saw one clearly, head on.

Intel was right. The Chinese couldn't get armor up here.

But these weren't tanks.

They were smaller than compact sedans, but larger than motorcycles. Remotely controlled, apparently. Or autonomous. The low-slung dark-green beetles ground along on wide, ridged rubber tracks. Multi-barreled guns pointed here and there as antennaed turrets rotated suspiciously. They bulldozed aside trees and climbed over rocks, and the grinding of their treads on wood and stone was like the chewing of gigantic insects. They were flanked and overheaded by gray-blue quadcopters, and behind them trotted troops in Associated Powers green with camo helmet covers, carrying rifles and light machine guns and RPGs. The drones held their positions like pilot fish on sharks, swaying as sheets of windblown rain trailed between them and Hector. Their high nasal hum overscored the deeper notes of treads and engines and the unending rumble of the mortars.

A coordinated assault: fliers, troops, and the new things. But the green beetles were leading the charge. Their first wave reached the base of the slope and started up. They rocked and nearly tipped backward, but recovered and kept climbing.

As if their progress had disturbed a nest there, suddenly small gray objects darted up, weaving and dipping above the slugs. They engaged the quads first, tongues of fire darting from the disks. A quad tilted and fell, bouncing down the slope, but the beetles still lumbered upward, occasionally firing, but mainly ignoring their mosquito-like attackers.

Then, as Hector watched, one of the disks dropped onto a turret. It clung there for a second. The machine tried to shake it off, but it detonated in a flash of light and puff of gray smoke.

The tracked vehicle emerged from the smoke, still climbing. A scar gleamed on its green painted hull, but otherwise it didn't seem to have been harmed.

Then it noticed him. A fixture atop the hull swung up to steady on him. Instantly other turrets swung up too.

Not only had he been seen, but they were communicating. Passing information. Which meant that though the Marines had no comms and no video, Allied jamming wasn't working on the enemy.

He pulled back from the edge as the world dazzled. A millisecond later automatic fire, 20mm or so by the sound of it, pulverized rock into powder. The edge sagged beneath him as he clawed backward. The Chad grabbed his load-bearing equipment and they rolled together back into the fighting hole.

Corporal Karamete was firing. But the boot was still hunched, shaking, gripping his rifle, but not aiming. He was muttering something over and over. A prayer, a curse . . . it didn't matter. Hector slammed the recruit's helmet into the side of the hole. "Return fire!" he screamed into the boy's face, shaking him. "Return fire, goddamn you, or I'll shoot your pussy fucking face myself!" He snatched the private's rifle, racked the bolt, and thrust it back into the kid's shaking hands.

Yet still the idiot didn't fire. Hector slapped him again, then turned away in disgust. "Climbing the cliff!" he yelled to the fire teams. "Pass it on. Little AFVs. AP and antiarmor." The cry went down the line, passed from mouth to mouth as the troops hastily reloaded magazines. But there were fewer voices now.

The squad was dying. One by one, like teeth from a beaten-in mouth. War was processing them one after the other. Disassembling their bodies into burnt blood and mangled flesh. Hanging them up to die. Like chickens on the Line . . .

The roar grew louder. The mortaring was sliding back toward the rear. A creeping barrage, to keep their heads down until the assault rolled over them. Grinding them into dirt and mud and blood.

He lifted his face to the rain. Watched it fall silver, endless, cold. He tongued his mike, then tried the PRC again. "Rampart 1, this is 1-2. Under attack. Troops and light armor. Need support. Artillery. Helos. Air. A missile strike. Anything. Over."

But all he got back was the drone and buzz of jamming.

A beetle thrust its nose over the edge of the cliff, hung there, treads scrabbling, then fell back. Hector slapped the cover down and pulled the bolt back, charging the 240. The C held the belt up and shook it in its metal hands, flinging the water off in a pewter cloud. They waited for an endless second.

The machine lunged up again, nose to the sky. As it exposed its underbelly Hector depressed the trigger. The butt of the gun jackhammered his shoulder as muddy spray obliterated the target. Every fifth round was tungsten cored. From up and down the line rifles banged, discharging projectiles fuzed to penetrate metal. The beetle faltered, quested this way and that, and at last exploded in a gout of orange fire. Burning, it toppled back out of sight.

But others were shouldering up behind it. The rain danced on their hulls. Their oculars searched the Marine line as they crunched heavily back down on rubberized treads and began to chew their way forward. As soon as they oriented they began firing. Their bullets kicked up mud and spray around the fighting holes.

The recruit bolted up and scrambled out of the hole. Hector grabbed for his harness, but missed. The coward pelted away.

Hector got back on the Pig. Firing and firing. Taking one target after the other. He was gunning for a mud-smeared machine on his right when another lurched up over the lip of the slope, rocked down, then spun its turret and charged for his hole.

At that moment the Pig ran through the last of its belt and stopped. Hector pulled a grenade and yanked the pin. He had his arm back to throw when something hit him.

The blow staggered him back, paralyzing him. The grenade dropped from his lifeless hand, puckered the mud, and slid gracefully down into their hole. Karamete shouted and kicked it into the sump. But too much dirt had fallen. The sump was full. The grenade lay exposed, and they all stared at it, horrified, unable to move.

"I have it," said 323. The Chad pivoted around Hector, pushed Karamete aside with a stiff-armed thrust, and fell on the grenade.

A hollow, subdued bang blew half its head off, and the side of the hole collapsed and caved in on top of it.

Screams rose from down the line as the beetles rolled over the fighting holes. One halted and spun, treads grinding down through the thin soil and mud like a mill to crush the screaming humans beneath. The marines fired from both sides, and its oculars flashed into splinters.

Blinded, the machine charged uphill. One tread ran up a fallen tree and it tipped over, crashed down a short drop, and landed on its side. Its tracks spun with a gnashing roar, like the grinding of steel teeth. Then it began crying out, a shrill, insistent beeping that went on and on beneath the clatter of fire and the growl of motors.

Hector lay half in and half out of the hole, dazed, gripping his arm. When he lifted his glove, blood pumped from the torn flesh beneath.

Beside him the C was stirring, digging itself out from the mudslide with finlike motions of its hands. Its wrecked, muddy head drooped askew. One eye was missing. Cables hung from its neck. Hector extended a hand. The head came around and studied it for a second before it seemed to recognize the gesture.

Hector pulled 323 to a sitting position, but when it tried to hoist itself one leg buckled. It sagged against the side of the hole.

He must have blacked out for a second or two then, because when he came back the assistant squad leader was working on his arm. "Hold it fucking out, Sergeant. Hold it straight." She slapped her belt around it, threaded the buckle, and yanked it tight. The arm felt weak. Dead. But it wasn't pumping blood now. Just a slow oozing. He blinked at the sliding orange mud in the bottom of the hole. His own blood, dripping into it. Turning it red.

"Another wave," the assistant squad leader shouted in his ear. Her voice was thin, almost inaudible over the roar of battle. "Milliron spotted another wave. Coming through the woods."

Hector shook rain off his Glasses to see that 323, mangled as it was, had worked itself upright. It stood half-propped against the front of the hole, one buckled knee thrust deep into the mud to keep it vertical. It patted the Pig. Brushed mud off the feed cover, inserted the end of a belt of linked cartridges into the feed tray, and charged the weapon.

It picked up the butt, and placed it carefully in its shoulder.

Snuggling its single good optic behind the rear sight, it traversed and pressed the trigger. The burst ripped into the turret of a beetle heading for the right flank. The armor-piercing slugs stitched its side, and the thing rolled to a stop and began its plaintive crying. A second burst silenced even that.

Hector hammered the robot's back with his good hand. "Nice shot. Just keep those bursts short," he yelled when the Chad's mangled head turned. He tucked a severed wire back into the chest armor. "Short, asshole, short bursts, you're gonna melt the fucking barrel."

His line was thinning. His guys were dying. Another assault would overrun them. Hector called Tac again, got nothing, tried the PRC but got only a thin high tormented squeal. “Fucking useless shit,” he growled, and stood in the hole. “Fall back!” he screamed.

The order caromed down the line. Marines began scrambling out of their fighting holes, so coated with mud they seemed to be born of the earth. The rain increased. He jerked the Pig out of the mud. Then rethought, set it back down, and told the C, “You’re the king. Machine gunner, he’s the king. The king fucks the queen. Copy me? You stand fast. You die, you die right here. At your weapon.”

It nodded, once, and slid behind the gun again. Hector yelled to Karamete, “If I don’t make it, set up at the military crest. Stand fast. Fight till we’re overrun. Then play dead. Maybe you can join up with Third Platoon after these things go past, take ’em from the rear.”

She nodded and turned away to climb, lurching uphill over the cratered, slippery ground.

Like maggots emerging from a rotten corpse, the rest of the platoon squirmed out of their holes and staggered, limped, crawled up the slope. They supported each other, or leaned on their rifles. Niegowski was dragging a body, one of his fire team guys. “Hustle, marines, hustle the fuck up!” Hector screamed. “Leave your claymores, wire ’em up.” A rifleman staggered past, gaze welded to some point in the infinite distance. He moved like one of the Chads, dragging his rifle-butt in the mud.

Hector grabbed him and shoved him along. “Move it!” he screamed. He walked the line again, making sure everyone got the word, then followed them up the hill. Pulling back, the marines clambered over fallen trees. They set up remote-det claymores as they went, antipersonnel charges that sprayed shrapnel when the integral radar sensed motion. They reached the top panting and scrambling on all fours, fell on their knees in the rain, and seized their entrenching tools once more.

WHEN he stumbled out at the crest the ridges spread below him, around them, open and exposed and rounded and smoking under a charcoal sky. Rain churned the ocher mud Chinese mortars had plowed. Jets thundered invisibly far above. Another battle, detached from yet somehow probably related to their lack of air support. All Hector could see was the clouds, lowering and black as Marine dress oxfords.

He trudged from one end of the line to the other, pegging each grunt to his or her place. His head reeled as if he'd been drinking. Sometimes he fell, but pushed himself to his feet again and went on. The grunts were too exhausted to dig, but he chivvied and kicked them into it. Those who'd lost their e-tools scooped with hands or Ka-Bars or rifle butts. He linked up his flanks with the squads to left and right. Several minutes went by without any hellish new development. It was actually a little breathing spell.

He tried to call Tac again, and to his astonishment got an only partially jammed channel. *"No, Sergeant. No more reinforcements available. Ammo's running short too. All we can do is pass requests for air support and artillery up the line."*

Just then he recognized a lone figure scrambling over an explosion crater to where he stood.

The recruit who'd run. White-faced, shaking, biting his lip. He carried two green steel ammo cans. Another was clamped under his arm. Hector waited, thumbs in his webbing. Said nothing. Until the guy blubbered, "Sergeant."

"Private."

"I'm sorry, I . . . lost it up there. I really—"

"You back now?" Hector snapped.

"Say again, Sergeant?"

"If you're done with your fucking piss break, let's see that fucking e-tool flying."

The boot hesitated. Stared, then nodded over and over with pathetic eagerness. "Aye aye, Sergeant. I'll dig you the best fucking hole—"

"Shut the fuck up," Hector said. "Give Milliron those cans. Fucking boot recruit. Greenie newbie asshole. *Pinche estúpido. Pinche* useless motherfucking abortion."

He was still muttering "Fucking boot" when the 240 went *kack kack kack*, down below, out of sight in the rain and smoke, and guilt stabbed him like a rooster's spur. He'd left C323 behind. "Die at your weapon," that's what he'd told it. After the thing had fallen on a grenade, to save them.

It felt . . . wrong.

But it had never been alive. So how could it die?

He strode along the line, kicking legs and shouting. They lay full length in the shallow scooped-out fighting holes, staring out over their weapons. They'd thrown away their useless Glasses and were blinking rain out of their eyes. Niegowski yelled that his team was out of ammo. Hector threw him the last can. The rain plonked on their helmets, mingled with their blood, trickled into the darkening mud.

At the far right of the line he ran into Glasscock, from Third, walking his own positions. The other NCO pointed wordlessly across the valley. Smoke rose from the far ridgeline. Green shapes lumbered eastward. Troops were streaming to the rear. The Nationalists were breaking.

Hector staggered. His head swam. He gripped his wounded shoulder with his good hand. Then forced himself on. His Pig. Where was his fucking Pig? Then he heard it again. Not short, but prolonged bursts. Practically a full belt. "Too fucking long!" he screamed, knowing the Chad couldn't hear him.

The gun stuttered on. And on.

Then suddenly fell silent.

The sky ripped open and shells screamed in. Hector couldn't tell if they were Allied or enemy. They burst ahead of his line. So, friendly, probably. But only a dozen or so.

Not enough. Not nearly enough.

"Here they come!" Karamete screamed.

Behind a walking wall of gray-white antitargeting smoke an army of green cockroaches lumbered up the slope. Gunflashes winked from their muzzles. Whistles blew. Lasers reached out, beams probing like antennae through rainfog and gunsmoke. Helmets bobbed behind the beetles. The troops were closed up on the robots this time, providing suppressing fire to keep the Gustav gunners down. Their cheers carried on the wind. The marines yelled back. Bullets puckered the top of the hill and whined overhead.

When the lead enemy was a hundred meters away Hector yelled, "Open fire!" The line opened up with a roar. He crawled from hole to hole, telling each fire team to conserve ammo. "We gotta hold this fucking hilltop. If we retreat, they'll fucking massacre us. Or I'll shoot you myself, no shit. Then I'll call in gunships on the position."

He didn't tell them there was no more support. That they were on their own. What would be the point?

Instead of a wide wave, this time four beetles came almost locked together, just enough space between them to see the troops crouching behind them, using the metal ovoids as cover. The battle-noise rose to a massive, roaring climax.

Hector was full length behind the boll of a fallen pine, firing, when a burst tore the wood apart, slashing splinters across his face and knocking him backward in a sticky rain of sap. He lay dazed. The universe smelled of turpentine. He waited dumbly to be crushed into the red soil. For it all to at last just fucking end.

Instead the howl of combat seemed to falter. Lessened.

He dragged a wet sleeve across his face and pulled it back covered with blood and pale splinters the color of canned tuna. Then sat up, gripping his empty rifle.

The beetles stood all around them. Their engines were running, but they weren't moving. Their turrets were canted upward, and a red light blinked below their lasers. Shouts and whistles came from down the hill.

Patterson took a knee beside him. "Sergeant. Y'okay? I'm gonna pull some of these big splinters out of your face. . . . Can ya stand? I'll help you up."

"What the fuck . . . What happened?"

"I don't know. They were about to overrun us, but just sort of . . . stalled out."

"Where's Karamete?"

"I'm slapping demo on them," his assistant yelled.

"Yeah. Blow the fuckers to hell, ASAP. Before they wake up again." He staggered up, clinging to the runner, and hobbled along the line. More wounded. Two more dead. He wasn't even sure who he had left anymore.

Leaning on Patterson, he tried to raise Tac again. The answer was nearly obliterated with static, but they seemed to be able to hear him. He reported casualties. Asked for ammo and water and reinforcements again.

Then he slumped to the mud, and nodded, stunned for a timeless time as the world spun viciously around him but he, himself, floated at a detached and motionless center.

A corpsman was bending over him. He took off the belt tourniquet, poured in clotting powder and antibiotic, and applied a field dressing. "Gonna have to evacuate you, Sergeant," he murmured.

Hector winced away as the medic plastered another bandage over his face. He shook his head. "No."

"Sorry, dude. Sendin' you to the rear."

"No, fuck that. *Ya valí madre.* Stayin' here, Doc."

The corpsman started to argue, then shrugged. "At least, some morphine."

"No. Gotta stay sharp. Gotta hold the line."

"Here, drink this. Drink it all. Hear me? Sergeant, can you hear me?"

Hector shook himself. Something was cradled in his hands. Something . . . to drink? He'd almost been asleep. "Gotta . . . hold. Take care of the other guys, Doc. Patch 'em up, so we can keep fighting."

ANOTHER hour crept past. The rain kept falling, now light, now heavy. His face was numb, as if a dentist had novocained it all over, but his arm was starting to really ache. A guy from H&S drove up with a cart. Rounds for the recoilless Gustavs, rifle ammo, flares, batteries, MREs, water. Hector yelled over to Glasscock, to coordinate, then told Karamete to move the platoon back down to the edge of the rise.

Stumbling, weaving between fallen trees, they filtered down toward their old holes. He could only stagger a few steps before he had to collapse and rest, head propped in his hands.

Corpses and parts of bodies lay tumbled along the bench where they'd fought. Below and around the fighting holes wrecked beetles stood burning, farting sparks as ammo cooked off.

Hector paused next to a twisted mass of metal and wires, torn apart and crushed into the mud behind a wrecked machine gun. He looked down at it for a few seconds.

Chads didn't have helmets, though their heads were vaguely helmet shaped, if you glimpsed one in the red-lit dark of an aircraft fuselage, hurtling toward battle.

They didn't have boots. Just plastic and alloy lower limb terminations that splayed out slightly when they pressed into soft ground, on the march.

He bent, and picked up a discarded rifle. Sorted through the wreckage in the hole.

When he stepped back the rifle stood upright in the mud, muzzle down. On top of it he hung the mangled wreck of what had once been 323's head. On the ground, he arranged a mangled foot assembly.

He stood there for a moment more, but found no words. What could he say? How could you envision an afterlife for something that had never lived? At last he just sighed and turned away, digging his fingers into his arm, which now felt like it had been plunged into boiling grease.

Their old fighting pits were shallow puddles now, nearly erased by treadmarks and shell-gouged craters. He ordered the fire team leaders to stack the dead, Marine and enemy both, in front of their positions for cover.

He sagged to half sit, half lean at the cliff, boots dangling over the edge, staring down at a smashed, annihilated forest. Quads and Gammas lay tumbled broken in the red mud. More dead lay down there too. Except for the rain falling on them all, the sky was empty.

AN hour later far-off whistles blew again. The grunts rousted from whatever rest they'd found, and charged their weapons. But Hector still sat by the cliff, contemplating his fields of fire as the whistles and cheers grew closer through the smoke and mist and rain.

He couldn't hear any more beetles. But another wave of troops was pushing up from the rising ground, as if growing from the soil itself up through the stumps and craters of the shattered jungle. But these shadowy forms looked different. Helmetless. Weaponless. He adjusted his Glasses.

No. Not troops. Old men, kids, women. Not uniformed, but in colored shirts and pants and dresses. They stumbled forward, glancing back fearfully as someone screamed at them from behind.

Hector pressed Transmit on the radio, and sent it in. He dragged a sleeve across his face, wiping away blood and tears, sweat and powder-grime.

The enemy was driving civilians ahead of them as shields. Taiwanese from the villages. They emerged from the smoke holding each other's hands, families clinging together, helping each other over fallen trees and along the ridges between shell holes.

The marines would have to machine-gun women, children, old men. Or else be overrun.

But they had to hold. Or the whole force could be pushed back, into the sea.

And then they would lose the war.

The fucking war, the endless *pinche* fucking war that got more desperate every day.

In his pocket, Sergeant Hector Ramos fingered the pink plastic rosary. Whether they held or not, he wouldn't be going home. He knew that now. He no longer cared. It didn't matter. But he knew.

Maybe Mirielle would remember him.

23

Cam Ranh, Vietnam

THE searing sun was impossible to look up into. It weighed on his shoulders like hot anvils. Heat boiled from the weathered tarmac. It burbled above the steel roofs of the stripside buildings, warping the scrub-covered hills that surrounded the airstrip.

Dan had helicoptered from *Peralta* to *Liscombe Bay* as the strike force retreated seaward after the Uppercut strike.

It had been costly but could have been much worse. *Kuklenski*'s Standards had taken out the cyberjacked Tomahawks, splashing them harmlessly at sea. The UAVs Dan had recalled from the coast had blunted the enemy air attacks. Chinese airfields, radars, jamming sites, and missile batteries along the coast had been destroyed. The main targets, the submarine bases, were damaged, though still operational.

Australian and Indian submarines had caught the enemy surface force sortieing from Hong Kong. They'd sunk the destroyer and an accompanying submarine, and a long-range Air Force strike had blown apart the catamaran missile boats.

Now he was at the principal Allied support facility in the southern theater of operations, taking a rattletrap taxi with a broken air conditioner from the international terminal, where the flight from the carrier had dropped him, across the base to headquarters.

The Corps of Engineers had built this airfield in 1965. During the U.S. involvement, most of the cargo to support American troops had been landed at the port, and fighter, bomber, and reconnaissance missions had flown from here to Laos, Cambodia, North Vietnam, and throughout the Republic of Vietnam.

Now Cam Ranh served the Allies. Contrails chalked a clear sky. A

C-5 trundled in from seaward, so huge and slow it hardly seemed to be moving at all. The cab passed fighters, their radomed noses just visible between revetments hastily Legoed of concrete castings ramped with bulldozed earth. An engine screamed, rising to full power. The taxi halted as a bomber rumbled in overhead, touching down with a whiff of smoke from its tires. Then, when the crossing gate came up, they proceeded across the strip, past a line of tractor trailers hauling wheeled bomb racks stacked with JDAMs and standoff missiles, to judge from the stenciling on the containers.

The headquarters lay east of the field, on a low hill surrounded by concertina. A sign at the entrance in various languages and scripts directed arriving personnel to different commands: Indian, Australian, U.S., Japanese. The driver braked at an upraised palm from the Vietnamese guarding the gate. A machine-gun team lounged by their weapon. Dan baked in the airless heat while the guards checked his ID and called in to confirm his access. At last they stepped back and gave him a whipcrack salute. He tapped one off in return, and the taxi, backfiring, jerked ahead again. A squad of Indian troops in turbans, khakis, and shorts, in a brisk, arm-swinging route step, snapped to "eyes left" as he passed.

"U.S., sir," the driver said, pulling in and braking so sharply Dan's head jerked forward. He passed a couple of bills over the seat back, probably too much, and the woman jumped out and scurried around to his door.

Headquarters, Allied Command, South China Sea/Forward Operating Base Cam Ranh Bay/Naval Facility Vietnam was a cluster of gray and tan prefabs separated by graveled walkways. A two-story barracks built out of containers rose on the far side of the hill. A blue sea, a glittering array of solar panels, and a beach were visible beyond, with more chain-link and guard masts. When he shaded his eyes his sea-trained gaze assembled a patrol boat from the hazy horizon. Closer in the sun glittered off creamy surf, vanilla sand, and the illuminating radar of an I-Hawk battery. Asians in green jumpsuits and red-billed caps were misting down the missiles.

A sergeant came out to welcome him, but Dan was early. He got to cool off in an air-conditioned corridor. Several other officers gathered, shepherded by aides. Short, dark men, mostly, in unfamiliar uniforms. A civilian employee, a Viet woman, headed past carrying a tray of fruit drinks and cookies.

He was crunching an orange wafer she'd rather grudgingly parted with when a familiar voice said, "Why, if it isn't my old buddy Dan."

He stood to shake Jack Byrne's hand. The civilian adviser to the commander in chief, Pacific, was in white tennis shorts and a bright orange short-sleeved shirt printed with outrigger canoes and palm trees. "Nice," Dan said, rubbing the material between two fingers. "Silk?"

"You bet. No point in a suit here, they told me."

"What *are* we doing here? Any idea?"

Byrne took off his sunglasses and peered at his cell. "You're early, but that's good. We're meeting with the deputy and the J-3 first."

Dan passed a hand over his wet hair, which felt icy in the cold air. "Tell me it's good news. Or am I on the carpet? For arrogating tactical command from Admiral Simko, I mean."

"AMPG. Above my pay grade. They asked me to sit in while they talked to you. Since we go back, I guess. You attending the 0900 briefing?"

Dan said he was here as directed, and that was all he knew.

The sergeant came back, led them down the passageway, knocked, and held open a door.

WHEN he snapped to attention three steps inside, a gaunt officer in Army tans and the three stars of a lieutenant general looked up from a ratty sofa beside a bamboo desk.

Randall Faulcon, deputy commander in chief, Pacific Command. They'd last met at Camp H. M. Smith, when he'd put Dan in charge of planning for the strike on the sub base. To his right a shorter, balding naval officer in trop whites sat with legs crossed. He wore three stars as well. Dan knew him too: Vice Admiral Bren Verstegen, the command's operations deputy. They both got up, and Faulcon saluted Dan's Congressional while Verstegen straightened to attention. Dan inclined his head to acknowledge the honor.

"Take a seat." Faulcon pointed to a rickety-looking folding chair. "Jack, another over there. You both know Admiral Verstegen, from our J-3."

Dan nodded and took the chair as the sergeant went to parade rest, still standing. Faulcon said, "Lenson, I see your wife occasionally. Very sharp woman. We're lucky she survived the crash."

"Thank you, sir."

Faulcon inspected the ceiling. "Let's get to business. I'm a student of General Grant's campaigns. Grant never abandoned a field, even after he was defeated. He renewed the action as soon as he could. And usually ended victorious.

"Today's meeting will coordinate a renewed assault on the South China coast. The APs already clobbered us there, so they won't expect us to push the same button again. Since they're heavily engaged in Taiwan, a major attack in the south should bring their remaining air and naval reserves to battle.

"Operation Rupture will be a major landing, not a raid. The objective is to seize and permanently hold Hainan Island."

Dan cleared his throat, suppressing a fidget. He liked the idea of hitting the same place twice. It didn't sound like he was going to be chewed out. But if not, then what the hell? Was he getting a ship again? "Yes, sir," he said, just to stay in the conversation.

Admiral Verstegen said, "We'll go into the planning at the meeting. It's already well advanced."

Byrne shifted in his chair. "Um, General, Admiral, I don't think Dan knows about his new orders yet. He just flew in off the carrier."

They looked surprised. Faulcon scratched his scalp. "Well . . . Admiral Simko was originally slated for this command. But as you know, he's sidelined for now. The heart attack. That clarify things?"

"Um, sorry, sir," Dan said. "I'm not exactly—"

Verstegen leaned forward. "DoD's reactivating Ninth Fleet to oversee operations in the south. I'll leave the planning staff to take command. You'll serve under me, in command of Task Force 91. Your expeditionary strike groups will carry out the softening-up strikes, pulling in as many enemy forces in South China as you can. Then, when they're attrited to an acceptable level, cover the amphibious assault."

He paused, frowning. "And cover the withdrawal, if it should fail."

Both men looked bleak then. Dan sucked air, searching for something to say. But could only come up with, "Um . . . Tim's in no danger, is he?"

Faulcon raised his eyebrows. "Simko? He's under medical care. As far as I know, he'll recover. But he's definitely not fit enough to run a major operation."

"He's a good officer," Dan said. His Academy classmate had been the only one between him and a cashiering, after Dan had transgressed his ROEs during the India-Iran conflict.

"Lenson deserves to know," Byrne put in. "Dan . . . he was warned in advance, about the possibility of bottom-laid missiles."

Dan turned that over. An oversight like that didn't sound like the guy he knew. But then again, Simko hadn't looked well. "Seriously? And didn't . . . ?"

The admiral uncrossed his legs. "Let's just say we need someone else for the next try. We've discussed this, but most of the people who are qualified to command are occupied elsewhere. Lee Custer's free, but there's no way we can have someone with that last name in charge of an operation this risky. So we'll probably slot him in for logistic support. Could be a bit awkward. He's senior to you. But the two of you'll just have to cope.

"Your name came up next. You're already read into enemy capabilities. You led Strike Seven effectively. And you always seem to come through under pressure . . . in my view, the most important attribute of a commander in wartime"

"I made one bad call," Dan said. "In the Central Pacific. Almost lost the task force."

Verstegen nodded. "We know. But you managed to bring the enemy's main submarine force to battle, when Admiral Lianfeng wanted them to stay covert. And you learned not to underestimate your enemy.

"Finally, I read the after-action reports on Uppercut. Your plan for the raid worked. And when you had to take over, calling the UAVs back saved us massive casualties. Possibly, forestalled a major defeat."

"Well done," Faulcon put in.

Dan touched a knuckle to his teeth. "Um, thank you, General, but . . . they had the advantage from the get-go in cyber. They penetrated our comms. Even turned our own missiles back on us."

The flag officers exchanged glances. Finally Verstegen murmured, "We needn't worry about that from here forward."

Dan blinked, not sure he'd heard that aright. "Are we certain of that? I mean . . . ?"

"It's been taken care of," said Byrne. "By a special operation. Deep in China."

Dan dropped his eyes, not wanting to argue, but not really eager to accept this cup, either. "So, not Tim. But what about Jennifer Roald? She's qualified. And the right rank."

Faulcon glanced at his watch. "She's good, I agree. But we have other plans for her."

Dan felt like he was protesting too much. "If those are the orders. What's the bad news?"

Verstegen grinned unwillingly. "The bad news. Yeah. We don't have enough forces. Not after our losses in the last two operations. Everything else, we've committed to Causeway. We have to prevail in Taiwan. They push us off there, this war's over.

"So, this next phase is going to get pretty much whatever we can scrape up. Allied ground forces, not American. Retreaded ships. Essentially, three expeditionary strike groups, built around *Hornet*, *Bataan*, and a combined Vietnamese/Indonesian force centered on *Makassar* and *Surabya*."

"Will we have carrier support?"

Faulcon said, "Two heavies, but they'll be held far back, out of DF-12 range."

"Sir, I'm still a captain," Dan said. Then realized how opportunistic that sounded, and wished he'd kept his damn mouth shut.

The J-3 nodded. "Two stars come with the job. That good enough for you?"

It felt unreal. Ping-ponging back to admiral, but this time with two stars instead of one? Making him a rear admiral, upper half. But it had happened before in wartime. Marshall had leapfrogged officers up two or even three ranks, to get the right man in the job. "Um, that's not my point, sir. I'm not negotiating here."

"Then let's play ball, goddamn it. The Indonesians know you. The Indians. The Viets respect your combat experience. You wouldn't be sitting here if Jim Yangerhans and Nick Niles didn't have confidence in you."

He looked away, trying to make sense of his feelings. Why was he wavering? This could be his last chance for a major command in wartime. What every naval officer was supposed to live for. Was it his fucking lack of self-confidence? Or that he really had lost his taste for battle?

Verstegen: "So. You aboard?"

"I guess I am, sir." He stiffened his tone. Faking, as so often before, assurance he didn't really feel. "Yes, sir. Of course. I'll do my best."

"Pick your staff. Just make it multinational."

A tap at the door. The sergeant again. "General, phone call."

Faulcon got up. So did Dan and Byrne. "It'll all be explained at 0900. So I'll ask you to excuse me." At the door, though, he turned back. "Bren, have you got—? We want him to rank his commanders."

"I brought a spare pair," Verstegen said. "Sergeant, can you help us out here?"

The J-3 took two sets of three five-pointed chromium-plated stars out of his pocket and rolled them on the desktop as if playing craps. They came to rest and lay glittering there. The sergeant unbent from parade rest and unclipped a Leatherman tool from his belt. He snapped off one star from each set, leaving two each. Verstegen added, "But the rank—"

"I know, sir. Duration only," Dan said, unpinning the eagles on his collar.

The other nodded. "Later I might be able to . . . well, let's see how it goes."

Faulcon was shaking Dan's hand when a short man in a tropical uniform peered into the room. Byrne waved him in. "General Pham Van Trong, Socialist Republic of Vietnam. Meet Admiral Daniel V. Lenson, one of our most highly decorated officers."

Dan tried his Naval Academy French on the Vietnamese, and they managed a few pleasantries before Verstegen led them down the hall.

THREE more men stood around the conference table, already making inroads on the fruit drinks and cookies. One had a violet beret and a truculent squint. Another was a small-featured, extremely short, dark-skinned officer in what looked like Royal Navy whites.

The one in whites spotted Dan and rushed over. "Daniel Lenson?"

They shook hands. "The same. And you are?"

"My name is Ramidin Madjid. You do not know me, but I served with you once! Yes! As executive officer of *Nala*."

"*Nala*," Dan said, not registering the name—a ship?—but not wanting to say so. "Of course." He caught his reflection in the glass surface of the table. Faint, almost ghostlike. But with two stars on each collar.

"You knew my mentor in the Indonesian Navy. Grand Admiral Waluyo Supryo Suriadiredja?"

Dan nodded then, remembering hazy days years before. In the Java Sea.

The Tiny Nation Task Force had hunted pirates while a geopolitical game unfolded around them. He'd chatted with Suriadiredja through a hot afternoon on the bridge of USS *Oliver C. Gaddis*, leading a higgle-piggle formation of Malaysian, Filipino, Singaporean, Indonesian, and Malaysian patrol vessels. Suriadiredja had predicted China's expansion southward. "I don't see it," Dan had said then. To which the leather-faced admiral had answered, "In the same way none of us can see a tree growing." The old Indonesian had anticipated China's step-by-step advance into the South China Sea, gradually supplanting U.S. power throughout Asia.

He cleared his throat and looked away from his reflection. "I knew him, yes. Have to admit, he saw further ahead than anyone else. How's he doing?"

Madjid said, "He is long retired, but well. And now we are involved in the war he foresaw. Together, as he expected we would be."

"I haven't seen much of your navy recently," Dan said. "I know you've modernized since I steamed with you. Your submarines have been active with our fleet. And with the Indian Navy."

The Indonesian nodded. "It took time for us to mobilize, and even more time to . . . you know we have a large enemy minority. Of Chinese ethnicity, I mean. I am happy to say now that issue is settled. We hope to lend our shoulders to the wheel more strongly, going forward. To support our allies, and lay the foundations for increased stature in the postwar world."

Dan was wondering what "settled" actually meant when an aide called, "Attention on deck."

Faulcon introduced himself, then Verstegen as commander, Ninth Fleet, and Dan as commander, Task Force 91. The deputy went around the table. "Our Allied members are Admiral Madjid, Republic of Indonesia Navy, with Major General Isnanta, commandant of the Korps Marinir—the Republic of Indonesia Marine Corps. General Pham Van Trong, chief of staff, People's Republic of Vietnam. And Admiral Vijay Gupta, commander, Indian navy operations in the South China Sea.

"Our countries, plus the heads of state of the Republic of Korea, Japan, and Australia, agreed on a combined strategy to end the war at the principals' meeting in Singapore. Welcome, everyone. I'll turn the floor over to Admiral Verstegen."

In laconic sentences, with printed handouts marked TOP SECRET, the new fleet commander outlined the renewed assault on the South China coast. "Operation Rupture will be a major landing, to seize and hold Hainan. First objective: further degrade enemy defensive and offensive assets. Two: land an Allied ground force and clear the island. And three, prepare for possible further operations to seize a foothold on the mainland." He glanced at Byrne. "Intel, any comment?"

Byrne said, "We're already seeing cracks in the monolith. Hong Kong's in revolt. Chemical weapons are being dropped on civilians. The enemy's fighting rebellions there, in Tibet, and in Xinjiang. He's sustaining heavy casualties in Taiwan and on the Vietnamese front. And in the Ryukyus, where the Japanese are retaking islands one by one."

Faulcon said, "This is the next step in bringing down our mutual enemy. Now we need to hear back from you about implementation, level of forces, readiness, and any support issues you may have.

"Let's hear from our hosts here in Cam Ranh first. General Trong?"

The Vietnamese looked pained. He muttered, in French, gaze on the table, "We are unable to furnish the ground forces we promised. I deeply regret this, but the battle south of Hanoi is absorbing all our reserves. That is how we can best contribute to the war."

Dan translated, hoping he didn't fumble anything. But Faulcon only nodded. "We understand. You made those commitments before the situation on your front degenerated. Perhaps the Socialist Republic can provide amphibious lift?"

Trong nodded. He said, in English, "I think . . . we in accord."

Verstegen turned to the Indonesians. "Your government's promised troops too."

The marine general said heavily, in more than passable English, "Indonesia has prepared an expeditionary force of three marine divisions for this operation. Each with three combat brigades. Also, combat and administrative support. But our reconnaissance and air support are not up to Allied standard. Also, we will need heavy artillery."

"Ours is fully committed," Trong stated, firmly, as if forestalling any request.

Faulcon only said quietly, "Our own marines are also fully engaged. In Taiwan. But the U.S. Army will furnish artillery and close air support. The Allies will strike with one fist, all five fingers together."

Dan rubbed his mouth, already uneasy with this plan. They'd stuck their fingers into the meat grinder off Hainan once, and barely gotten them back whole. Plus, from the history he'd read, mixing national commands had seldom led to effective coordination.

But no one had asked him, and Verstegen went on to discuss assembly points, troop movement, escorts, and the movement to assault. Finally Faulcon checked his watch. "Let's break for fifteen, then reconvene. A reminder: Do not discuss the plan or its target with anyone not cleared to the highest level. Or on any digital channel whatsoever. Lives depend on our maintaining security."

The Americans clustered at the juice tray. Byrne muttered, "So we're going with the jayvees."

Verstegen looked insulted. "I wouldn't call them that. They'll bring fresh resolve. Especially the Indonesians. They need to bleed, to buy in for the postwar settlement. They'll give us the bodies on the ground to take on the Chinese." He swirled pineapple juice, looking reflective. "Dan, forces aren't quite as skimpy as PACOM makes out. We have Spruances coming out of mothballs. Light carriers. Plus new ships."

"Any of the new cruisers?"

Before the vice admiral could answer, Faulcon came back in, the sergeant with him. "It's time, sir," the enlisted man said.

The screens lit with the angular, almost deformed features of Justin Yangerhans. Commander, Pacific Command. Dictator of half the globe. The man making the decisions, for both peace and war, that seemed no longer available from a paralyzed national leadership.

"Welcome," he said. *"I'm glad we're going to be working together in this operation."*

LATER that day an aide called Dan out of a logistics subconference for a call. It was the chief of naval operations, Barry "Nick" Niles. Dan's old adversary, but lately, a supporter. A communicator set up the call on the lavender Ultra Secure phone in the Comm Room. *"Dan?"* Niles opened, his booming voice sounding oddly thin and wavery on the quantum-entangled circuit. *"We all on the same page out there?"*

"Pretty much, Admiral. Focusing on the specifics now."

A lag of a second or two, then, *"Good. I just saw Blair. She's okay, no need to worry about her."* Another voice gabbled faintly behind him on the circuit. *"Just a sec, important call here. But I want to get one thing across."*

"Sir?" Dan frowned at the handset.

A pause, as words bounced and echoed between networked microsatellites, were downloaded and decoded. *"The public's patience is exhausted. And the administration isn't backing us up. This southern attack . . . Rupture . . . will be our last gasp before we have to either compromise, or escalate. I only hope China's as tapped out as we are."*

Dan took a deep breath. If Zhang Zurong was finally cornered . . . did they really expect him to go down without all-out nuclear war? If not to win, at least to seek a final, despairing vengeance? And what about his even more truculent and isolated fellow dictator, in North Korea?

He wished the CNO had an answer. But no one did. Maybe not even Zhang himself.

Niles congratulated him on the fleet-up, and told him to call if he needed anything. Then he signed off.

Dan set the handset down gently. Then asked the communicator, "Can I place a call with this? To a cell in CONUS?"

"I can arrange that, sir. But it won't be on a covered circuit."

He called Nan's number. Her cell rang and rang, but his daughter never picked up.

Finally her "leave a call" message came up. He started to speak a couple of times, but couldn't muster the right words. What could he say that wouldn't either violate classification, or else just come across as a vague worry?

She wouldn't listen, anyway. He'd already advised her to leave Seattle. Her work was too important, she said.

Anyway, how could he in good conscience ask her to leave, when millions of others would still be there, hostages to the god of war?

A war that seemed to be approaching its climax, one way or another. And grow only more perilous to everyone involved, as it drew near a final resolution.

Holding the phone, he squeezed his eyes shut. Remembering her as a child. Holding her, promising silently, but with his whole being and without reservation, that he would always be there for her. That he would protect her, no matter what happened.

But how could he?

Would their actions, no matter how carefully planned and well intentioned, bring down catastrophe on them all?

Shouldn't he be with her now? Or with Blair?

No. They didn't need him.

His duty was clear.

Yeah. His fucking . . . duty.

So that finally he just said, forcing the words through a closing throat, "This is your dad. I'm . . . okay. Sorry I missed you.

"I love you. Take care of yourself.

"And . . . I'll try to call you again."

The story of the war with China will continue in David Poyer's Overthrow.

ACKNOWLEDGMENTS

EX nihilo nihil fit. I began this novel with the advantage of copious notes accumulated for previous books as well as my own experiences in Asia, the Pentagon, and the Pacific. The following new sources were also helpful.

For Marine Corps passages: On the robotic target range, live-firing MGs, and Overmatch rifles: http://www.scout.com/military/warrior/story/1765379-army-pursues-guided-shoulder-fired-weapon?utm_source=Sailthru&utm_medium=email&utm_campaign=EBB%203.24.17&utm_term=Editorial%20-%20Early%20Bird%20Brief); also MCWP 3-11.2, "Marine Rifle Squad," Marine Corps Combat Development Command, and Todd South, "New Gear for Squad-Level Marines Will Help Adapt for New Enemies," *Defense News*, September 18, 2017. Hector's chapters were reviewed and commented on by Katie and Peter Gibbons-Neff, for which many thanks, as well as to Drew Davis.

For Navy passages: Previous research aboard USS *San Jacinto*, USS *George Washington*, USS *Wasp*, with Strike Group One, plus a visit to USS *Rafael Peralta* just after her commissioning, where Aaron Demeyer was especially helpful. A deep bow to all! Also, interview with James A. Kirk, *Surface Sitrep*, December 2016. Jennifer McDermott, "The Seal Whiskerers: Navy Looks to Sea Life for New Ships," Associated Press, March 15, 2017. Some of the specs for the "Savo Island–class cruiser" were adapted from the CG(X) program.

Naval History and Heritage Command, *Dictionary of American Naval Fighting Ships*, "USS *Savo Island*, CVE-78." Cheryl's speech owes a bit to articles by James Kirk and Edward Lundquist in the Surface Navy Association's December 2016 *Surface Sitrep.* Also, Roger

Ellis, "Electromagnetic Railgun," Office of Naval Research, https://www.onr.navy.mil/en/Science-Technology/Departments/Code-35/All-Programs/air-warfare-352/Electromagnetic-Railgun, accessed March 22, 2017. Jen Judson, "US Army Gets World Record–Setting 60-kW Laser," *Defense News*, March 16, 2017. Adam Stone, "Tactical Data System Almost Ready for Prime Time," C41SRNET, March 23, 2017. Halon breakdown products: Kevin McNesby et al., "Optical Measurement of Toxic Gases Produced During Firefighting Using Halons," U.S. Army Research Laboratory, Aberdeen Proving Ground, *Applied Spectroscopy*, vol. 51, No. 5, 1997.

References on influenza: https://www.cdc.gov/flu/avianflu/h7n9-virus.htm; Baylor College of Medicine, "Influenza Virus," https://www.bcm.edu/departments/molecular-virology-and-microbiology/emerging-infections-and-biodefense/influenza-virus-flu. Also, National Center for Biotechnology Information, "The Threat of Pandemic Influenza: Are We Ready?," https://www.ncbi.nlm.nih.gov/books/NBK22148. Also, Lee Ratner, "Phase II Trial of Induction Therapy with EPOCH Chemotherapy and Maintenance Therapy with Combivir/Interferon ALPHA-2a for HTLV-1 Associated T-Cell Non-Hodgkin's Lymphoma," National Cancer Institute. Also, L. Rudenko et al., "H7N9 Live Attenuated Influenza Vaccine in Healthy Adults: A Randomised, Double-Blind, Placebo-Controlled, Phase 1 Trial," *Lancet Infectious Diseases*, March 2016.

The Dublin scenes were based on personal research. Details of diplomatic protocol were reviewed by Donna Hopkins and Liz McManus.

The following sources were valuable as background for tactics, mind-sets, and strategic decisions: *Joint Publication 5-0, Joint Operation Planning*, August 2011; Kevin McCaney, "DARPA's Gremlins Could Cut the Costs of Attack Drones," 2015, August 31, *Defense Systems*, https://defensesystems.com/articles/2015/08/31/darpa-gremlins-reusable-attack-drones.aspx; Leigh Giangreco, "DARPA Narrows Down Gremlins Competition," FlightGlobal.com, March 20, 2017, https://www.FlightGlobal.com/news/articles/darpa-narrows-down-gremlins-competition-435372/; Hans Kristensen, "China SSBN Fleet Getting Ready—but for What?," Federation of American Scientists, April 25, 2014, https://fas.org/blogs/security/2014/04/chinassbnfleet/; David McDonough, "Unveiled: China's New Naval Base in the South China Sea," *The National Interest*, March 20, 2015, http://nationalinterest.org/blog/the-buzz/unveiled-chinas-new-naval-base-the-south-china-sea-12452; Franz-Stefan Gady, "China Unveils New Submarine-Launched Anti-Ship

Cruise Missile," *The Diplomat*, April 21, 2016, http://thediplomat.com/2016/04/china-unveils-new-submarine-launched-anti-ship-cruise-missile/; John R. Allen et al., "On Hyperwar," *Naval Institute Proceedings*, July 2017.

The scene of an airliner being cyberjacked was commented on by my esteemed classmate Mike Hichak.

For Teddy Oberg's strand of the story, the references listed in *Hunter Killer*, plus Muhammad Mumtaz Khalid, *History of Karakoram Highway* (Rawalpindi, 2011), especially volume 1; Shirley Kan, "U.S.-China Counterterrorism Cooperation: Issues for U.S. Policy," Congressional Research Service, July 15, 2010; Also, Department of the Army FM 3-05.201, "Special Forces Unconventional Warfare Operations." *The U.S. Army Ranger Handbook* was also useful.

For overall help, I owe recognition to the Surface Navy Association, Hampton Roads Chapter; to Charle Ricci and Stacia Childers of the Eastern Shore Public Library; to Matthew Stroup and Corey Barker of the Navy Office of Information, East; with bows to Mark "Dusty" Durstewitz, Aimee Brennan, Bill Dougherty, Bill Doughty, James W. Neuman, Phil Wisecup, Aaron Demeyer, John T. Fusselman, Dick Enderly, and others (they know who they are), both retired and still on active duty, who put in many hours adding additional perspective. If I left anyone out, apologies!

Let me reemphasize that these sources were consulted for the purposes of *fiction*. The specifics of tactics, units, and locales are employed as the materials of story, not reportage. Some details have been altered to protect classified capabilities and procedures.

My deepest gratitude goes to George Witte, editor and friend of over three decades, without whom this series would not exist. And Sally Richardson, Ken Silver, Sara Thwaite, Young Jin Lim, Naia Poyer, and Staci Burt at St. Martin's/Macmillan. And finally to Lenore Hart, kindest critic, anchor on lee shores, and my North Star when skies are clear.

As always, all errors and deficiencies are my own.